# THE BLIND CONSPIRACY

*SECRETS IN THE DARK-BOOK 1*

MICHEL BATTLES SR.

This is a work of fiction. Names, characters, businesses, places, events, and incidents are either the products of the author's imagination or used in a fictitious manner. Any resemblance to actual persons, living or dead, or actual events is purely coincidental.

Published by Iron Cane Media, Kansas, USA

First Edition

ISBN: 979-8-9948726-1-1

Printed in the United States of America

## DEDICATION

I dedicate this book to my wife Sonia. I know it is not easy being married to a crazy blind man. This book is for all the blind operators across the United States who are not being heard and are fed up with conflict. Thanks to all the SLA and committee members that really care about the blind and the program. This book is only fiction. Is it really?

— Michel Battles

# Table of Contents

## CHAPTER ONE

# The Audit Letter

Detective Michael Miguel could tell a serious letter by its weight.

Not the weight of the paper itself—paper was thin now, cheap, designed to be touched once and forgotten—but the weight of intention behind it. This envelope resisted being ignored. It lay on the kitchen table perfectly squared with the edge, aligned with the grain of the wood as if someone had measured the placement twice before letting go.

That kind of care never meant courtesy.

Kansas State Licensing Agency.

The return address sat centered, clean, printed in a font that suggested authority without urgency. No warning stamps. No bold type. Michael stared at it longer than necessary, feeling the familiar pressure build behind his right eye—the one that still worked. His left eye, covered by the worn black patch he'd carried back from the war, offered no distraction. It was the stillness that unsettled him, the quiet confidence of a system that didn't have to shout to be obeyed.

The envelope arrived midweek. Not Monday, when urgency could still pretend to matter. Not Friday, when responsibility could be postponed. Wednesday—when bureaucracy moved efficiently, assuming no one was paying attention.

Behind him, the kitchen had its own steady language: the refrigerator exhaled as it cycled on; the old wall clock ticked with stubborn consistency; the coffee maker clicked once as it warmed the plate. Ordinary sounds. Predictable sounds. They were the kinds of sounds Michael collected, the way some people collected sunlight.

He heard Sonia before he saw her—soft steps, a quick breath, the faint rustle of fabric being adjusted. She stood in the doorway in her uniform pants and undershirt, duty belt draped over one arm like a reminder. Her hair was pinned back with the disciplined speed of someone who never allowed the day to start sloppy.

She was watching him, not the envelope.

“You’re doing that thing,” she said.

“What thing?” Michael asked, without looking up.

“That stillness,” Sonia replied. “The one where you’re getting mad, but you’re trying to stay calm enough to think.”

Michael exhaled slowly. He hated that she could read him like that. He loved it, too—because she wasn’t guessing. She knew him the way he knew a room by sound.

He opened the envelope slowly, careful not to tear it, as if the paper could serve as evidence later. The letter inside was polite. Carefully, deliberately polite.

It informed him that Antony Grumpton, a licensed blind vending operator in the Kansas Blind Business Vending Program, had been placed under a compliance review. The language referenced an audit, a temporary reassignment, and a review determination date that had already passed.

Michael read the date.

Then he read it again.

Three days old.

Anger flared, sharp and immediate, before he forced it down. Delay was never accidental. Delay meant conversations had already happened. Decisions had already been made. Delay existed so the record could age just enough to look routine before anyone outside the process noticed the absence it created.

Sonia stepped closer and leaned over his shoulder. "BBVP?" she asked.

"Yes."

Her jaw tightened. "That's the third one this month."

"And the third one with the same reassignment code," Michael replied, tapping the letter with more force than necessary. "They're not even trying to hide the pattern anymore."

Sonia's eyes tracked the lines, the way she read police reports—looking for the moment language turned slippery. "The program handles discipline internally," she said. "Blind committee votes. Administrative hearings. SLA oversight. You told me law enforcement usually isn't involved."

"That's the theory," Michael said. "But this isn't discipline. This is movement."

He pointed to the signature block at the bottom. No name. Just a title.

A name could hesitate. A name could be questioned. A title existed to absorb blame and redirect anger into appeals that went nowhere.

Sonia straightened, frustration surfacing now. "Antony is completely blind," she said. "He runs his route by memory. He doesn't miss days. He doesn't wander off. And he sure doesn't volunteer for reassignment without calling someone."

"No," Michael agreed, voice low. "And he doesn't disappear unless someone helps him."

The word sat between them—disappear—uglier than arrest, more dangerous than death. Disappearance meant control.

Michael folded the letter once, precisely, aligning the edges until they matched perfectly. That detail annoyed him. Systems loved precision. Precision made abuse look organized.

Sonia lifted the folded page from his hand and unfolded it again, slower, like she wanted to see the letter refuse to change. "Read the part about 'committee discretion' again," she said.

Michael did, and his voice hardened as he spoke. The letter was written in the familiar language of governance: compliance, integrity, review, temporary adjustments. It framed a person's livelihood like a removable part.

Sonia's mouth tightened. "They call it 'temporary' like it's a favor."

"It's a lever," Michael said. "They move people with it."

He didn't say the rest out loud: They could move anyone.

Sonia set the letter down, and for a second her professional mask slipped. The fear in her eyes wasn't for the program. It was for him.

"You remember the last time you crossed a system that didn't want to be questioned," she said softly.

Michael's hand hovered over his eye patch, a habit he didn't notice until Sonia's voice pulled him back. The war had taken his left eye and left him with a kind of permanent alertness. He didn't need to see a threat clearly to recognize when one was near.

"I remember," he said.

"You came home with a patch," Sonia continued, voice tightening, "and you told me you were fine. Like losing part of your body was just paperwork. Like it was just a line in a report."

Michael looked up at her, and the anger he'd been aiming at the letter shifted, sharpened, turned inward. "I didn't want you to carry it," he said.

"I carry you," she answered, and her voice trembled just enough to make him feel it in his chest. "That's what marriage is. So don't ask me to pretend this doesn't matter."

Michael stood, pacing now. It was the controlled pace of a man trying not to explode. "This program is supposed to protect blind operators," he said. "It's supposed to give them stability—routes, income, dignity. The committee is supposed to represent them to the SLA, like a board. And when it works, it works."

Sonia nodded. "And when it doesn't, it becomes a weapon."

Michael stopped by the sink and stared out the window without seeing the yard. "Antony isn't just a name on a letter," he said. "He's a man who built his whole life around a route he can't see. He built it around timing, touch, sound. He built it around trust that the system wouldn't pull the floor out from under him."

Sonia's hands clenched and unclenched at her sides. "The cruelest part," she said, anger rising, "is that everyone calls it 'help.' They call it ‘support.’ They call it ‘program integrity’ while they take away the one thing these operators can’t replace overnight.”

Michael turned back toward the table. “And they do it because it looks legal,” he said. “It looks clean.”

He picked up the letter again and ran his thumb along the reassignment code. “This code,” he said, “isn’t a place. It’s a step.”

Sonia frowned. “A step to what?”

Michael’s voice dropped. “A step to a file that lives somewhere else. A place where names turn into numbers. Where people become ‘cases’ and then become ‘closed.’”

Sonia leaned against the counter, fighting for steadiness. “We’ve dealt with missing persons cases,” she said. “But this feels different.”

“It is,” Michael replied. “This is disappearance with permission. Disappearance with policy language wrapped around it like a blanket.”

He hated how excited part of him felt—because excitement meant the hunt had started, the puzzle had teeth. He hated that he’d been built for this. He loved that it meant he could do something about it.

“I’m going to talk to Antony,” he said.

Sonia’s frustration sharpened into fear. “You’re not assigned to BBVP cases, Mike. You know how territorial that program is. The blind committee guards its authority like a board of directors. The SLA backs them because it keeps everything ‘contained.’ They don’t want outsiders asking questions.”

“I’m assigned to missing people,” Michael snapped, then immediately regretted the edge in his voice. He stepped closer and took her hands. “I’m sorry. I’m not mad at you.”

"I know," Sonia said, but her eyes were wet. "I'm mad, too. And I'm scared."

Michael squeezed her hands. "I'll be careful," he said, hearing how hollow it sounded even to himself.

Sonia pulled her hands back and brushed her fingers along his jaw, a small, grounding gesture. "You always say that," she whispered. "And then you go and do the brave thing that makes enemies."

"That's not brave," Michael replied. "That's necessary."

Sonia's voice sharpened again. "Necessary gets you killed, Mike. Or worse—disappeared."

The word made Michael's stomach turn. He looked back down at the letter, and for a moment he saw not just Antony's name but a line of names, a quiet list. He saw folders closing. He saw doors labeled PROGRAM REVIEW. He saw a system that worked like a machine—smooth until it caught you in its gears.

Michael inhaled slowly. "I'm not going to let them do this to him," he said.

Sonia's eyes locked onto his. "Then let me in," she said. "Not as your partner on the job—because I already am. As your wife."

He nodded once. "You're in."

Sonia's shoulders loosened slightly, relief mixing with dread. "Okay," she said, forcing air into her lungs. "Then we do this smart. We don't storm the program. We don't give them excuses. We gather facts."

Michael's anger surged again, but he harnessed it. "We start with Antony," he said. "We confirm he's missing, not 'reassigned.' We find out who covered his route. We find the paperwork trail they think no one can see."

Sonia picked up her duty belt and began fastening it with quick, practiced motions. "And if they try to stand you down?" she asked.

Michael folded the letter, not as neatly this time, and shoved it into his jacket pocket. "Then we keep moving," he said. "Because movement is the only thing they can't lock down without admitting what they're doing."

Sonia stepped close, and before the day could swallow her again, she pressed her forehead against his for a brief moment—an intimate, silent promise.

"Come home," she murmured. "Even if you come home angry. Even if you come home tired. Just... come home."

Michael held her there a second longer than he should have. "I will," he said, knowing he could not guarantee it, but needing the words anyway.

Outside, a car passed on the street. Wichita went on with its morning.

Inside, the case had already begun.

And it had already begun to bite back.

# CHAPTER TWO

## No Voice on the Line

Antony Grumpton's phone rang until it handed Detective Michael Miguel to voicemail.

The sound cut off too cleanly.

No static. No background noise. No hint of motion. Just silence, followed by a calm, evenly paced recorded greeting spoken by a man who believed his life was still governed by routine.

"Hello, this is Antony. I'm probably on my route. Please leave your name and number, and I'll call you back."

The message ended with a soft click.

Michael did not hang up right away.

He stayed on the line, counting his breaths, listening to the dead air stretch after the recording as if the phone itself might confess something. Silence had its own language. In his line of work, it often spoke louder than panic. Panic made noise. Panic left mistakes. Silence meant someone had been removed cleanly—or had never been given the chance to react.

Antony didn't break through it.

There was no hurried intake of breath. No whispered warning. No coded plea disguised as casual conversation. Just absence—complete and deliberate.

Michael finally disconnected and wrote the time in his notebook. He wrote slowly, carefully, pressing the pen just hard enough to leave an impression on the next page. He wrote the voicemail wording verbatim. Exact language mattered. Systems lived and died on phrasing, and this system already felt like one built to survive scrutiny.

He tried again an hour later.

Same result.

The message played identically, down to the cadence and timing. No update. No revision. No subtle change that suggested Antony knew something was wrong. It was the voice of a man who expected to come home and check messages at the end of a normal day.

Across the kitchen table, Sonia Miguel watched him work. Her coffee sat untouched, cooling by degrees she did not seem to notice. She knew better than to interrupt too early. Michael built cases in layers, and he hated admitting a case existed before he had control of the frame.

"That message sounds old," she said finally.

Michael nodded without looking up. "Recorded when things were normal."

"That's what bothers me," Sonia replied, irritation sharpening into anger. "People change their voicemail when something's wrong. Even blind operators do. They warn route contacts. They leave instructions. He didn't."

Michael capped the pen and leaned back in his chair. "Which means he didn't see it coming."

The words settled between them like a bruise.

Michael thought about routine—the invisible architecture that allowed blind vending operators to function independently in a world designed for sighted people. Antony ran his route by sound, touch, and memory. He counted steps in hallways. He recognized elevators by the sigh of their doors. He identified buildings by acoustics, airflow, and the echo of his cane.

Routine wasn't comfort.

Routine was survival.

Sonia's fingers tightened around the mug. "They act like it's just a job," she said. "But it's not. It's his whole system. You take that from a blind operator and you're not 'reassigning' him. You're ripping out the floor."

Michael's irritation flared—at the letter, at the delay, at the careful politeness of all of it. "And the worst part," he said, "is they'll call it support while they do it."

Sonia's eyes lifted to his. "And you're going to walk into their building and ask for honesty."

"I'm going to walk into their building and ask for records," Michael corrected.

"Records they control," Sonia shot back, anger rising. "And if they control them, they control the story."

Michael's jaw tightened. "Then we don't let them write it."

Sonia leaned forward, emotion breaking through her professional discipline. "Mike, I'm not arguing because I want you to stop," she said. "I'm arguing because I want you to come home."

The word home hit him harder than the voicemail.

For a second, his mind flashed back—not to a battlefield, but to a hospital hallway. The smell of antiseptic. The dull pressure bandage across his face. The moment he realized his left eye was gone and the world would never look the same. He remembered the first time he tried to walk without depth perception and misjudged a step—how helpless the body felt when it could not trust itself.

He remembered Sonia sitting beside him, her hand steady on his wrist, refusing to let him pretend it didn't matter.

Blindness changed the world. Not the person. The world.

Michael opened his notebook again. "We start with the route," he said, voice low. "We start where Antony's life is loudest."

They drove to Antony's vending site just after midmorning. The building was already alive with foot traffic—employees coming and going, coins dropping, buttons pressed without thought. Michael paused just inside the entrance, letting the soundscape map itself in his head before he moved closer.

Everything hummed evenly.

Too evenly.

The motors were smooth. The coin mechanisms responsive. Snack spirals aligned with obsessive precision. Someone had serviced these machines recently—and carefully.

Michael closed his eyes for a moment. In the war, he'd learned to trust sound when vision failed him. Machines neglected by distracted hands told on themselves. These didn't. Whoever had touched them knew exactly what they were doing—and had been given time to do it.

The building manager approached with polite impatience already baked into his posture. "Machines are working fine," he said, as if that should end the conversation before it began.

"I'm not here about the machines," Michael replied evenly. "I'm here about the operator."

The manager blinked. "Antony?"

"Yes."

"He hasn't been around in a few days," the manager said. "But service hasn't lapsed."

"Who serviced the machines?" Michael asked.

The man hesitated—just long enough to matter. "Blind guy. Knew the route. Didn't give a name. Said he was covering temporarily."

Temporary.

The word struck Michael like a slap. It was always the same word in these letters, these programs, these clean little processes. Temporary made harm sound harmless.

"Did Antony tell you he was leaving?" Michael asked.

The manager shook his head. "No. He loved this route. Took pride in it. Always early. If he stopped coming, something stopped him."

Michael stepped closer to the machines and listened again, then ran his fingertips along the coin return, feeling for residual warmth. Recently handled. Different rhythm. Different pressure. Antony had a particular way of working—efficient but cautious. This was someone else.

Someone else had learned the route.

Michael asked to see the backroom where supplies were stored. The manager hesitated again, then led him down a hallway. Boxes of snacks sat stacked with clean edges. Labels faced outward. Inventory sheets were clipped to a board like a badge of order. Too neat.

"Antony keep it like this?" Michael asked.

"Pretty much," the manager said. "He was meticulous."

Michael ran a finger across the top of one box. No dust. Recently moved.

He pointed to the clipboard. "Who signs these?"

The manager glanced away. "Whoever covers. It's not a big deal."

"It's a big deal when the operator is missing," Michael said, sharper than he intended.

The manager stiffened. "I'm telling you, the service isn't broken."

"That's not the question," Michael replied. "The question is: who has authority to be here?"

The manager's impatience hardened into caution. "I don't know anything about authority. I get told a schedule. Machines get filled."

Michael let it go—for now. Pushing the manager would make him defensive. Defensive people lied. Michael needed people to talk.

Outside, Sonia leaned against the hood of the cruiser, arms crossed tight against her chest. She didn't wait for him to speak.

"They replaced him," she said, anger breaking through restraint.

"Yes," Michael replied. "Cleanly."

"Like he was a defective part," Sonia snapped. "A human being running a state route, and they swap him out like a coin mechanism."

"Yes," Michael said again. "Which means this wasn't sloppy. It was sanctioned."

He pulled the audit letter from his jacket and studied the reassignment code. It wasn't a location. It wasn't a building. It was procedural—a marker indicating authority transfer rather than destination.

"A process marker," Sonia said quietly, the implication sinking in.

"Exactly," Michael replied. "Which means Antony didn't go somewhere public. He went somewhere administrative."

Sonia's jaw clenched. "They're hiding him in paperwork."

"They're hiding him behind authority," Michael corrected. "And authority is harder to arrest."

They drove next to the State Licensing Agency annex—a building designed to look harmless. Beige walls. Neutral signage. No sense of urgency anywhere. Michael requested reassignment logs at the front desk.

The receptionist's smile tightened the moment she heard the operator's name. "Those records fall under blind committee oversight," she said.

"I'm not asking for contents," Michael replied evenly. "I'm asking for dates."

"Dates still fall under oversight," she said, as if repeating it made it more true.

Michael held her gaze. "A blind business owner is missing. I'm requesting basic confirmation that he was reassigned and where the authority moved."

Her smile thinned. "You'll need to speak to the BBVP administrator."

"Then call them," Michael said.

"I can't," she replied quickly. "Not without... not without a request form."

Sonia's voice cut in, sharp. "A request form to confirm a person exists?"

The receptionist's cheeks flushed. "Ma'am, this is procedure."

"Procedure is not a shield," Sonia snapped. "It's not a reason to hide behind a counter while people disappear."

Michael put a hand up—quiet command, not dismissal. "We do this smart," he murmured to Sonia. Then to the receptionist: "I'll take the form."

The receptionist slid a page across the counter and pointed to fields labeled in small print: operator name, program number, request purpose, justification, supervisory signature. Paperwork designed to slow questions until questions gave up.

Michael filled it out with measured strokes. When he handed it back, the receptionist disappeared into the back and returned with a clipboard—redacted, sanitized, stamped after Antony's voicemail recording.

Delay again.

Michael scanned the timestamps, feeling anger rise. "These dates don't match field activity," he said. "There's a three-day gap."

The receptionist lifted her chin. "That's what's on file."

Sonia's breath came out sharp. "Because you wrote the file after you moved him," she said under her breath.

The receptionist stiffened, pretending she hadn't heard.

Outside, Sonia leaned against the wall and squeezed her eyes shut for a moment. "They're moving faster than the paper," she said, voice trembling with rage.

"They always do," Michael replied. "Paper exists to make it look slow."

Before leaving, Michael requested access logs. Denied. Visitor records. Denied. Each refusal was polite. Each one airtight. Procedure weaponized into a cage.

He called John Lizzardo, the department records clerk, from the parking lot. John answered on the second ring, his voice cautious and sleepy, as if he already suspected why Michael was calling.

"Lizzardo," he said.

"Mike Miguel," Michael replied. "I need a cross-reference on a reassignment code. BBVP related."

A pause. "Those aren't in my section."

"Everything's in your section," Michael said flatly. "You just decide what's visible."

Another pause, longer this time. "You're stepping into an internal program. They don't like that."

Michael's anger flashed. "Blind people are missing, John. Not paperwork."

John lowered his voice. "Listen. I can tell you this: the reassignment codes don't map to locations. They map to processes. If you're looking for a place, you won't find it in my system."

"Then where?" Michael demanded.

John hesitated. "There are 'review destinations.' That's what they call them. Like a holding pattern. They're not public. They're not... recorded in a way that leads back to a door."

Michael felt his stomach tighten. "Are you telling me a state program has a way to move people without leaving a trail?"

John exhaled. "I'm telling you the trail exists, but it's layered. And you're not authorized to peel it."

"Authorization doesn't matter," Michael said. "A man is gone."

John's voice went quieter. "Be careful, Miguel. When you pull on the wrong thread, you don't always get the truth. Sometimes you get cut."

The line clicked dead. John hadn't hung up. Someone else had ended the call.

Sonia stared at Michael. "Did you hear that?" she asked.

"Yes," Michael said, voice tight. "And now they know we're not just asking."

They returned to the vending site near closing time to see if anything changed when the building emptied. A janitor mentioned an unmarked van earlier that week—early morning, no logos, doors closed quickly. He hadn't thought much of it. Vans came and went every day.

"What color?" Sonia asked.

"White," the janitor said. "Maybe. Could've been gray. No writing. No company name. Just… plain."

"Did anyone get out?" Michael asked.

The janitor shrugged. "Two guys. Moved quick. Didn't chat. Didn't laugh. Like they were on a timer."

It wasn't proof. But it was pattern. Pattern was what you built cases on when people were smart enough to avoid leaving evidence.

Back in the cruiser, Michael wrote carefully:

No voice.

No warning.

No consent.

Beneath it, he added:

Replacement authorized without operator contact.

Process code hides destination.

Records clerk call terminated by unknown.

He stared at the words longer than necessary, the weight of them settling into his chest.

For the first time since opening the letter, Michael felt something colder than anger take hold.

Fear.

Not for himself.

For how easy this had been.

If the system could erase Antony Grumpton this quietly, it could do it again.

And again.

And no one would ever hear the moment it happened.

Michael closed his notebook and looked at Sonia. "We're past routine now," he said.

Sonia's eyes were bright with anger and something sharper. "Good," she said. "Because I'm done being polite."

Michael started the engine.

And the city kept moving, unaware that a man had vanished without noise—and that the noise was coming next.

CHAPTER THREE

# The Committee Door

Michael Miguel had learned long before becoming a detective that the most dangerous rooms were the ones that pretended to be reasonable.

The hallway outside the BBVP committee chamber smelled faintly of disinfectant and old carpet glue, the kind of institutional scent that suggested permanence without accountability. The lighting was even, soft, designed to calm. Nothing in the space looked hostile, and that was precisely what made it dangerous. This building had been designed to slow people down, to make them feel small and procedural, to remind them that nothing urgent ever happened here.

Sonia stood beside him, arms folded tight across her chest. Her posture was disciplined, professional, but Michael knew her well enough to see the tension beneath it. She had reviewed the Kansas Blind Business Vending Program manual twice the night before, not because she believed it would protect them, but because she wanted to understand exactly how authority would be used against them.

“They’re not going to say no,” Sonia said quietly. “They’ll say ‘not here,’ or ‘not now,’ or ‘that’s handled.’”

Michael adjusted the strap of the patch over his left eye, an old habit that surfaced when pressure closed in. "Then we listen for what they don't say."

Sonia exhaled slowly. "This committee isn't advisory, Mike. They're a board. They control audits, site assignments, reviews. If they decide someone is a problem, they don't have to touch them directly. They just move the ground out from under their feet."

Michael nodded. "Which is why Antony didn't get a warning."

"And why you're standing here instead of knocking on a door that says 'Missing Persons,'" Sonia added, frustration bleeding through control.

Michael turned slightly toward her, lowering his voice so the hallway microphones—real or imagined—couldn't steal the moment. "Say what you're really saying."

Sonia's jaw worked once, like she was chewing down the sentence before it could escape. "I'm saying they know how to take people apart without touching them." Her eyes fixed on his patch. "And I'm saying you don't get to act like you're indestructible just because you've survived worse."

The anger in her voice wasn't directed at him. It was directed at the idea that he might not come back from this one.

Michael felt that old war memory try to rise—dust, heat, a flash of pain—and he pushed it down. "I'm not trying to be indestructible," he said. "I'm trying to be useful."

"You can be useful without being reckless," Sonia snapped, then immediately softened, like she'd caught herself stepping too hard on a bruise. "Mike... if this committee has friends in the building, they can ruin your career with one phone call. Or worse."

Michael held her gaze. "Then we keep it tight. Facts. Procedure. We make them say something."

Sonia shook her head. "They won't. They'll make you the problem for asking."

"Then we let them," Michael said. "Because if they're willing to make me the problem, it means we're close."

Before Sonia could answer, a woman stepped out from behind a frosted glass partition. Her badge identified her as administrative support. She smiled politely, the way people did when policy had already decided the outcome.

"The committee is in session," she said. "They weren't expecting law enforcement."

"I'm not here for the committee," Michael replied evenly. "I'm here for an operator who hasn't been heard from in six days."

The woman hesitated. "This is a program matter."

Sonia's voice cut in, sharp but controlled. "A blind business owner is missing. That makes it a people matter."

The woman lowered her voice. "Detective, if you enter that room, it will be noted."

Michael met her gaze. "Good."

She didn't move immediately. Her polite expression held, but her eyes flicked toward the ceiling corner—toward a camera that didn't need to be obvious to be real.

"Sir," she said, softer now, "I'm not telling you not to go in. I'm telling you what happens after you do."

Sonia leaned closer, her tone all business. "What happens?"

The woman swallowed. "You'll get a letter. A complaint. Something about interference. It'll sound official." Her voice dropped again. "And it won't be from them. It'll be from somebody above them."

Michael nodded once. He'd heard that exact pattern in other cases: the warning delivered with a smile so no one could accuse the messenger of hostility. "Thank you," he said. "That's enough."

The woman stepped aside.

The door ahead of them was labeled PROGRAM REVIEW.

The sign was printed in neutral font, bolted flush to the wall, and mounted at a height that assumed the reader could see it clearly.

Michael paused for half a second, letting the irony land. A room governed entirely by blind operators, marked for sighted convenience.

He knocked once, deliberately, then opened the door.

Inside, the room was quiet in a way that felt rehearsed.

Not silent—never silent—but regulated.

Chairs were arranged with geometric precision around a long conference table. Name placards sat in front of each seat, embossed and tactile, readable by touch. Audio-assist devices rested at measured intervals.

Everything in the room spoke of competence, preparation, and authority.

This was not a group that needed help navigating power. This was a group that wielded it.

Demetrius Giller sat at the head of the table.

He did not stand.

Demetrius was blind, like the others, but authority had taught him how to occupy space without vision. His posture was relaxed, shoulders back, hands folded. His cane rested against the table not as a mobility aid, but as punctuation.

"Detective Miguel," Demetrius said. "You're early."

"I didn't schedule," Michael replied. "I'm here because Antony Grumpton is missing."

The word missing altered the air.

Darrius Johnson, seated to Demetrius's right, straightened slightly.

Maykayla Peterson, the vice chair, tilted her head as if listening beyond the word itself. Ida Glitter and Ryean Trotter sat farther down the table, hands folded, faces neutral. All of them were blind. All of them were BBVP operators. All of them represented hundreds of others who trusted this committee to speak when they could not.

"Missing is an assumption," Demetrius said calmly. "Operators undergo reviews. Reassignments happen."

Michael remained standing. He did not take the chair that had been subtly angled toward him. "Antony's phone is dead. His route was reassigned without notice. His audit letter was backdated."

Demetrius smiled. "That's interpretation."

Michael felt irritation flare, then forced it down. Anger was expected.

Precision was not. “I need the destination,” he said. “Where was Antony reassigned?”

There was a pause—not confusion, not surprise, but coordination.

Darrius spoke next. “Destinations are confidential during review.”

“And after review?” Michael asked.

Maykayla answered. “After review, the operator either returns to their route or exits the program.”

“Exits how?” Michael pressed.

Demetrius leaned forward slightly. “That depends on the findings.”

Michael scanned the room, reading posture instead of faces. Silence here wasn’t awkward. It was procedural. Silence was how votes happened without raised hands.

“Who authorized the reassignment?” Michael asked.

“The committee,” Demetrius replied. “In accordance with the BBVP manual.”

“Show me the vote,” Michael said.

Demetrius’s smile thinned. “Votes are internal.”

Sonia stepped forward, anger breaking through restraint. “A blind business owner is missing. You’re hiding behind policy.”

Every head turned toward her voice.

Demetrius nodded politely. “Officer Miguel. You’re welcome to sit.”

"I'm fine standing," Sonia replied. "So was Antony, last time anyone heard him."

The temperature in the room dropped.

Ida Glitter shifted in her chair. Ryean Trotter inhaled sharply, then said nothing. Darrius tapped the table once—one sharp sound that ended discussion before it could spread.

Michael leaned forward, placing both hands flat on the table. "Let's stop pretending this is normal. Antony didn't resign. He didn't request leave. He didn't violate policy. Yet his livelihood was reassigned and his voice disappeared."

Demetrius's tone hardened. "This committee exists to protect blind operators."

Michael's reply was immediate. "Then where is he?"

Silence.

"By erasing them?" Sonia snapped.

"That's enough," Demetrius said coldly. "This is not a law enforcement proceeding."

"It is when someone goes missing," Michael replied.

Demetrius reached for a folder and tapped it once. "You don't understand how this program works. Operators agree to oversight. Audits. Committee discretion."

"They do not agree to vanish," Michael said.

The scrape of Demetrius's chair echoed as he stood. "You are interfering with a state-regulated program."

Michael straightened. "And you are obstructing an investigation."

Maykayla spoke carefully, voice smooth. "Detective, your concern is noted. There are channels."

Michael's frustration rose again. "Channels don't answer phones," he said. "Channels don't return families their loved ones."

Darrius's voice stayed low, controlled. "Detective, you're misreading the structure. This committee cannot be compelled by tone."

"No," Michael replied. "You can be compelled by law. And by conscience."

Ida Glitter shifted again, more noticeably. Her hands moved in her lap, fingers tightening. Michael watched her posture. She wasn't calm—she was contained. It was the same containment he'd seen in witnesses who wanted to speak but were afraid of the cost.

Demetrius angled his head slightly. "Are you implying wrongdoing?"

Michael placed Antony's audit letter on the table. "I'm implying a man's name became a code. I'm implying you backdated paperwork to make a removal look normal."

No one reached for the letter.

No one denied the date.

A staff member entered quietly and leaned toward Demetrius, whispering something Michael couldn't hear. Demetrius nodded once, then his mouth tightened as if the whisper had turned a dial inside him.

"This meeting is adjourned," Demetrius said. "You will receive a written response."

Sonia laughed once, sharp and incredulous. "Written by who? After how many days?"

Demetrius ignored her. "Detective, you should leave before you misunderstand your role."

Michael didn't move. "Explain the backdated timestamp," he said again, slower this time, forcing the question to sit in the room like a stain.

Darrius finally spoke, voice low. "Records reflect process, not emotion."

Michael's laugh was bitter. "That's the problem."

Two men appeared at the doorway—security, not police. Their presence was quiet and deliberate. Not a threat delivered with fists, but a reminder delivered with bodies.

Sonia's hand touched Michael's arm. Not pulling him back—anchoring him.

"Mike," she said softly, and he heard the plea under the discipline: come out of this room.

Michael stepped back, one measured step at a time, refusing to be hurried. If the committee wanted control, he would deny them the satisfaction of seeing it work quickly.

They were escorted into the hallway by the same administrative aide. Her voice was quiet now, barely above a whisper. "You didn't hear this from me," she said, "but they don't like attention."

Sonia's anger snapped. "People are missing."

The aide swallowed. "And now you're noticed."

They walked away from the door, and the corridor seemed longer than it had before, as if the building itself had expanded to keep distance between them and the truth.

When they reached the elevator, Sonia finally let the emotion spill in a controlled burst. "They sat in there like a board meeting," she said, voice shaking with fury. "Like it was a spreadsheet. Like Antony is a line item."

Michael pressed the elevator call button and listened to the soft ding. "That's what they've turned it into," he said.

Sonia stepped closer, lowering her voice. "You heard that whisper. You saw the security." Her eyes flicked to the cameras again. "They're not just defending a program. They're defending a pipeline."

Michael's chest tightened. "And pipelines have destinations."

Sonia's hand slid into his, quick and subtle, a gesture that carried more than comfort. It carried a promise: I'm here. I'm with you. "I'm angry," she said. "But I'm also scared. Don't make me say that twice."

Michael squeezed her hand once. "You won't have to."

The elevator arrived. They stepped inside. The doors began to close, and for a second Michael watched the hallway disappear—smooth, polished, innocent-looking.

Sonia exhaled. "What now?"

Michael opened his notebook and wrote three bullet points, each one short enough to feel like a verdict.

No destination.

No consent.

No appeal.

He closed the notebook slowly.

"This committee doesn't just govern routes," he said. "It governs disappearance."

Sonia's voice was quiet. "So how do we fight something that doesn't leave a body?"

Michael stared at the closing doors, feeling the system tighten around them. "We find the one person inside who still remembers what the manual can't hide," he said.

The doors sealed shut.

And somewhere on the other side, the machinery of the program kept moving—quiet, polite, and hungry.

## CHAPTER FOUR

# Kail's Warning

The elevator doors closed with a cushioned, hydraulic sigh that felt heavier than the sound itself. Michael Miguel remained still as the car began its descent, the illuminated numbers above the door sliding downward at a pace that felt deliberate, almost watchful. Each floor passing beneath them felt like another layer of insulation being sealed between what they had just challenged and whatever consequences were already forming above.

Sonia stood at his side, arms folded tightly across her chest. Her posture was controlled, professional, but Michael had learned long ago to read the signs beneath the uniform. The tension in her shoulders. The way her jaw stayed set, as if she were holding words back by force.

Neither of them spoke.

The silence stretched, thick and uncomfortable, until Sonia finally broke it.

"They already called someone," she said quietly.

Michael nodded once. "Before we left the room."

"No," she corrected, her eyes flicking briefly toward the mirrored wall.

"Before we opened our mouths."

That landed heavier than he wanted to admit. The committee had been ready. Not just defensive, but prepared. That meant this wasn't reactionary. It was rehearsed.

The elevator chimed and the doors opened onto the main lobby of the State Licensing Agency building. Sunlight filtered through tall glass panes, illuminating polished floors and the steady movement of employees and visitors. Phones rang. Conversations overlapped. Life moved forward in neat, orderly patterns.

None of it felt real.

Sonia slowed her pace just enough to speak without drawing attention.

"From this moment on, we assume everything we do is logged. Phones, computers, reports. Even conversations that look casual."

"I already do," Michael replied. "The question is who's reading the logs—and who they're sharing them with."

They didn't head toward the exit. Instead, Michael veered toward a side corridor marked EMPLOYEE ACCESS ONLY. Sonia followed without question.

Years of working together—and years of marriage—had taught her when to trust his instincts without needing an explanation.

Halfway down the corridor, Sonia reached out and caught his sleeve.

"You didn't sit," she said.

Michael stopped. "I wasn't going to."

"They wanted you to," she pressed. "That was the test. Sit down. Let them control the pace. Let them define the rules of the conversation."

Michael glanced back toward the committee wing, now hidden by a turn in the hallway. "I've watched too many people disappear because they agreed to rules designed to erase them."

Sonia's voice sharpened, anger cracking into fear. "And I've watched good cops get buried because they underestimated how quietly a system can retaliate."

He turned to face her fully. "You think I don't know that?"

"I think you know it," she said, lowering her voice, "and you keep acting like surviving the worst already means you're immune to what comes next."

Michael took a breath. "I'm not immune. I just refuse to let fear decide who matters."

Before Sonia could respond, a voice called out behind them.

"Detective Miguel."

Michael turned.

Kail McDow stood near a recessed doorway, his white cane angled lightly against his leg. He wore no jacket, no visible badge—nothing that marked him as part of the institutional machinery surrounding them. Despite his blindness, he carried himself with a precision that came from memorizing space and sensing presence rather than relying on sight.

"You shouldn't be here," Kail said evenly. "And you definitely shouldn't have gone into that room."

Michael studied him. Kail was blind—completely—but navigated the building with a confidence that suggested deep familiarity. He was also the only blind person the State Licensing Agency had ever hired and retained.

"You heard," Michael said.

Kail smiled thinly. "Everyone hears."

Sonia stepped closer. "We're looking for Antony Grumpton."

Kail's jaw tightened. "I know."

The air shifted.

"Then tell us what you know," Michael said.

Kail tilted his head slightly, listening—not to them, but to the building itself. The hum of ventilation. The distant echo of footsteps.

The faint electrical buzz in the walls.

"Not here," Kail said. "Not standing."

He turned and began walking without waiting for them to follow.

They did.

The corridor narrowed as they moved deeper into the building's service arteries. Carpet gave way to industrial tile, and the lighting grew harsher, stripped of decorative intent. Kail stopped near a maintenance alcove filled with cleaning supplies and access panels—an invisible space designed to be overlooked.

"This program wasn't built to hurt people," Kail said quietly. "But it was built to move them."

"Move them where?" Sonia asked.

Kail shook his head. "That's the wrong question. There isn't a place.

There's a process."

Michael leaned in. "Explain it."

"The BBVP manual authorizes audits, reassignments, temporary removals pending review," Kail said. "The committee has authority to 'stabilize operations.' That language is vague by design."

"Vague enough to erase people," Sonia said.

"Isolate them," Kail corrected. "Isolation is cleaner. Quieter. No scenes."

Michael felt his jaw tighten. "Are they alive?"

Kail hesitated, the silence stretching long enough to answer the question before words arrived.

"Yes," he said finally. "At first."

The words struck like a blow.

Sonia turned away, pressing her palm flat against the wall, grounding herself. "How many?"

"I don't know," Kail replied. "More than the files show. Fewer than the rumors claim."

Michael's voice hardened. "Where are they being held?"

"I don't know," Kail said. "And if I did, I wouldn't say it in this building."

"Then why warn us?" Michael demanded.

"Because you didn't sit down," Kail said. "That made you dangerous."

"And you?" Sonia asked. "What does that make you?"

Kail smiled faintly. "Temporary."

The word carried weight. A reminder that even insiders were disposable.

"You need to stop," Kail continued. "Officially. Loudly. Make it look like you backed off."

"I can't," Michael said.

"I know," Kail replied. "That's why I'm warning you."

Sonia stepped between them, protective without being obvious. "What happens if he doesn't?"

Kail lowered his voice. "Then he gets moved. Just like the operators."

Sonia froze. "They'd remove a detective?"

"They already started," Kail said, pulling a folded document from his jacket. "Internal inquiry. Your name isn't on it yet—but the structure is there."

Michael scanned the page. "Interference. Overreach."

"Once paperwork exists," Kail said, "reality follows."

Sonia looked up. "Why help us?"

“Because I’m blind,” Kail said simply. “And because I still remember what this program was supposed to be.”

“You need proof,” Kail continued. “Something external. Something alive.”

Sonia’s eyes widened. “You know someone.”

Kail didn’t answer. “Go quiet. Let them think you’re scared.”

Footsteps echoed down the corridor. Kail stepped back.

“Be careful who you trust,” he said. “Even people who love you.”

Then he was gone, cane tapping softly as he merged back into the building.

They stepped outside into the sunlight, the brightness almost painful after the controlled interior.

“My access is delayed,” Sonia said suddenly, staring at her phone.

“System lag.”

Michael checked his own. “My case notes won’t sync.”

Sonia let out a bitter laugh. “That was fast.”

They reached their cruiser and stopped. Sonia finally let herself shake.

“I won’t lose you to paperwork,” she said. “Promise me you won’t go alone.”

Michael took her hands. “I promise.”

She rested her forehead against his. “Then we do this together.”

Michael opened his notebook and wrote three lines:

No destination.

No consent.

No appeal.

He closed it.

This wasn't just a missing persons case.

It was a system built to erase people.

And now it had chosen him.

## CHAPTER FIVE

# Families Left Behind

The Grumpton house sat at the end of a quiet street where trees older than the neighborhood leaned over fences and cast shadows that moved with the wind. Michael Miguel stood on the front porch longer than necessary, his hand hovering near the doorbell, aware that what he was about to do would crack open grief that had barely begun to settle.

He pressed the button.

Inside, footsteps approached—slow, careful, the gait of someone who had learned to move through a world that no longer made sense. The door opened to reveal Martha Grumpton, Antony's wife. She was younger than Michael expected, maybe forty, with dark hair pulled back and eyes that had cried themselves dry days ago.

She looked at his badge without surprise.

"You're late," she said.

Michael blinked. "Ma'am?"

"I called the police four days ago," Martha said, her voice steady but brittle. "They told me my husband was reassigned. That it was program business. That I should contact the committee."

“And did you?” Michael asked.

Martha’s laugh was sharp and humorless. “I tried. They told me Antony signed paperwork. That he agreed to temporary relocation for program enhancement.” She stepped back, opening the door wider. “He didn’t sign anything, Detective. He didn’t agree to anything. And he sure didn’t leave without telling me.”

Michael entered the house. It was neat, organized in the specific way that homes with blind residents often were—everything in its place, nothing left to chance. Photos lined the hallway: Antony at his vending site, smiling beside a machine he couldn’t see but had mastered through touch and memory. Antony at what looked like a BBVP conference, surrounded by other operators. Antony and Martha on their wedding day, his hand on her shoulder, her hand covering his. “When did you last see him?” Michael asked.

Martha led him to the kitchen and gestured to a chair. She didn’t offer coffee. This wasn’t a social visit.

“Tuesday morning,” she said. “Three weeks ago. He left for his route at five-thirty like always. He liked to get there early, check inventory, make sure everything was perfect before the building opened.” Her voice caught. “He took pride in his work.”

“Did he mention anything unusual?” Michael asked. “Any concerns? Anyone watching him?”

Martha’s eyes sharpened. “How did you know?”

Michael leaned forward. “Know what?”

“About the watching,” Martha said. She stood and walked to a desk in the corner, opening a laptop. “Antony kept notes on his computer. He said operators who didn’t document things got forgotten.”

She opened a file marked with a date. "Two weeks before he disappeared, he typed this. I heard him using his screen reader late at night."

She turned the laptop toward Michael.

Michael read the text on screen—typed in clean, structured paragraphs: Feel like someone's tracking my movements. Not customers. Someone else. Asked building manager if security changed. He said no. Route patterns feel monitored. Committee called yesterday asking about "efficiency metrics." Never asked before. Michael's jaw tightened. "He felt watched."

"For two weeks," Martha confirmed. "He didn't want to worry me, but I could tell. He'd come home tense. Quiet. He'd check his phone constantly, like he was waiting for something."

"Did he receive any official communication from the BBVP?" Michael asked.

"Not until the day before he disappeared," Martha said. "A letter. He had me read it to him. It said he was being audited. That someone would be reviewing his operation. That he should prepare documentation."

"Do you still have the letter?"

Martha's expression hardened. "No. Two days after he disappeared, a man came to the door. Said he was from the SLA. Said the letter had been sent in error and he needed to collect it for program records." She crossed her arms. "I was stupid enough to give it to him."

Michael felt anger coil in his chest. "What did this man look like?"

"Suit. Tie. Carried a briefcase. Very polite. Very official." She paused. "And very thorough. He asked if Antony had left any other documents. Any correspondence with the committee. Any complaints."

"What did you tell him?"

"I told him no," Martha said. "But Antony did leave something."

She walked to a shelf and removed what looked like a decorative box. Inside were audio recordings—small digital files organized by date.

"Antony recorded his routes," Martha explained. "Not for work. For himself. He'd narrate what he was doing, what he was feeling, like a diary. He said it helped him process." She selected one file dated three days before his disappearance. "Listen to this."

She pressed play.

Antony's voice filled the kitchen, warm and familiar despite the recording's compression: "Thursday route. Everything serviced on time. Met new operator today—or at least, I think he was an operator. He was blind, knew the terminology, but something felt wrong. He asked about my committee relationships. Asked if I'd ever disagreed with a vote. Asked if I considered myself 'cooperative.' Strange questions. I didn't answer. He left quickly after that." The recording ended.

Michael's mind raced. "Did Antony tell anyone about this?"

"Just me," Martha said. "He was going to mention it to his route supervisor, but then the audit letter came, and then..." She stopped, swallowing hard. "Then he was gone."

Michael pulled out his notebook. "This new operator—did Antony describe him?"

Martha shook her head. "Just that he seemed to know too much. Like he'd been briefed."

“Briefed on what?”

“On Antony,” Martha said quietly. “On his personality. His habits. His relationships with other operators.” Her voice broke. “Detective, they weren’t auditing his vending machines. They were auditing him.”

The words landed like a verdict.

Michael closed his notebook slowly. “Mrs. Grumpton, I need you to understand something. What’s happening to the operators isn’t random. It’s systematic. And the people behind it have resources.”

Martha’s eyes filled with tears she refused to let fall. “Is my husband alive?”

Michael met her gaze. “I don’t know. But I’m going to find out.”

“The committee told me to stop asking questions,” Martha said. “They said I was interfering with program operations. That if I kept calling, I’d be listed as a disruptive contact.”

Michael felt rage flash hot and immediate. “They threatened you?”

“Not in those words,” Martha replied. “But the message was clear: stop looking, or there will be consequences.”

Michael stood. “I need copies of those recordings.”

Martha began transferring files to a USB drive. As she worked, she spoke without looking up. “Detective, there’s something else. Antony told me that if anything ever happened to him, I should contact Kail McDow at the SLA. He said Kail was one of the good ones.”

Michael’s pulse quickened. “Did Antony say why?”

"He said Kail understood what the program was supposed to be," Martha replied. "And what it had become."

She handed Michael the USB drive. Their eyes met, and in that moment, an unspoken agreement passed between them: she would not stop looking for her husband, and he would not stop until the system that had taken Antony was torn apart.

"Be careful, Detective," Martha said as he reached the door. "They made my husband disappear without leaving a trace. They can do the same to you."

Michael stepped onto the porch. The afternoon light was harsh, unforgiving. "Mrs. Grumpton, they're going to wish they'd left your husband alone."

As he walked to his car, Michael glanced back once. Martha stood in the doorway, Of the home she'd built with a man who'd been erased by paperwork and lies.

He started the engine and sat for a moment, listening to the first of Antony's recordings.

The voice was steady, competent, proud. The voice of a man who'd mastered a difficult profession. The voice of someone who'd believed the system would protect him.

Michael knew that belief had killed him.

Or worse—kept him alive in a place where dying would be mercy.

He pulled away from the curb and drove toward the next name on his list. The investigation had shifted. This wasn't about finding a missing operator anymore.

This was about documenting a crime that hadn't finished happening yet.

## CHAPTER SIX

# The Route Replacement

The building that housed Antony Grumpton's vending route was generic in the way government buildings often were—functional, beige, designed to be forgotten. Michael entered through the main doors and immediately felt the hum of bureaucratic routine: footsteps echoing on tile, voices murmuring behind office doors, the soft mechanical sounds of productivity.

The vending machines sat in an alcove near the elevators. Three of them, aligned with precision, stocked with the efficiency that came from someone who knew exactly what they were doing.

Someone who wasn't Antony Grumpton.

Michael approached the machines slowly, studying them the way a detective might study a crime scene—because that's what this was. Not dramatic. Not violent. But a crime scene nonetheless.

The coin mechanisms gleamed. The selection buttons responded instantly. Snack rows sat perfectly aligned, not a single bag crooked or misplaced. Everything hummed with the kind of sterile perfection that suggested recent and thorough maintenance.

Too thorough.

Antony had been meticulous, according to his wife. But meticulous had its own fingerprints—small personal touches that came from pride and habit. Michael didn't see those touches here. He saw efficiency without personality.

"Can I help you?"

Michael turned. A man stood near the elevators, holding a clipboard and wearing an expression of polite suspicion. He was in his thirties, clean-cut, dressed in casual business attire. A white cane rested against his hip, folded and carried more like a credential than a mobility aid.

"Detective Michael Miguel," Michael said, showing his badge. "I'm looking into the previous operator who serviced these machines."

The man's face tightened almost imperceptibly. "I'm covering this route temporarily."

"Your name?"

"Marcus Torres." He shifted his weight. "Is there a problem with the service?"

"No," Michael said. "The machines look perfect. That's actually what I wanted to ask about."

Marcus's jaw worked once. "I don't understand."

Michael gestured to the machines. "You took over this route when?"

"Two and a half weeks ago," Marcus replied. "The committee reassigned me after the previous operator's review."

"Antony Grumpton."

"Yes."

Michael noted the careful neutrality in Marcus's tone—no surprise, no curiosity, just professional distance. "Did you know him?"

"We'd met at operator meetings," Marcus said. "Briefly."

"What did the committee tell you about why you were taking over his route?"

Marcus's fingers tightened around the clipboard. "They said his operation was under review. That temporary coverage was needed. That I was selected based on my performance metrics."

"And you didn't ask questions."

It wasn't phrased as a question, and Marcus heard it. His face flushed. "Detective, when the committee gives you a route, you take it. That's how the program works."

Michael stepped closer, lowering his voice. "Marcus, I'm not here to get you in trouble. But I need to understand something: did anyone tell you what to do if law enforcement asked about Antony?"

The silence stretched too long.

"Marcus," Michael pressed. "Did they?"

The operator's shoulders sagged. "I was told that if anyone came asking, I should refer them to the committee. That Antony's reassignment was confidential program business."

"Who told you that?"

Marcus hesitated. "Darrius Johnson. Committee secretary."

Michael's pulse quickened. "When?"

"The day I got the route," Marcus replied. "He called me personally. Said this was a sensitive situation. That discretion was essential." His voice dropped further. "He said operators who couldn't be discreet didn't keep their routes."

There it was—the threat wrapped in advice, the coercion disguised as guidance.

Michael pulled out his notebook. "Walk me through your first day on this route. Everything."

Marcus listened to the lobby nervously, as if expecting committee members to materialize. "I arrived at five-thirty AM. The machines had already been serviced."

"Already serviced?" Michael repeated. "By who?"

"I don't know," Marcus said. "I assumed Antony had done it before leaving, but..." He paused. "When I checked the inventory logs, the last entry was dated the day before. Antony's handwriting. Everything accounted for."

"So someone serviced the machines between Antony's last entry and your arrival."

"Yes."

Michael felt pieces clicking into place. "Did you report this?"

Marcus shook his head. "I was told the transition was already handled. That my job was just to maintain operations going forward."

"And you didn't think that was strange?"

Marcus's frustration broke through his caution. "Detective, everything about this was strange. But when the committee tells you to be grateful for an assignment, you don't question the logistics."

Michael studied him. "You're scared."

"Yes," Marcus admitted. "Because operators who make the committee uncomfortable get reassigned. And reassignment in this program doesn't just mean losing your route—it means losing everything."

"Is that what happened to Antony?"

Marcus looked away. "I don't know what happened to Antony. But I know he wasn't the first."

Michael's attention sharpened. "What do you mean?"

Marcus lowered his voice to barely above a whisper. "There's talk among operators. Quiet talk. About people disappearing. Not leaving the program—disappearing. Good operators. Experienced ones. People who'd been running successful routes for years."

"How many?"

"I've heard five names in the last six months," Marcus said. "But no one keeps records. No one wants to be the person asking questions."

"Why not?"

Marcus met his gaze. "Because asking questions is how you become the next name on the list."

The words hung in the air between them, heavy with the weight of survival instinct.

Michael leaned forward slightly. "I need to ask you about someone. Do you know a man named Kail McDow?"

Marcus's expression shifted—recognition mixed with caution. "Kail. He works for the SLA. Only blind person they've ever hired into administration. Why?"

"Have you talked to him recently?" Michael asked.

Marcus shook his head. "Not in a couple weeks. He keeps to himself mostly. Doesn't really associate with operators outside of official business. Why are you asking about Kail?"

"I'm trying to understand how the system works from the inside," Michael said carefully. "Kail might have information about the reassignment process."

Marcus's voice dropped. "If you're thinking about approaching Kail, be careful. He's loyal to the SLA. He might report back to the committee that you're asking questions."

"Noted," Michael replied. "But right now, I need allies anywhere I can find them."

Marcus stepped back, his hand instinctively finding his cane. "Detective, I've told you everything I can. If the committee finds out I talked to you—"

"They won't," Michael interrupted. "But I need one more thing."

"What?"

"If you hear anything—anything at all—about operators being contacted, reassigned, or moved, I need you to call me." Michael handed him a card with his direct number.

Marcus took the card hesitantly, running his fingers over the embossed text. "You're asking me to spy."

"I'm asking you to survive," Michael corrected. "Because right now, keeping your head down isn't keeping you safe. It's just making you easier to move when they decide you've served your purpose."

Marcus pocketed the card, his hand shaking slightly. "What do you think is happening to them?"

Michael wanted to lie, to offer reassurance he didn't have. But Marcus deserved truth. "I think they're being taken somewhere. Held. Used."

"For what?"

"I don't know yet," Michael admitted. "But I will."

Marcus slipped the card into his pocket. "Detective, be careful. The committee doesn't just control routes. They control reputations. Careers. If they decide you're the problem..."

"Then I'll deal with that when it comes," Michael said.

He left Marcus standing beside the machines, surrounded by the evidence of Antony's erasure—perfect inventory, flawless operation, no trace of the man who'd built it.

Outside, Michael sat in his car and called Sonia.

She answered on the first ring. "Tell me you found something."

"Antony was being watched," Michael said. "Profiled. Someone interviewed him days before the audit letter. Someone who knew too much about him."

"The committee?"

"Or someone working with them," Michael replied. "And Marcus Torres, the operator who took over his route, was explicitly told not to cooperate with law enforcement."

Sonia's voice tightened. "That's obstruction."

"It's also smart," Michael said. "Because they're not obstructing specific questions—they're creating a culture where operators police themselves."

"Fear as policy," Sonia murmured.

"Exactly."

There was a pause. "Mike, I did some digging on the other missing operators. Three of them filed complaints with the committee in the six months before they disappeared."

Michael's grip tightened on the phone. "Complaints about what?"

"Equipment failures. Route safety issues. Discriminatory treatment by building managers."

Sonia's voice carried an edge of anger. "All legitimate grievances. All dismissed."

"And then they vanished."

"Yes."

Michael closed his eyes, the pattern crystallizing with brutal clarity. "They're not taking random operators. They're taking the ones who push back."

"Which means you were right," Sonia said quietly. "This isn't about program integrity. It's about control."

Michael started the engine. "Where are you?"

"Records office," Sonia replied. "Trying to find the original complaint documents."

"Be careful," Michael said. "If they're watching operators, they're watching us too."

"I know," Sonia said. "I love you."

"I love you too."

The line went dead.

Michael pulled onto the street, his mind churning through the evidence. Antony's recordings. Martha's testimony. Marcus's fear. The pattern of complaints followed by disappearances.

This wasn't a mystery anymore.

This was a system designed to disappear people—and it was working exactly as intended.

His phone buzzed. A text from an unknown number: Stop asking about Antony. For your own good.

Michael stared at the message, then deleted it.

He'd been warned before, in a war that had cost him half his vision. Warnings didn't stop him then. And they sure wouldn't stop him now.

## CHAPTER SEVEN

# Records Clerk's Silence

The Records Division of the Kansas Department of Public Safety occupied a windowless basement that smelled of old paper and electronic ozone. Michael had been there dozens of times over his career, navigating the fluorescent-lit corridors and the bureaucratic gatekeepers who controlled access to the files that made or broke cases.

John Lizzardo had been his contact for five years—a career clerk who understood that information wasn't just data, it was power, and power meant knowing when to share and when to stay quiet.

Michael trusted him.

Past tense.

The desk where John usually sat was empty. Not vacant-for-lunch empty, but cleared empty. No coffee mug. No family photos. No sticky notes with cryptic reminders. The desktop was wiped clean, the drawers removed entirely, the computer terminal dark. Michael stood there longer than necessary, staring at the absence.

"Can I help you, Detective?"

Michael turned. A young woman in a visitor's badge stood near the entrance, holding a tablet and wearing the kind of practiced smile that belonged to someone trained in deflection.

“I’m looking for John Lizzardo,” Michael said.

Her smile didn’t waver. “Mr. Lizzardo is no longer with the department.”

“Since when?”

“I’m not at liberty to discuss personnel matters,” she replied smoothly. “But I’d be happy to assist you with any records requests.”

Michael stepped closer, lowering his voice. “Where did he go?”

The smile finally cracked. “Detective, I really can’t—”

“I’m not asking for his life story,” Michael interrupted. “I’m asking why a career records clerk with fifteen years of service suddenly doesn’t exist.”

The woman glanced toward the doorway, then back at Michael. Her voice dropped. “He resigned. Four days ago. No notice. Cleared out his desk after hours.”

“Did he say why?”

“No.”

“Did anyone talk to him before he left?”

She hesitated. “I wasn’t here, but... I heard he had visitors earlier that day.”

“What kind of visitors?”

“I don’t know,” she said, and Michael heard the truth in it. “But after they left, John looked...” She searched for the word. “Shaken.”

Michael pulled out his notebook. "I need to see the visitor log."

"I'll have to check with my supervisor—"

"I don't have time for supervisors," Michael said, his tone sharpening. "A man I've worked with for five years disappeared from this building, and you're telling me he just decided to retire on a Tuesday afternoon?"

The woman's professional mask slipped further. "Detective, I'm just a temp. They brought me in to cover his shifts. I don't know anything beyond what I was told: John Lizzardo resigned for personal reasons, and all requests should be directed through the new system."

"New system?"

"Automated records portal," she explained. "Everything digital now. No more walk-in requests. You have to submit forms online and wait for approval."

Michael felt the walls closing in. "How long does approval take?"

"Three to five business days. Sometimes longer if the request is flagged."

"Flagged for what?"

She shifted uncomfortably. "I don't have that information."

Michael took a breath, forcing himself to stay calm. "I need John's contact information. His phone number. His home address."

"I can't provide personal information about former employees—"

"Then connect me with whoever can," Michael demanded.

The woman backed toward the door. "I'll see what I can do. Please wait here."

She disappeared into the hallway, moving faster than necessary.

Michael stood alone in the records division, surrounded by the machinery of institutional memory—servers humming behind locked doors, filing cabinets sealed with digital locks, cameras tracking every movement.

This was where truth lived.

And someone was killing it.

He pulled out his phone and dialed John's number from memory.

It rang once, then disconnected.

He tried again. Same result.

On the third attempt, an automated message played: The number you have dialed is no longer in service. Michael felt anger coil in his chest. Phone disconnected. Desk cleared. No forwarding information. John Lizzardo had been erased as thoroughly as Antony Grumpton.

He walked to the main records counter and flagged down another clerk—an older man Michael recognized from previous visits.

"I need to speak to your supervisor," Michael said.

The clerk didn't look up from his terminal. "She's in a meeting."

"Then interrupt it."

Now the clerk looked up, irritation flashing across his face. "Detective, you can't just demand—"

"John Lizzardo," Michael said. "Why did he leave?"

The clerk's expression shifted—not to confusion, but to something closer to fear. "I can't discuss personnel matters."

"Can't or won't?"

"Both."

Michael leaned against the counter. "You worked with John for years. You're telling me he just walked out without saying goodbye?"

The clerk's fingers stopped moving on the keyboard. "Detective Miguel, I suggest you submit your records requests through the proper channels."

"Why?"

"Because that's policy."

Michael lowered his voice. "What happened to him?"

The clerk met his eyes for just a second—long enough for Michael to see the warning there. "Nothing happened. He resigned. People resign."

"Not like this," Michael pressed.

"Like what?"

"Like they're running."

The clerk closed his terminal and stood. "I have work to do."

He walked away before Michael could respond.

Michael stood at the counter, feeling the weight of institutional silence press down around him. Every person he'd talked to had the same look in their eyes: we know something's wrong, but we're not stupid enough to say it out loud.

He turned and nearly collided with a woman in a maintenance uniform. She was older, maybe sixty, pushing a cart loaded with cleaning supplies.

"Excuse me," Michael said automatically.

She didn't move. "You looking for John?"

Michael's attention snapped to her. "Yes."

She glanced around quickly, then leaned closer. "He came to me before he left. Asked me to hold something for him."

Michael's pulse quickened. "What?"

The woman reached into her cleaning cart and pulled out a small envelope, sealed and marked with Michael's name in John's distinctive handwriting.

"He said if a man with a patch over his left eye came asking about him, I should give him this," she said. "Only to you."

Michael took the envelope carefully, as if it might disintegrate. "Did he say anything else?"

"Just that he was sorry." Her voice dropped. "And that you should be careful who you trust."

She pushed her cart away before Michael could ask more.

He walked to his car in the parking garage, got inside, and locked the doors. His hands shook slightly as he opened the envelope.

Inside was a single flash drive and a handwritten note: Miguel—

They came for me. Not cops. Not SLA. Something else. They knew I helped you with the BBVP records. They knew before I did anything traceable. That means someone in your department is feeding them information.

The flash drive has everything I could pull before they locked me out: operator files, reassignment codes, budget transfers. It's not complete, but it's enough. Don't trust the system. Don't trust your chain of command. And for God's sake, don't trust anyone who tells you to back off "for your own good." I'm leaving Kansas. I don't know where yet. Just far.

They told me if I talked, my family would pay the price. I believe them.

Find the reassignment facility before they make you disappear too.

—John

Michael read the note three times, each word sinking deeper.

The reassignment facility.

John had heard about it. He'd found something.

And it had scared him enough to run.

Michael plugged the flash drive into his laptop and opened the files. What he saw made his blood run cold.

Operator names. Dozens of them. Reassignment dates stretching back two years.

Financial transfers labeled "Program Enhancement Initiative." And coordinates—latitude and longitude—pointing to a location in the middle of the Pacific Ocean.

Far from any shipping lanes.

Far from any surveillance.

Far from any hope of rescue.

Michael's phone buzzed. A text from Sonia:

Just left records office. John's gone. What happened?

Michael stared at her message, John's warning echoing in his mind: Don't trust anyone.

But Sonia wasn't anyone. She was his wife. His partner.

He typed back:

Meet me at home. I found something.

Her response came immediately:

On my way.

Michael pulled out of the parking garage, checking his mirrors obsessively. The note had been clear: someone in the department was feeding information to whoever was behind the disappearances.

That meant every call he made, every file he accessed, every person he talked to—all of it could be monitored.

He thought about Martha Grumpton, alone in her house with her husband's voice recordings.

He thought about Marcus Torres, terrified of losing his route.

He thought about Kail McDow at the SLA—the only blind person they'd hired into administration, and Michael's best hope for an inside perspective.

And now John Lizzardo, running from Kansas with his family, leaving behind fifteen years of service because saying the wrong thing meant paying with blood.

This wasn't an investigation anymore.

This was war.

And Michael was walking into it half-blind, surrounded by people who might be allies or enemies, with a target on his back he couldn't see but could feel closing in. He drove home, gripping the steering wheel tight enough to hurt.

The flash drive sat in his pocket like a bomb.

And somewhere in the Pacific Ocean, on an island that shouldn't exist, operators were being held for reasons Michael was only beginning to understand.

John's final words haunted him:

Find the reassignment facility before they make you disappear too.

Michael intended to. The question was whether he'd find it as a detective—or as its next prisoner.

# CHAPTER EIGHT

## Sonia's Instinct

The kitchen table had become their war room.

Michael spread out printed documents from John Lizzardo's flash drive while Sonia stood at the counter, laptop open, cross-referencing financial records she'd pulled from the State Licensing Agency's public budget reports.

The late afternoon sun slanted through the window, casting long shadows that made the paperwork look like evidence at a crime scene.

Which, Michael supposed, it was. "These numbers don't match," Sonia said without looking up. Her fingers flew across the keyboard, pulling up spreadsheets and PDFs. "The BBVP reports sixty-three licensed operators currently active in the program."

"And?" Michael prompted.

"And I count seventy-two names in last year's budget allocation," she replied. "Nine operators are being funded who don't officially exist."

Michael stood and moved to her side, studying the screen over her shoulder. The spreadsheet was dense with line items, codes, and dollar amounts that blurred together into bureaucratic noise. But Sonia had highlighted the discrepancies in yellow—nine entries with operator ID numbers that didn't correspond to anyone in the current roster.

"Ghost operators," Michael murmured.

"Or hidden ones," Sonia corrected. She opened another window, comparing the phantom ID numbers against John's data. "Look at this. Every single one of these ghost IDs shows up in John's reassignment logs."

Michael felt his pulse quicken. "Meaning they're not ghosts. They're operators who were removed from official records but still being paid."

"Paid for what?" Sonia asked, but they both knew the answer.

"For labor," Michael said. "Somewhere off the books."

Sonia closed the laptop and turned to face him. In the fading light, he could see the strain in her face—the tension that came from weeks of digging into a system that fought back with bureaucratic violence.

"Mike, this is funded through the state budget," she said carefully. "That means legislative oversight. Approved expenditures. Someone in the governor's office signed off on this."

Michael's jaw tightened. "Governor Dickens."

"Or his chief of staff," Sonia replied. "Ron Spillwind. He controls budget allocations."

Michael walked back to the table and pulled up the list of financial transfers John had flagged. Hundreds of thousands of dollars moving through accounts labeled "Program Enhancement," "Facility Maintenance," and "Operator Support Services."

"These aren't support services," Michael said. "These are operational costs. Food. Transport. Security."

Sonia joined him at the table, studying the documents with the kind of focused intensity she brought to every case. "Security for what? The program operates in public buildings. Operators work independently. Why would they need private security?"

"Because the operators aren't in public buildings anymore," Michael said. "They're somewhere else. Somewhere that needs guards."

Sonia's hand moved to her mouth, a gesture of unconscious anxiety. "the reassignment facility."

Michael nodded. "John's coordinates point to the middle of the Pacific. No commercial routes nearby. No civilian infrastructure. Just ocean."

"But there's something there," Sonia said. "These financials prove it."

Michael pulled up satellite imagery on his phone, zooming in on the coordinates. The resolution wasn't great—government satellites didn't prioritize empty ocean—but there was something: a dark smudge that could have been cloud cover or could have been land.

"I need better imaging," Michael said. "Military grade."

Sonia shook her head. "You'll never get clearance. Not for a location that far out. Not without explaining why."

"Then I'll find another way."

Sonia reached across the table and took his hand. "Mike, we need to be smart about this. If the governor's office is involved, we're not just fighting the committee anymore. We're fighting the state."

"I know."

"And if they find out what we know—"

"They won't," Michael interrupted. "Not until we're ready."

Sonia's grip tightened. "When will we be ready?"

Michael didn't have an answer. Ready meant having proof so overwhelming that corruption couldn't hide behind procedure. Ready meant having allies who couldn't be bought or intimidated. Ready meant being certain that exposing the truth wouldn't just make them the next names on the disappearance list.

They weren't ready.

Not even close.

"Sonia," Michael said carefully, "John warned me. He said someone in the department is feeding information to whoever's running this."

Sonia's expression hardened. "Do you know who?"

"No. But it means every file I access, every call I make—it's all potentially monitored."

"Then we go dark," Sonia said immediately. "No official channels. No department resources. We work this like an undercover op."

Michael studied her face, seeing the determination there but also something else—something that looked like fear poorly disguised as resolve.

"Are you okay?" he asked.

Sonia's smile was quick and brittle. "No. But I will be when we stop this."

Michael wanted to believe her, but something in her tone felt rehearsed, like she'd been practicing the answer.

Before he could press further, her phone buzzed. She glanced at the screen and her expression shifted—just for a second, but Michael caught it.

"Who is it?" he asked.

"Work," Sonia said, silencing the call. "I'll deal with it later."

"Sonia—"

"Mike, focus," she said, cutting him off. "We have nine ghost operators and financial proof of an off-books facility. What's our next move?"

Michael let it go, filing the moment away for later examination. "We identify the operators. Match names to the ghost IDs. Confirm they're actually missing."

"And if they are?"

"Then we have a pattern of state-sanctioned kidnapping," Michael said. "And we take it public."

Sonia stood and walked to the window, staring out at their quiet street where nothing ever happened, where life moved at the pace of routine and normalcy.

"Public means media," she said. "Media means exposure. Exposure means whoever's behind this will either shut it down or bury us."

"Then we make sure we're buried with enough evidence that it can't stay hidden," Michael replied.

Sonia turned back to him, and for a moment she looked like she wanted to say something else—something important. But instead she just nodded.

"I'll start matching names," she said, returning to her laptop.

They worked in silence for another hour, the only sounds the click of keyboards and the rustle of paper. Michael cross-referenced John's operator IDs against BBVP rosters going back one year. Sonia tracked financial transfers, building a timeline of when money started flowing to the ghost accounts.

Finally, Sonia broke the silence.

"Mike."

He looked up.

"I matched five of the nine ghost IDs to names," she said, her voice tight. "Antony Grumpton. Justin Jones. De'Osha Davenport. Two others I don't recognize yet."

"All confirmed missing," Michael said.

"Yes." Sonia turned her laptop toward him. "And look at the budget allocations for their ghost IDs. They're still being paid monthly. Not their original salaries—these are coded as 'facility allowances.'"

Michael scanned the numbers. "They're not allowances. They're maintenance costs. Food. Housing. Medical."

"Medical for what?"

Michael thought about the coordinates. The secrecy. The ghost operators being funded years after their official disappearances.

“For keeping them alive,” he said. “Alive and working.”

Sonia’s face went pale. “Working at what?”

Michael pulled up the satellite image again, zooming in on the dark smudge in the Pacific.

“Something that requires blind labor. Something so valuable that it’s worth maintaining an entire reassignment facility.”

“Mining,” Sonia said suddenly. “The budget line items mention ‘resource operations’ and ‘geological survey.’”

Michael’s mind raced. “John mentioned the reassignment facility in his note. An island would have geology. Resources.”

“What kind of resources require blind workers?” Sonia asked.

“The kind that make seeing people go blind,” Michael replied.

The implication hung between them.

Sonia closed her laptop slowly. “If they’re mining something toxic—something that causes blindness—then using operators who are already blind...”

“Is the only workforce that makes sense,” Michael finished. “Because they’ve already lost what the job would take from anyone else.”

Sonia stood abruptly and walked to the sink, gripping the edge like she needed something solid to hold onto. “That’s not just criminal, Mike. That’s evil.”

“Yes.”

“And it’s been happening for years.”

"Yes."

She turned to face him, tears threatening but not falling. "How do we stop something this big?"

Michael gathered the documents into a folder, organizing them with the methodical care of someone building a case that couldn't fall apart under scrutiny.

"We prove it exists," he said. "We identify every missing operator. We trace every dollar. We find out exactly what's being mined and why it's worth enslaving people."

"And then?"

"Then we make it so expensive to keep the secret that destroying it becomes cheaper than maintaining it."

Sonia crossed her arms, and Michael saw her shift from frightened wife to focused detective. "We'll need allies. People we can trust absolutely."

"James Simmons," Michael said. "My partner. He's solid."

Sonia hesitated. "Mike, if there's a leak in the department—"

"It's not James," Michael said with certainty. "I've known him for ten years. He's saved my life twice."

"People change when the pressure's right," Sonia said quietly.

Michael met her eyes. "Do you trust him?"

Sonia considered, then nodded slowly. "Yes. But we tell him only what he needs to know. Compartmentalize everything."

"Agreed."

Her phone buzzed again. Same unknown number. She silenced it without looking.

"Sonia," Michael said carefully. "Who keeps calling?"

"I don't know," she replied. "Probably spam."

But her voice carried a note of something Michael couldn't quite identify—not quite a lie, but not quite truth either.

"If someone's trying to reach you—"

"Mike, let it go," she said, sharper than necessary. Then, softer: "I'm sorry. I'm just tired."

Michael nodded, but doubt planted itself like a seed in his mind.

They cleaned up the kitchen, hiding the documents in a locked safe Michael kept in the bedroom closet. As they worked, Michael caught Sonia glancing at her phone twice more, her expression unreadable.

That night, lying in bed with the lights off and Sonia beside him, Michael stared at the ceiling and tried to quiet the questions circling in his mind.

John Lizzardo's warning echoed: Don't trust anyone.

But that was impossible. Trust was how partnerships worked. How marriages worked.

How investigations moved forward.

Michael rolled toward Sonia, watching her breathe in the darkness.

She was his partner. His wife. The person he trusted more than anyone.

But something had shifted.

Something small and barely noticeable, like a crack in ice that hadn't spread yet but would—inevitable as gravity.

Michael told himself he was being paranoid.

He told himself the pressure was making him see threats where none existed.

He told himself Sonia would never betray him.

But in the darkness, with his one good eye adjusted to the shadows, he couldn't shake the feeling that someone was already ahead of them—watching, waiting, preparing to move.

And the thought that kept him awake wasn't about the committee or the governor or even the reassignment facility.

It was simpler and more terrible:

What if the person watching was someone he loved?

## CHAPTER NINE

# The Second Disappearance

Morning came too early and without mercy.

Michael woke to his phone vibrating on the nightstand—a call from a number he recognized as belonging to Chief Joe Donetelli. He answered before the second ring, already knowing the news wouldn't be good.

"Miguel," the chief's voice was gravel and exhaustion. "We've got another one."

Michael sat up, careful not to wake Sonia. "Another operator?"

"Justin Jones. Thirty-eight. Licensed BBVP operator for six years. His wife called it in an hour ago. He didn't come home last night."

Michael was already moving, pulling on clothes in the dark. "Same pattern?"

"Audit letter arrived yesterday morning," Donetelli confirmed. "Reassignment code. Committee notification. The whole script."

"Where's his route?"

"State office complex downtown. I'm sending you the address."

Michael's phone buzzed with the incoming text. "I'm on my way."

"Miguel," Donetelli said, his tone shifting. "This is the second operator in three weeks. People are starting to ask questions."

"Good," Michael replied. "They should be asking questions."

"I'm not talking about civilians," the chief said. "I'm talking about upstairs. The governor's office called yesterday. They want to know why we're investigating program operations."

Michael stopped moving. "The governor's office knows I'm investigating?"

"They know someone is," Donetelli replied carefully. "They didn't mention you by name, but they made it clear that law enforcement involvement in BBVP matters is unwelcome."

"Operators are disappearing, Chief. That makes it law enforcement business."

"Not according to the state," Donetelli said. "According to them, these are voluntary reassignments within a federally protected program. Any interference constitutes obstruction of program operations."

Michael felt anger flash hot. "They're threatening to charge us with obstruction?"

"They're reminding us to stay in our lane," Donetelli corrected. "Which is their way of saying back off before someone gets hurt."

"Someone is already hurt," Michael snapped. "Multiple someones. They're just not around to file complaints anymore."

There was a long pause. "Miguel, I'm not telling you to stop. I'm telling you to be smart. Whatever you're digging into, it's got reach. High reach."

"I know."

"Do you?" Donetelli's voice hardened. "Because from where I'm sitting, it looks like you're about to kick a hornet's nest with your eyes closed."

Michael almost smiled at the unintended accuracy. "I'll be careful."

"That's not what I'm asking for," Donetelli said. "I'm asking for you to think about what happens if you're right. If this conspiracy goes as high as you think. What happens to the evidence? What happens to you?"

"The evidence gets protected," Michael said. "And I survive."

"In that order?"

Michael didn't answer.

Donetelli exhaled slowly. "Check out the Jones case. Report back. And Miguel—watch your back. The committee's already filed a formal complaint about your conduct. I can hold them off for now, but not forever."

The line went dead.

Michael finished dressing and walked quietly to the kitchen. Sonia was already awake, sitting at the table with coffee and her laptop open.

"Another one?" she asked without looking up.

"Yes. Justin Jones."

Sonia's jaw tightened. "That's number two in our timeline. There appears to be a schedule."

Michael grabbed his keys. "I'm heading to his route site. You want to come?"

Sonia shook her head. "I'm meeting with Ralph Barefoot at the medical examiner's office. I want to review any recent deaths among BBVP operators. See if anyone else disappeared without making our list."

"Good thinking," Michael said. He paused at the door. "Sonia—Chief says the governor's office is watching us."

She looked up then, and Michael saw something flash across her face—concern, maybe, or something deeper. "How closely?"

"Close enough to know we're investigating," Michael replied. "Close enough to threaten obstruction charges."

Sonia stood and crossed to him, putting a hand on his arm. "Then we're doing something right. They only push back when you're close to the truth."

"Or close to something they can make us regret," Michael said.

Sonia's hand slid down to his, squeezing once. "We'll be careful."

Michael wanted to believe her, but something in her eyes suggested she was trying to convince herself as much as him.

He left before the doubt could take root deeper.

The state office complex was already bustling with morning activity when Michael arrived.

Government employees streamed through security checkpoints, badge scanners beeping approval in rhythmic succession. The building was newer than most—glass and steel designed to project efficiency and transparency.

Michael knew better. Transparency was performance. Truth lived in basements and locked filing cabinets.

He found Justin Jones's vending machines on the third floor, positioned near a break room that smelled of burned coffee and microwaved lunches. Three machines, perfectly maintained, recently serviced.

Just like Antony's.

Michael approached slowly, studying the setup. Coins moved smoothly through mechanisms. Selection buttons responded instantly. Inventory aligned with geometric precision.

Too perfect.

A woman in a business suit stopped nearby, inserting bills and selecting a granola bar.

She glanced at Michael's badge.

"Problem with the machines?" she asked.

"No," Michael replied. "I'm looking for information about the operator who services them."

The woman collected her snack. "Justin? Nice guy. Always professional."

"When did you last see him?"

She thought for a moment. "Yesterday morning. Early. He was restocking when I got my coffee."

"How did he seem?"

"Fine," she said. "Maybe a little distracted. But he did his job."

"Did you see anyone with him? Anyone unusual?"

The woman's expression shifted slightly. "There were two men. Not building staff. They were talking to Justin near the freight elevator."

Michael's attention sharpened. "What did they look like?"

"Business casual. Clipboards. One of them was blind—I noticed the cane. They seemed official."

"Official how?"

"Like auditors," she said. "They had that governmental look. Checking things off, asking questions."

"What kind of questions?"

"I didn't hear," the woman replied. "But Justin looked uncomfortable. He kept checking his Braille watch, like he wanted them to leave."

"Did they give you their names?"

"No. They weren't interested in me. Just Justin."

Michael pulled out his notebook. "Would you recognize them if you saw them again?"

The woman hesitated. "Maybe. But honestly, they looked like a thousand other government employees. Forgettable on purpose."

Michael thanked her and moved to the freight elevator. The area was service-only—no cameras visible, no foot traffic. The perfect place for a conversation that needed to stay private.

He pulled out his phone and called the building security office.

"This is Detective Miguel. I need to see surveillance footage from the third-floor freight elevator area. Yesterday morning, between five and seven AM."

The security supervisor's voice came through cautious. "I'll need authorization."

"This is a missing persons investigation," Michael said.

"I understand, Detective. But our system requires written requests. Liability issues."

Michael's frustration spiked. "A man is missing. I need that footage today."

"Then file the paperwork," the supervisor replied. "I'll expedite it."

Michael hung up and resisted the urge to throw the phone. Paperwork meant delay. Delay meant footage disappearing. Footage disappearing meant another dead end.

This was how the system protected itself—not with violence, but with procedure.

He called John Lizzardo's number out of habit, forgetting for a moment that John was gone. The disconnected message played, and Michael cursed under his breath.

His phone buzzed. A text from an unknown number: Stop investigating Jones. This is your last warning.

Michael stared at the message, rage replacing fear. They were watching. They knew he was here, at this building, asking questions.

Which meant someone in this building—maybe security, maybe staff, maybe another operator—was reporting back.

He typed a response:

Come say it to my face.

The reply came instantly:

Soon.

Michael pocketed the phone and returned to the machines. He examined the front of the vending units where an operator's contact info typically should be located.

Someone had replaced the service tags.

Not carefully—torn off, leaving adhesive residue. Someone had stripped Justin's signage from the machines he'd maintained for six years.

Erasure, one detail at a time.

Michael stood and photographed everything—the machines, the break room, the freight elevator entrance. He interviewed four more building employees. All confirmed Justin had been there yesterday morning. None had seen anything suspicious after the two men left.

He called Sonia.

"Justin was here yesterday," Michael said. "Working normally until two men showed up. One was blind. They did not look friendly. Asked questions. Justin looked uncomfortable."

"Committee?" Sonia asked.

"Or people working with them," Michael replied. "Building security won't release footage without paperwork. By the time I get approval, it'll be gone."

"Then we bypass security," Sonia said. "I'll call in a favor with IT. See if we can pull the feeds remotely."

"Be careful," Michael warned. "Someone's watching us."

"I know," Sonia said. "I got a call this morning. No voice, just breathing. Then they hung up."

Michael's stomach tightened. "Intimidation."

"Confirmation," Sonia corrected. "We're close enough that they're worried."

"Which makes us targets."

"We were always targets, Mike. Now they're just admitting it."

Michael heard voices in the background on her end. "Where are you?"

"Medical examiner's office," Sonia replied. "Ralph's pulling files on BBVP operator deaths over the last two years. So far we've got three suicides and one accidental drowning."

"Suicides?" Michael repeated.

"All ruled self-inflicted," Sonia said. "All within six months of filing complaints with the committee."

Michael closed his eyes, the pattern crystallizing with brutal clarity. "They don't just disappear people. They suicide them too."

"Looks that way," Sonia said quietly. "Ralph's doing secondary reviews. Seeing if the medical evidence supports the rulings."

"And if it doesn't?"

"Then we've got murdered operators being covered up as suicides," Sonia said. "Which means this conspiracy has reach into the coroner's office."

Michael leaned against the wall, feeling the weight of how deep this went. "How many people are in on this?"

"Enough," Sonia replied. "Too many."

They were both silent for a moment, the impossibility of the task settling over them like gravity.

"Mike," Sonia said finally, "I need to tell you something."

His pulse quickened. "What?"

"Internal Affairs opened an investigation into you this morning. Officially."

Michael's world tilted. "On what grounds?"

"Harassment of committee members. Unauthorized access to program records. Conduct unbecoming." Sonia's voice was steady, but Michael heard the fear beneath it. "They're building a case to suspend you."

"When?"

"Soon. Days, maybe."

Michael pushed off the wall, pacing. "This is retaliation. The committee complained because I'm getting too close."

"I know," Sonia said. "But knowing it and proving it are different things. Right now, you're on borrowed time."

"Then I work faster."

"Mike—"

"I'm not backing off," he said. "Not when operators are dying. Not when the evidence is right there."

"Evidence doesn't matter if you're suspended," Sonia replied. "They'll lock you out of everything. Badge, files, contacts. You'll be blind."

The irony wasn't lost on Michael. "Then help me see before the lights go out."

There was a long pause. "I will. But promise me something."

"What?"

"Promise me you'll come home tonight," Sonia said, her voice breaking slightly. "Even if you don't find Justin. Even if the case falls apart. Promise me you'll come home."

Michael heard the fear in her voice—real and raw. "I promise."

"I love you," she said.

"I love you too."

The line went dead.

Michael stood in the break room, surrounded by the evidence of Justin Jones's erasure, and felt the clock ticking down.

Two operators gone. More disappearing every week. Internal Affairs circling. The governor's office watching.

And somewhere in the Pacific Ocean, on an island that shouldn't exist, blind people were mining something so valuable that their lives had become expendable.

Michael walked out of the building into harsh morning sunlight.

He had days—maybe less—to find the truth.

And if he failed, the next person to disappear wouldn't be an operator.

It would be him.

## CHAPTER TEN

# Committee Patterns

The conference room at the police station felt smaller than usual, crowded with suspicion and the weight of evidence that refused to stay buried. Michael had commandeered the space for the afternoon, spreading documents across the table in organized chaos that made sense only to him.

Sonia sat across from him, laptop open, cross-referencing dates and committee votes.

James Simmons, Michael's partner and best friend for a decade, stood near the whiteboard where Michael had started mapping connections with dry-erase markers.

James was a big man—six-three, former college linebacker, with hands that could palm a basketball and a voice that carried natural authority. But right now he looked uncertain, staring at the web of names and dates like they might rearrange themselves into something less damning.

"Walk me through this again," James said carefully. "Because what you're suggesting is..."

"Conspiracy," Michael finished. "State-sanctioned kidnapping. Forced labor. Murder covered up as suicide."

James turned to face him. "That's a heck of an accusation, Mike."

"It's also the truth," Sonia said without looking up from her screen. "The pattern is undeniable."

She projected her laptop display onto the conference room screen. A spreadsheet appeared, color-coded and annotated: Operator disappearances mapped against committee votes.

Red rows indicated missing operators. Blue columns showed committee meeting dates.

Yellow highlights marked unanimous votes for "reassignment pending review."

Every single disappearance had been preceded by a unanimous committee vote within two weeks.

Every. Single. One.

James studied the data, his jaw working as he processed the implications. "Unanimous votes aren't unusual. Committee members tend to vote as a bloc."

"On routine matters, yes," Michael replied. "But these aren't routine. Look at the vote descriptions."

He pointed to specific entries:

- Operator 47–Compliance Review–Vote: 5-0 Approve–Operator 53–Performance Audit–Vote: 5-0 Approve–Operator 61–Program Enhancement Assessment–Vote: 5-0 Approve "These are all different names for the same thing," Michael said. "Removal without cause."

James crossed his arms. "Or they could be legitimate program oversight."

"Then where are the operators?" Sonia challenged. "If this is legitimate oversight, why can't we find a single person who's been 'reassigned'? Why do their families have no contact information? Why do their routes get taken over immediately without going up for bid?"

James's expression hardened. "You think the entire committee is corrupt."

"Yes," Michael said flatly.

"All five members?"

"Yes."

James walked to the window, staring out at the parking lot. "Mike, if you're right—and I'm not saying you are—but if you're right, this goes beyond the committee. Someone's authorizing the funding. Someone's providing the facility. Someone's protecting the operation from oversight."

"Governor Dickens," Sonia said. "Or people working directly under him."

James turned back sharply. "You want to accuse the governor of kidnapping blind people? On what evidence?"

"Financial transfers," Sonia replied, pulling up another spreadsheet. "Budget allocations to ghost operator IDs. Payments for 'facility maintenance' and 'geological services' that don't correspond to any public program."

James studied the screen, his skepticism warring with the evidence. "Where'd you get these files?"

"John Lizzardo," Michael said. "Before he disappeared."

James's head snapped toward him. "John's gone?"

"Four days ago," Michael confirmed. "Resigned without notice. Phone disconnected. Left a flash drive with me containing files he'd pulled before getting locked out of the system."

"And you didn't think to mention this sooner?" James's voice carried an edge of betrayal.

"I'm mentioning it now," Michael said. "Because I need help. And I need to know if you're in or out."

James's face flushed with anger. "Don't give me that ultimatum. You're asking me to believe that a state-run program is trafficking blind people to a secret island. That the governor's office is involved. That multiple agencies are complicit. That's not 'help'—that's career suicide."

"It's also the truth," Sonia said quietly.

"Then prove it," James shot back. "Show me one operator who can testify. One witness who can corroborate. One piece of physical evidence that this island exists."

Michael stood and walked to the whiteboard. "I can't. Because everyone who knows is either missing, dead, or too scared to talk."

"Then you've got nothing," James said.

"I've got financial records," Michael countered. "I've got unanimous committee votes preceding every disappearance. I've got families who haven't heard from their loved ones in months. I've got coordinates to an island that shouldn't exist but does."

James shook his head. "Coordinates aren't proof. They're dots on a map."

"Then help me connect them," Michael said. "Come with me. Investigate with me. Prove me wrong if you can."

James looked between Michael and Sonia, seeing the exhaustion in their faces, the desperation barely held in check. "You're obsessed with this. Both of you."

"We're dedicated," Sonia corrected.

"Dedication has limits," James replied. "Obsession doesn't know when to stop."

Michael stepped closer. "James, I've known you for ten years. You've saved my life. I've saved yours. You're the closest thing I have to a brother. So I'm asking you—not as your partner, but as your friend—do you trust me?"

James met his gaze for a long moment. "I trust that you believe what you're saying."

"That's not an answer."

"It's the only answer I've got right now," James said. He pointed to the spreadsheet. "Show me one operator who can verify they were taken against their will. One person who escaped. One piece of testimony that stands up to cross-examination."

"Marcus Torres," Michael said. "He's covering Antony Grumpton's route. He was told explicitly not to cooperate with law enforcement."

"That's hearsay," James replied.

"Then come with me and interview him," Michael said. "Let him tell you directly."

James considered, then nodded slowly. "Fine. But if this turns out to be a misunderstanding—if these operators really are in legitimate reassignment—you need to let it go."

"Deal," Michael said, knowing he wouldn't have to keep that promise.

They drove to Antony's vending site in James's cruiser. The afternoon traffic was light, and the silence between them carried the weight of friendship strained by belief.

James finally spoke. "Mike, I need you to consider something."

"What?"

"That you might be wrong," James said carefully. "That you're seeing conspiracy where there's just incompetence. That the system isn't evil—it's just broken."

Michael stared out the window. "I've considered that. Every day. And every day the evidence points the other way."

"Evidence can be misleading," James said. "Patterns can be coincidence."

"Not this many," Michael replied. "Not this consistently."

They arrived at the building and found Marcus Torres servicing the machines. He paused immediately when he heard footsteps approaching—two sets, purposeful, the kind of stride that suggested authority.

"Marcus Torres?" James said.

Marcus turned toward the voice, his posture tensing as he recognized the formal tone. "Yes?"

"I'm Detective Simmons. This is Detective Miguel. I understand you've been covering this route temporarily."

"Yes," Marcus said carefully.

“Can you tell me why?” James asked.

Marcus glanced at Michael, then back at James. “The previous operator was reassigned. The committee asked me to cover until a permanent replacement could be found.”

“And you didn’t think that was unusual?” James pressed.

“It’s unusual,” Marcus admitted. “But the committee has authority to make route assignments.”

“Did anyone tell you not to talk to law enforcement about this?” James asked directly.

Marcus’s face went pale. “I don’t want trouble.”

“You won’t get any,” James assured him. “Just answer the question.”

Marcus’s hands tightened on his cane. “Yes. Darrius Johnson, the committee secretary, told me that if anyone asked questions, I should refer them to the committee. He said discretion was essential.”

“Discretion or silence?” James asked.

“He used the word discretion,” Marcus said. “But I understood the message.”

“Which was?”

Marcus looked directly at James. “That operators who cooperate keep their routes. Operators who talk lose everything.”

The words hung in the air.

James turned to Michael, and something shifted in his expression—not quite belief, but no longer dismissal.

"Thank you, Mr. Torres," James said. "If you think of anything else, call me." He handed Marcus his card.

They walked back to the cruiser in silence. James got behind the wheel but didn't start the engine.

"That was a threat," he said finally. "Clear and unambiguous."

"Yes," Michael replied.

"From a committee secretary representing a state program."

"Yes."

James gripped the steering wheel. "That changes things."

"Does it change enough?" Michael asked.

James started the engine. "It changes enough that I'm willing to look deeper. But Mike—and I mean this—if we do this, we do it by the book. Chain of evidence. Documented interviews. Legal authority for every move."

"Agreed," Michael said.

"And if I find out you've been cutting corners, withholding evidence, or breaking procedure to make the case fit your theory—"

"I'll walk away," Michael said, knowing it was a lie.

James pulled onto the street. "Where to next?"

"Committee meeting records," Michael replied. "I want to see every vote that preceded a disappearance. I want names attached to approvals."

"That's public record," James said. "They can't hide committee votes."

"They can if they don't record them properly," Sonia said from the backseat, where she'd been silently reviewing notes. "Ralph Barefoot confirmed three operators were ruled suicides despite evidence suggesting otherwise. That means someone's altering reports."

James's jaw tightened. "The medical examiner's office?"

"Or someone with access to their files," Sonia replied.

They drove to the State Licensing Agency building where committee records were maintained. The receptionist recognized Michael immediately and her smile tightened.

"Detective Miguel," she said. "How can I help you?"

"We need to review committee meeting minutes," James said, taking the lead. "Last two years. Public record request."

The receptionist's fingers moved across her keyboard. "I'll need to check availability."

"It's public record," James repeated. "It's available."

She picked up the phone and spoke quietly to someone on the other end. A minute later, she hung up and smiled apologetically. "I'm sorry, but those records are currently being digitized. They're not accessible."

"When will they be accessible?" James asked.

"The timeline hasn't been established," she replied.

"That's convenient," Michael said.

The receptionist's smile didn't waver. "It's procedure."

James pulled out his badge. "This is a law enforcement request in connection with an active investigation. Those records need to be produced."

"I understand, Detective," she said. "But without a subpoena, I can't override the digitization hold."

"A subpoena for public records?" James's voice rose slightly.

"New policy," the receptionist said smoothly. "Implemented last week."

Michael and James exchanged glances. New policy meant someone had anticipated this request.

"Who authorized the new policy?" Sonia asked.

"The SLA administrator," the receptionist replied. "Cynthia Delancey."

"We need to speak with her," James said.

"She's in a meeting."

"Then we'll wait."

They sat in the lobby for ninety minutes. Employees came and went, eyeing the three detectives with curiosity and caution. Finally, a woman in her fifties emerged from the administrative wing.

"Detective Simmons?" she said. "I'm Cynthia Delancey. I understand you're requesting committee records?"

James stood. "Yes, ma'am. Public records related to operator reassignments."

"Those records are being updated," Cynthia said pleasantly. "We're implementing a new digital archiving system to improve access."

"By denying access?" Sonia said.

Cynthia's smile thinned. "By ensuring accuracy and completeness. The old paper records had inconsistencies. We're correcting those before making the files publicly available."

"What kind of inconsistencies?" Michael asked.

"Missing signatures. Incorrect dates. Transcription errors." Cynthia folded her hands. "We take accuracy seriously."

"When will the records be available?" James pressed.

"I can't provide a specific timeline," Cynthia replied. "But I assure you, transparency is our priority."

"Then provide the original paper records," James said.

"They've already been transferred to digitization," Cynthia said. "They're not accessible in their original format."

Michael felt frustration surge. "You're telling us that public records documenting how blind operators are removed from the program are suddenly unavailable the same week we request them?"

Cynthia's expression hardened. "Detective Miguel, I'm aware of your investigation. I'm also aware that you've made several committee members uncomfortable with your inquiries. This program serves vulnerable people. Disrupting operations serves no one."

"Neither does hiding evidence," Michael shot back.

"I'm not hiding anything," Cynthia said coldly. "I'm protecting program integrity."

"By obstructing justice," Sonia said.

"By following procedure," Cynthia corrected. She pulled a business card from her pocket and handed it to James. "File a formal records request. We'll respond within the legal timeframe."

"Which is?" James asked.

"Ten business days," Cynthia said. "Per state statute."

They left the building empty-handed.

Outside, James leaned against the cruiser. "That was a coordinated cover-up."

"Yes," Michael said.

"She knew we were coming," Sonia added. "The new policy. The digitization. The timing. All of it was designed to delay us."

James pulled out his phone. "I'm calling the chief. We need a subpoena."

"He won't authorize it," Michael said. "The governor's office already warned him off."

James looked at him sharply. "How do you know that?"

"Donetelli told me this morning," Michael replied. "The state's threatening obstruction charges if we keep investigating."

James's face flushed with anger. "And you didn't think to mention that before we drove out here?"

"Would it have changed your mind?" Michael asked.

James didn't answer.

They stood in the parking lot, three detectives with a case that was being killed by procedure, watching the sun set on another day without justice.

"Mike," James said finally, "I believe something's wrong. I believe there's a pattern. But believing isn't enough. We need evidence that can stand up in court."

"I know," Michael said.

"Do you?" James challenged. "Because right now all we have is suspicious timing and uncooperative bureaucrats. That's not proof of conspiracy. That's proof of government."

"It's both," Sonia said quietly.

James shook his head. "I'm going back to the station. I'll try to get the subpoena authorized. But Mike—you need to be ready for the possibility that this goes nowhere."

"It's already somewhere," Michael replied. "People are missing. That's not nowhere."

James got in his cruiser and drove away, leaving Michael and Sonia standing in the parking lot.

"He's scared," Sonia said.

"He should be," Michael replied.

"Are you?"

Michael looked up at the SLA building, thinking about the operators who'd passed through those doors trusting the system to protect them.

"No," he said. "I'm angry."

They walked to their car and drove home in silence, both knowing that the pattern was clear, the conspiracy was real, and the evidence was being erased faster than they could collect it.

That night, Michael updated his whiteboard at home with one new entry: Committee Pattern: 15 disappearances. 15 unanimous votes. 0 survivors located.

Underneath, he wrote in red marker:

Time remaining: Unknown.

Sonia watched from the doorway, her phone buzzing in her pocket with another call she didn't answer.

"Mike," she said softly.

He turned.

"What if we can't stop this?" she asked.

Michael set down the marker. "Then we document it so thoroughly that someone else can."

"And if they come for us before we finish?"

Michael crossed the room and took her hands. "Then we make sure the evidence survives even if we don't."

Sonia pulled him close, and for a moment they stood together in the growing darkness, holding onto each other while the machinery of conspiracy turned around them.

Somewhere in the Pacific, operators were being exploited.

Somewhere in Kansas, the committee was voting.

And somewhere between those two points, a system was deciding who would disappear next.

Michael held his wife and tried not to think about how the statistics kept suggesting it would be him.

## CHAPTER ELEVEN

# Chief Donetelli's Warning

The chief's office always smelled like old coffee and quiet compromise. Michael sat in the chair across from Joe Donetelli's desk—the same chair where he'd received commendations, promotions, and once, a letter of reprimand for punching a suspect who'd spit in his face.

That reprimand had been warranted.

This one wouldn't be. Donetelli was fifty-eight, career law enforcement, with gray hair cut military-short and eyes that had seen too many bodies to believe in easy answers. He'd been chief for twelve years, navigating politics and policing with the kind of pragmatic wisdom that kept departments funded and officers alive.

Right now, he looked tired.

"Close the door," Donetelli said.

Michael did.

"Sit."

Michael sat.

Donetelli opened a folder on his desk and turned it so Michael could see. Inside were copies of complaint forms, each one bearing the letterhead of the Kansas Blind Business Vending Program Committee.

"Harassment," Donetelli read. "Intimidation. Unauthorized contact with program participants. Interference with state operations. Conduct unbecoming." He looked up. "That's five formal complaints filed against you in the last ten days."

"All from the committee," Michael said.

"Yes."

"The same committee whose members are making operators disappear."

Donetelli closed the folder. "Miguel, I'm going to ask you a question, and I need you to think before you answer."

"Okay."

"Are you investigating a crime, or are you building a theory?"

Michael met his gaze. "What's the difference?"

"A crime has victims, suspects, and evidence," Donetelli said. "A theory has patterns, suspicions, and assumptions. One leads to arrests. The other leads to paranoia."

"Operators are missing," Michael said. "That's not theory."

"Operators are reassigned," Donetelli corrected. "According to the BBVP manual, which is federally protected under the Randolph-Sheppard Act, the committee has authority to review, audit, and relocate operators as needed for program integrity."

"And if I told you those relocations lead to a secret facility in the Pacific Ocean?"

Donetelli's expression didn't change. "I'd ask for proof."

"I have financial records," Michael said. "Ghost operator IDs being paid after official reassignment. Budget transfers to coordinates that don't correspond to any known facility."

"Financial records from where?"

Michael hesitated. "A source."

"John Lizzardo," Donetelli said.

Michael felt his stomach tighten. "How did you know?"

"Because I got a call from the Department of Public Safety yesterday," Donetelli replied.

"They wanted to know if I was aware that one of my detectives was in possession of stolen government files."

"They're not stolen," Michael said. "They're evidence."

"Of what?" Donetelli challenged. "Show me one operator who says they were taken against their will. Show me one facility with an address I can send patrol units to. Show me one piece of physical evidence that isn't just numbers on a spreadsheet."

"I'm working on it," Michael said.

"You're out of time," Donetelli replied. He pulled another document from his desk drawer.

"Internal Affairs is opening a formal investigation. You'll be placed on administrative leave pending review."

Michael's hands clenched. "When?"

"End of the week," Donetelli said. "Maybe sooner if the committee pushes harder."

"So they get to make me disappear too," Michael said bitterly. "Just with paperwork instead of vans."

Donetelli leaned back in his chair. "Miguel, I've known you for eight years. You're a good detective. One of the best I've had. But you've got a blind spot."

"Funny choice of words," Michael said.

"I'm serious," Donetelli continued. "You see injustice and you can't let it go. That makes you great at the job. It also makes you reckless."

"Reckless would be ignoring this," Michael shot back.

"Reckless is charging ahead without backup, without authorization, without a plan that doesn't end with your career in a dumpster," Donetelli said, his voice rising. "You want to take down a state program? Fine. But you do it with airtight evidence, legal authority, and political cover. Not with stolen files and conspiracy theories."

"It's not a theory if it's true," Michael said.

Donetelli stood and walked to the window, staring out at the parking lot where patrol units sat in neat rows. "You know what the governor's office told me yesterday?"

"What?"

"That Detective Michael Miguel is a rogue investigator pursuing a vendetta against blind operators and the committee that protects them," Donetelli said. "That I should consider whether his war injury affected his judgment. That maybe he's projecting his own disabilities onto a program he doesn't understand."

Michael felt rage flash white-hot. "They're using my eye against me?"

"They're using everything," Donetelli said, turning back. "Your service record. Your injury. Your wife's involvement. They're building a narrative where you're the problem, not them."

"And you believe it?"

"No," Donetelli said. "But belief doesn't matter. Proof matters. And right now, they've got more documentation of your misconduct than you have of their conspiracy."

Michael stood. "Chief, operators are being held somewhere against their will. Families are being lied to. The committee is complicit. The governor's office is funding it. If I stop now—"

"Then you survive to fight later," Donetelli interrupted. "If you keep pushing, they'll bury you so deep you'll never see daylight again."

"I've been buried before," Michael said, touching his eye patch. "I dug myself out."

"This isn't a battlefield, Miguel. This is politics. And in politics, the people with power don't kill you—they make you irrelevant."

Michael walked to the door, then stopped. "Chief, what would you do?"

Donetelli was quiet for a long moment. "Honestly?"

"Yes."

“I’d make a choice,” Donetelli said. “Either accept that some systems are too big to break, or accept that breaking them means sacrificing everything.”

“And if I choose to sacrifice everything?”

Donetelli’s expression softened. “Then I’d tell you to make sure the evidence survives even if you don’t.”

Michael nodded once and left the office.

In the hallway, Sonia was waiting. She’d clearly been listening.

“He’s right,” she said quietly.

“I know.”

“Mike, we need to talk about what happens when you’re suspended.”

“I keep investigating,” Michael said.

“How?” Sonia challenged. “You’ll have no badge, no access, no authority. They’ll lock you out of everything.”

“Then I work off the books,” Michael replied. “The way they do.”

Sonia grabbed his arm, stopping him. “And what happens to us? To our careers? To our future?”

Michael looked at her—really looked—and saw the fear beneath the determination.

“Sonia, if we stop now, those operators stay wherever they are. Forever.”

"And if we don't stop, we join them," Sonia said, her voice breaking. "Because that's how this ends, Mike. They don't negotiate. They don't compromise. They erase."

"Then let them try," Michael said.

Sonia's eyes filled with tears. "You're willing to lose everything?"

Michael pulled her close, holding her in the middle of the precinct hallway while other officers walked past pretending not to notice.

"I already lost something in the war," he said quietly. "I lost half my vision and a piece of my soul. I came home and I told myself I'd never look away from injustice again. Not for comfort. Not for safety. Not even for love."

Sonia pulled back, anger mixing with grief. "So I'm supposed to just watch you walk into a trap?"

"No," Michael said. "You're supposed to help me spring it."

"How?"

Michael lowered his voice. "The evidence survives. We make copies. We distribute them. We create a dead man's switch so if anything happens to us, everything goes public."

"That's not a plan," Sonia said. "That's suicide insurance."

"It's the best I've got," Michael admitted.

They stood there, two detectives at the end of a hallway that suddenly felt like a precipice.

"I love you," Sonia said finally.

"I love you too."

"But I'm terrified," she continued. "Not of them. Of losing you."

Michael kissed her forehead. "You won't."

"You can't promise that."

"I can promise I'll fight," Michael said. "I can promise I won't disappear quietly."

Sonia wiped her eyes and straightened her uniform. "Then we need to move faster. Before the suspension kicks in. Before they lock us out completely."

"Agreed," Michael said. "What's next?"

"The security footage from Justin Jones's building," Sonia replied. "I called in a favor with IT. They're pulling it from the backup servers before it gets deleted."

"When?"

"Tonight," Sonia said. "After hours. Off the record."

Michael checked his watch. "Then we have six hours to document everything we know. Create a timeline. Build a case file that can stand alone."

They returned to their desks and worked in focused silence, typing reports and cross-referencing data with the urgency of people who knew time was running out.

Around them, the precinct carried on with normal business—arrests processed, reports filed, coffee consumed in quantities that bordered on addiction. Life continued as if the world wasn't fracturing.

But Michael felt the fracture widening with every keystroke.

At five o'clock, James Simmons stopped by Michael's desk.

"Chief told me," he said simply.

"Yeah."

"You've got until Friday before suspension kicks in," James said. "That's four days."

"I know."

James sat on the edge of the desk. "Mike, I ran the numbers. Fifteen operators disappeared over two years. All committee votes unanimous. All relocations coded to coordinates that don't exist on any official map."

"And?" Michael prompted.

"And that's enough for probable cause," James said. "Enough to justify a deeper investigation. But not enough for a warrant. Not enough for raids. Not enough to arrest anyone."

"So we need more," Michael said.

"We need a body," James replied bluntly. "Or a living operator who can testify. Without that, everything else is circumstantial."

Michael's phone buzzed. A text from an unknown number: You have 72 hours to stop asking questions. After that, the questions stop asking themselves. Michael showed it to James.

"Threat," James said immediately. "Document it. Report it."

"To who?" Michael asked. "The same department that's about to suspend me?"

James's jaw tightened. "Then what do you want to do?"

Michael forwarded the text to his personal email, then deleted it from his phone. "I want to make them nervous enough to make mistakes."

"That's dangerous," James said.

"Good," Michael replied. "Dangerous means they're worried."

James stood. "I'm with you until Friday. After that, I can't officially help. But unofficially..."

He trailed off.

"Unofficially?" Michael pressed.

"Unofficially, I'll keep digging," James said. "Just don't tell me anything that could make me an accessory."

Michael nodded. "Thank you."

"Don't thank me yet," James said. "Thank me when we're not all in prison."

He walked away, leaving Michael alone with his computer screen full of evidence that proved everything and nothing at once.

Sonia returned with coffee and a grim expression.

"IT says the footage is corrupted," she said.

Michael's stomach dropped. "Corrupted how?"

"Server failure. Complete data loss. Happened this afternoon." She set the coffee down with more force than necessary. "Right after I requested it."

"That's not coincidence," Michael said.

"No," Sonia agreed. "That's someone with access to city IT infrastructure actively destroying evidence."

Michael leaned back in his chair, feeling the walls close tighter. "They're inside our systems. They can see what we're doing. They can erase what we find."

"Which means we need to work outside the system," Sonia said.

"How?"

"I don't know yet," Sonia admitted. "But we have four days to figure it out."

Michael looked at his computer screen, then at Sonia, then at the precinct around them—a place that had once felt like home and now felt like enemy territory.

"I'm not giving up," he said.

"I know," Sonia replied. "That's what scares me."

They worked until late that night, building case files, printing documents, creating backups of backups. When they finally left the precinct, the parking lot was dark and empty except for their cars.

Michael held Sonia's hand as they walked.

"Whatever happens," he said, "we're in this together."

Sonia squeezed his hand. "Together."

But even as she said it, her phone buzzed in her pocket with another call she didn't answer.

And Michael felt the first seed of doubt bloom into something darker.

## CHAPTER TWELVE

# Unmarked Vehicles

The morning came with fog so thick it turned the world into suggestion rather than fact.

Michael sat in his car across from Antony Grumpton's old vending site, watching the building through curtains of gray while nursing coffee that had gone cold an hour ago.

He'd been there since four AM.

Waiting.

The text message had been specific: Watch the buildings. Early morning. White vans.

You'll see. The number was blocked. The sender unknown. But Michael had learned to trust warnings from people too scared to identify themselves.

At 5:47 AM, the van appeared.

White. No logos. No company markings. Just smooth panels and tinted windows that reflected fog like mirrors. It pulled into the service entrance at the back of the building and stopped with the engine running.

Michael lifted his camera and started shooting.

Two men emerged from the front—both wearing maintenance coveralls, both moving with the kind of practiced efficiency that suggested this wasn't their first delivery. One was Black, maybe forty, with the build of someone who'd done manual labor. The other was white, younger, with a clipboard and the air of someone following a checklist.

They opened the back doors of the van.

A third man climbed out. He was blind—Michael could tell by the way he hesitated at the edge of the van, cane in hand, head tilted listening before moving. He wore the same coveralls as the others, but his posture was different. Tense. Uncertain.

Afraid.

The man with the clipboard said something Michael couldn't hear. The blind operator nodded and followed them toward the building's service entrance. They moved quickly, glancing at their watches, clearly on a schedule.

Michael photographed everything: the van's license plate, the men's faces, the operator's reluctant compliance. He checked the timestamp on each photo, making sure the metadata would hold up in court.

If this ever made it to court.

The service door opened and they disappeared inside. Michael waited, engine off, barely breathing.

Seventeen minutes later, they emerged. The blind operator was no longer with them. The two men locked the service entrance, returned to the van, and drove away at exactly the speed limit.

Michael started his car and followed.

The van wound through early morning streets where delivery trucks and garbage collectors were the only traffic. Michael kept two cars back, using the fog as cover, documenting every turn.

The van stopped at two more buildings—both state facilities, both with vending operations.

The pattern repeated: two men, service entrance, blind operator left behind, departure.

By the time the van headed toward the highway, Michael had thirty-seven photographs and a sick certainty in his gut.

They were moving operators. Not to some distant facility. Right here in Wichita. Replacing people with people. Erasing identities while maintaining operations.

But why?

Michael followed the van to an industrial park on the edge of town. It pulled into a warehouse complex surrounded by chain-link fencing and cameras that looked newer than the buildings they protected.

No signage. No company names. Just numbered warehouses stretching in neat rows.

The van disappeared into Warehouse 7.

Michael parked a block away and approached on foot, camera ready. The fence was topped with barbed wire but not electrified. The gate had a keycard reader and a guard station that was currently empty.

He photographed the entrance, the security cameras, the layout. Then he circled the complex, looking for weak points.

What he found was more vans—eight of them, parked in a lot behind Warehouse 7. All white. All unmarked. All identical.

This wasn't a one-time operation.

This was infrastructure.

Michael's phone buzzed. A call from Sonia.

"Where are you?" she asked immediately.

"Industrial park off Highway 54," Michael replied. "Following a white van. They're moving operators between buildings. I've got photos."

"Mike, you need to get back here now," Sonia said, urgency cutting through her voice.

"Why?"

"Internal Affairs moved up the suspension hearing," she said. "It's happening today. Noon."

Michael checked his watch. 8:23 AM. "That's in four hours."

"Yes."

"They're trying to shut me down before I can finish," Michael said.

"They're trying to shut you down before you get arrested," Sonia corrected. "Chief Donetelli just told me there's a warrant being drafted. Criminal trespass. Theft of government property. Obstruction."

Michael felt ice run through his veins. "A warrant? For what?"

"For the files John gave you," Sonia said. "They're calling it stolen classified information. If they serve it, you go to jail. Not suspension—actual jail."

Michael stared at the warehouse complex, at the evidence sitting right in front of him. "I'm not leaving."

"Mike—"

"If they arrest me, fine," Michael said. "But I'm not walking away from this. Not when I'm this close."

"Close to what?" Sonia demanded. "You've got photos of vans. That's not proof of kidnapping. That's not proof of anything except deliveries."

"It's proof of a pattern," Michael insisted.

"Patterns aren't enough!" Sonia's voice cracked. "They need to be more than enough, and you don't have time!"

Michael closed his eyes, frustration and desperation warring in his chest. "Then what do you want me to do?"

"Come back," Sonia said quietly. "We'll figure this out together. But you need to be here. In the building. With witnesses. When the warrant comes, you need to not be alone in an industrial park photographing unmarked vans."

She was right. Michael knew she was right.

But something held him there—something deeper than logic, deeper than survival instinct.

He'd followed orders before. He'd been careful before. And he'd come home from war with half his vision and a permanent reminder that caution only protected you until it didn't.

"I'm coming back," Michael said. "But I need one more thing."

"What?"

"I need to see inside that warehouse."

"Mike, no—"

"Just one look," Michael pressed. "Just confirmation of what they're doing. Then I'll come back. I promise."

Sonia was silent for so long Michael thought she'd hung up.

"One look," she finally said. "Then you get back here. Understood?"

"Understood."

"And Mike?"

"Yeah?"

"I love you. Don't do anything that makes me regret saying that."

The line went dead.

Michael pocketed his phone and studied the warehouse. The loading bay door was closed. The regular entrance had a keycard reader and a security camera pointed directly at it. The windows were too high to reach and probably alarmed.

But there was a ventilation grate on the north side, half-hidden by overgrown weeds.

Michael approached carefully, checking for cameras. The angle was blind—unusual for a secure facility, but lucky for him.

He removed the grate cover using a multi-tool from his car. The opening was tight, barely wide enough for shoulders, but Michael had been in tighter spaces before. He pulled out his phone, turned on the video recording function, and squeezed through.

The duct was dark and claustrophobic, smelling of dust and industrial cleaner. Michael crawled forward, using his phone's light to navigate. After twenty feet, the duct opened onto a ventilation shaft that looked down into the warehouse floor.

What Michael saw made his blood run cold.

The warehouse had been converted into a dormitory. Rows of bunk beds stretched across the space—maybe forty beds total, most of them occupied. Blind operators sat on bunks or stood in small groups, talking in low voices. Some wore the same coveralls the men from the van had worn. Others wore street clothes that looked slept in. Guards patrolled the perimeter. Not police. Not security company uniforms. Just men in dark clothes with radios and weapons visible on their hips.

This wasn't a facility.

This was a holding cell.

Michael recorded everything, panning slowly across the space, capturing faces, layout, conditions. His hand shook slightly as the full horror of it crystallized.

These operators weren't being relocated to distant facilities.

They were being held here. In Wichita. Right under everyone's noses.

A voice echoed from below: "Next transport in three hours. Make sure they're ready."

Michael zoomed in on the speaker—one of the guards, checking a list on a tablet.

"Ready for what?" another guard asked.

"Processing," the first guard replied. "Then island deployment."

There it was. the reassignment facility.

Not a rumor. Not a theory. A real destination where operators were being sent after processing in this warehouse.

Michael's heart hammered as he continued recording. He got footage of the guards, the conditions, the operators' faces. He got audio of the conversation about island deployment.

Then his phone buzzed—loud in the enclosed space.

One of the guards looked up.

"What was that?" he said.

Michael froze, phone still recording.

The guard walked directly beneath the ventilation shaft, looking up.

Michael held his breath, pressing himself flat against the metal duct.

The guard stared for a long moment, then shook his head. "Probably rats."

"Get pest control," the other guard said.

They moved away.

Michael carefully backed out of the ventilation shaft, moving as silently as possible. Every scrape of fabric against metal felt deafening. Every breath felt like a siren.

He made it back to the exterior grate, squeezed through, and replaced the cover. Then he ran—low and fast—back to his car.

His hands shook as he started the engine. He pulled out his phone and texted Sonia: Got it. Video evidence. Operators being held in Warehouse 7. Guards. Armed. Island deployment mentioned. Her response came immediately: Get back here NOW. Warrant just issued.

Michael drove away from the industrial park, checking his mirrors constantly. No one followed. No cars appeared behind him with lights flashing.

But he felt the walls closing anyway.

He'd just trespassed on private property, illegally recorded people without consent, and violated half a dozen laws in the process. Everything he'd captured would be inadmissible in court. Fruit of the poisonous tree.

But it was proof.

Real, undeniable proof.

And proof was worth the risk.

He called Sonia as he drove.

"I'm coming in," he said. "But I need you to do something first."

"What?"

"Take this video and upload it to a secure cloud," Michael said. "Not department servers. Something they can't access."

"Mike—"

"If they arrest me, this evidence disappears," Michael interrupted. "You know that. You need to protect it."

Sonia was quiet. "Send it to me."

Michael pulled over and texted her the video file. "Got it?"

"Downloading now," Sonia replied. "Mike, this is incredible. But it's also illegal. You can't use this."

"I don't need to use it in court," Michael said. "I need to use it as leverage. Show them we have proof. Make them negotiate."

"Or make them come after us harder," Sonia said.

"Then we go public first," Michael replied. "Media. Press conference. Release everything before they can suppress it."

"That ends your career," Sonia said.

"My career's already over," Michael replied. "I just haven't signed the paperwork yet."

He hung up and drove toward the precinct, knowing that the moment he walked through those doors, everything would change.

The warrant would be served.

The suspension would be enforced.

And the choice between justice and survival would become binary.

But he'd made that choice the moment he opened Antony Grumpton's audit letter.

He just hadn't known how much it would cost.

Now he did.

And he was willing to pay it.

## CHAPTER THIRTEEN

# The Reassignment Facility

The Internal Affairs conference room was designed to make people uncomfortable. Hard chairs. Fluorescent lighting that flickered just enough to notice. A recording device on the table that might or might not be active. Michael had conducted interviews in this room. He'd never been interviewed in it.

Until now.

Lieutenant Rebecca Brennan sat across from him, flanked by a union lawyer Michael had met once at a retirement party. The lawyer—Gerald something—looked like he'd rather be anywhere else.

Chief Donetelli stood near the door, arms crossed, expression unreadable.

"Detective Miguel," Brennan said, opening a folder. "Do you understand why you're here?"

"I assume it's related to the multiple complaints filed against me," Michael replied evenly.

"Correct," Brennan said. "Five formal complaints from the Kansas Blind Business Vending Program Committee. Three informal complaints from state officials. And one warrant for your arrest currently being reviewed by the district attorney."

Michael felt Sonia tense beside him. She'd insisted on being present—not as a witness, but as his wife.

"What's the warrant for?" Gerald asked.

"Theft of classified government documents," Brennan replied. "Possession of stolen property. Obstruction of government operations."

"Those documents were given to me by a government employee concerned about corruption," Michael said.

"John Lizzardo was not authorized to remove files from the Department of Public Safety,"

Brennan countered. "And you were not authorized to retain them."

"I'm a detective investigating missing persons," Michael said. "Those files are evidence."

"Of what crime?" Brennan challenged. "Show me one operator who's filed a complaint about being forcibly relocated. Show me one family who's reported an actual kidnapping. Show me anything beyond circumstantial pattern-matching."

Michael pulled out his phone and placed it on the table. "I have video evidence of operators being held against their will in an unmarked warehouse. I have audio of guards discussing island deployment. I have documentation of systematic erasure."

Brennan didn't touch the phone. "How did you obtain this video?"

Michael hesitated.

"Detective Miguel," Brennan pressed. "How did you obtain this evidence?"

"I followed a lead," Michael said.

"Did you trespass on private property?"

"I was investigating—"

"Did you break into a secured facility without a warrant?" Brennan's voice sharpened.

Michael met her gaze. "I did what was necessary to find the truth."

"That's a confession of criminal trespass," Gerald said quickly. "Lieutenant, my client is invoking his right to remain silent until we've reviewed the circumstances of this alleged—"

"There's nothing alleged about it," Brennan interrupted. "Detective Miguel just admitted to breaking into a private warehouse and illegally recording people without consent."

"In pursuit of evidence of a larger crime," Michael said.

"Which makes all of that evidence inadmissible," Brennan replied. "You know that. You've testified in enough cases to understand how evidence law works."

"I understand that people are disappearing and no one else is doing anything about it,"

Michael snapped.

Brennan closed the folder. "Detective Miguel, you're suspended effective immediately. Badge and weapon, please."

The words landed like a physical blow.

Michael slowly removed his badge and placed it on the table. His service weapon followed—unloaded, safety on, a piece of him he'd carried for eight years.

"You'll remain on administrative leave pending further investigation," Brennan continued.

"You're prohibited from entering any police facility, accessing any department resources, or conducting any investigation related to the BBVP."

"For how long?" Gerald asked.

"Until the DA decides whether to file charges," Brennan said.

"And if he does?" Sonia asked quietly.

"Then Detective Miguel will be arrested and prosecuted to the fullest extent of the law,"

Brennan replied. She stood. "This interview is concluded."

Michael remained seated. "Lieutenant, there are blind operators being held in Warehouse 7 off Highway 54. Right now. While we're sitting here playing procedural games. Every hour we delay is another hour they're imprisoned."

"That's an allegation I'll pass along to the appropriate authorities," Brennan said.

"You are the appropriate authority," Michael said.

"No," Brennan corrected. "I'm Internal Affairs. I investigate officers. If you believe a crime is being committed, file a report through proper channels."

"I did," Michael said. "I filed multiple reports. They were all ignored."

"Then that's a policy issue, not a criminal one," Brennan replied.

She left the room. Chief Donetelli followed without meeting Michael's eyes.

Michael sat at the table, staring at his badge. Eight years. Dozens of cases. Hundreds of victims helped. All reduced to a piece of metal on a conference room table.

Sonia's hand found his. "Mike..."

"I know," he said.

Gerald cleared his throat. "Detective, I strongly advise you to cease all investigation into this matter. The warrant is serious. If you continue pushing, you will be arrested. And given the circumstances, bail might not be granted."

"Meaning?" Michael asked.

"Meaning you could spend months in jail waiting for trial," Gerald said. "And your illegal evidence means you'll likely be convicted."

Michael stood. "Thank you for your advice."

"Will you follow it?" Gerald pressed.

Michael picked up his phone. "No."

"Then I can't help you," Gerald said, gathering his papers. "Good luck, Detective."

He left.

Sonia and Michael stood alone in the conference room, surrounded by the machinery of accountability that had been turned against them.

"What now?" Sonia asked.

"Now we use what we have," Michael replied. "The video. The audio. The documentation. We make it public before they can suppress it."

"That's career suicide," Sonia said.

"My career's already dead," Michael replied. "I'm just deciding how to bury it."

They left the precinct together. Officers Michael had worked with for years looked away as he passed. Some out of discomfort. Some out of solidarity they couldn't voice. Some because they believed the complaints.

James Simmons met them in the parking lot.

"Mike," he said simply.

"James."

"You know you're radioactive now," James said. "Anyone who helps you gets burned."

"I know."

James pulled out a flash drive and handed it to Michael. "Then you didn't get this from me."

"What is it?" Michael asked.

"Everything I could pull before my access got restricted," James replied. "Committee meeting transcripts. Financial transfers. Operator files going back one year."

Michael took the drive. "They'll know you copied it."

"Probably," James agreed. "But proving it is different than knowing it."

"Thank you," Michael said.

James looked at Sonia. "Take care of him. He's got a habit of running toward trouble."

"I know," Sonia said.

James got in his car and drove away, leaving Michael standing in a parking lot that was no longer his to stand in. They went home. Michael set up his laptop on the kitchen table and began uploading everything—the video, the audio, the documents—to encrypted cloud storage. Multiple copies. Multiple locations. Insurance against erasure.

Sonia made coffee and stood at the window, watching the street.

"Mike," she said suddenly.

"Yeah?"

"There's a car parked across from our house. It's been there for twenty minutes."

Michael joined her at the window. A sedan. Dark blue. Two people inside.

"Surveillance," Michael said.

"Or intimidation," Sonia replied.

Michael's phone buzzed. Another unknown number: We tried to warn you. Now you're the problem we solve.

He showed Sonia the message.

Her face went pale. "Mike, they're not just watching. They're threatening."

"Good," Michael said. "Threats mean we matter."

"Threats mean we're in danger," Sonia corrected.

Michael returned to his laptop and finished the uploads. Then he opened a new document and began typing: PUBLIC STATEMENT Re: Kansas BBVP Operator Disappearances I am Detective Michael Miguel, formerly of the Wichita Police Department. I am making this statement to document evidence of a systematic conspiracy to kidnap and imprison blind vending operators... He typed for two hours, documenting everything. Every operator. Every committee vote.

Every piece of evidence. He included links to the encrypted files. He named names: Demetrius Giller. Governor Bruce Dickens. Cynthia Delancey.

When he finished, he had a ten-page statement that would either expose the conspiracy or get him killed.

"I'm going to release this," he told Sonia.

"When?"

"Tomorrow morning," Michael said. "I'll send it to every media outlet in Kansas. Then we wait."

"For what?" Sonia asked.

"For them to either deny it and get exposed, or admit it and face consequences," Michael replied.

Sonia crossed her arms. "Or they arrest you before morning and the statement never gets sent."

Michael set up an automated email to send at 6 AM if he didn't cancel it. "Then it goes out anyway."

"That's your dead man's switch," Sonia said.

"Yes."

She walked to him and took his face in her hands. "I love you. I've loved you since the day you came home from the war with that patch and that determination to keep fighting. But Mike—I'm scared. Really scared."

"I know," Michael said.

"Promise me something," Sonia said.

"What?"

"Promise me that if it comes down to saving the operators or saving us, you'll choose us."

Michael couldn't make that promise. They both knew it.

Sonia saw the answer in his silence. Her hands dropped. "That's what I thought."

"Sonia—"

"I'm going to take a shower," she said. "When I come out, maybe you'll have figured out how to save everyone without sacrificing the person you love."

She left him alone in the kitchen, surrounded by evidence that proved everything and solved nothing.

Michael stared at his statement. Ten pages. Dozens of names. Hundreds of hours of investigation distilled into a document that would either change everything or mean nothing.

He thought about the operators in Warehouse 7. About Antony Grumpton. About Justin Jones. About the families waiting for answers that never came.

He thought about Sonia, upstairs, wondering if her husband would choose justice over love.

And he realized, with crushing certainty, that there was no choosing.

There was only forward.

Into the truth.

Into the fire.

Into whatever consequences came next.

Tomorrow morning, the statement would send.

And everything would change.

Michael just hoped he'd survive long enough to see it.

## CHAPTER FOURTEEN

# Kail Goes Dark

The voice on the other end of the phone was steady but strained, like someone trying to maintain composure while drowning.

"Detective Miguel, I need to talk to you. But not over the phone. Not anywhere they can hear."

Michael recognized Kail McDow's voice immediately. "Kail, where are you?"

"Parking garage. Third level. Southwest corner. Come alone."

The line went dead.

Michael checked his watch. 9:47 PM. Sonia was already asleep—or pretending to be—upstairs. The house felt like a cage, and the surveillance car across the street felt like a countdown timer.

He left through the back door, cutting through two neighbors' yards before doubling back to his car parked a block over. Old tactics from old wars. If they were watching the front, they'd miss the side exit.

The parking garage was downtown, attached to an office building that emptied after business hours. Michael climbed to the third level and found Kail standing near a concrete pillar, white cane in hand, head tilted listening.

"I know you're there," Kail said without turning.

Michael approached slowly. "How?"

"Your footsteps," Kail replied. "Different weight distribution than most people. Favoring your right leg. Probably from the war injury."

Michael stopped a few feet away. "You wanted to talk."

"I'm leaving," Kail said. "Tonight. I wanted to give you this first."

He pulled out a folded envelope and extended it toward Michael.

Michael took it. "What is this?"

"Everything I could document before they locked me out," Kail said. "Personnel files. Committee communications. Internal memos from the SLA administrator. And something else."

"What?"

"Proof that Blind Island exists," Kail said quietly, his voice dropping as he spoke the name. "Not just coordinates. Actual documentation. Shipping manifests. Supply orders. Personnel transport logs."

Michael felt his pulse quicken. The name hit him like a punch. "Blind Island. You know the actual name."

"I found it buried in encrypted files," Kail said. "They call it 'Site 7' in most documents. But in the oldest files—the ones from when the operation started—they called it by its real name. Blind Island."

Michael felt his pulse quicken. "Why didn't you give this to me before?"

"Because I was scared," Kail admitted. "Because I wanted to believe I could survive inside the system by keeping my head down. Because I thought being the only blind person working for the SLA meant something. That they needed me. That I was safe."

"What changed?" Michael asked.

Kail's jaw tightened. "This morning, Cynthia Delancey called me into her office. She said my position was being eliminated due to budget restructuring. She gave me thirty days' notice and a severance package."

"They're firing you?"

"They're removing me," Kail corrected. "Politely. Legally. With paperwork that makes it look like standard budget cuts." He paused. "But I know what happens to blind people this program decides are inconvenient."

Michael opened the envelope and scanned the documents inside. His breath caught.

Shipping manifests showing regular supply runs to coordinates labeled "Site 7—Pacific Operations." Personnel transport logs listing operator names and deployment dates. Facility maintenance budgets for "island infrastructure."

And photographs.

Grainy, taken from a distance, but clear enough: a volcanic island with industrial structures. Workers in gas masks. Guards with weapons.

Blind Island.

"Where did you get these?" Michael asked.

"I've been copying files for months," Kail said. "Every time I had access to the director's computer. Every time Cynthia left her office unlocked. I didn't know what I was looking for, but I knew something was wrong."

"This is proof," Michael said, almost breathless. "Real, documented proof."

"It's also incomplete," Kail warned. "The island coordinates aren't in these files. Neither are the names of everyone involved at the state level. This proves the island exists, but not who's running it or why."

"It's enough," Michael said. "With this and what I already have, we can force an investigation."

Kail shook his head. "You still don't understand. They don't care about investigations. They care about control. You can have all the evidence in the world, but if they control who sees it, it doesn't matter."

"Then we make sure everyone sees it," Michael replied.

"How?" Kail challenged. "You're suspended. Your partner's under scrutiny. The media won't touch this without corroboration from officials who are all involved." His voice rose with frustration. "Detective, I'm giving you this because you're the only person crazy enough to keep fighting. But I'm also telling you: this fight might not be winnable."

Michael folded the documents back into the envelope. "I don't need winnable. I just need right."

Kail's expression softened. "That's what Antony used to say. He believed the system was supposed to protect us. That our rights meant something. That being blind didn't make us disposable."

"What happened to him?" Michael asked quietly.

"He questioned a committee vote," Kail said. "Publicly. At an operator meeting. He said the reassignment process wasn't transparent enough. That operators deserved to know where their colleagues were being sent." Kail's voice cracked. "Two weeks later, he got an audit letter."

Michael felt anger coil in his chest. "They made him disappear for asking questions."

"Yes," Kail said. "Just like they'll make me disappear if I stay. Just like they'll make you disappear if they get the chance."

"Where are you going?" Michael asked.

"Far," Kail replied. "I've got family in Detroit. A brother who doesn't ask too many questions. I'll start over. Find work that doesn't involve state programs or blind committees or people who treat disability like a weakness to exploit."

"You could testify," Michael said. "With your position at the SLA, your testimony would carry weight."

"My testimony would get me killed," Kail corrected. "Or worse—sent to the island with everyone else who became inconvenient."

Michael wanted to argue, but he understood. Kail had survived this long by being careful.

Asking him to stop now was asking him to sacrifice everything.

"Thank you," Michael said. "For the files. For the warning. For caring when it would've been easier not to."

Kail extended his hand. Michael shook it.

"Detective," Kail said, "one more thing. The warehouse you found—Warehouse 7. That's not the only holding facility."

Michael's breath caught. "There are others?"

"At least three more in Kansas," Kail said. "Maybe more nationwide. The BBVP operates in every state. If Kansas is doing this, other states might be too."

Michael felt the scope of the conspiracy expand like a detonation. "How many operators?"

"I don't know," Kail admitted. "But if I had to guess? Hundreds. Maybe thousands. Spread across the country. All disappeared through legitimate-looking processes. All held until they can be transported."

"Transported where? Just Blind Island?"

"I think there are multiple sites," Kail said. "Island operations are mentioned in the files, but so are mainland facilities. Mining sites. Processing centers." He paused. "Detective, this isn't just about Kansas. This is bigger than you know."

Michael stared at the envelope in his hands, feeling the weight of evidence that was both salvation and doom.

"Go," he told Kail. "Get to Detroit. Stay safe."

"What will you do?" Kail asked.

"Finish this," Michael said.

Kail nodded once, then walked to the stairwell, his cane tapping a rhythm that faded into echo and then silence.

Michael stood alone in the parking garage, surrounded by concrete and the unsettling thought of That there would be more disappearing operators.

His phone buzzed. A text from Sonia:

Where are you?

He typed back:

Getting evidence. Be home soon.

We need to talk.

Michael stared at those four words. They carried the weight of something broken or about to break.

Okay.

He drove home carefully, watching his mirrors, taking random turns to detect surveillance.

No one followed. Or if they did, they were better at it than he was at spotting them.

Sonia was waiting in the kitchen. She'd made tea—chamomile, the kind she drank when she was trying to stay calm.

"Where were you?" she asked.

"Meeting Kail McDow," Michael replied. He set the envelope on the table. "He's leaving. Gave me these before he goes."

Sonia opened the envelope and scanned the documents. Her expression shifted from concern to shock to something darker.

"Mike, these are classified SLA documents."

"Yes."

"If you use these, you'll be charged with espionage," Sonia said. "Not just trespassing. Not just obstruction. Actual federal charges."

"I know."

Sonia set the papers down carefully, like they might explode. "And you're going to use them anyway."

"Yes."

"Why?" Sonia's voice rose. "Why are you so determined to destroy yourself for this?"

"Because no one else will," Michael said. "Because the system is designed to protect itself, not the people it's supposed to serve. Because operators are dying and everyone is looking away."

"I'm not looking away," Sonia said. "I'm standing right here. Fighting with you. Risking my career with you. Loving you through this obsession that's going to get you killed."

Michael reached for her hand. "Sonia—"

She pulled away. "No. You don't get to comfort me while you're planning your own destruction."

"What do you want me to do?" Michael asked. "Walk away? Let them keep making the blind operators disappear?"

"I want you to choose me!" Sonia shouted. "For once in this investigation, I want you to choose our life over your crusade!"

The words echoed in the kitchen.

Michael stared at his wife—his partner, his anchor—and saw the pain he'd been too focused to notice before. "I can't," he said quietly.

Sonia's eyes filled with tears. "Then you've already chosen."

She walked upstairs without another word.

Michael sat at the kitchen table, surrounded by evidence that proved everything and saved no one.

His phone buzzed. Another unknown number:

Kail McDow's car was found abandoned at the Detroit border. His driver is missing. He won't make it to testify. Neither will you.

Michael's blood ran cold. He immediately called Kail's number.

No answer.

He tried again. Straight to voicemail.

Michael stood and paced, adrenaline spiking. They'd gotten to Kail. Intercepted him before he could reach safety.

Which meant they were watching everyone. Tracking everyone. Moving pieces on a board Michael couldn't see but could feel closing around him.

He looked at the documents spread across the table.

Evidence.

Proof.

And a death sentence.

Tomorrow, his public statement would send. The media would get it. The documents would be released. And either the conspiracy would crumble or he would.

Michael walked to the window and stared out at the surveillance car, still parked across the street.

Two people inside. Waiting.

For what?

For him to run?

For him to fight?

For him to make one more mistake they could use to justify what came next?

Michael turned away from the window and climbed the stairs. Sonia was in bed, facing away from him, shoulders tight with anger and fear.

He lay down beside her without touching her. "I love you," he said to her back.

She didn't respond.

"I'm sorry," he continued. "For all of this. For being the person who can't walk away. For choosing justice over safety. For making you watch."

Sonia's voice came quiet and broken. "I know you're sorry. I just wish sorry was enough."

Michael stared at the ceiling, listening to his wife breathe and feeling the distance between them grow.

Tomorrow, everything would change.

Tonight, he just wanted to hold onto what he still had. But Sonia didn't turn around.

And Michael didn't reach for her. They lay in the dark, together but separate, while the clock ticked toward morning and the consequences neither of them could escape.

## CHAPTER FIFTEEN

# Internal Affairs Intervenes

Morning came with the sound of knocking.

Not polite knocking. Not tentative. The kind of knocking that announced authority and didn't care about convenience.

Michael opened his eyes to gray dawn light filtering through the bedroom curtains. Sonia was already awake, sitting up in bed, staring at the door.

"They're here," she said.

The knocking continued, harder now, accompanied by a voice: "Detective Miguel! Open the door!"

Michael got up and pulled on clothes. His hands were steady—muscle memory from situations where panic meant death. He checked his phone. 5:47 AM. The automated email with his public statement hadn't sent yet.

He had thirteen minutes.

He walked downstairs and opened the front door to find four officers in tactical gear and Lieutenant Rebecca Brennan from Internal Affairs standing behind them.

"Detective Miguel," Brennan said, "we have a warrant for your arrest."

She held up the document so he could see the seal.

Michael scanned it quickly: Possession of stolen government property. Criminal trespass.

Obstruction of justice. Unauthorized access to classified information. "You have the right to remain silent," Brennan continued, her voice flat and professional.

"Anything you say can and will be used against you in a court of law..."

The Miranda warning played like background music while Michael's mind raced. Thirteen minutes until the email sent. If they arrested him now, they'd seize his phone, his computer, his access to everything.

The statement would die.

The evidence would disappear.

And the operators would stay forgotten.

"I understand my rights," Michael said. "I need to get dressed properly."

"You're dressed enough," Brennan replied.

"I need my shoes," Michael said. "And my medication."

Brennan hesitated, then nodded to one of the tactical officers. "Escort him. Two minutes."

Michael walked back upstairs with the officer following. Sonia stood in the hallway, her eyes wide with fear barely held in check.

"Mike," she whispered.

Michael pulled her close for one second, speaking directly into her ear. "The statement. Six AM. Make sure it sends."

She nodded against his shoulder.

"I love you," he said.

"I love you too."

The tactical officer cleared his throat. "Time's up."

Michael released Sonia and put on shoes. He grabbed his medication bottle from the bathroom—unnecessary, but buying time. Eleven minutes now.

He walked back downstairs slowly, each step deliberate. Ten minutes.

"Detective Miguel," Brennan said, "turn around and place your hands behind your back."

Michael complied. The handcuffs closed around his wrists with a metallic click that felt final.

"You're making a mistake," Michael said.

"You made the mistake," Brennan replied. "We're just cleaning it up."

They walked him to a patrol car. The surveillance sedan across the street was gone—its job complete. Neighbors peered out windows, watching a detective get arrested in his own driveway.

Michael checked the digital clock on the patrol car's dashboard as they pushed him into the back seat: 5:52 AM.

Eight minutes.

The drive to the station took twelve.

By the time they processed him—mugshot, fingerprints, property inventory—it was 6:17 AM.

The statement had sent.

To forty-seven media outlets across Kansas.

To every state and federal law enforcement agency.

To civil rights organizations and advocacy groups.

To everyone Michael could think of who might care that blind operators were systematically disappearing.

The email contained links to the encrypted files. Photos. Video. Audio recordings.

Financial documents. Kail's classified files.

Everything.

Michael sat in the holding cell and waited for the explosion.

It came at 6:43 AM.

The detective who'd processed him returned, face pale. "Miguel, what did you do?"

"Told the truth," Michael replied.

"You just accused the governor of kidnapping," the detective said. "You just released classified SLA documents. You just committed about fifteen federal crimes."

"Sixteen," Michael corrected. "I also illegally recorded people without their consent."

The detective shook his head. "You're done. You know that, right? Your career. Your freedom. Everything."

"I know," Michael said.

"Was it worth it?"

Michael thought about Antony Grumpton. About Justin Jones. About the operators in Warehouse 7 and Blind Island and wherever else they were being held.

"Ask me after they're free," Michael said.

The detective left without another word.

The morning stretched into afternoon. Michael was moved to a different cell, then to a conference room where his lawyer—not Gerald, but someone from the police union—explained in careful detail how thoroughly he'd destroyed himself.

"Federal prosecutors are already reviewing the case," the lawyer said. "The governor's office is demanding maximum penalties. The SLA is filing civil suits for damages. And the committee is calling for congressional oversight of local law enforcement."

"What about the operators?" Michael asked.

"What about them?"

"Has anyone investigated the warehouses? The shipping manifests? The island coordinates?"

The lawyer shifted uncomfortably. "That's not my area."

"It should be everyone's area," Michael said.

At 2:17 PM, Sonia was allowed to visit.

She sat across from him in the visitation room, separated by plexiglass and monitored by cameras.

"The media is going crazy," she said. "Every outlet in the state is covering it. Some national networks picked it up. They're calling it the biggest government corruption scandal in Kansas history."

"Good," Michael said.

"The governor's office issued a statement denying everything," Sonia continued. "They're claiming you fabricated evidence. That you're a disgruntled detective with a vendetta. That your war injury affected your judgment."

"Let them deny it," Michael replied. "The evidence speaks for itself."

"Mike, they're not investigating the warehouses," Sonia said, her voice dropping. "State police say they need more than your illegally obtained video to justify raids. Federal authorities say it's a state matter. Everyone's passing the buck."

Michael felt his chest tighten. "So nothing's changed."

"Everything's changed," Sonia corrected. "You're in jail. Your statement made you radioactive. And now the only people willing to help are conspiracy theorists and activists who don't have the power to actually do anything."

Michael leaned forward. "Then we make them care. We keep pushing. We—"

"We?" Sonia interrupted. "Mike, there is no we anymore. You're in here. I'm out there. And I've been told that if I continue investigating, I'll join you."

The words landed like a punch.

"They threatened you?" Michael asked.

"Internal Affairs called me in this morning," Sonia said. "Told me I'm under review for aiding your illegal activities. That I need to distance myself from you and the case if I want to keep my job."

"And what did you say?"

Sonia's eyes filled with tears. "I said I'd think about it."

"Sonia—"

"Don't," she said. "Don't make this harder. I love you. I support what you're trying to do. But I can't throw away my career for a case that might not win."

"It will win," Michael insisted. "The truth always wins."

"No it doesn't," Sonia said quietly. "Power wins. And right now, power wants you gone and wants me silent."

Michael stared at his wife through the plexiglass, seeing the fear and exhaustion in her face.

"What are you saying?" he asked.

"I'm saying I need time," Sonia replied. "Time to figure out how to help without destroying myself. Time to see if your statement actually changes anything." She wiped her eyes. "I'm not abandoning you. But I can't fight beside you right now. Not when the cost is this high."

Michael nodded slowly. "I understand."

"Do you?"

"Yes," he lied.

Sonia stood. "They're arraigning you tomorrow. The union lawyer says bail will be denied. You could be in here for months."

"I know."

"Mike..." She pressed her hand against the plexiglass. "Come back to me. Please. Don't disappear into this fight."

Michael placed his hand against the glass, matching hers. "I'll try."

But they both knew he wouldn't.

Sonia left.

Michael returned to his cell.

That night, lying on a thin mattress that smelled of disinfectant and defeat, Michael thought about the statement he'd released. Forty-seven media outlets. Dozens of law enforcement agencies. Civil rights organizations.

Someone would act.

Someone would care.

Someone would investigate.

But as the hours stretched and the silence grew, Michael felt doubt creep in. What if he'd destroyed himself for nothing?

What if power really did win?

What if the operators were not saved, and the only thing that changed was Michael joining them—not on an island, but in a cell where the crime was caring too much about justice?

His phone was gone. His badge was gone. His freedom was gone.

All he had left was the certainty that he'd been right.

But certainty didn't open doors.

It didn't free prisoners.

It didn't stop systems designed to protect themselves at all costs.

Michael closed his eyes and tried to sleep.

Tomorrow was arraignment.

After that, months of waiting.

And somewhere in the Pacific Ocean, on an island he'd never see, operators continued Imprisoned on a hidden island while the world debated whether the detective who'd tried to save them was a hero or a criminal.

Michael knew the answer.

He just hoped someone else would figure it out before it was too late.

For the operators.

For him.

For everyone who'd disappeared into silence and shadows while the system looked away.

But hope was a luxury.

And Michael was running out of everything else.

## CHAPTER SIXTEEN

# Sonia's Secret Calls

The arraignment lasted eleven minutes.

Michael stood in an orange jumpsuit before Judge Patricia Hammond, hands cuffed, while a federal prosecutor outlined charges that sounded like a terrorist indictment: theft of classified documents, obstruction of federal operations, criminal trespass, unauthorized surveillance, conspiracy to commit fraud.

"The defendant poses a significant flight risk," the prosecutor said, her voice carrying the confidence of someone who'd already won. "He's demonstrated a complete disregard for legal authority. He's disseminated classified government information to the public. And he's made it clear through his own statement that he believes himself above the law."

Michael's union lawyer—a man named Robert Hayes who looked perpetually exhausted—stood to respond. "Your Honor, Detective Miguel is a decorated war veteran with eight years of exemplary service. He has no prior criminal record. He's not a flight risk—he's a public servant who believed he was investigating legitimate crimes."

"By breaking multiple laws," Judge Hammond said dryly.

"By following evidence," Hayes countered. "Evidence that suggests systematic human rights violations."

“Evidence obtained illegally,” the prosecutor interrupted. “Which makes it inadmissible and irrelevant.”

Judge Hammond adjusted her glasses and studied the file in front of her. “Mr. Hayes, your client released classified State Licensing Agency documents to the media. He trespassed on private property. He conducted unauthorized surveillance. These aren’t judgment calls—these are crimes.”

“Yes, Your Honor,” Hayes said. “But we believe the circumstances warrant consideration of bail—”

“Bail is denied,” Hammond said flatly. “Detective Miguel will remain in custody pending trial. Given the severity of charges and the volume of evidence to review, trial is set for...” She checked her calendar. “April seventeenth. Four months.”

Michael felt the words land like a physical blow. Four months in jail. Four months while operators remained imprisoned. Four months while the conspiracy continued.

“Your Honor,” Michael said, breaking protocol.

Hammond looked up sharply. “Detective Miguel, your attorney is speaking for you.”

“Your Honor, people are being held in warehouses across Kansas,” Michael continued.

“Right now. While we’re sitting here debating procedure, blind operators are being transported to forced labor camps. Every day we delay is another day they suffer.”

“Detective,” Hammond’s voice hardened, “you will remain silent or I will hold you in contempt.”

"I'm already in contempt," Michael said. "Of a system that protects itself instead of the vulnerable."

"That's enough," Hammond said. "Bailiff, remove the defendant."

Two officers moved forward, gripping Michael's arms.

"Check Warehouse 7," Michael said as they pulled him away. "Off Highway 54. You'll find—"

The courtroom doors closed, cutting off his words.

Michael was returned to his cell in the county jail—a concrete box eight feet by ten, with a metal toilet, a thin mattress, and a window too high and narrow to see anything but sky.

He'd been there three days. It felt like three years.

The other inmates left him alone. Word had spread that he was a cop, which made him both untouchable and vulnerable. He existed in a strange limbo where no one spoke to him but everyone watched.

At two o'clock, a guard appeared at his cell. "Miguel. Visitor."

Michael was escorted to the visitation room and placed in a booth with plexiglass separating him from the outside world. The chair was bolted to the floor. The phone receiver smelled like disinfectant and fear.

Sonia sat on the other side, wearing her uniform. She looked tired—the kind of tired that went deeper than missed sleep.

Michael picked up the phone. "Hey."

"Hey," Sonia replied.

They stared at each other for a moment, the plexiglass between them both literal and metaphorical.

"Four months," Sonia said finally.

"Yeah."

"Mike, that's... that's a long time."

"I know."

Sonia looked down at her hands. "The media coverage is dying down. The governor's office did a press conference yesterday. Said your allegations are baseless. That you fabricated evidence to justify illegal actions. That you're a disturbed individual who needs mental health treatment, not a platform."

"And people believed him?" Michael asked.

"Some did," Sonia said. "Others are demanding investigations. Civil rights groups are calling for federal oversight. But the momentum is fading. Without new evidence, without someone corroborating your claims..." She trailed off.

"Did anyone check Warehouse 7?" Michael asked.

Sonia shook her head. "State police say they need more than illegally obtained video to justify a raid. Federal authorities say it's a local matter. Everyone's passing responsibility."

Michael felt frustration coil in his chest. "So the operators are still there. Still being held."

"Probably," Sonia said. "But Mike, even if they raided the warehouse and found operators, the defense would claim they're there voluntarily. For training or processing or whatever story the committee feeds them. Without operators willing to testify that they were taken against their will—"

"They're too scared to testify," Michael interrupted. "That's the point. Fear is how this system works."

"I know," Sonia said quietly.

They sat in silence for a moment, the weight of impossibility pressing down.

"How are you?" Michael asked.

Sonia's eyes filled with tears. "Terrible. Internal Affairs is investigating me. They're reviewing every case I've worked on for the last two years, looking for misconduct. My access is restricted. My partner won't talk to me. And everyone looks at me like I'm an accomplice in your crimes."

"I'm sorry," Michael said.

"I know you are," Sonia replied. "But sorry doesn't fix this."

Michael leaned forward. "What do you need me to do?"

Sonia wiped her eyes. "I need you to accept a plea deal."

Michael froze. "What?"

"The prosecutor offered a deal," Sonia said. "You plead guilty to reduced charges. Serve two years. Probation after that. In exchange, you agree to never speak publicly about the BBVP case again."

"They want to silence me," Michael said.

"They want to move on," Sonia corrected. "And Mike, if you go to trial, you'll lose. The evidence against you is overwhelming. You admitted everything. The illegal trespass, the surveillance, the document theft. A jury will convict you, and the judge will give you the maximum sentence. Ten years, maybe more."

Michael shook his head. "I can't plead guilty. That makes everything I did a crime instead of an investigation."

"It was both," Sonia said. "Mike, I love you. I support what you were trying to do. But you broke the law. Multiple laws. And you did it knowing the consequences."

"Because no one else would act," Michael said.

"And now you're in jail and nothing has changed," Sonia shot back. "The operators are still missing. The committee is still operating. The governor is still in power. You sacrificed everything and accomplished nothing."

The words hit harder than Michael wanted to admit.

"What do you want me to do?" he asked.

Sonia's voice broke. "I want you to come home. I want us to have a life. I want to stop feeling like I'm watching you destroy yourself for a fight you can't win."

Michael stared at his wife through the plexiglass, seeing the pain and exhaustion in her face.

"I can't take the deal," he said quietly.

Sonia closed her eyes. "Why not?"

"Because if I do, they win," Michael said. "They keep making operators disappear, I try to expose it, they jail me and silence me, and the world moves on pretending nothing happened. That's not justice. That's surrender."

"Sometimes surrender is survival," Sonia said.

"And sometimes survival isn't worth the cost," Michael replied.

Sonia stood abruptly. "I have to go."

"Sonia—"

"I can't do this right now," she said, her voice tight with emotion. "I can't sit here and watch you choose martyrdom over me."

"That's not what I'm doing," Michael said.

"Yes it is," Sonia replied. "And I understand why. I really do. But understanding doesn't make it hurt less."

She hung up the phone and walked away before Michael could respond.

Michael sat alone in the booth, phone receiver still pressed to his ear, listening to dial tone until a guard told him his time was up.

Back in his cell, Michael lay on the thin mattress and stared at the ceiling. Four months until trial. Maybe ten years after that. And for what? Operators were still imprisoned. The conspiracy was still protected. And the only thing that had changed was that Michael was now caged instead of hunting.

His cellblock neighbor—a man named Craig serving time for drug possession—spoke through the vent between cells.

"You the cop who went after the blind people?" Craig asked.

"I went after the people hurting them," Michael corrected.

"Same difference to most folks," Torres said. "They hear 'blind program' and they think you was attacking disabled people."

"The media spin," Michael said bitterly.

"Yeah, well, spin is all that matters," Torres replied. "Truth don't mean nothing if people don't believe it. And people believe what the TV tells them to believe."

Michael closed his eyes. "You think I'm wrong?"

"I think you're screwed," Craig said. "But that don't make you wrong. Just makes you unlucky."

"Thanks," Michael said dryly.

"Hey, man, I'm just saying—sometimes the system is bigger than one person. Sometimes you gotta know when to quit."

"I don't know how," Michael admitted.

Craig laughed without humor. "Yeah. I can see that."

The lights went out at nine PM. Michael lay in darkness, listening to the sounds of the jail: coughs, shouts, the rattle of bars, the hum of fluorescent lights in distant corridors.

He thought about Sonia. About the distance growing between them. About how love couldn't bridge the gap between his need for justice and her need for safety.

He thought about the operators in Warehouse 7. About Antony Grumpton and Justin Jones and Kail McDow. About all the people who'd disappeared while the system looked away.

And he thought about the choice he'd made—the choice to fight even when fighting meant losing everything.

Was it worth it?

Michael didn't know anymore.

All he knew was that stopping felt like betrayal. And continuing felt like drowning.

He fell asleep sometime after midnight, dreaming of islands he'd never seen and people he couldn't save.

# CHAPTER SEVENTEEN

## The Governor's Connection

Three weeks into his incarceration, Michael received an unexpected visitor.

James Simmons walked into the visitation room wearing civilian clothes and an expression that Michael couldn't quite read. He sat down across from Michael and picked up the phone.

"You look like crap," James said.

"Four weeks in county jail will do that," Michael replied.

"It's been three," James corrected.

"Feels like four."

James set a folder on the counter between them. "I brought something fascinating."

Michael looked at the folder. "What is it?"

"Evidence you're not crazy," James said.

Michael leaned forward. "What did you find?"

"Financial connections," James replied. "Between the governor's office and the BBVP committee. Between the SLA and a shell corporation called Pacific Mineral Holdings. Between that corporation and Advanced Semiconductor Technologies—one of the biggest AI chip manufacturers in the country."

Michael's pulse quickened. "Keep going."

James opened the folder, showing Michael pages of bank transfers, corporate filings, and email exchanges. "Governor Dickens's chief of staff, Ron Spillwind, sits on the board of Pacific Mineral Holdings. The company was incorporated six months before the first operator disappearances started."

"What does the company do?" Michael asked.

"According to the filing, mineral acquisition and processing," James said. "But there's no public record of any mining operations. No environmental permits. No site locations. It's a ghost company funded by state budget transfers disguised as program enhancements."

Michael scanned the documents through the plexiglass. "How did you find this?"

"I've been digging for three weeks," James said. "Off the clock. Using sources that can't be traced. This is clean evidence, Mike. Legal. Admissible. It proves the governor's office is connected to whatever's happening with the operators."

"Does it prove Blind Island?" Michael asked.

James hesitated. "Not directly. But it proves the money is real. That the program is funded through state channels. That officials are connected to it at the highest levels."

"That's not enough to free the operators," Michael said.

"No," James agreed. "But it's enough to force real investigations. Federal investigations. The kind that can't be blocked by local politics."

Michael felt hope flare—small and fragile, but real. "What do we do with this?"

"We give it to someone who can use it," James said. "A federal prosecutor. An investigative journalist. Someone outside Kansas who isn't compromised."

"And you trust that person won't bury it?" Michael asked.

"I trust that with enough eyes on this, someone will act," James replied.

Michael studied his friend's face. "Why are you doing this? You could lose your job. Your pension. Everything."

James was quiet for a moment, then met Michael's eyes directly through the glass. "I owe you an apology, Mike. A real one. I doubted you. I questioned your judgment. I let procedure blind me to what was happening right in front of me." He paused. "You were right. About all of it. And I'm sorry it took me this long to see it."

Michael felt the weight of those words. "You're here now. That's what matters."

"Because you were right," James continued. "I didn't believe you at first. I thought you were seeing patterns where there were only coincidences. But I kept digging, and the more I found, the more I realized—this conspiracy is real. And it's bigger than we thought."

"How big?" Michael asked.

"Nationwide," James said. "I found similar shell corporations in Florida, Texas, Oregon. All connected to state BBVP programs. All funded through budget transfers. All incorporated within months of operator disappearances starting in those states."

Michael felt ice run through his veins. "They're doing this everywhere."

"Not everywhere," James corrected. "But in enough states that it's coordinated. Someone is running this at the federal level. Someone with access to multiple state programs and the authority to move operators across state lines."

"Who?" Michael asked.

"I don't know yet," James admitted. "But I'm working on it."

Michael's hands shook slightly. "James, if they find out what you're doing—"

"They won't," James interrupted. "I'm being careful. Using encrypted communications. Meeting sources in person. Covering my tracks."

"That's what Kail said," Michael replied. "They still got to him."

James's expression darkened. "I heard about that. His car found at the Detroit border. No body. No trace."

"Because they took him," Michael said. "The same way they're taking operators. And if they're willing to make a government employee disappear, they'll do the same to a detective."

"Then I'll be careful," James said.

"Careful isn't enough," Michael pressed. "These people have resources. Surveillance. Connections. They're inside law enforcement, inside government agencies. They know what we're doing before we do it."

James leaned closer to the plexiglass. "Then we stop telling them. We work completely dark. Off-grid communications. Cash transactions. Face-to-face meetings only. We treat this like a deep cover operation."

"And Sonia?" Michael asked. "Does she know what you're doing?"

James hesitated. "No."

"Why not?"

"Because she's under investigation," James said carefully. "Internal Affairs is watching her. Monitoring her communications. If she knows what I'm doing, they'll use it against her."

Michael felt his chest tighten. "So she's alone."

"She's surviving," James corrected. "Which is what she needs to do right now."

"Has she visited you?" James asked.

Michael shook his head. "Not since the arraignment. She wanted me to take a plea deal. I refused. Now she's..." He trailed off.

"Distant," James finished.

"Yeah."

"She's scared, Mike," James said. "And I don't blame her. This case has already destroyed your career. It's threatening hers. She's trying to figure out how to love you without losing herself."

"I don't want her to choose," Michael said.

"You already made her choose by refusing the plea," James replied. "Now she's living with the consequences of your decision. And that's not fair to her."

Michael looked away, guilt mixing with anger. "What was I supposed to do? Roll over and let them win?"

"I don't know," James admitted. "But I know that marriage means considering your partner's needs alongside your principles. And right now, you're choosing principles."

"Because the operators need someone to fight for them," Michael said.

"And Sonia needs someone to come home to," James countered.

They sat in uncomfortable silence for a moment.

"One more thing before I go," James said. "I've arranged for you to receive a special prison-issued tablet through the warden's office. It's approved for legal research and communication. Your IT contact—the one Sonia mentioned—pulled some strings with the prison's network security."

Michael raised an eyebrow. "How special?"

"It'll have secure access capabilities," James explained, keeping his voice low. "The warden thinks it's for your legal defense. What he doesn't know is that it's configured to access your secure cloud via VPN. You'll be able to communicate with me through encrypted messaging. Text 'blue' if you need me urgently, and I'll respond through the secure channel."

"When?" Michael asked.

"Should be delivered to you within forty-eight hours," James said. "Standard protocol—the warden's office will present it as part of your legal defense package. No one will question it."

Michael nodded. It was risky, but far more believable than smuggling contraband.

"There's also a reporter," James continued. "Sarah Chen from the Kansas City Star. She's been covering your case. She doesn't believe the governor's version. I think she'd be willing to publish the financial evidence if it came from a credible source."

"Would she protect her source?" Michael asked.

"She's gone to jail before for refusing to reveal sources," James said. "She's solid."

"Then give her the documents," Michael said. "Everything you found. Make sure it's published before they can suppress it."

"That'll expose the connection to the governor," James said. "It'll create a political firestorm."

"Good," Michael replied. "Fires spread. Maybe someone will get burned."

James stood. "I'll be in touch. Stay strong, Mike."

"Wait," Michael said. "The third operator. De'Osha Davenport. Have you found anything about where she was taken?"

James's expression tightened. "She's in Warehouse 7. I confirmed it through a confidential source. She's alive, but..." He paused. "She's scheduled for transport next week."

"Transport where?"

"The manifest says 'Site 7—Pacific Operations,'" James replied. "I'm guessing that's Blind Island."

Michael felt urgency spike. "We have to stop it. If she gets transported—"

"I know," James said. "I'm working on it. But Mike, even if we prove operators are being held in the warehouse, proving they're being transported to an illegal facility is different. We need more than manifests. We need testimony. We need someone willing to go on record."

"Then find someone," Michael said desperately. "Please, James. De'Osha has a family. Kids. We can't let her disappear."

"I'm doing everything I can," James said. "But this system is designed to be airtight. Every person involved is either corrupt, scared, or both."

Michael pressed his fist against the plexiglass. "There has to be someone. Someone with a conscience. Someone willing to risk themselves to stop this."

James met his gaze. "You were that someone. And look where it got you."

The words landed heavy.

"I'd do it again," Michael said quietly.

"I know," James replied. "That's why you're in here and I'm out there. You don't know when to quit."

"Quitting means they win," Michael said.

"And fighting means you lose everything," James countered. "Including the people who love you."

He stood and walked away before Michael could respond.

Michael returned to his cell and Laid down and stared at the ceiling, thinking about connections and conspiracies and the web that kept growing larger the more they investigated.

Governor Dickens. Ron Spillwind. Pacific Mineral Holdings. Advanced Semiconductor Technologies.

And somewhere at the center of it all: Blind Island.

A place where operators were sent to mine something valuable enough to justify systematic kidnapping. Something dangerous enough that only blind workers could safely extract it. Something profitable enough that state governments and corporate interests would conspire to traffic human beings.

What was it?

What mineral was worth all this suffering?

Michael didn't have answers. But he had time—four months until trial, maybe years after that. Time to think.

Time to plan.

Time to figure out how to fight a system that had already beaten him.

The prison tablet lay on his chest— a link to the outside world, a reminder that even in jail, the fight wasn't over.

Just changed.

Just harder.

Just more dangerous than before. Michael closed his eyes and tried to sleep.

Tomorrow, James would give the financial documents to Sarah Chen.

Tomorrow, the governor's connection would become public.

Tomorrow, everything would escalate.

And Michael, locked in a concrete cell with no badge and no freedom, would watch it happen from behind bars.

Helpless.

Desperate.

And still refusing to quit.

## CHAPTER EIGHTEEN

# The Third Disappearance: De'Osha

The prison tablet displayed an alert with a notification at 3:17 AM.

He jolted fully awake, disoriented, before remembering where he was. County jail. Cell block D.

Week four of pre-trial detention.

The prison-issued tablet had a reminder alert.

Michael picked it up and checked the screen. A text from James's encrypted number through the secure channel: De'Osha being moved tonight. Warehouse 7. 4 AM. Can't stop it officially. Wanted you to know. Michael's heart hammered. He typed back: Where are they taking her?

The response came immediately:

Airport. Private terminal. Flight plan filed for Pacific coordinates. This is her last night on US soil. Michael stared at the screen, helpless rage flooding through him. De'Osha Davenport—thirty-four years old, blind since birth, mother of two—was being transported to Blind Island in two hours, and Michael was sitting in a cell unable to do anything about it.

He typed:

Can you intercept?

James's response:

Not without a warrant. And no judge will sign one based on what we have. I'm sorry, Mike. Michael wanted to scream. Wanted to pound on the bars until his hands broke. Wanted to do anything except sit here powerless while another operator disappeared.

He typed:

Sarah Chen. Tell her. Tell her to be at the airport. Document the transport. Get photos.

Video. Anything.

Three dots appeared, then: Already contacted her. She's on her way. But Mike—even with photos, we can't prove De'Osha is being taken against her will. Not without her testimony. And if she's scared or coerced... Michael finished the thought: They'll say she's going voluntarily.

Exactly.

Michael sat on the edge of his bunk, tablet in hand, watching the minutes tick toward four AM. Somewhere across town, De'Osha was being loaded into a van. Driven to a private airport. Placed on a plane that would carry her thousands of miles away from her family, her home, her life.

And no one could stop it.

Because the system protected itself before it protected people.

Because power moved in shadows while justice struggled in light.

Because operators were disposable and investigators were jailed.

The tablet had a new message. Another message from James: The governor's press conference is scheduled for 10 AM. In response to the financial documents Sarah published this morning. He's going to deny everything and accuse us of fabricating evidence. Michael hadn't known the article was already published. He'd lost track of time in jail—days blurred together, marked only by meals and sleep and the slow erosion of hope.

What does the article say? Michael typed.

Everything. The shell corporation. The board connections. The budget transfers. Pacific Mineral Holdings. Ron Spillwind's involvement. It's front page. Creating significant pressure. Will it stop De'Osha's transport?

A long pause, then: No. The wheels are already turning. But it might stop future transports. Might force real oversight. Michael wanted to believe that. Wanted to think that exposure meant accountability.

But he'd learned that exposure and accountability were different things.

The tablet just received a new message. Not from James. Unknown number: Detective Miguel. This is Sarah Chen, Kansas City Star. Your partner gave me this number. I'm at the private terminal now. I see the plane. I see security. I see a white van approaching. I'm going to document everything. But I need you to understand—whatever I photograph, they'll claim it's legitimate transport. I need proof this is coerced. Do you have that? Michael typed: Interview De'Osha's family. Her kids. Document that she didn't tell them she was leaving.

That she didn't pack. That she didn't say goodbye. Prove this wasn't planned. Already did that yesterday. Her daughter told me that she's been worried about her mom for weeks. That two men in suits came to their house asking questions. Michael's chest tightened. What kind of questions?

Questions about De'Osha's relationship with the committee. Whether she'd ever complained. Whether she was "cooperative." The daughter said her mom was scared after that visit. That was the pattern. The same pattern Antony had experienced. Justin. All of them.

Assessment. Profiling. Then removal.

Michael typed:

Get that on record. Video interview with the daughter. Get her to tell the story exactly as she told you. Make sure it's timestamped. That's proof of coercion. Will do. Stand by. I'm going to try to photograph the transport.

The tablet went silent.

Michael sat in his cell, staring at the tablet, feeling seconds tick into minutes. Four AM came and went. 4:15. 4:30.

At 4:47, a message arrived:

Got photos. De'Osha being escorted onto plane by two men. She's wearing coveralls.

Carrying nothing. No luggage. No personal items. She looked terrified. I tried to get closer but security blocked me. Threatened to arrest me for trespassing on private property. Did she see you? Michael typed.

No. I used a long lens. But Mike—she wasn't walking freely. One of the men had his hand on her arm. Guiding her. Maybe restraining her. Hard to tell from distance. Michael closed his eyes. Send the photos to James. Post them with your article. Make sure people see this. I will. But you should know—the governor's office just issued a statement claiming De'Osha Davenport requested reassignment for advanced training at a specialized facility.

They're preempting criticism.

They knew you were there, Michael realized. They knew you'd photograph it.

Probably. Which means they planned their narrative in advance.

Michael felt the trap tighten. Every move documented. Every response anticipated. The conspiracy wasn't reacting to exposure—it was adapting to it.

What now? Sarah typed.

Michael thought for a long moment, then replied: Keep digging. The financial documents prove connection to the governor. The transport photos prove operators are being moved. Now we need to prove where they're going and why. Find out what Pacific Mineral Holdings actually does. What they're mining. What makes it valuable enough to justify all this. I'll try. But Mike—I'm getting pressure from my editor. The governor's office threatened legal action if we keep publishing "unverified allegations." They're calling it defamation.

Threatening to sue the paper.

That's intimidation, Michael typed. Don't let them silence you.

I won't. But you should know—this fight is getting expensive. For everyone.

The messages stopped.

Michael deleted the messages. Then he lay back on his bunk and listened to the jail wake up around him: cell doors opening, guards calling names, inmates shuffling toward breakfast.

Another day.

Another operator gone.

Another piece of evidence that proved everything and changed nothing.

At seven AM, a guard appeared at Michael's cell. "Miguel. You got mail."

Michael took the envelope. No return address. Postmarked from Wichita two days ago.

Inside was a single photograph.

De'Osha Davenport, standing with her two daughters at what looked like a school event.

She was smiling, one arm around each girl, the three of them pressed close together like they were trying to fit all their love into a single frame.

On the back, written in careful handwriting:

Her name is De'Osha. She has a family who loves her. She is not a case number. She is not a statistic. She is a human being who deserves dignity and freedom. Please don't let them make her disappear. Michael flipped the photo over and stared at De'Osha's face. The smile. The warmth. The Overwhelming joy of a mother with her children.

And he thought about where she was now. On a plane over the Pacific Ocean. Flying toward an island where she'd be enslaved until her body gave out or her spirit broke.

Because the system decided she was expendable.

Because the committee marked her as difficult.

Because asking questions had become a crime.

Michael pressed the photo against his chest and closed his eyes.

"I'm sorry," he whispered. "I tried. I'm still trying. But I don't know how to save you."

The photograph didn't answer.

It just showed him what he'd failed to protect.

At ten AM, Michael was escorted to the common area where inmates were allowed to watch television. The governor's press conference was already playing.

Governor Bruce Dickens stood at a podium, flanked by American and Kansas flags, wearing a suit that cost more than most operators made in a month.

"Let me be absolutely clear," Dickens said, his voice carrying practiced authority. "The allegations made by the Kansas City Star this morning are categorically false. There is no conspiracy. There is no trafficking. There is no Blind Island."

The camera flashed to a graphic showing the newspaper headline: GOVERNOR CONNECTED TO SHELL CORP IN BLIND OPERATOR CASE.

"What you're seeing is a coordinated smear campaign orchestrated by a disgraced detective and enablers in the media who care more about sensationalism than truth," Dickens continued. "Detective Michael Miguel illegally obtained documents, fabricated evidence, and has now convinced others to spread his delusions."

Michael watched, feeling anger burn cold and steady.

"Pacific Mineral Holdings is a legitimate investment company," Dickens said. "My chief of staff, Ron Spillwind, serves on its board in a personal capacity. There is nothing improper about this. And the suggestion that this company is somehow connected to human trafficking is not just false—it's defamatory."

A reporter called out: "Governor, what about the photographs of De'Osha Davenport being placed on a plane this morning?"

Dickens didn't miss a beat. "Ms. Davenport requested reassignment to a specialized training facility. The BBVP regularly provides advanced education opportunities for operators who want to expand their skills. She went voluntarily. With full knowledge and consent."

"Where is this facility?" another reporter asked.

"That information is confidential for security purposes," Dickens replied. "Just as all operator training locations are confidential to protect their privacy and safety."

"Can we speak with Ms. Davenport?" a reporter pressed.

"When her training is complete, I'm sure she'll be happy to speak about her experience,"

Dickens said smoothly. "But right now, she's focused on her education. We ask that you respect her privacy during this time."

Michael watched the reporters accept these answers—not because they believed them, but because they couldn't prove otherwise. De'Osha was gone. Her location was classified.

Her testimony unavailable.

The perfect trap.

"I want to be clear about something else," Dickens said, his tone hardening. "This administration will not tolerate attacks on programs that serve vulnerable populations. The Blind Business Vending Program has operated successfully since 1935, providing independence and income to blind operators across Kansas. Detective Miguel's reckless allegations has harm this program's good reputation and hurt the very people he claims to help."

The camera cut to protesters outside the governor's mansion—a mix of disability rights advocates and BBVP operators holding signs: JUSTICE FOR BLIND OPERATORS INVESTIGATE DICKENS WHERE IS DE'OSHA?

But there were other signs too:

SUPPORT GOVERNOR DICKENS STOP THE LIES PROTECT THE BBVP The conspiracy had supporters. People who believed the official narrative. People who trusted the system.

And why wouldn't they? The system had badges and lawyers and press conferences. It had procedure and protocol and the weight of authority.

Miguel had a cell and a tablet and diminishing hope.

The press conference ended. Dickens walked away from the podium without taking more questions.

Michael returned to his cell and lay down, the photograph of De'Osha and her daughters clutched in his hand.

Somewhere over the Pacific, she was flying into her new life of cruel blind slavery and a slow sickly death.

And Michael, the detective who'd sworn to protect people, could only watch from behind bars as another human being disappeared into silence.

The prison-issued tablet displayed an alert hours later. A message from James: Sarah's article is trending. Millions of views. People are demanding investigations.

Federal prosecutors are reviewing the financial documents. This is working, Mike. Slowly. But it's working. Michael typed back: De'Osha is on a plane to Blind Island. How is that working?

James's response was delayed, then: Because now everyone knows her name. Everyone knows she's missing. They can't make her disappear quietly anymore. Whatever they do to her, the world is watching. Michael wanted to believe that mattered.

But he'd seen what the world did with its attention: move on. Today's crisis became tomorrow's footnote became next week's forgotten story.

And operators who vanished while the world watched stayed vanished.

Michael put down the tablet and tucked De'Osha's photograph under his pillow.

Then he closed his eyes and tried not to think about what she was feeling right now.

Alone.

Scared.

Flying toward an island where hope went to die.

## CHAPTER NINETEEN

# The Tech Company Link

Five weeks into his incarceration, Michael received a visitor he didn't expect: a woman in an expensive suit carrying a briefcase that looked like it cost more than his car.

"Detective Miguel," she said, sitting across from him in the visitation booth. "My name is Dr. Elena Vasquez. I'm a consultant for Advanced Semiconductor Technologies."

Michael studied her through the plexiglass. Mid-thirties, hair pulled back in a severe bun, eyes that carried the kind of sharp intelligence that made people uncomfortable.

"I don't talk to corporate representatives," Michael said.

"I'm not here representing the company," Vasquez replied. "I'm here representing my conscience."

Michael raised an eye brow. "I'm listening."

Vasquez opened her briefcase and pulled out a tablet. She angled it so Michael could see the screen. "Do you know what Tenorite is?"

Michael shook his head.

"It's a rare mineral found in specific volcanic formations," Vasquez explained. "When processed correctly, it produces semiconductors with computational capacity thousands of times greater than traditional silicon. It's revolutionary for AI chip manufacturing."

"And?" Michael prompted.

"And it's also one of the most dangerous substances on earth," Vasquez continued.

"Unprocessed Tenorite produces a crystalline dust. When inhaled or exposed to eyes, it causes rapid cellular degeneration. Irreversible blindness within hours. Neurological damage. Eventually death."

Michael felt his pulse quicken. "How do you mine something that causes blindness?"

Vasquez met his gaze. "You use workers who are already blind."

The words landed like a bomb.

"Advanced Semiconductor Technologies has been purchasing processed Tenorite for three years," Vasquez said. "We pay top dollar. The material is delivered through a supplier called Pacific Mineral Holdings."

"The governor's shell corporation," Michael said.

"Yes," Vasquez confirmed. "We didn't question the source. We were told it came from a legitimate mining operation with proper environmental and safety protocols. We had no reason to doubt that."

"Until?" Michael pressed.

"Until your allegations became public," Vasquez said. "Until I started looking into where our Tenorite actually comes from. And what I found..." She paused, her professional composure cracking slightly. "What I found is that Pacific Mineral Holdings operates multiple extraction sites. Most are legitimate mines in South America and Africa. But one site is different."

"Blind Island," Michael said.

"Site 7," Vasquez corrected. "That's how it's labeled in the procurement manifests. No geographic information. Just 'Site 7—Pacific Operations.' The materials from that site are flagged as 'specialty labor source.'"

"Meaning blind workers," Michael said.

"I believe so," Vasquez replied. "Though the company has been careful not to explicitly document that. They use code words. Specialty labor. Enhanced safety protocols. Pre-adapted workforce."

"Pre-adapted," Michael repeated. "Because they're already blind, so the dust can't hurt them."

"Exactly," Vasquez said. "It's elegant, from a corporate perspective. The workers are protected from the substance's most devastating effect. The company gets access to high-value materials that would be too dangerous to extract otherwise. Everyone wins."

"Except the workers aren't there voluntarily," Michael said.

Vasquez's jaw tightened. "That's what I'm here to verify. Detective Miguel, I need to know—are blind operators actually being trafficked to this island and forced to mine Tenorite?"

"Yes," Michael said flatly.

"How do you know?"

“I’ve seen the warehouses where they’re held before transport,” Michael said. “I’ve documented systematic disappearances. I’ve traced financial flows from the Kansas government through Pacific Mineral Holdings. And I’ve watched operators vanish while state officials claim they went voluntarily for training.”

Vasquez absorbed this, her expression hardening. “If what you’re saying is true, Advanced Semiconductor Technologies has been partnering in human trafficking. Unknowingly, but affiliated nonetheless.”

“So stop buying Tenorite from Pacific Mineral Holdings,” Michael said.

“It’s not that simple,” Vasquez replied. “We have contracts. Legal obligations. And Site 7 accounts for less than ten percent of our Tenorite supply. Cutting them off would make a moral statement, but it wouldn’t stop the operation.”

“Then go public,” Michael said. “Hold a press conference. Admit your company has been purchasing materials extracted through forced labor. Demand federal investigations.”

Vasquez shook her head. “Our legal team would never allow it. Admitting knowledge opens us to massive liability. Criminal charges. Civil suits. The company could collapse.”

“So instead you protect yourselves and let the operators suffer,” Michael said bitterly.

“No,” Vasquez replied sharply. “Instead I give you the evidence I’ve compiled. Internal procurement documents. Shipping manifests. Chemical analyses that prove Site 7 materials come from Tenorite extraction. Communication logs between Pacific Mineral Holdings and state officials. Everything I could access before my company realized I was investigating.”

"I sent you instructions for accessing a secure cloud folder. I've uploaded everything there. The credentials are included—memorize them and delete them. "Why are you doing this?" Vasquez's composure cracked further. "Because I have a daughter. She's twelve. And I want her to grow up in a world where corporations can't traffic human beings for profit without consequences." She paused. "And because when I read your statement—the one you released before your arrest—I recognized the kind of desperation that comes from knowing the truth and being powerless to make people believe it." "I'm still powerless," Michael said. "No," Vasquez corrected. "You're just caged. But cages don't stop information from spreading. They just make the messenger more sympathetic." Michael folded the paper carefully. "Thank you." "Don't thank me," Vasquez said. "Just stop this. Whatever it takes. And Detective—if you need to get this information to someone outside, your wife Sonia can access the same cloud folder. The credentials will work for her too." Michael nodded, understanding. If something happened to him, Sonia could continue the fight. "One more thing," Vasquez continued. "Tenorite isn't just rare—it's finite. The known deposits will be exhausted within five years. Maybe less. Which means whoever controls the current supply has a monopoly on the most valuable material in technology." "And that means they'll do anything to protect it," Michael said. "Yes," Vasquez replied. "Including making people disappear. Including jailing detectives who ask too many questions. Including destroying anyone who threatens their control." "I'm already in jail," Michael said. "What else can they do?" Vasquez's expression turned grave. "They can make sure you stay there. Or worse—they can make sure you never get out. Jail isn't just punishment, Detective. It's isolation. It's a way to remove your voice from the conversation. And if you become too inconvenient..." She didn't finish the sentence. She didn't have to. Vasquez left the visitation room. " and the growing certainty that he was now more valuable dead than alive.

Back in his cell, Michael sat on his bunk and thought about Tenorite.

A mineral that caused blindness.

A mineral so valuable that corporations and governments would conspire to extract it using the only workers who couldn't be further harmed by its primary hazard.

A mineral that turned blind operators from people into resources.

Expendable.

Replaceable.

Invisible.

The logic was brutal. Efficient. Monstrous.

And it explained everything.

The conspiracy was not just about immense cruelty of the blind operators. It was about economics. The operators weren't victims of random evil—they were casualties of calculated greed.

Michael's tablet displayed a message. A text from James: Did you just meet with someone from Advanced Semiconductor?

Yes. How did you know?

Because their legal team just called the DA's office demanding to know why you're being allowed to meet with unauthorized visitors. They're claiming you're attempting to extort the company. Michael's blood ran cold. They know she gave me information.

Probably. Which means she's in danger. And so are you. They'll spin this as you fabricating more evidence. Threatening corporations to support your conspiracy theories. She gave me proof, James. Procurement documents. Shipping manifests. Everything that connects Advanced Semiconductor to Pacific Mineral Holdings to the island operations. Can you get it to me?

Michael sent the credentials to James and Sonia. They already knew to make back ups of the data.

Be careful. They're watching you closer now. Any mistake gives them justification to put you in isolation. Or worse. The tablet went silent.

Michael stared at the ceiling, feeling walls close from every direction.

Advanced Semiconductor Technologies knew one of their consultants had leaked. They'd be investigating Vasquez now. Reviewing her communications. Tracking her movements.

She'd risked everything to give him evidence.

Only if he could survive long enough to make it matter.

Too many ifs.

Not enough certainty.

Michael closed his eyes.

Tomorrow he'd figure out how to use the evidence to get out of jail.

Tonight he'd just try to stay alive.

Because the conspiracy wasn't just fighting him anymore.

It was hunting him.

And the cage he was in made him an easy target.

## CHAPTER TWENTY

# Operator Testimony

The breakthrough came from an unexpected source.

Michael was in the common area, half-watching television while inmates argued about sports, when his name was called over the intercom.

"Miguel. Visitor."

Michael returned to the visitation booth expecting James or maybe his lawyer. Instead, he found a woman he didn't recognize sitting on the other side of the plexiglass.

She was blind—he could tell by the white cane resting against her chair and the way her eyes didn't track movement. She wore business casual clothing and carried herself with the kind of controlled nervousness that suggested this visit had taken significant courage.

Michael picked up the phone. "I'm Michael Miguel."

"I know," the woman said. "I'm Ida Glitter. I'm on the BBVP committee. Western Director."

Michael's breath caught. "You're committee?"

"Yes," Ida said. "And I need to tell you what's really happening. Before I lose my nerve."

Michael leaned forward. "I'm listening."

Ida took a deep breath. "The committee didn't start corrupt. When I joined five years ago, we genuinely tried to advocate for operators. We fought for better working conditions, fair pay, protection from discrimination. We believed in the program."

"What changed?" Michael asked.

"Demetrius Giller became chairman," Ida replied. "Two years ago. He came in with... connections. Political connections. Corporate connections. He knew people in the governor's office. People who wanted to 'modernize' the program."

"Modernize how?"

"By making it profitable," Ida said, bitterness creeping into her voice. "The BBVP has always been self-sustaining through vending profits. But Demetrius said we could do more. Generate revenue beyond what operators made. Become a real economic force."

"Through Tenorite mining," Michael said.

Ida's head snapped toward him. "How do you know about Tenorite?"

"I have sources," Michael replied. "Tell me what the committee knows."

Ida's hands tightened around the phone. "About a year ago, Demetrius told us about an opportunity. A private corporation wanted to hire blind operators for specialized work. Mining rare materials in environments where sighted workers couldn't safely operate. He said it was dangerous but lucrative. That operators who participated would make five times their normal income."

"And you believed him?" Michael asked.

"At first, yes," Ida admitted. "He showed us contracts. Legal documents. Volunteer agreements signed by operators who wanted to participate. Everything looked legitimate."

"What made you question it?"

Ida's voice dropped to barely above a whisper. "When operators started disappearing. When families stopped hearing from them. When the 'voluntary' assignments became permanent with no communication allowed."

"Why didn't you report this?" Michael demanded.

"I tried," Ida said, anger breaking through fear. "I went to the SLA administrator. She told me it was being handled internally. I contacted the Kansas Attorney General's office. They said they'd investigate but I never heard back. I even tried calling the FBI."

"What did they say?"

"That they'd review the complaint," Ida said. "Then nothing. Silence. Like my report disappeared into a black hole."

"Because they're all compromised," Michael said. "The oversight is controlled by the people running the operation."

"Yes," Ida confirmed. "That's when I realized how deep this goes. It's not just Demetrius. It's not just the committee. It's state officials, federal agencies, corporations. Everyone's either Involved or looking the other way."

"Why are you here now?" Michael asked.

Ida met his gaze, her sightless eyes somehow piercing. "Because you're the only person who tried to stop this and I watched them destroy you for it. Because three more operators disappeared last week and I helped vote to approve their reassignments. Because I can't live with myself anymore."

Michael felt hope flare. "Will you testify?"

"In court?" Ida's voice shook. "Against the committee? Against the governor?"

"Yes," Michael said. "Your testimony could break this open. You're inside the system. You have direct knowledge of how operators are selected, how votes are manipulated, how the process works."

"They'll destroy me," Ida said.

"They already have," Michael countered. "You just haven't admitted it yet. Right now you're a part of the corruption. But if you testify, you become a witness. A whistleblower. Someone trying to make things right."

Ida was quiet for a long moment. "If I testify, I lose my position. My reputation. Maybe my freedom. They'll claim I'm lying. That I'm trying to deflect blame."

"Probably," Michael agreed. "But you'll also save lives. Operators who haven't been taken yet. Future victims. And you'll expose a conspiracy that's bigger than both of us."

"I'm scared," Ida whispered.

"So am I," Michael said. "But fear is what they count on. Fear is how this system works. They make people too scared to speak, too scared to act, too scared to resist. And as long as we stay scared, they keep winning."

Ida's hands shook as she gripped the phone. "What do you need from me?"

"Everything," Michael said. "Committee meeting records. Vote tallies. Communications with Demetrius. Any documentation of how operators are selected for reassignment. Financial information if you have access. And most importantly—your sworn testimony about what you've witnessed."

"The records are controlled by Darrius Johnson, the secretary," Ida said. "After he died—"

"Wait," Michael interrupted. "Darrius died?"

"Two months ago," Ida confirmed. "They said it was suicide. But Darrius didn't kill himself. He was terrified in the weeks before his death. Said he knew too much. That they were going to silence him."

"Who's they?" Michael asked.

"He never said," Ida replied. "But after he died, all his personal files disappeared. His home was cleaned out. His computer wiped. Everything gone."

Michael felt ice run through his veins. "They killed him."

"I think so," Ida said quietly. "And if I testify, they'll kill me too."

"We can protect you," Michael said. "Witness protection. Federal custody. We can—"

"You can't even protect yourself," Ida interrupted. "You're in jail, Detective. Your career is destroyed. Your evidence has been ruled inadmissible. What protection can you possibly offer me?"

The words cut deep because they were true.

"I can offer you truth," Michael said finally. "Not safety. Not comfort. Just truth. And the knowledge that you did the right thing even when it cost you everything."

Ida sat in silence, weighing an impossible choice.

"I need time," she said finally. "Time to gather what I can. Time to prepare. Time to say goodbye to the life I have."

"How much time?" Michael asked.

"Two weeks," Ida replied. "Give me two weeks to collect evidence and get my affairs in order. Then I'll go on record."

"Two weeks is a long time," Michael said. "A lot can happen."

"I know," Ida said. "But I can't just walk out of here and destroy my life without preparation. I have family. Obligations. I need to protect them first."

Michael understood. "Two weeks. But Ida—be careful. If they suspect what you're doing—"

"I know," she interrupted. "I'll be careful. I'll be smart. And in two weeks, I'll tell you everything."

She stood to leave.

"Ida," Michael called out.

She paused.

"Thank you," Michael said. "For your courage. For caring. For being willing to risk everything when everyone else looked away."

Ida's expression softened. "Don't thank me yet, Detective. I haven't actually done anything. I've just promised to. And promises are easy. Following through is hard."

She walked away, leaving Michael alone in the booth with hope and dread warring in his chest.

Back in his cell, Michael immediately texted James: Committee member came to see me. Ida Glitter. Western Director. Wants to testify. Says she has evidence of how operators are selected. Says Darrius Johnson was murdered two months ago. James's response came fast: Darrius Johnson died? When?

Two months ago. Ruled suicide. Ida says he was scared before his death. Files disappeared after. That's another murder covered as suicide. We're up to four now.

Michael felt the pattern solidify. They're killing witnesses. Anyone who knows too much.

Which means Ida is in danger. Can you protect her?

Michael typed: She won't testify for two weeks. Says she needs time to prepare.

Two weeks is too long. They'll find out. They'll stop her. I know. But she won't move faster. She's scared.

Then we prepare for her to disappear too, James typed. And we figure out how to stop this with or without her testimony. Michael sat on his bunk, feeling the weight of certainty: Ida wouldn't survive two weeks.

The conspiracy wouldn't let her. They'd already killed Darrius Johnson. Made Kail McDow disappear without a trace. Jailed Michael.

One more voice wouldn't be allowed to speak.

Not when silence was the only thing protecting the operation.

Michael pulled out the prison-issued tablet and sent one more message to James: Put surveillance on Ida. 24/7. If they move against her, I want to know immediately.

That's not legal.

Neither is human trafficking. Do it anyway.

James didn't respond, but Michael knew he would do it. Because they were past legal now. Past procedure. Past everything except desperate measures and diminishing hope.

Two weeks.

Fourteen days.

Three hundred and thirty-six hours until Ida Glitter either saved the case or became its next victim.

Michael lay down and tried to sleep.

But all he could see was the growing list of people who'd tried to help and paid with their lives.

And the terrible knowledge that he was adding names faster than he could save anyone.

CHAPTER TWENTY-ONE

# James Simmons' Doubt

James Simmons sat in his car outside the precinct at two in the morning, staring at a photograph he shouldn't have.

The photo showed Ida Glitter entering her home at 10:47 PM. A man stood on her porch—tall, wearing a dark suit, face partially obscured by the porch light's shadow. The timestamp was from three hours ago.

James had put surveillance on Ida like Miguel requested. Twenty-four hour watch rotation. Two officers he trusted absolutely, working off the books, using personal vehicles and equipment that couldn't be traced to the department.

And now he had proof that someone else was watching her too.

He zoomed in on the photograph, trying to identify the man. The angle was wrong. The resolution insufficient. But something about the posture felt familiar—law enforcement familiar. The way he stood. The way his jacket hung. The bulge at his hip that suggested a weapon.

James's phone buzzed. A call from Officer Linda Martinez, one of his surveillance team.

"Simmons," he answered.

“The man just left,” Martinez said. “Stayed inside Ida’s house for eighteen minutes. Left alone. Got into a black sedan, no plates visible. Drove north.”

“Did you follow?”

“Lost him in traffic,” Martinez admitted. “He knew how to disappear.”

James cursed under his breath. “Did Ida seem distressed when he left?”

“Couldn’t tell,” Martinez said. “She didn’t come to the door. He let himself out.”

“He had a key?” James asked.

“Or she left it unlocked for him.”

That suggested familiarity. Trust. Or coercion.

“Keep watching,” James ordered. “Document everyone who approaches. Get photos. Plates when possible.”

“Simmons,” Martinez said carefully, “you know this surveillance is illegal, right? We’re following a committee member without warrant. If this comes out—”

“It won’t,” James interrupted. “Not unless we find something that justifies it.”

“And if we don’t?”

“Then we bury it and pretend it never happened.”

Martinez was quiet. “You’re starting to sound like Miguel.”

"Good," James said. "Because Miguel was right."

He hung up and texted Michael:

Someone visited Ida tonight. Male. Suit. Law enforcement posture. Stayed 18 minutes. She let him in voluntarily.

Michael's response came immediately—he was awake, unable to sleep in jail:

Can you ID him?

Not from the photo. But I'll try to match it against known personnel.

James, if they're already monitoring her, she won't survive two weeks.

I know. I'm trying to figure out how to protect her without revealing we're watching.

You can't. The moment you intervene, they know we have surveillance.

James stared at his phone, feeling the impossible choice crystallize: protect Ida and expose the surveillance, or maintain operational security and watch her get silenced.

What do I do? James typed.

Move faster. Get her testimony now. Before they stop her.

She said she needs two weeks.

She won't get two weeks, Michael replied. Push her. Tell her the timeline collapsed. Get her on record tonight if possible.

James checked the time: 2:34 AM. Too late to visit Ida without terrifying her. Too early to call. He'd have to wait until morning.

I'll contact her at 7 AM, James texted. Try to accelerate the timeline.

Thank you. And James—be careful. If they're watching her, they might be watching you too.

James looked up at his rearview mirror, scanning the empty street. No cars. No movement. But Miguel's warning settled into his gut like ice.

How long had he been compromised without knowing it?

How many of his moves had been anticipated?

How many steps ahead were they?

James drove home, checking his mirrors obsessively. No one followed. Or if they did, they were better at it than he was at detecting them.

At home, his wife Danielle was asleep. He stood in the doorway of their bedroom for a long moment, watching her breathe, thinking about what he was risking.

His career. His pension. His marriage. His freedom.

All for a case that might not be winnable.

But Michael had risked everything. Kail had run. Elena Vasquez had leaked. Ida was preparing to testify.

People were sacrificing themselves.

And James couldn't do less.

He pulled out his laptop and began cross-referencing the photograph of the man who'd visited Ida. Height: approximately six feet. Build: athletic. Age: forties, maybe early fifties. Suit quality: expensive. Posture: trained.

James ran the physical description against department personnel databases. Then state police. Then federal agents assigned to Kansas.

At 4:17 AM, he found a match.

Agent Thomas Rutledge. FBI. Assigned to the Kansas City field office. Specialty: public corruption investigations.

James felt his stomach drop.

The FBI was involved. Which could mean two things: either they were investigating the conspiracy, or they were part of it.

James called a contact at the field office—a friend from the academy who owed him favors.

"Mark Raider," James said when the call connected. "I need information on Thomas Rutledge."

"It's four in the morning," Mark replied, groggy.

"I know. This is urgent."

Mark sighed. "What do you want to know?"

"Is he working the BBVP case?" James asked.

There was a long pause. "Who told you about that?"

James's pulse quickened. "So he is."

"James, that investigation is classified," Mark said carefully. "I can't talk about it."

"I'm not asking for details," James pressed. "I just need to know whose side he's on."

"What kind of question is that?" Marcus demanded. "He's FBI. He's on the side of justice."

"Is he investigating Governor Dickens?"

Another pause. "I really can't—"

"Rader, please," James interrupted. "A woman's life might depend on this. Is Rutledge investigating the governor or protecting him?"

Mark lowered his voice. "Off the record?"

"Off the record."

"Rutledge was assigned to review the allegations made by Detective Miguel," Mark said. "Determine if there's federal jurisdiction. But his investigation has been... slow. Lots of requests for clarification. Lots of procedural delays. Some people think he's stalling."

"Why would he stall?" James asked.

"Because political corruption cases are career killers," Mark replied. "You go after a sitting governor, you better be absolutely certain. Otherwise, you're the one who gets destroyed."

"So he's scared," James said.

"Or smart," Marcus corrected. "Or both."

James thanked him and hung up.

Rutledge's visit to Ida made sense now. He was working the case—officially. But whether he was working it to expose the conspiracy or bury it remained unclear.

At seven AM, James called Ida Glitter.

She answered on the third ring, her voice cautious. "Hello?"

"Ms. Glitter, this is Detective James Simmons. We need to talk."

"About what?" Ida asked, wariness in her tone.

"About your visit to Detective Miguel," James said. "About your offer to testify. And about the FBI agent who visited you last night."

Ida's breath caught. "How do you know about that?"

"Because I'm trying to keep you alive," James replied. "And right now, your timeline is too slow. We need your testimony immediately."

"I told Detective Miguel I need two weeks," Ida said.

"You won't get two weeks," James replied bluntly. "The FBI knows you talked to Miguel. The committee knows you're wavering. The conspiracy knows you're a threat. Every day you delay is another day they have to silence you."

"Agent Rutledge said he'd protect me," Ida said. "He said if I cooperate with the federal investigation—"

"Did he ask you to testify?" James interrupted.

Ida hesitated. "He asked me to... reconsider. He said my allegations could be damaging to the program. That I should think carefully before making accusations I couldn't prove."

James felt anger spike. "He's not protecting you. He's threatening you."

"He was very polite," Ida said. "Very professional."

"That's how intimidation works at the federal level," James replied. "They don't yell. They don't threaten directly. They just make sure you understand the consequences of speaking out."

"What if he's right?" Ida asked. "What if I'm wrong? What if the program really is legitimate and I'm just confused?"

"Are you confused?" James challenged. "Or are you scared?"

Ida was quiet.

"Ms. Glitter," James continued, "I have evidence that operators are being held in warehouses before transport. I have financial documents linking the governor to shell corporations. I have testimony from a corporate whistleblower about Tenorite mining. What I don't have is someone inside the committee willing to explain how operators are selected for disappearance. That's you. You're the missing piece."

"And if I testify and they're not convicted?" Ida asked. "If the jury doesn't believe me? If the judge rules the evidence inadmissible? Then I've destroyed my life for nothing."

"Then at least you tried," James said. "Which is more than most people can say."

Ida's voice broke. "I'm not brave like Detective Miguel. I can't just throw everything away for principle."

"You already did," James replied. "The moment you visited him in jail, you chose a side. The only question now is whether you follow through or back down."

“And if I back down?”

“Then operators keep disappearing,” James said. “And eventually, when the committee decides you’re too much of a liability, you disappear too.”

The line was silent except for Ida’s breathing.

“Come to the precinct today,” James said. “Give a formal statement. On the record. With a lawyer present if you want. But do it today. Before they stop you.”

“And if Agent Rutledge finds out?”

“He already knows you talked to Miguel,” James said. “This just makes it official.”

Ida was quiet for a long time. “Okay.”

“Okay?” James repeated.

“I’ll come in,” Ida said. “This afternoon. Three o’clock. But I need something from you.”

“What?”

“I need you to promise that if something happens to me, you’ll finish this,” Ida said. “Promise me that my testimony won’t be for nothing. That someone will see this through.”

“I promise,” James said.

“No,” Ida interrupted. “Say the whole thing. Promise me you’ll finish this even if I die.”

James felt the weight of the words. “I promise I’ll finish this even if you die.”

"Thank you," Ida said quietly. "I'll see you at three."

She hung up.

James sat in his car, feeling the enormity of what he'd just committed to. Not just investigating a case. Not just gathering evidence. But finishing a fight that had already consumed Miguel's career and might consume James's life.

He texted Michael:

Ida's coming in today. 3 PM. She'll give formal testimony.

Michael's response:

That's too public. They'll know immediately.

That's the point. Once it's on record, they can't make her disappear quietly.

Or they make her disappear loudly and call it an accident.

James stared at the message, then typed:

I'll protect her.

You can't protect everyone, James. Eventually, they'll find an opening.

Then I'll make sure they don't find one today.

James drove to the precinct and began preparing. He booked an interview room. Arranged for a stenographer. Contacted the union lawyer who'd represented Miguel. Set up recording equipment with redundant backups.

And he called Linda Martinez. "I need you at the precinct this afternoon. Three o'clock. Plainclothes. Armed."

"What's happening?" Martinez asked.

"A witness is coming in," James said. "And I think someone might try to stop her."

"You want me as security?"

"I want you as insurance," James corrected. "If anything happens to this witness, I need someone who saw it. Someone who can testify that it wasn't an accident."

Martinez was quiet. "You really think they'd kill someone inside a police station?"

"I think they've killed people in more secure places than that," James replied.

At 2:45 PM, James positioned himself in the lobby. Martinez stood near the entrance, pretending to check her phone. Two other officers James trusted were stationed at exits.

At 2:58 PM, Ida Glitter walked through the front doors.

She was alone. No escort. No lawyer. Just her white cane and a small bag containing, James hoped, the evidence she'd promised.

"Ms. Glitter," James said, approaching. "Thank you for coming."

Ida's face was pale. "Let's do this before I lose my nerve."

James led her to the interview room. The stenographer was already seated. Recording equipment active. Lawyer present—Hayes, who'd represented Miguel.

"Ms. Glitter," Robert said, "before we begin, I want to make sure you understand your rights. Anything you say here can be used in legal proceedings. You're not under arrest, but your testimony could implicate you in—"

"I understand," Ida interrupted. "I'm guilty. I've been corrupt for a year. I voted to approve reassignments I knew were wrong. I stayed silent when I should have spoken. I'm not here to avoid responsibility. I'm here to stop this."

James nodded. "Then let's begin."

For the next three hours, Ida talked.

She explained how operators were selected: those who complained, who questioned, who showed independence. She detailed the committee's internal discussions—how Demetrius Giller had pushed for cooperation with "external partners." How financial incentives were offered to committee members for each operator successfully "transitioned." How the votes were always unanimous because dissent meant losing your position.

She described Darrius Johnson's growing fear in the weeks before his death. How he'd told her the program had become "a machine that eats blind people." How he'd tried to resign and been told resignation wasn't an option.

She provided names, dates, vote tallies, financial records she'd secretly copied.

And she cried. Often. As she described operators she'd known personally. Families she'd lied to. Lives she'd helped destroy through silence and cowardice.

By six PM, they had enough testimony to justify federal charges against the committee, the SLA administrator, and potentially the governor.

"This is good," Robert said. "This is actionable."

"This is suicide," Ida replied quietly. "They'll kill me for this."

"We'll protect you," James assured her.

"You can't," Ida said. "You're just one detective. They're an entire system."

She wasn't wrong.

James escorted Ida to her car, Martinez walking behind them as security. The parking lot was empty except for a few civilian vehicles. A man waited by a dark sedan—Ida's driver, patient and professional.

"Thank you," James said as Ida's driver opened the rear door. "What you did today—"

"Don't," Ida interrupted, one hand finding the car's frame to orient herself. "Don't make it noble. I'm just trying to sleep at night."

She got in the back seat. Her driver closed the door and returned to the driver's seat. The sedan pulled away smoothly.

James and Martinez stood in the parking lot, watching the taillights disappear.

"You think she'll make it home?" Martinez asked.

"I don't know," James admitted.

His phone buzzed. A text from an unknown number:

Detective Simmons. You should have stayed out of this. Now you're just another problem to solve.

James showed the message to Martinez.

"That's a threat," she said.

"That's a promise," James corrected.

They returned to the precinct. James immediately sent copies of Ida's testimony to multiple recipients: the DA's office, the FBI field office, the Kansas Attorney General, and Sarah Chen at the Kansas City Star.

If something happened to Ida, the testimony would survive.

If something happened to James, the testimony would survive.

That was all he could do.

At nine PM, James's phone rang. Unknown caller.

He answered. "Simmons."

"Detective," a calm male voice said. "This is Agent Thomas Rutledge, FBI. I understand you conducted an interview with Ida Glitter today."

"Yes," James said carefully.

"That interview was conducted without notifying federal investigators," Rutledge continued. "Which interferes with an ongoing federal investigation."

"There's no law requiring local police to notify the FBI before interviewing witnesses," James replied.

"There is when that witness is part of a federal case," Rutledge countered. "I need copies of that testimony. Immediately."

“Submit a formal request,” James said. “Through proper channels.”

“Detective Simmons,” Rutledge’s voice hardened. “I’m trying to help you. You’re playing in waters deeper than you understand. People who push too hard on this case tend to have very bad accidents.”

“Is that a threat?” James asked.

“That’s a warning,” Rutledge replied. “The same warning I gave Ms. Glitter. The same warning that should have been given to Detective Miguel before he destroyed his career.”

“Miguel destroyed his career by doing the right thing,” James said.

“And where is he now?” Rutledge asked. “In jail. Awaiting trial. Separated from his wife. Facing ten years in prison. Is that what you want for yourself?”

James felt ice run through his veins. “What do you want, Agent Rutledge?”

“I want you to stop interfering,” Rutledge said. “I want you to let federal investigators handle this. I want you to go back to your regular duties and forget about blind operators and conspiracies and everything else that isn’t your problem.”

“It’s everyone’s problem,” James replied.

“No,” Rutledge corrected. “It’s a problem for people with authority to address it. You’re a city detective. You have no jurisdiction over federal programs, interstate commerce, or national security matters.”

“National security?” James repeated. “What does Tenorite mining have to do with national security?”

Rutledge was silent for a moment. "Goodbye, Detective Simmons. I hope you make better choices than your friend Miguel did."

The line went dead.

James sat at his desk, feeling walls close from every direction.

The FBI wasn't investigating the conspiracy.

They were protecting it.

And now James was on their list.

He texted Miguel:

FBI Agent Rutledge called. Threatened me. Said this is a national security matter. I think the conspiracy goes higher than we thought.

Michael's response came fast:

How high?

Federal level. Maybe Department of War. Maybe intelligence agencies. Tenorite isn't just valuable—it's strategic.

Which means they'll do anything to protect it.

Yes, James typed. Including making us all disappear.

Then we go nuclear. Release everything. All of Ida's testimony. All the documents. Everything we have. Make it so public they can't suppress it.

That destroys any chance of prosecution. Everything becomes public record. Inadmissible in court.

Court doesn't matter if we're dead, Michael replied. Survival matters. Truth matters. Justice matters even if we don't survive to see it.

James stared at the message, feeling the choice crystallize: play by rules and get destroyed, or break every rule and hope truth was enough protection.

"I'm going to release it," James typed. "Tomorrow morning. Sarah Chen will publish. Then we see what happens."

I'll be ready, Michael replied.

But neither of them knew what ready meant anymore.

Because the fight had stopped being about evidence and started being about survival.

And survival didn't follow rules.

It just fought.

With everything.

Until there was nothing left to fight with.

## CHAPTER TWENTY-TWO

# Shipping Manifests

Sonia Miguel hadn't visited her husband in jail for three weeks.

The choice haunted her—made her stomach clench every morning when she woke up alone in their bed. Made her hands shake when she passed the hallway where his eye patch still hung on a hook. Made her hate herself a little more each day.

But she'd made a calculation: distance kept her employed. Employment gave her access. Access meant she could help in ways Miguel couldn't see.

So she stayed away.

And she dug deeper.

Tonight, she sat in a windowless records room at the Department of Transportation, surrounded by shipping manifests going back one year. The room smelled like old paper and industrial cleaner. The only sound was the hum of fluorescent lights and the rustle of pages as she worked.

She'd called in every favor she had to get access to these files. Promised her contact in the DOT that she was investigating fraud, not conspiracy. Sworn she'd be careful, quiet, invisible.

And now, at eleven PM on a Thursday, she was finally seeing the pattern Miguel had known existed but couldn't prove.

Pacific Mineral Holdings. Shipments classified as "geological materials." Weekly deliveries to coordinates labeled simply: 22.4°N, 157.8°W.

Sonia pulled up a map on her phone and entered the coordinates.

Middle of the Pacific Ocean. Two thousand miles from any major landmass. No charted islands. No official territory.

But the manifests were real. Signed. Documented. Verified.

Someone was shipping supplies to a location that officially didn't exist.

Sonia photographed every manifest with her phone, working quickly. The DOT closed at 5 PM and she'd promised to be gone by then.

The manifests showed deliveries every Monday: food, medical supplies, fuel, industrial equipment. And once a month: personnel transport.

Personnel.

That was the word that made Sonia's chest tighten.

Not cargo. Not materials. Personnel.

People.

Being shipped to coordinates in the middle of the Pacific.

She cross-referenced the personnel transport dates against the operator disappearance timeline she and Miguel had built. Every single disappearance was followed by a personnel transport within seventy-two hours.

Antony Grumpton: disappeared June 8th. Personnel transport: June 11th.

Justin Jones: disappeared July 3rd. Personnel transport: July 5th.

De'Osha Davenport: disappeared three weeks ago. Personnel transport: same week.

The pattern was perfect. Mechanical. Undeniable.

Sonia felt rage and grief war in her chest. Miguel had been right. About everything. And she'd asked him to take a plea deal. Asked him to give up. Asked him to choose her over the operators who were being shipped like cargo to an island that didn't exist.

She'd been selfish.

Cowardly.

Wrong.

Her phone buzzed. A text from James Simmons:

Are you at DOT?

Sonia froze. How did James know where she was?

Yes, she typed swiftly.

Get out. Now. Building security just got a call about an unauthorized person in records division.

Sonia's pulse spiked. I have authorization.

Not anymore. They're coming to escort you out. And report you to Internal Affairs.

Sonia looked around the records room, feeling the trap close. Someone knew she was here. Someone had called security. Someone was watching.

She quickly photographed the last dozen manifests, shoved her phone in her pocket, and headed for the door.

Two security guards met her in the hallway.

"Ma'am," one said, "you need to come with us."

"I have authorization from DOT Deputy Director Pieren," Sonia said, keeping her voice steady.

"That authorization was revoked ten minutes ago," the guard replied. "We need to escort you out of the building."

Sonia wanted to argue but knew it would only make things worse. She followed the guards to the lobby, where they confiscated her temporary access badge and logged the incident.

"This will be reported to your supervisor," the guard said. "Standard protocol."

Sonia nodded and walked out into the parking lot, feeling eyes on her back.

Her phone buzzed again. James:

Did you get what you needed?

Yes. Photos of shipping manifests. Personnel transports to Pacific coordinates matching operator disappearances.

Good. Send them to me. Then delete them from your phone.

Why delete them?

Because they're going to seize your phone. Internal Affairs. Tomorrow morning. They'll claim you stole government documents.

Sonia felt ice run through her veins. How do you know?

Because that's what they do. They isolated Miguel. Now they're isolating you. Removing your access. Building a case. They want you discredited before Ida's testimony becomes public.

Sonia sat in her car, hands shaking. I'm not going to let them.

You might not have a choice, James replied. Upload the photos to the encrypted cloud Miguel set up. Then wipe your phone. Factory reset. Make it look like you never had them.

That destroys evidence.

The evidence is in the cloud. Safe. Distributed. They can't suppress what they can't find.

Sonia pulled out her laptop and began uploading the manifest photos. The progress bar moved agonizingly slowly: 37%... 48%... 61%...

Her phone rang. Caller ID showed: Chief Donetelli.

Sonia's stomach dropped.

She answered. "Chief."

"Officer Miguel," Donetelli's voice was tense. "I need you to come to the station. Right now."

"It's eleven-thirty at night," Sonia said.

"I'm aware," Donetelli replied. "This can't wait until morning."

"What's this about?" Sonia asked, though she already knew.

"It's about unauthorized access to DOT records," Donetelli said. "It's about your husband's illegal investigation. And it's about whether you're fit to remain on active duty."

"I'll be there in twenty minutes," Sonia said.

"Bring your badge and weapon," Donetelli replied. "This is a formal inquiry."

The line went dead.

The upload hit 100%. Files secured in the encrypted cloud.

Sonia wiped her phone's recent photos, deleted the upload history, and reset to factory default. The process took three minutes. When it was done, her phone was clean—no evidence she'd ever photographed anything.

Sonia drove to the precinct, feeling the weight of inevitability. They were going to suspend her. Maybe fire her. Maybe charge her with crimes like they'd charged Michael.

The system was eating everyone who tried to fight it.

At the precinct, she was escorted to the same Internal Affairs conference room where Miguel had been suspended. Lieutenant Brennan sat waiting, flanked by two people Sonia didn't recognize.

"Officer Miguel," Brennan said. "This is Special Agent Thomas Rutledge from the FBI, and Assistant Attorney General Catherine Flores."

Sonia felt her stomach turn. FBI and state AG. This wasn't just a suspension hearing. This was a prosecution.

"Sit down," Brennan said.

Sonia sat.

"You were observed tonight entering the Department of Transportation records division," Flores said. "You accessed shipping manifests without proper authorization. You photographed government documents. And you've been coordinating with Detective Simmons on an illegal investigation."

"I had authorization from Deputy Director Pieren," Sonia said.

"That authorization was issued based on false pretenses," Flores replied. "You told Director Martinez you were investigating fraud. You didn't mention blind operators or conspiracy theories."

"Because calling it a conspiracy theory doesn't make it false," Sonia said.

Rutledge leaned forward. "Officer Miguel, your husband is in jail awaiting trial for serious crimes. You're under investigation for aiding his illegal activities. Right now, you have a choice: cooperate with us, or face charges alongside him."

"Cooperate how?" Sonia asked.

"Tell us everything you know about your husband's investigation," Rutledge said. "Every source. Every piece of evidence. Every contact. Give us access to his files, his communications, his plans."

"So you can destroy the evidence," Sonia said.

"So we can conduct a proper investigation," Rutledge corrected. "Free from the illegal methods your husband employed."

Sonia laughed bitterly. "You're not investigating. You're covering up."

Flores's expression hardened. "That's a serious accusation."

"It's a serious crime," Sonia shot back. "Blind operators are being trafficked to a mining facility in the Pacific Ocean. They're extracting Tenorite under conditions that would kill sighted workers. And everyone from the governor down to federal agents is protecting the operation because it's profitable."

"You have no proof of that," Flores said.

"I have shipping manifests," Sonia replied. "Personnel transports to coordinates that match—"

"Manifests you obtained illegally," Flores interrupted. "Which makes them inadmissible. Which makes them worthless."

"They're not worthless," Sonia said. "They're proof."

"Proof of what?" Rutledge challenged. "That someone ships supplies to Pacific coordinates? That's not evidence of trafficking. That's evidence of commerce."

"Commerce in human beings," Sonia said.

"Prove it," Rutledge replied. "Show me one operator who says they were taken against their will. Show me one witness who can testify to coercion. Show me anything beyond circumstantial patterns."

"Ida Glitter gave testimony today," Sonia said. "To Detective Simmons. Three hours of detailed testimony about how operators are selected, how votes are manipulated, how the committee facilitates disappearances."

Rutledge's jaw tightened. "That testimony was obtained improperly. Without notifying federal investigators. It's tainted."

"It's true," Sonia said.

"Truth and evidence are different things," Flores replied. "And right now, you have neither."

Brennan placed a document on the table. "Officer Miguel, you're suspended effective immediately. Pending investigation into unauthorized access to government records, conspiracy to obstruct justice, and aiding a criminal enterprise."

Sonia stared at the document. "Criminal enterprise? You're calling my husband a criminal?"

"We're calling his methods criminal," Brennan corrected. "And we're calling you a suspected accomplice."

"Badge and weapon," Flores said.

Sonia's hands trembled slightly as she unclipped her badge and set it on the table. Her weapon followed—cleaned just yesterday, maintained with the same discipline she'd applied to everything in her career. Every case closed. Every victim protected. Every promise kept.

Now surrendered to people who saw justice as paperwork.

"This doesn't change what's true," Sonia said, her voice steady despite the anger burning in her chest.

"No," Rutledge replied. "You made the mistake. You chose loyalty to your husband over loyalty to the law."

"I chose truth over corruption," Sonia corrected. "And I'd make the same choice again."

“That’s what your husband said,” Flores replied. “And now he’s in jail. And you’re unemployed. Was it worth it?”

Sonia stood. “Ask me when the operators are free.”

She walked out of the conference room, out of the precinct, into the parking lot where she’d parked her car next to Miguel’s empty spot for eight years.

And she cried.

Not because she’d been suspended. Not because her career was over. But because Michael had been right, and she’d doubted him. Because operators were being trafficked, and she’d asked him to stop fighting. Because she’d chosen safety over justice.

And now safety was gone anyway.

Her phone buzzed—the new phone, clean of evidence. A text from James:

I’m sorry. I heard what happened.

They suspended me, Sonia typed. FBI threatened prosecution.

Same happened to me an hour ago. We’re being systematically removed.

What do we do now?

James’s response took a moment:

We go public. Tomorrow. Sarah Chen publishes everything. Ida’s testimony. The shipping manifests. The financial documents. All of it. We burn it all down.

That ends any chance of criminal prosecution, Sonia typed.

Criminal prosecution was never going to happen, James replied. The system protects itself. The courts protect power. The only weapon we have left is publicity. So we use it.

Sonia sat in her car, staring at her badge on the passenger seat—confiscated, but she'd palmed her personal backup before leaving the conference room.

She drove home. The house felt empty without Michael. She climbed the stairs and lay down on their bed fully clothed, staring at the ceiling.

Her phone buzzed one more time. A text from an unknown number:

You should have stayed quiet. Now you're just another loose end.

Sonia deleted the message and closed her eyes.

Tomorrow, the world would know everything.

Tomorrow, the conspiracy would be forced to respond.

Tomorrow, she'd either be vindicated or destroyed.

But tonight, she was just a suspended cop lying alone in a too-big bed, married to a man in jail, fighting a system that was bigger and meaner and more patient than she'd ever imagined.

And she realized, with crushing certainty, that Michael had known this would happen.

He'd known they'd separate them.

Suspend them.

Isolate them.

He'd known and he'd fought anyway.

Because some fights were worth losing everything.

Even love.

Even safety.

Even each other.

Sonia pressed Michael's t-shirt against her face smelling his cologne and let herself break.

Just for tonight.

Tomorrow, she'd fight again.

But tonight, she mourned everything they'd lost and everything they might never get back.

## CHAPTER TWENTY-THREE

# Volcanic Activity

The article published at six AM on Friday morning.

EXCLUSIVE: Inside the Blind Island Conspiracy

By Sarah Chen, Kansas City Star

Shipping manifests obtained by the Star reveal systematic transportation of blind vending operators to undisclosed Pacific coordinates. Internal testimony from BBVP committee member Ida Glitter details how operators are selected for forced labor. Financial documents connect Governor Bruce Dickens's administration to shell corporations profiting from Tenorite extraction...

The article ran ten thousand words. It included photographs of the shipping manifests. Excerpts from Ida's testimony. Financial charts. Corporate documents. Everything.

By seven AM, it had two million views.

By eight AM, it was trending nationally.

By nine AM, Governor Dickens called an emergency press conference.

Michael watched it from the jail common area, surrounded by inmates who'd suddenly become interested in his case.

"That's you," Craig said, pointing at the screen where Miguel's photograph appeared alongside text reading: DETECTIVE WHO EXPOSED CONSPIRACY JAILED FOR ILLEGAL METHODS.

"Yeah," Michael said.

"You look better in jail than in that photo," Craig commented.

"Thanks," Michael replied dryly.

Governor Dickens stood at his podium, flanked by lawyers instead of flags this time.

"The allegations published this morning by the Kansas City Star are categorically false," Dickens said, his voice tight with controlled anger. "They are based on stolen documents, coerced testimony, and a coordinated campaign by disgraced law enforcement officers to destroy this administration."

A reporter called out: "Governor, what about the shipping manifests showing personnel transports to Pacific coordinates?"

"Those manifests are legitimate commerce," Dickens replied. "Pacific Mineral Holdings operates mining facilities across international waters. Personnel transport is standard practice."

"What about Tenorite?" another reporter asked. "Is it true that blind operators are being forced to mine a substance that causes blindness?"

Dickens's jaw tightened. "Tenorite is a valuable industrial mineral used in semiconductor manufacturing. It is mined using appropriate safety protocols. No one is being forced to do anything."

"Then where is Blind Island?" a reporter pressed. "Can we visit the facility?"

"The facility's location is proprietary information," Dickens said. "Revealing it would compromise commercial interests and national security."

"National security?" the reporter challenged. "How does mining relate to national security?"

"Advanced semiconductor technology is critical to defense applications," Dickens replied smoothly. "Tenorite enables AI systems that protect American interests. Compromising supply chains compromises security."

Michael watched the governor transform the narrative in real time: from human trafficking to national defense. From conspiracy to patriotism.

It was masterful.

Terrifying.

And effective.

Already, the comments section under Sarah Chen's article was filling with debate:

If this helps national security, isn't it worth it?

Blind people can work just like anyone else

The detective broke the law to get this evidence–he's the real criminal This is a conspiracy theory–where's the proof?

Michael felt sick.

The truth was public. Documented. Undeniable.

And people were still finding ways to doubt it.

His prison-issued tablet flashed a new message. James:

The governor's narrative is gaining traction. People are choosing to believe him.

Why? Michael typed.

Because believing him is easier than accepting that the government traffics people. Cognitive dissonance. Patriotism. Fear of conspiracy theories. Pick your reason.

What do we do?

We need proof that can't be spun. We need photographs of the island. Video of operators working. Something so visceral people can't rationalize it away.

How do we get that? Michael asked. The island is thousands of miles away in international waters. We have no jurisdiction. No resources. No access.

James's response took several minutes:

I'm working on something. Can't say more over text. But Mike—we might have one chance to get physical evidence. If it works, everything changes. If it fails, we're done.

What are you planning?

Something stupidly brave or bravely stupid. I'll know which when it's over.

As usual the conversation went silent from James.

Michael stared at his tablet, feeling dread mix with hope.

That afternoon, a new visitor appeared at the jail: Dr. Elena Vasquez, the Advanced Semiconductor consultant who'd given Michael the cloud folder.

She sat across from him looking shaken.

"They fired me," she said without preamble. "Escorted me out of the building this morning. Told me I violated my NDA. Threatened legal action if I ever speak about the company again."

"I'm sorry," Michael said.

"Don't be," Vasquez replied. "I expected it. But Detective, there's something you need to know about Tenorite."

"What?"

Vasquez pulled out papers—handwritten notes, not corporate documents. "I've been researching the geology. Tenorite only forms in specific volcanic conditions. High pressure. Extreme heat. Rapid cooling. The mineral crystallizes in lava tubes deep underground."

"So?" Michael prompted.

"So Blind Island isn't just any island," Vasquez continued. "It's a volcanic island. Probably active or recently active. The operators aren't mining surface deposits. They're going into volcanic formations. Into lava tubes where the mineral formed millions of years ago."

Michael felt his chest tighten. "How deep?"

"Based on the quality of material I've analyzed? Hundreds of feet underground," Vasquez said. "Maybe deeper. These aren't open-pit mines. These are tunnel systems. Confined spaces. Limited ventilation. And the Tenorite dust is everywhere."

"How dangerous?" Michael asked.

"Extremely," Vasquez replied. "Unprocessed Tenorite becomes unstable when exposed to moisture—like human sweat or breath. It creates toxic gas. The operators aren't just risking blindness from dust. They're risking poisoning from breathing contaminated air."

"So they need gas masks," Michael said.

"Yes," Vasquez confirmed. "But gas masks only protect against inhalation. They don't protect against skin contact. And in confined volcanic tunnels, with limited airflow, the concentration builds. Eventually, even protection fails."

"How long can someone survive working in those conditions?" Michael asked.

Vasquez met his gaze. "Based on exposure models? Six months. Maybe a year if they're rotated out regularly. But Detective—I analyzed the procurement manifests from your shipping documents. Medical supplies. High volumes of respiratory medication. Treatment for chemical burns. Antibiotics for infections."

"They're not rotating operators out," Michael realized.

"No," Vasquez said. "They're keeping them there until they can't work anymore. Then..." She trailed off.

"Then what?" Michael pressed.

"Then they disappear from the manifests entirely," Vasquez said quietly. "Personnel transport goes one direction only. There's no record of anyone ever leaving the island."

Michael felt horror crystallize into certainty. "They're working operators to death."

"Yes," Vasquez said. "And replacing them with new operators as needed. It's not just trafficking, Detective. It's systematic murder disguised as employment."

Michael's hands shook. "Can you testify to this?"

"My company will sue me into oblivion if I do," Vasquez replied. "But yes. I'll testify. Because this isn't just corporate negligence. This is mass murder for profit."

Michael felt the case transform. They weren't just exposing trafficking anymore. They were exposing a death camp. A facility where blind people were sent to die slowly while corporations profited and governments looked away.

"I need you to write everything down," Michael said. "Every detail about Tenorite. The volcanic geology. The exposure risks. The medical evidence from the manifests. Everything."

"I already did," Vasquez said. "Forty pages. Footnoted. Referenced. Enough for an expert witness testimony. I've uploaded it to the same secure cloud folder where I put the other evidence. The document is titled 'Tenorite Medical Analysis.'"

Michael nodded, memorizing the file name. "Thank you."

"Don't thank me," Vasquez said. "Just stop them. Before more people die."

She left.

Michael returned to his cell and accessed the cloud folder on his prison issued tablet. He open Vasquez's report and read it cover to cover. The technical detail was overwhelming, but the conclusion was clear:

Blind Island wasn't just a sinister mining operation.

It was an execution chamber disguised as employment.

And every operator sent there was on a countdown to death that started the moment they arrived.

Michael texted James:

Got new evidence from Vasquez. Tenorite extraction is killing operators. Six months to a year survival time. This is murder, not just trafficking.

James responded immediately:

That changes everything. Murder has no statute of limitations. Federal jurisdiction is automatic. This isn't just a state conspiracy anymore—it's serial killing.

Will that get operators rescued?

It will get the FBI off the fence, James replied. Murder investigation can't be buried like corruption. Rutledge might be protecting the conspiracy, but his superiors won't protect mass murder. Too public. Too explosive.

So we give this to the media?

Not yet. First we need physical proof. Photos from the island showing conditions. Then we release Vasquez's report alongside visual evidence. Make it impossible to deny.

James, how are you planning to get photos from an island in the middle of the Pacific?

A long pause, then:

I'm going there.

Michael felt his blood run cold.

What?

I found a cargo ship captain who does supply runs to the coordinates. He's willing to take me. For a price.

That's insane. If they catch you—

Then I'm dead, James replied. But if I don't go, operators keep dying. And you stay in jail. And the conspiracy wins. So I'm going.

When?

Tomorrow night. Ship leaves from Long Beach. Four-day voyage. I'll have 48 hours on the island before the return trip.

You can't do this alone, Michael typed desperately.

I'm not. Martinez is coming with me. Two witnesses. Two cameras. Two chances to get evidence that sticks.

Michael wanted to argue. To demand James stop. To find another way.

But there was no other way.

James was risking his life because Michael couldn't.

Because Michael was caged while operators died.

Because someone had to witness what was happening before all the victims disappeared.

Be safe out there, Michael typed. And James—stay sharp. They'll be watching.

I know, James replied. If something goes wrong, if I don't make it back—you have to see this through. No matter what.

I will, Michael typed.

Swear it to me, James insisted. Everything we've worked for, everything these operators have suffered—it can't be for nothing. Swear you'll finish what we started.

Michael's eyes burned as he typed:

I swear I'll see this through. No matter what happens to either of us, the truth comes out. The operators get justice.

Good, James replied. That's all I needed to hear. I'll contact you when I'm back on land. Two weeks, Mike.

The connection ended.

Michael sat in his cell, staring at the tablet screen, feeling everything slip toward an ending he couldn't control.

Tomorrow, James would board a cargo ship heading into the Pacific.

In four days, he'd reach Blind Island.

And in forty-eight hours, he'd either document genocide or become its next victim.

Michael pressed his forehead against the cool concrete wall and tried not to think about all the ways this could go wrong.

Tried not to imagine James's body dumped in the ocean.

Tried not to calculate the odds of anyone surviving exposure to a system that had killed everyone else who got too close.

But the math was simple.

And the odds were terrible.

And Michael could do nothing except wait.

And hope.

And pray to a God he wasn't sure he believed in that James Simmons would survive doing the bravest and stupidest thing anyone had attempted in this entire cursed case.

## CHAPTER TWENTY-FOUR

# Fourth Disappearance: Micah

The notification came at three in the morning.

Michael's prison tablet displayed a bright alert, pulling him from restless sleep. He checked the screen: a secure message from Sonia.

They hadn't communicated in three weeks.

Micah Mitchell is missing. The message was blunt, professional. Her husband called me twenty minutes ago. She didn't come home from her route. Phone's dead. Route supervisor says she finished her day normally, but building security footage shows two men escorting her to a van at 6:47 PM.

Michael sat up, instantly alert. He typed back:

When?

Yesterday evening. Her husband waited until tonight to call because Micah sometimes works late. But when she didn't answer her phone by midnight, he got scared.

Michael open his cloud file named disappearance. He typed:

Who is Micah?

Micah Mitchell. Forty-two. Blind since age seven. BBVP operator for nine years. Runs a site at the county administrative building. Married. Three kids. She filed a complaint with the committee six weeks ago. About unsafe working conditions and discrimination from building management.

And now she's gone. Michael typed, the pattern clicking into place.

Same as the others. Committee voted unanimously last week to approve a 'performance review.' Audit letter arrived yesterday morning. Disappearance by evening. They're not even pretending anymore, Mike. They're just taking people.

Michael felt rage burn cold and steady. He typed: How many does that make?

Twenty-three. Twenty-three documented disappearances in two years. Plus however many we don't know about from other states.

Where are you? Michael asked.

Outside Micah's house. I came when her husband called. I know I'm suspended. I know I shouldn't be investigating. But Mike—I couldn't just ignore it.

You did the right thing, Michael typed.

Did I? Because investigating didn't stop them from taking Micah. It didn't save Antony or Justin or De'Osha. It didn't keep you out of jail or keep me employed. What did it accomplish except destroying our lives?

Michael stared at the screen, reading the exhaustion between the words—the slow erosion of someone who'd fought too hard for too long with too little success.

He typed carefully: It documented the truth. That's not nothing.

It feels like nothing. It feels like we're just collecting names for a memorial no one will build.

Michael wanted to argue. Wanted to reassure her. But he understood the fatigue. The despair that came from watching people disappear while the system protected itself.

He typed: Sonia, I know this is hard. I know it feels hopeless. But James is getting proof. Real, physical proof from the island. When he comes back—

If he comes back, came her immediate response.

When he comes back, we'll have evidence that can't be dismissed. Photos. Video. Testimony from someone who actually saw the conditions. That changes everything.

A long pause. The three dots appeared and disappeared several times before her message finally came through:

And if he doesn't come back? If James becomes another name on the list?

Michael stared at the tablet screen, unable to type an answer.

Because the possibility was too real.

Too likely.

Too close.

He changed the subject: Is Micah's husband willing to make a statement?

Yes. I recorded his testimony on my phone. He describes two men in suits. Official looking. They showed Micah paperwork. She looked confused but went with them voluntarily. Or what looked like voluntarily. Hard to tell from security footage.

Same pattern, Michael typed, writing it down in his notebook. Coercion disguised as compliance.

Her husband also said something else. He said Micah told him last week that she felt watched. That someone had been asking her coworkers questions about her. About her attitude. Her relationship with the committee. Whether she was 'cooperative.'

Michael paused. Then He typed: They profiled her.

Yes. Just like Antony. Just like all of them. Someone assessed Micah, determined she was a problem, and marked her for removal.

Who does the assessment? Michael typed.

I don't know. But it's systematic. Organized. Someone has authority to investigate operators, profile their attitudes, and flag them for reassignment.

Michael thought about Ida Glitter's testimony—how committee members received financial incentives for each operator successfully transitioned. How Demetrius Giller had connections to state officials. How the system was designed to identify and remove "difficult" operators before they could organize resistance.

He typed: It's the committee. They're not just approving removals. They're recommending targets.

Which makes them a direct hand in murder. If Vasquez is right about the survival time on the island.

She is. I've seen her research. It's airtight.

A pause, then Sonia's message came through: Mike, what are we going to do when James gets back? Assuming he gets back. What's the plan?

We hold a press conference, Michael typed. We release everything. Photos from the island. Vasquez's medical research. Ida's testimony. The shipping manifests. Financial documents. Everything at once. Make it so overwhelming the conspiracy can't suppress it.

And then?

Then we force federal investigations. Murder investigations. International trafficking. War crimes if we can make the case. We bring enough charges that someone has to act.

The FBI is compromised. Rutledge proved that.

Then we go above Rutledge. Justice Department. Congressional oversight. International human rights organizations. We make this too big for one corrupt agent to bury.

You make it sound possible.

It is possible, Michael typed.

No. It's necessary. That's different than possible. Necessary just means we have to try. It doesn't mean we'll succeed.

Michael stared at the screen, wanting to argue. Wanting to promise her that justice would prevail. That their sacrifices would matter. That operators would be rescued and conspirators would face consequences.

But he'd learned that promises were cheap and outcomes were expensive.

He typed: I love you.

Several minutes passed. Michael watched the screen, wondering if she'd respond.

Finally: I love you too. But Mike—I don't know if love is enough anymore. Not against this.

It has to be. Because it's all we have left.

No. We have each other. And we have truth. Love is just the reason we keep fighting when both seem worthless.

The message conversation ended.

Michael sat in his cell, feeling the weight of another name added to the list. Another family destroyed. Another operator transported to an island where death came slowly, measured in contaminated breaths and tunnel collapses and the gradual failure of bodies pushed beyond endurance.

Micah Mitchell.

Mother of three.

Nine-year veteran of a program that had betrayed him.

Gone.

Michael grab his tablet and wrote carefully:

Operator #23: Micah Mitchell

Disappeared: [today's date]

Last seen: County Administrative Building, 6:47 PM Committee action: Performance review approved [date] Complaint filed: 6 weeks prior—unsafe conditions

He stared at the entry, then at all the entries above it. Twenty-three names. Twenty-three people. Twenty-three families trying to understand how someone could disappear in America in 2026.

And the list would keep growing.

Every week, the committee would vote. Every week, another operator would be marked. Every week, vans would arrive and people would vanish and families would be told it was voluntary, it was training, it was for the good of the program.

Every week, the machinery of conspiracy would grind forward.

Unless James came back with evidence that stopped it.

Unless the press conference forced investigations that couldn't be buried.

Unless someone—anyone—with authority decided that blind lives mattered as much as corporate profits.

Michael closed his notebook and lay back on his bunk.

Craig spoke through the vent: "Another one disappeared?"

"Yeah," Michael replied.

"How many does that make?"

"Too many."

Craig was quiet for a moment. "You know what the worst part is?"

"What?"

"Even if you stop them," Craig said, "even if you expose everything and they all go to jail—the people who already disappeared are still gone. You can't bring them back. You can't undo what happened. Best you can do is stop it from happening to others."

"I know," Michael said.

"That enough for you?" Craig asked. "Knowing you can't save the ones already taken?"

Michael thought about Antony Grumpton. Justin Jones. De'Osha Davenport. Micah Mitchell. All the others.

"It has to be," Michael said. "Because stopping it from happening again is the only justice they'll ever get."

Craig grunted an agreement sound. "You're either stupid or a saint, cop. I can't tell which."

"I'm just angry," Michael replied.

"Anger runs out," Craig said. "What keeps you going after that?"

Michael stared at the ceiling, thinking about Sonia and James and Ida and everyone else who'd sacrificed themselves to expose the conspiracy.

"Stubbornness," he finally said.

Craig laughed—a real laugh, not bitter. "That I believe."

The lights went out.

Michael lay in darkness, listening to the jail settle into night sounds.

Somewhere across the country, James Simmons was preparing to board a cargo ship.

Somewhere in Kansas, Micah Mitchell's husband was trying to explain to three kids why their mother wasn't coming home.

Somewhere in the Pacific Ocean, operators were descending into volcanic tunnels to mine poison while guards watched and corporations profited and governments looked away.

And somewhere in a concrete cell in Wichita, a detective with one eye and too much stubbornness refused to quit fighting a system that had already destroyed him.

Because quitting meant the operators died for nothing.

And Michael Miguel—suspended, jailed, separated from his wife, awaiting trial that might send him to prison for a decade—couldn't live with that.

So he didn't quit.

He just lay in the dark.

And waited.

And prepared for the moment when James came back with proof.

Or didn't come back at all.

Either way, the fight would continue.

Because some things were worth losing everything.

Even when everything was already gone.

CHAPTER TWENTY-FIVE

# The Committee's Fear

Ida Glitter was scared.

Not the normal kind of scared—the flutter of nerves before public speaking or the worry about making mistakes. This was deeper. Existential. The kind of fear that came from knowing powerful people wanted you silent and had resources to make silence permanent.

She sat in her living room at four in the morning, unable to sleep, listening to her house settle around her. Every creak was a footstep. Every wind gust was a door opening. Every distant car was them coming to finish what they'd started.

Two days ago, she'd given testimony to Detective Simmons. Three hours of detailed confession about committee corruption, operator selection, Demetrius Giller's connections, Darrius Johnson's murder.

Yesterday, Sarah Chen's article had published. Ida's testimony—excerpted, anonymized, but clearly hers to anyone who knew the program—had been read by millions.

And today, the committee would respond.

Ida knew how the committee responded to threats.

Quietly.

Permanently.

Her phone buzzed. A text from an unknown number:

We need to talk. Committee meeting. Emergency session. 10 AM. Your attendance is required.

Ida's hands shook as she read the message.

Required.

Not requested. Required.

She knew what that meant.

They were going to remove her. Vote her out. Strip her position. And then—if Darrius Johnson's fate was any indication—ensure she couldn't testify again.

Ida called Detective Simmons. It went to voicemail.

She tried Michael Miguel's number—the one he'd given her during their jail visit. Also voicemail.

She tried Sonia Miguel. Nothing.

Everyone was suddenly unreachable.

Which meant everyone was suddenly unavailable to protect her.

Ida sat in her living room, as the sun rose painting her walls orange and gold, and considered running.

She had a sister in Tennessee. She could buy a bus ticket. Disappear into a rural town where the committee couldn't reach her. Live quiet and invisible until this blew over.

Except it wouldn't blow over.

Because testimony couldn't be un-given. Articles couldn't be un-published. And committees didn't forget members who betrayed them.

She'd made her choice when she visited Miguel in jail.

Now she had to live with the consequences.

Or die with them.

At nine-thirty, Ida dressed carefully. Business casual. Professional. She pinned her BBVP committee badge to her jacket—a small defiance. They might remove her, but she'd walk in wearing the authority they'd given her.

She called a ride service and gave the address of the SLA building where emergency committee meetings were held.

The driver tried to make small talk. Ida couldn't hear him over the roar of her own heartbeat.

At 9:58 AM, she walked into the SLA building.

The receptionist looked surprised. "Ms. Glitter. I didn't think you'd come."

"Why wouldn't I?" Ida asked, keeping her voice steady.

"Because..." The receptionist trailed off. "Never mind. Conference room C. Third floor."

Ida found the elevator by memory and sound. Rode up. Walked down the carpeted hallway where acoustic tiles dampened her cane's tap.

Conference room C's door was closed.

Ida paused outside, hearing voices within. Low. Tense. Angry.

She knocked.

The voices stopped.

"Come in," Demetrius Giller's voice called.

Ida opened the door and stepped inside.

The committee was already seated: Demetrius at the head of the table. Maykayla Peterson, vice chair. Ryean Trotter, eastern director. And two empty chairs—one that had been Darrius Johnson's, one that would be Ida's.

Or had been Ida's.

Past tense.

"Sit down, Ida," Demetrius said.

Ida sat.

"You know why you're here," Demetrius continued. "So let's not pretend otherwise."

"I'm here because you called an emergency meeting," Ida replied, forcing steel into her voice.

"You're here because you betrayed this committee," Maykayla said sharply. "You went to the police. You gave testimony. You helped that detective destroy everything we've built."

"I helped expose what this committee became," Ida corrected. "There's a difference."

"Is there?" Demetrius asked. "Because from where I'm sitting, you took an oath to represent blind operators. To protect the program. To maintain committee solidarity. And you violated all of it."

"I took an oath to represent operators," Ida agreed. "Not to help them disappear."

The temperature in the room dropped.

"Careful," Demetrius said quietly. "Accusations have consequences."

"So does trafficking," Ida shot back.

Ryean spoke for the first time: "Ida, you've been under a lot of stress. The responsibilities of committee service can be overwhelming. Maybe you need time away. Medical leave. A chance to recover perspective."

Ida recognized the offer for what it was: a way out. Resign quietly. Recant her testimony. Claim mental health issues. Disappear from the narrative before she could do more damage.

"I don't need time away," Ida said. "I need this committee to stop killing people."

Maykayla slammed her hand on the table. "We're not killing anyone!"

"Then where are the operators?" Ida challenged. "Antony Grumpton. Justin Jones. De'Osha Davenport. Micah Mitchell. Twenty-three people in two years. Where are they?"

"Reassigned," Demetrius said. "To advanced opportunities. Training programs. Better positions."

"Prove it," Ida said. "Show me documentation. Show me contracts. Show me anything that proves they're alive and well and working voluntarily."

“That information is confidential,” Demetrius replied.

“That information doesn’t exist,” Ida corrected. “Because those operators aren’t in training. They’re in volcanic tunnels mining Tenorite until their bodies fail and then they’re disposed of like industrial waste.”

The room went silent.

Demetrius stood slowly. “You have no proof of that.”

“I have Dr. Vasquez’s research,” Ida said. “I have shipping manifests. I have financial documents. I have Detective Simmons’s investigation. And I have my own conscience.”

“Your conscience is misinformed,” Demetrius said.

“My conscience is finally awake,” Ida replied.

Demetrius walked around the table until he stood behind Ida’s chair. She felt his presence—large, intimidating, calculated to make her feel small.

“Ida,” he said, voice dropping to something almost gentle, “I understand you’re upset. I understand the media attention has been stressful. But you need to think about your future. Your family. Your position. If you continue down this path, you lose everything.”

“I already lost everything,” Ida said. “The moment I realized what we were doing.”

“Then let me be clear about what happens next,” Demetrius continued. “This committee votes unanimously to remove you from your position. Effective immediately. You’re stripped of all authority, all access, all privileges. Your testimony to Detective

Simmons is discredited as the ramblings of a disgruntled former member. And if you continue speaking to the media or law enforcement..."

He left the threat unfinished.

"You'll kill me," Ida said flatly. "Like you killed Darrius."

"Darrius killed himself," Maykayla said quickly. "The medical examiner—"

"Lied," Ida interrupted. "Or was pressured. Or was paid. I don't know which. But Darrius didn't kill himself. He was terrified in the weeks before his death. He knew too much. And you silenced him."

"That's a serious accusation," Ryean said.

"It's a serious crime," Ida replied.

Demetrius returned to his seat. "All in favor of removing Ida Glitter from the committee for gross misconduct, violation of confidentiality, and actions detrimental to the program?"

Three hands rose.

Unanimous.

Of course.

"The vote is recorded," Demetrius said. "Ida, you're no longer a committee member. Please surrender your badge and leave this building."

Ida unpinned her badge slowly. Looked at it. Five years of service. Hundreds of hours in meetings. Countless operators she'd tried to help before the committee became corrupted.

She placed it on the table.

"I'll leave," she said. "But I won't be silent. Everything I told Detective Simmons is true. Everything Dr. Vasquez documented is true. Everything Detective Miguel exposed is true. And no vote you take will change that."

"The only thing that vote changes," Demetrius said, "is whether you're part of the solution or part of the problem."

"I'm already part of the problem," Ida replied. "I was part of it the moment I stayed silent while operators disappeared. But I'm trying to become part of the solution. Even if it kills me."

She stood and walked to the door.

"Ida," Demetrius called.

She paused.

"Be careful going forward," he said. "Blindness makes people vulnerable. Accidents happen."

There it was. The threat. Polite. Professional. Unmistakable.

"I'll be careful," Ida said. "You be afraid."

She left the conference room and walked out of the SLA building for the last time.

Outside, the morning was bright and warm. Traffic moved normally. People walked past absorbed in their phones and coffee and ordinary concerns.

Ida called Detective Simmons again. Still voicemail.

She called Sonia Miguel. Nothing.

She called Michael Miguel's lawyer. No answer.

Everyone was suddenly unreachable.

Which meant she was alone.

Ida stood on the sidewalk, feeling the weight of isolation. No job. No protection. No allies currently available.

Just her testimony already given and the knowledge that powerful people wanted her dead.

She pulled out her phone and recorded a video:

"My name is Ida Glitter. I was western director of the Kansas BBVP committee until this morning when I was removed for telling the truth. If you're watching this, it means something happened to me. An accident. A suicide. A disappearance. Don't believe it. I'm not suicidal. I'm not careless. I'm scared but determined. If I die, it's because the committee—specifically Demetrius Giller, Maykayla Peterson, and Ryean Trotter—had me killed to protect their involvement in operator trafficking. Detective Michael Miguel was right about everything. The conspiracy is real. Blind Island is real. Operators are being murdered for profit. And I'm probably going to die for saying this. But someone needs to say it. Someone needs to—"

A hand grabbed her shoulder.

Ida spun, heart hammering.

A man stood there—middle-aged, professional attire.

"Ms. Glitter?" the man said. "I'm Special Agent Andre Park, FBI. I've been assigned to protect you."

Ida felt tears of relief threaten. "Protect me from what?"

"From the people who've killed witnesses before," Park replied. "Agent Rutledge has been reassigned. I'm taking over the investigation. And right now, you're in danger."

"I know," Ida said.

"No," Park corrected. "You don't. The committee just put out an alert claiming you're mentally unstable and may harm yourself or others. They're setting up your death to look like suicide or police intervention."

Ida felt ice run through her veins. "How long do I have?"

"Hours," Park said. "Maybe less. We need to get you into protective custody. Now."

"And then?" Ida asked.

"Then you testify," Park replied. "In federal court. Under oath. With full immunity and protection. We're building a case against the committee, the governor's office, and Pacific Mineral Holdings. But we need you alive to make it."

Ida wanted to believe him. Wanted to trust that the FBI would protect her where local police couldn't.

But she'd learned that systems protected themselves first.

"How do I know you're really FBI?" Ida asked.

Park showed her credentials. "Call the Kansas City field office. Verify my identity. But do it fast. Because the longer we stand here, the more vulnerable you are."

Ida pulled out her phone and called the FBI field office. The receptionist confirmed Agent Andre Park was assigned to the BBVP investigation and authorized to provide witness protection.

"Okay," Ida said. "Where are we going?"

"Somewhere safe," Park replied. "Somewhere they can't reach you. You're going dark for a few weeks. No phone. No contact with anyone. Not even Detective Simmons or the Miguels."

"They'll think I'm dead," Ida said.

"Better they think you're dead than you actually are dead," Park replied.

They walked to an unmarked sedan. Park opened the passenger door.

Ida hesitated. "Agent Park, if this is a trap—if you're working with them—"

"Then you're dead already," Park said bluntly. "But I'm not. And you're not. So get in the car and let me save your life."

Ida got in.

They drove away from the SLA building, away from the city, toward a safe house that Ida hoped actually existed.

And she thought about Michael Miguel, locked in jail, waiting for testimony that might never reach trial because the witness might not survive protection.

She thought about all the operators already gone.

And she thought about how the committee's fear meant she'd been right.

Because they only killed people who threatened them.

And she'd become a threat.

Which meant everything she'd said was true.

Even if it got her killed proving it.

## CHAPTER TWENTY-SIX

# Blind Island

The cargo ship left Long Beach at 11:47 PM on a Saturday.

James Simmons stood on the deck, watching California's lights fade into darkness, feeling the enormity of what he'd committed to. Four days at sea. Forty-eight hours on the island. Documentation that could either save the case or get him killed.

Officer Linda Martinez stood beside him, camera equipment secured in waterproof cases at their feet.

"Last chance to change your mind," Martinez said.

"I changed my mind six times already," James replied. "Kept coming back to the same conclusion: this is necessary."

"Necessary and suicidal aren't mutually exclusive," Martinez pointed out.

"I know."

The captain—a grizzled man named Duane Elliot who'd taken cash without asking questions—approached from the bridge. "You two should get below deck. Storm's coming in from the west. We'll be riding rough seas for the next day or two."

"How rough?" James asked.

"Rough enough that staying topside is dangerous," the captain replied. "Especially for passengers who aren't experienced sailors."

They followed him below to cramped quarters that smelled of diesel and salt. Two bunks. A porthole too small to see much through. A door that locked from the inside—which gave James some comfort but not much.

"We arrive at the coordinates in four days," Captain Elliot said. "I drop you at the supply dock. You have exactly ten hours before I leave. If you're not at the dock when I leave, I will without a doubt leave without you. Understood?"

"Understood," James said.

"And if you get caught?" Elliot asked. "If they question you about who brought you?"

"We've never met," James assured him. "We chartered a private boat. It broke down. We drifted to the island. We have no idea who you are."

The Captain nodded. "Good. Because I have a family. And this run pays well enough that I don't want to lose it."

He left them alone in the cabin.

Martinez sat on one of the bunks and pulled out her camera equipment, checking batteries and memory cards. "You realize we're probably going to die, right?"

"Probably," James agreed. "But probably isn't certainly."

"That's not as comforting as you think," Martinez said.

James pulled out his own equipment: two cameras, backup batteries, satellite phone programmed with Miguel's direct cloud upload, and a small drone with a camera attachment—something he'd bought online and hoped would work for aerial documentation.

"If we get photos," James said, "real photos of operators working in those conditions, of the guards, of the facilities—that changes everything."

"And if we get caught before we get photos?" Martinez asked.

"Then Miguel finishes this," James replied. "He promised."

Martinez was quiet for a moment. "You trust him? Even locked up in jail, suspended, with no resources?"

"I trust his stubbornness," James said. "That's more reliable than resources."

The ship rolled as they hit rougher water. Martinez gripped the bunk frame.

"You get seasick?" James asked.

"We're about to find out," Martinez replied.

They spent the next thirty-six hours below deck while the storm raged. James tried to sleep but mostly lay awake, thinking about everything that could go wrong. The list was long and specific.

They could be caught immediately upon arrival. Arrested. Killed. Made to Disappear like the operators they were trying to document.

The island security could be too tight to penetrate. Guards everywhere. Surveillance cameras. Perimeter defenses.

They could document everything and have the equipment confiscated before leaving. All evidence lost.

The captain could betray them. Turn them over to island security in exchange for payment or immunity.

The cargo ship could sink in the storm and none of this would matter.

James ran through contingency plans, backup plans, emergency protocols. But every scenario ended the same way: success required luck as much as skill.

On the third day, the storm broke. James and Martinez returned to deck and stared out at endless ocean.

"Four thousand miles from anywhere," Martinez said. "If something goes wrong, no one's coming to help."

"Then we make sure nothing goes wrong," James replied.

That night, James used the satellite phone to text Miguel:

24 hours from island. Everything ready. If you don't hear from me in 6 days, assume the worst.

Miguel's response came immediately:

Be careful. Document everything. Come back alive.

I'll try. How are you holding up?

Still in jail. Trial date moved up to next month. DA is pushing for maximum sentence. But if you get proof from the island, that changes the case.

I'll get proof, James typed.

Good. Because without it, I'm going to prison for ten years and operators keep disappearing.

James stared at the message, feeling the weight of expectation. Miguel's freedom depended on this. Sonia's vindication. Ida's testimony. The operators' lives.

Everything hinged on the next forty-eight hours.

I won't let you down, James typed.

You never have, Miguel replied. That's why I trust you with this.

James returned to the cabin where Martinez was organizing their equipment for the third time—nervous energy needing outlet.

"You ready for this?" James asked.

"No," Martinez admitted. "But I'm going anyway."

They tried to sleep. Couldn't. Just lay in their bunks listening to the ship's engine and ocean sounds and the quiet terror of approaching the unknown.

At dawn on the fourth day, Captain Elliot knocked on their door.

"We're here," he said. "Come see."

James and Martinez climbed to the deck and stared at the horizon.

Blind Island rose from the ocean like a scar on the water's surface.

Volcanic rock. Black and jagged. Steam rising from vents. Industrial structures clinging to the slopes like metal barnacles. A dock extending into the water where other cargo ships sat at anchor.

And movement. People. Dozens of them. Wearing coveralls. Moving between buildings. Some wearing gas masks. Some being escorted by guards with weapons.

James lifted his camera and started photographing.

The island was real.

Visible.

Documented.

"That's it," Martinez breathed. "That's actually it."

Captain Elliot approached, his expression grim. "You've got two days. There's a supply schedule. I deliver cargo, pick up processed materials, and leave. You'll blend in with the dock workers during unloading. After that, you're on your own."

"What about getting back?" James asked.

"Be at the dock Captain Elliot replied. "I leave in 8 hours whether you're there or not."

The ship approached the dock. James and Martinez watched as the island grew larger, more detailed, more real.

Operators in gas masks moved in organized lines between a mine entrance and a processing building. Guards stood at intervals, watching. Radio communication between them suggested tight coordination.

This wasn't a small operation.

This was industrial scale.

The ship docked. The Captain's crew began unloading cargo—food supplies, fuel drums, medical equipment, industrial machinery.

James and Martinez shouldered their equipment bags and joined the dock workers, moving with purpose but not urgency. Just two more bodies in the organized chaos of a supply delivery.

No one stopped them.

No one questioned them.

They were invisible in the machinery of commerce.

James felt adrenaline spike as they reached the dock and stepped onto Blind Island's volcanic rock.

The air smelled like sulfur and industrial chemicals. The ground radiated heat. Steam vents hissed nearby.

And everywhere—operators. Dozens of them. Moving with practiced efficiency through a landscape designed to extract their labor until there was nothing left to extract.

James lifted his camera and began documenting.

Because this was why he'd come.

This was what Miguel needed.

This was proof.

And if it killed him, at least it would matter.

## CHAPTER TWENTY-SEVEN

# The Island's Purpose

The mine entrance yawned like a wound in the volcanic rock—a tunnel descending into darkness where portable lights failed to reach the depths.

James crouched behind a processing building, camera raised, photographing operators as they emerged from the tunnel. Each one wore a gas mask. Each one carried a container filled with glittering silverish-yellow dust. Each one moved with the exhaustion of people pushed beyond endurance.

Tenorite.

James could see it in the containers, in the dust coating the operators' coveralls, in the way guards kept their distance from the contaminated workers.

Martinez positioned herself fifty yards away, filming from a different angle. They'd agreed to document independently—if one got caught, the other might escape with evidence.

Through his telephoto lens, James focused on faces. Looking for anyone he recognized. Antony Grumpton. Justin Jones. De'Osha Davenport. Micah Mitchell. Twenty-three names from Miguel's list.

He saw De'Osha first.

She emerged from the tunnel, gas mask obscuring most of her face, but James recognized her from photographs Miguel had shown him. She moved slowly, deliberately, like someone conserving energy for survival. A guard prodded her toward the processing building and De'Osha complied without resistance.

James photographed everything. Her face. Her number—stenciled on her coveralls: 0089. Her physical condition—thin, moving with pain, clearly deteriorated from the photographs her family had provided.

She was alive.

But barely.

James moved closer, using cargo containers as cover, trying to get audio. A small microphone hidden in his jacket picked up fragments of conversation between guards:

"—shipment ready by Thursday—"

"—three more showing respiratory failure—"

"—disposal protocols same as last month—"

Disposal protocols.

James felt ice run through his veins.

They weren't talking about waste management. They were talking about operators who could no longer work.

He kept filming.

An hour passed. Then two. The sun climbed higher, making the volcanic rock radiate heat that shimmered in waves. James drank water sparingly from bottles he'd brought, knowing he couldn't afford dehydration.

Martinez circled to the eastern side of the facility, documenting the dormitory buildings where operators were housed. James stayed focused on the mine entrance and processing building—the heart of the operation.

At midday, a new group emerged from the tunnel. These operators weren't carrying containers. They were being supported by guards, their movements unsteady. Even through gas masks, James could see distress.

The guards escorted them not toward the dormitories but toward a separate building—smaller, isolated, marked with a red cross.

Medical facility.

James photographed the transfer, zooming in on faces. He recognized Justin Jones—one of the early disappearances from Miguel's list. Justin could barely walk. His coveralls were stained with what looked like blood.

The guards deposited Justin and three other operators inside the medical building and left them there.

James watched for twenty minutes. No one entered or exited. No doctors. No nurses. Just a building where sick operators were placed and forgotten.

Not a hospital.

A waiting room for death.

James's hands shook as he photographed the scene. This wasn't just forced labor. This was systematic extermination. Work operators until they broke, then abandon them to die while new operators were brought in to replace them.

His satellite phone buzzed. A text from Martinez:

Found dormitories. Conditions horrific. Overcrowded. No climate control. Basic sanitation. Photographing everything but need to move soon—guards patrol every 30 minutes.

James typed back:

Medical building on west side. Operators being left to die. Document if you can. Meet back at dock in 3 hours.

Copy that.

James moved position, circling toward the medical building. He needed to see inside. Needed evidence of what happened to operators who could no longer work.

The building had windows—small, high up, designed for ventilation not visibility. James found a maintenance ladder leaning against a storage shed and quietly moved it to the medical building's side wall.

He climbed carefully, camera ready.

Through the window, he saw six operators lying on cots. No medical equipment. No monitoring. No treatment. Just bodies waiting to stop breathing.

James photographed each face. Matched them against the list Miguel had provided.

Justin Jones.

Operator 0047—name unknown.

Operator 0063—name unknown.

Three he didn't recognize, but their coveralls bore numbers that James documented meticulously.

One operator wasn't moving. Wasn't breathing. Dead for hours, based on the stillness.

No one had removed the body.

James felt rage and grief war in his chest as he photographed the scene. This was murder. Documented. Undeniable. Criminal.

A voice called out below him.

"Hey! What are you doing?"

James's heart stopped. A guard stood at the base of the ladder, hand on his weapon.

James made a split-second decision.

He jumped.

The drop was fifteen feet. James hit the ground hard, rolled, came up running. The guard shouted into his radio. Footsteps pounded behind him.

James sprinted between buildings, using cargo containers and equipment as cover. His ankle screamed pain from the landing but adrenaline overrode it.

More guards appeared, converging from multiple directions.

James dove behind a fuel storage tank and pulled out the satellite phone.

He texted Martinez:

Compromised. Guards alerted. Get to dock NOW. Upload photos to cloud before they catch you.

Martinez's response was immediate:

On my way. You?

I'll try. If I don't make it, get the evidence out. That's priority.

James—

Go. That's an order.

James pocketed the phone and checked his camera. Hundreds of photos. Evidence that could destroy the conspiracy. Evidence worth dying for.

He pulled the memory card and swapped it for a blank one. Tucked the real card inside his sock. If they searched him, they'd find the camera with blank card and assume that's all he had.

The guards were closer now. James could hear radio chatter coordinating the search.

He had two choices: run for the dock and hope Martinez could escape, or create a distraction that gave her time.

James chose distraction.

He stood and ran toward the mine entrance—away from the dock. Guards spotted him immediately and gave chase.

"Stop! Hands up!"

James kept running. The mine entrance loomed ahead—a dark mouth leading into volcanic depths.

He thought about Miguel in jail. About Sonia suspended. About Ida in hiding. About twenty-three operators who'd disappeared trusting the system to protect them.

He thought about the memory card in his sock—proof of everything.

And he ran faster.

Guards closed the distance. James could hear their breathing, their boots on volcanic rock, their weapons being drawn.

He reached the mine entrance and plunged into darkness.

The temperature dropped immediately. The air turned thick with dust. Emergency lights cast weak yellow illumination every fifty feet.

James ran deeper, using his phone's flashlight to avoid obstacles. Tunnel walls pressed close. The sound of pursuit echoed behind him.

He found a side tunnel—unmarked, narrow—and squeezed into it. Turned off his light. Held his breath.

Guards pounded past. Radio chatter: "Lost visual. Continuing pursuit deeper."

James waited. One minute. Two. Five.

Silence.

He turned his light back on and examined his surroundings. The side tunnel branched into a network of passages. Lava tubes formed millions of years ago, now being mined for the mineral that had caused all this suffering.

James pulled out his camera and kept documenting. Evidence of mining conditions. Tunnel instability. Lack of safety equipment. This was what operators worked in—dark, unstable, contaminated passages where every breath was toxic.

He photographed for twenty minutes, moving deeper into the tunnel system, documenting everything he could before running out of time.

His phone buzzed. Martinez:

At dock. Ship preparing to leave early. Captain says guards alerted port authority. We have 10 minutes before lockdown.

James checked the time. He was at least twenty minutes from the dock. Running.

Go without me, he typed. Get the evidence out.

Negative. We leave together or not at all.

Martinez, that's not—

10 minutes, James. Move quickly.

James ran.

Through tunnels. Up toward the entrance. Out into blinding sunlight. Across the facility grounds where operators watched him pass with empty expressions.

Guards spotted him immediately.

"Stop!"

James didn't stop.

He sprinted toward the dock, legs burning, lungs screaming. The cargo ship was pulling away from the dock—thirty feet of water already between hull and pier.

Martinez stood at the dock's edge. "Jump!"

James hit the end of the dock and leaped.

For a terrible moment he hung suspended over dark water, arms windmilling, gravity pulling him down.

Hands grabbed him. Captain Elliot and two crew members hauled him aboard.

Guards reached the dock and raised weapons.

"Go!" James shouted. "Now!"

The ship's engines roared. Distance opened. Guards shouted and radioed but didn't shoot—gunfire would attract attention

James collapsed on deck, gasping for air, checking his sock.

The memory card was still there.

Martinez knelt beside him. "You're insane."

"I'm documented," James corrected, pulling out the card. "Everything. The tunnels. The operators. The medical building. Bodies. All of it."

Martinez pulled her own memory cards from a hidden pocket. "Me too. Dormitories. Processing facilities. Guards. Probably a thousand photos between us."

Captain Elliot appeared, his face pale. "You two just made me an accessory to whatever that was. If island security traces this ship—"

"They won't," James said. "You never saw us. We were never here. You just did a regular supply run."

The Captain didn't look convinced. "Get below deck. Stay there until we're a hundred miles out. And pray they don't send patrol boats after us."

James and Martinez retreated to their cabin. Martinez immediately pulled out her laptop and began uploading photos to the encrypted cloud Miguel had set up.

Progress bar: 3%... 7%... 12%...

James did the same with his photos. Duplicating evidence across multiple secure locations. Making it impossible to suppress even if they were caught.

18%... 24%... 31%...

Hours passed. The ship sailed west, away from the island, into open ocean.

No patrol boats appeared.

No helicopters.

No pursuit.

By midnight, all photos were uploaded. Backed up. Distributed.

James and Martinez sat in their cabin, staring at laptops displaying hundreds of images that proved everything Miguel had said.

Operators working in toxic conditions.

Guards armed and watching.

Bodies left to die in a medical building that provided no medicine.

A volcanic island where human beings were disposable resources.

“We did it,” Martinez said quietly.

“Yeah,” James replied. “Now comes the hard part.”

“What’s harder than getting these photos?” Martinez asked.

“Making people believe them,” James said. “Making people care enough to act.”

He pulled out the satellite phone and texted Miguel:

Mission complete. Evidence secured. Coming home.

Miguel’s response came immediately:

Thank God. I’ll be ready.

James leaned back against the bunk and closed his eyes, feeling adrenaline finally drain away.

They’d survived.

They’d documented.

They’d proven Miguel right.

Now they just had to make it matter.

Before the conspiracy erased them like it had erased everyone else who got too close to the truth.

## CHAPTER TWENTY-EIGHT

# Sonia's Betrayal Begins

Sonia Miguel sat alone in a coffee shop three blocks from the precinct she was no longer allowed to enter.

Suspended. Investigated. Isolated.

Her phone buzzed. Unknown number. She'd been getting unknown numbers for days—threats, warnings, blocked calls that played silence or breathing.

She answered anyway. "Hello?"

"Officer Miguel." The voice was male, calm, professional. "This is Assistant Attorney General Ken Flores. We need to talk."

Sonia's stomach tightened. "talk about what?."

"something that will make both of us very happy Flores replied. "Because I have something to offer you."

"I'm not interested in—"

"Your husband's freedom," Flores interrupted. "I'm offering Michael Miguel's freedom."

Sonia went still. "What?"

“Detective Miguel is facing ten years in federal prison,” Flores said. “Multiple felony charges. The evidence against him is overwhelming. But it doesn’t have to end that way.”

“What are you proposing?” Sonia asked carefully.

“Cooperation,” Flores replied. “You help us, we help him. Simple.”

“Define ‘help,’” Sonia said.

“Detective Simmons just returned from an unauthorized trip to international waters,” Flores said. “He’s in possession of illegally obtained photographs from a private facility. Those photographs were taken without warrant, without jurisdiction, without legal authority.”

“Those photographs prove blind operators are being trafficked,” Sonia said.

“Those photographs prove Detective Simmons committed multiple crimes,” Flores corrected. “Trespassing. Espionage. Violation of international maritime law. If those photos become public, he faces prosecution.”

“So you want me to stop him from releasing them,” Sonia said.

“I want you to retrieve the photos before they’re distributed,” Flores replied. “Bring them to me. Testify that they were obtained illegally. Help us neutralize Simmons’s investigation.”

“And in exchange?” Sonia asked.

“Your husband’s charges get reduced,” Flores said. “Plea deal. Suspended sentence. He serves no time. You get your life back.”

Sonia felt her chest tighten. “Why would you offer that?”

"Because we want this case closed quietly," Flores said. "Not dramatized in media. Not turned into a political circus. Detective Miguel started something he can't finish. Detective Simmons is making it worse. You can end it."

"By betraying everyone who fought to expose this conspiracy," Sonia said.

"By saving your husband from a decade in prison," Flores corrected. "That's not betrayal. That's love."

Sonia closed her eyes. "I need time to think."

"You have twenty-four hours," Flores replied. "After that, the plea offer expires and your husband goes to trial. With maximum sentence recommendations."

The line went dead.

Sonia sat in the coffee shop, staring at her phone, feeling walls close from every direction.

She called James. He didn't answer—probably still at sea, satellite phone turned off to avoid detection.

She called Michael's lawyer. Robert Hayes's assessment was blunt: "They're serious. Michael will be convicted if he goes to trial. The plea offer is the best option."

"But the photos James took—" Sonia began.

"Are inadmissible," Robert interrupted. "Just like Michael's evidence. Just like everything else. You can have justice or you can have your husband. You can't have both."

Sonia hung up and walked to her car.

She drove home—to the house that was empty without her husband. Climbed the stairs. Sat on their bed.

His army photo sat on the bedside stand. She picked it up, running her fingers over the engraved wood.

He'd lost half his vision fighting for something he believed in.

Now he was losing his freedom.

And she had the power to save him.

All she had to do was betray everyone else.

Her phone buzzed. A text from an unknown number:

Officer Miguel. This is Agent Park. Ida is safe. But we need the photos from Detective Simmons's island trip. They're evidence in a federal investigation. Can you help us secure them?

Sonia stared at the message. Agent Park—the FBI agent who'd taken Ida into protective custody.

Were they working together? Park and Flores? FBI and state AG? Or was this a separate request?

Sonia texted back:

Why do you need them? James documented genocide. That should support your investigation, not threaten it.

Park's response:

The photos were obtained illegally. If Simmons releases them publicly, they become tainted. We need them secured through proper channels. Official custody. Then we can use them in prosecution.

But if I give them to you, how do I know you won't destroy them?

You don't. You have to trust the system.

Sonia laughed bitterly. The system. The same system that had jailed Miguel, suspended her, killed witnesses, and let operators disappear for two years.

She typed:

I don't trust the system. I trust evidence.

Then help us preserve it properly, Park replied. Before Simmons ruins any chance of ending this conspiracy right now.

Sonia didn't respond.

She sat on the bed, holding Miguel's photo, trying to figure out who was lying and who was telling truth and whether there was any difference anymore.

Her phone rang. Not unknown this time. James Simmons.

She answered. "James."

"Sonia. I'm back. I have everything. Photos. Video. Proof of everything Miguel said. I'm meeting with Sarah Chen tomorrow to release it."

"Wait," Sonia said. "Don't release it yet."

"Why not?" James asked, suspicion in his voice.

"Because I got a call," Sonia said. "From the assistant AG. They offered me a deal. If I help them stop the photos from going public, they'll reduce Michael's charges. He won't go to prison."

Silence.

"James?" Sonia prompted.

"They're trying to silence us," James said flatly. "They're using Michael to pressure you. It's a trap."

"Or it's a way to save him," Sonia replied.

"By letting operators die," James said. "Sonia, I saw them. I saw De'Osha. I saw Justin Jones dying in a medical building with no medicine. I saw the tunnels. The conditions. The bodies. If we don't release this evidence, those people have suffered for nothing."

"And if we do release it, Miguel goes to prison for ten years," Sonia shot back. "How is that just?"

"It's not," James admitted. "None of this is just. But Sonia—if you help them suppress this evidence, you become their partner in murder. Not just future murders. Past ones. All of it."

Sonia felt tears threaten. "I can't lose him, James. I can't watch him spend a decade in prison knowing I could have stopped it."

"And I can't watch operators keep dying knowing I had proof and buried it," James replied.

They sat in silence, connected by phone but separated by impossible choices.

"What would Miguel want you to do?" James asked finally.

Sonia closed her eyes. "He'd want me to release the photos. To finish the fight. To choose justice over him."

"Yeah," James agreed. "He would."

“But I’m not Miguel,” Sonia said. “I don’t have his certainty. His willingness to sacrifice everything.”

“You don’t have to be him,” James replied gently. “You just have to decide what you can live with. And I can’t make that choice for you.”

“What are you going to do?” Sonia asked.

“I’m releasing the photos,” James said. “Tomorrow morning. With or without your support. Because those operators deserve someone to witness what happened to them. Even if it costs me everything.”

“It will,” Sonia said. “They’ll prosecute you. Espionage. Trespassing. Every charge they can file.”

“I know,” James said. “But I can’t unknow what I saw. And I can’t pretend it doesn’t matter.”

Sonia heard the finality in his voice. “James—”

“I’m sorry, Sonia,” he said. “I’m sorry you have to choose between Miguel and doing the right thing. But that’s the choice. And tomorrow morning, I’m making mine.”

He hung up.

Sonia sat alone in her bedroom, phone in one hand, Miguel’s photo in the other.

She had twenty-four hours before Flores’s offer expired.

Twenty-four hours before James released evidence that would destroy any chance of a plea deal.

Twenty-four hours to decide whether love meant protection or truth.

She pulled out her laptop and opened the encrypted cloud where James had uploaded his photos.

She watched herself type in the access code.

Watched the files load.

Watched hundreds of images appear—documentation of systematic murder disguised as employment.

And she thought about Michael in jail, believing she'd choose justice.

About James on a ship, trusting she'd support the exposure.

About Ida in hiding, hoping her testimony would matter.

About operators dying, waiting for someone to care enough to save them.

She thought about all of it.

And she made her choice.

She called Flores back.

"I'll do it," Sonia said. "I'll get the photos. I'll testify they were obtained illegally. I'll help you close this case."

"Smart decision," Flores said. "Meet me tomorrow. Nine AM. Bring everything Simmons collected."

"And Miguel's charges get reduced?" Sonia confirmed.

"Immediately," Flores promised. "New plea deal. No prison time. He'll be home within weeks."

"Okay," Sonia said quietly. "I'll see you tomorrow."

She hung up and immediately called James back.

Voicemail.

She texted:

James, I'm sorry. I can't let Michael go to prison. I'm giving the photos to the AG tomorrow. Please understand.

She sent the message and waited.

No response.

Sonia lay down on the bed, still clutching the photo, and cried.

Not because she'd made the wrong choice.

But because she'd made the only choice she could live with.

And it meant betraying everyone who'd trusted her.

Just like every person in history who chose love over principle.

She'd save Michael.

And operators would keep dying.

And she'd have to live with that knowledge for the rest of her life.

But at least Michael would be free.

At least they'd have a chance at a future.

Even if that future was built on silence and complicity and the abandoned bodies of people who'd trusted the system to protect them.

Sonia closed her eyes and tried to convince herself she'd made the right choice.

But deep down, in the part of her that had become a cop to help people, she knew the truth.

She'd chosen wrong.

She'd chosen love over justice.

And tomorrow, when she handed those photos to the attorney general, she'd become exactly what the conspiracy needed her to be.

An accomplice.

## CHAPTER TWENTY-NINE

# The Trap Closes

James Simmons read Sonia's message three times, each reading making his stomach tighten more.

*James, I'm sorry. I can't let Miguel go to prison. I'm giving the photos to the AG tomorrow. Please understand.*

He understood.

He just didn't accept it.

He immediately called Sarah Chen. "We need to move up the release. Tonight. Right now."

"What happened?" Sarah asked.

"Sonia's been compromised," James said. "She's giving the AG my photos tomorrow morning. If we don't publish first, they'll suppress everything."

"How long do I have?" Sarah asked.

"Hours," James replied. "I'll send you everything now. Get it online before midnight."

"That's not enough time to verify—"

"There's no time for verification," James interrupted. "Either we publish tonight and force the truth out, or it gets buried tomorrow. Your choice."

Sarah was quiet for a moment. "Send me everything. I'll have it online in two hours."

James hung up and began uploading. Photos. Video. Audio recordings. Everything he and Martinez had documented on Blind Island.

Progress bar: 11%... 23%... 38%...

His phone rang. Unknown number.

He answered. "Simmons."

"Detective Simmons." The voice was male, calm, familiar. "This is Agent Thomas Rutledge. FBI. We need to talk about your recent international travel."

James felt ice run through his veins. "I don't know what you're talking about."

"You boarded a cargo ship in Long Beach six days ago," Rutledge said. "You traveled to coordinates in international waters. You trespassed on private property. You illegally photographed a secure facility. And now you're planning to release classified material to the media."

"Classified?" James repeated. "Since when is genocide classified?"

"Since it involves national security interests," Rutledge replied. "Tenorite is a strategic resource. The facility you photographed is a legally sanctioned operation under international commerce law."

"Legally sanctioned murder," James said.

"Legal nonetheless," Rutledge replied. "And your photographs constitute espionage. Which carries a twenty-year sentence."

James kept uploading. 52%... 61%... 70%...

"If you're calling to threaten me, you're too late," James said. "The evidence is already distributed."

"Not distributed," Rutledge corrected. "Uploading. To servers we're currently monitoring. Detective, I'm offering you one chance: stop the upload. Delete the files. Cooperate with federal investigators. And we'll reduce charges to misdemeanor trespass."

"And if I refuse?" James asked.

"Then we arrest you tonight," Rutledge said. "Seize all your equipment. Confiscate the evidence. And prosecute you for espionage against United States interests."

"Blind operators aren't United States interests," James said.

"The mineral they extract is," Rutledge replied. "Which makes your actions a threat to national security."

The upload hit 88%... 93%... 97%...

"Too late," James said. "Evidence is secured."

"We'll see," Rutledge replied.

The line went dead.

James's laptop screen flickered. Then froze. Then went black.

"No," James whispered. "No, no, no—"

He rebooted. The files were gone. Corrupted. Deleted remotely.

They'd hacked him.

Federal agents. Remote access. Wiped his upload mid-transfer.

James grabbed his backup drive and tried again from a different computer.

Same result. Files corrupted.

Someone had access to his cloud storage. Someone was deleting evidence as fast as he uploaded it.

His phone rang again. Sarah Chen.

"James, I'm being blocked," she said. "Every file you send gets corrupted before I can download it. Someone's intercepting the transfer."

James felt panic rise. "Try different servers. Different protocols. Anything."

"I'm trying," Sarah said. "But they're one step ahead. It's like they have admin access to everything."

Because they did. Federal agencies. NSA surveillance. The full weight of government cyber capabilities turned against one detective trying to expose murder.

James grabbed the memory cards—physical media they couldn't delete remotely—and ran to his car.

If digital distribution was compromised, he'd do this the old way. Physical delivery. Hand Sarah the cards in person. Let her publish from air-gapped computers they couldn't reach.

He drove toward the Kansas City Star offices, checking mirrors obsessively.

No pursuit.

No lights.

No obvious surveillance.

Which meant they were being subtle.

Or they were waiting.

James called Martinez. "Linda, they're onto us. Federal agents. They're blocking the upload. I'm delivering physical media to Sarah Chen. If something happens to me—"

"Nothing's going to happen," Martinez interrupted. "Where are you?"

"Heading to Kansas City," James replied. "ETA forty minutes."

"I'll meet you there," Martinez said. "Backup."

"No," James said. "If they catch both of us, there's no one left to—"

The car behind him turned on its lights. Not police lights. Just headlights. Bright. Blinding in the rearview mirror.

"James?" Martinez's voice carried concern.

"Someone's following me," James said.

"Get to a public place," Martinez ordered. "Cameras. Witnesses. Make it in plain view for them to grab you."

James took the next exit, heading toward a well-lit gas station. The car followed.

He pulled into the station. Bright lights. Security cameras. A clerk visible through the window.

The following car parked beside him.

Two men got out. Suits. Badges visible.

Federal agents.

James grabbed the memory cards and shoved them in his jacket pocket. Stepped out of his car with hands visible.

"Detective Simmons," one agent said. "I'm Agent Morrison. We need you to come with us."

"Am I under arrest?" James asked.

"Not yet," Morrison replied. "But you're wanted for questioning regarding violations of federal law."

"I'm not going anywhere without a lawyer," James said.

"That's your right," Morrison agreed. "But the longer you delay, the more charges accumulate. Right now, it's trespassing. Tomorrow, it might be espionage."

James felt the trap close. "I want to call my lawyer."

"After we secure the evidence," Morrison said. "We know you have photographs and video from the island facility. Those need to be turned over immediately."

"They're evidence of murder," James said.

"They're classified material obtained illegally," Morrison corrected. "Hand them over or we'll search you."

James's hand moved toward his pocket. Morrison's hand moved toward his weapon.

"Slowly," Morrison said.

James slowly pulled out the memory cards. Held them up. "This is proof that blind operators are being murdered on Blind Island. Proof that can save lives."

"This is stolen property," Morrison said. "That can send you to prison."

A third car pulled into the gas station. Sonia Miguel got out.

James felt his heart sink. "Sonia. What are you doing here?"

"I'm sorry, James," Sonia said, her voice tight. "They offered me a deal. Michael's freedom for the evidence. I can't let him go to prison."

"So you sold us out," James said.

"I saved my husband," Sonia corrected.

Morrison extended his hand. "The memory cards, Detective Simmons."

James looked at Sonia. At the agents. At the gas station cameras that would document this moment forever.

And he made his choice.

While Morrison's attention was on the cards in James's hands, James subtly shifted his weight, using the motion to press his heel against his opposite ankle. The tiny micro SD card he'd hidden in his sock—so small the agents wouldn't find it in a pat-down—slipped free and dropped into the dirt beneath his feet.

He dropped the visible memory cards and crushed them under his boot—deliberately grinding his heel in the exact spot where the micro SD card had fallen, pressing it deeper into the gravel where it disappeared from view.

Morrison lunged forward, but too late. The cards shattered. Circuitry exposed. Data destroyed.

"You just destroyed evidence in a federal investigation," Morrison said.

"I just destroyed your cover-up," James corrected.

Morrison grabbed James's arm, twisting it behind his back. "You're under arrest. Destruction of evidence. Obstruction of justice. Espionage."

James didn't resist. He let himself be handcuffed, his eyes tracking the exact spot in the gravel where the final card lay hidden—invisible beneath dust and tire tracks. The agents pushed him toward the federal vehicle, none of them noticing the infinitesimal glint of black plastic buried in the dirt.

"I'm sorry," Sonia said again.

"No you're not," James replied. "You just chose wrong."

"I chose love," Sonia said.

"Love doesn't mean silence," James replied. "It means sacrifice. And you sacrificed everyone except Miguel.

Morrison shoved James into the back of the vehicle. The door closed.

Through the window, James watched Sonia stand alone in the gas station parking lot, surrounded by agents collecting the destroyed memory cards, trying to salvage data that was already gone. None of them looked at the ground beneath their feet. None of them knew that fifty photographs—the most damning evidence—lay buried in gravel just yards away.

He'd destroyed the visible evidence. But the real evidence remained.

If Martinez got his message. If she knew where to look. If she understood his final words: Under my heel at the station.

The vehicle drove away from the gas station, toward federal detention.

James memorized the name of the gas station, the intersection, the exact parking spot. He'd get one phone call. One chance to tell someone where to dig.

The micro SD card contained fifty photographs. Bodies in the medical building. De'Osha's face. The mine entrance. Guards with weapons.

Not everything.

But enough.

The agents would search the gas station eventually. But by then, Martinez would have his message. She'd know where to look. She'd recover the card.

And fifty photographs would survive.

Because fifty was better than zero.

And zero was what the conspiracy wanted.

The vehicle drove through the night toward an uncertain future.

James closed his eyes and thought about Miguel in jail.

About Sonia choosing wrong.

About Martinez still free, still fighting.

About fifty photographs hidden in the dirt.

And about whether any of it would be enough to stop a system designed to crush anyone who challenged it.

He didn't know.

He just hoped.

Because hope was all that was left.

Hope and fifty photographs.

And the stubborn refusal to quit even when quitting was the smart choice.

CHAPTER THIRTY

# Operator Death: Ida

Michael Miguel got the news at 6:23 AM.

A guard appeared at his cell door. "Miguel. Visitor."

Too early for normal visitation. Which meant something had happened.

Michael followed the guard to the visitation room expecting his lawyer or Sonia or maybe James with news about the island photos.

Instead, FBI Agent Andre Park sat waiting.

"Detective Miguel," Park said when Michael picked up the phone. "I'm sorry to inform you that Ida Glitter died last night."

Michael felt the world tilt. "What?"

"Apparent suicide," Park said, her voice carefully neutral. "She was found in the safe house where we'd placed her under protective custody. Single gunshot wound. Self-inflicted."

"that's a lie," Michael said immediately. "Ida didn't kill herself."

"That's what the preliminary investigation suggests," Park replied.

“Then your investigation is wrong,” Michael said. “Or compromised. Or both.”

Park met his gaze through the plexiglass. “Off the record? I agree with you. Ida Glitter was scared but determined. She had plans to testify. She had hope. People like that don’t suddenly decide to end their lives.”

“So what really happened?” Michael demanded.

“I don’t know,” Park admitted. “I left the safe house at eleven PM for a shift change. When my replacement arrived at eleven-thirty, Ida was dead. Thirty minutes. That’s the window.”

“Someone got to her,” Michael said. “Someone inside your protection detail.”

“Possibly,” Park agreed. “Or someone with access we didn’t anticipate. The safe house location was classified. Only four people knew where it was.”

“And one of them was compromised,” Michael said.

“Or all of them,” Park replied. “I’m being pulled from the case this morning. Reassigned to counter-terrorism in Detroit. My entire team is being scattered. The investigation is being shut down.”

Michael felt rage burn cold. “Because Ida’s death closes the only insider testimony you had.”

“Yes,” Park confirmed. “Without her, we have financial documents that can be explained. Shipping manifests that prove commerce, not trafficking. Photographs that were obtained illegally. Nothing that stands up in court.”

“What about the photos James took on the island?” Michael asked.

Park's expression darkened. "Detective Simmons was arrested last night. The photographs were destroyed. What little data survived the remote wipe is too fragmented to use as evidence."

Michael felt the floor drop out from under him. "James was arrested?"

"Federal custody," Park confirmed. "Espionage charges. He'll likely spend the next twenty years in prison."

"And Sonia?" Michael asked, though he already knew.

"Officer Miguel cooperated with federal agents," Park said carefully. "She helped secure the scene where Detective Simmons destroyed evidence. She's been offered immunity in exchange for testimony against him."

Michael closed his eyes, feeling everything collapse. James arrested. Ida dead. Evidence destroyed. Sonia turned informant.

"Why are you telling me this?" Michael asked.

"Because you're next," Park replied. "Your trial is scheduled for next month. The prosecution is seeking maximum sentence. And without Ida's testimony or Simmons's photographs, you have no defense. You'll be convicted."

"I know," Michael said quietly.

"Then why are you smiling?" Park asked.

Michael opened his eyes. "Because they think they won. They think destroying evidence means destroying truth. But truth doesn't die when evidence gets suppressed. It just goes underground. And eventually, it resurfaces."

"That's optimistic," Park said.

"That's inevitable," Michael corrected. "Conspiracies collapse. Always. They get too big. Too many people know. Too many loose ends. Eventually, someone talks. Someone breaks. Someone's conscience catches up."

"And if that doesn't happen before you're sentenced?" Park asked.

"Then I do my time," Michael said. "And I wait. Because I've got ten years to wait. And the conspiracy has to be perfect for ten years. All I need is one mistake."

Park studied him. "You really believe that."

"I have to," Michael replied. "Because the alternative is accepting that operators die and conspiracies win and justice doesn't exist. And I can't live with that."

Park stood to leave. "For what it's worth, Detective—I believe you. I believe every word you said. I believe the conspiracy is real. But believing isn't enough. And I'm sorry."

"Don't be sorry," Michael said. "Be angry. And when you get to Detroit, don't forget what you learned here. Because this isn't just Kansas. This is everywhere power meets vulnerability."

Park nodded once and walked away.

Michael returned to his cell and lay on his bunk, staring at the ceiling.

Ida was dead.

James was arrested.

Sonia had cooperated.

The evidence was destroyed.

And Michael had one month until trial that would send him to prison for a decade.

Everything had failed.

Every plan. Every hope. Every sacrifice.

And operators were still dying on an island in the Pacific while the world moved on pretending nothing was wrong.

Michael pulled out his tablet—where he documented every disappearance—and added a new entry:

Witness Death: Ida Glitter

Date: [last night]

Ruled: Suicide

Actual: Murder

He stared at the entry, then at all the other names above it.

Twenty-three operators disappeared.

Four witnesses dead: Darrius Johnson. Kail McDow (presumed). John Lizzardo (missing). Ida Glitter.

One detective jailed: Michael Miguel.

One detective arrested: James Simmons.

One officer compromised: Sonia Miguel.

The cost kept rising.

The bodies kept accumulating.

And the conspiracy kept winning.

Michael put his tablet down and tried to find some reason to keep fighting when everything suggested fighting was pointless.

He thought about Antony Grumpton, the first name on his list.

About Martha Grumpton, still waiting for a husband who would never come home.

About De'Osha Davenport's daughters, wondering where their mother went.

About every family destroyed by a system that treated human beings as disposable.

And he realized something.

Fighting wasn't about winning.

It was about refusing to surrender.

Even when surrender was smart.

Even when surrender was safe.

Even when surrender meant survival.

Because some things were more important than survival.

Like truth.

Like justice.

Like the stubborn insistence that blind lives mattered as much as corporate profits.

Michael opened his eyes and sat up.

He still had one month until trial.

One month to figure out how to fight a system that had destroyed everyone else.

One month to find one piece of evidence they'd missed.

One month to make one mistake count.

It wasn't much.

But it was enough.

Because enough wasn't about quantity.

It was about persistence.

And Michael Miguel—suspended detective, jailed investigator, abandoned husband—was nothing if not persistent.

He pulled out his prison-issued tablet and sent one final message to Martinez:

James is arrested. Ida is dead. Evidence is destroyed. I'm going to trial next month. This is probably our last chance. If you have anything—any fragment of evidence, any witness, any thread we haven't pulled—now is the time.

Martinez's response came an hour later:

I have something. Not much. But something. Give me two weeks. I'll either find a way to save this or confirm it's unsavable.

What do you have? Michael typed.

James hid a micro SD card before arrest. 50 photos from the island. Not enough to prove genocide. But enough to prove the island exists. Enough to force questions. I'm going to find a way to leak them without getting arrested myself.

Michael felt hope flare—small, fragile, but real.

Be careful. They're hunting everyone connected to this case.

I know, Martinez replied. Which is why I'm doing this off the books. Ghost protocols. Complete dark. If this works, you won't hear from me until trial. If it doesn't work, you won't hear from me at all.

Thank you, Michael typed.

Don't thank me yet. Thank me when you're free and operators are rescued.

Michael lay back on his bunk and closed his eyes.

One month until trial.

Fifty photographs hidden somewhere James had planted them.

Martinez working completely dark to leak them without attribution.

And Michael, locked in a cell, waiting to see if one final gambit would save everything or confirm that nothing could stop a conspiracy willing to kill anyone who threatened it.

He fell asleep thinking about volcanic islands and toxic dust and operators who'd never see justice.

And he dreamed about a world where truth mattered more than power.

Where evidence destroyed couldn't stay destroyed.

Where fifty photographs were enough to change everything.

It was a nice dream.

He just hoped it wasn't only a dream.

## CHAPTER THIRTY-ONE

# Governor's Denial

Governor Bruce Dickens stood at his podium, bathed in camera lights, projecting the calm authority of a man who'd never lost control of a narrative.

Behind him: the Kansas state seal. American flag. The machinery of legitimacy.

Before him: forty-seven journalists, cameras, and the weight of fifty leaked photographs that had appeared online at 3 AM that morning.

The photos showed everything. Operators in gas masks. Volcanic tunnels. Bodies in a medical building. Guards with weapons. Blind Island, documented and undeniable.

Except Dickens was about to deny it anyway.

"Let me be absolutely clear," Dickens began, his voice measured and confident. "The photographs released by anonymous sources this morning are a deliberate attempt to undermine a legitimate government program using doctored images and false context."

Michael watched from jail, feeling rage burn cold.

The TV showed side-by-side images: one of James's photographs showing an operator in a gas mask, the other showing what Dickens claimed was "stock footage from training exercises."

"These images," Dickens continued, "were taken out of context and manipulated to suggest conditions that simply do not exist. The BBVP operates with the highest safety standards. Operators work in controlled environments with full protective equipment and medical oversight."

A reporter called out: "Governor, what about the bodies shown in the medical facility?"

"There are no bodies," Dickens replied smoothly. "Those images have been identified as staged photographs using actors. We have forensic analysis proving digital manipulation."

Another reporter: "Can you explain the volcanic setting? The island visible in the photographs?"

"The so-called 'Blind Island' is a fabrication," Dickens said. "A conspiracy theory promoted by disgraced law enforcement officers and amplified by media outlets more interested in sensationalism than truth."

Michael felt his stomach turn as he watched the governor lie with absolute confidence.

The TV cut to "expert analysis"—a digital forensics consultant who claimed the photographs showed signs of manipulation. Lighting inconsistencies. Shadow angles. Metadata corruption.

All lies.

All convincing.

All designed to make truth look like fiction.

Michael's prison-issued tablet shined with a message. Martinez:

They're dismissing the photos as fake. Forensic experts saying they're manipulated.

They're not manipulated, Michael typed back. You know that. I know that.

But the public doesn't, Martinez replied. And without original files to verify, we can't prove authenticity. The federal agents who wiped James's computers destroyed the metadata we needed to establish provenance.

So the conspiracy planned for this, Michael realized. They knew photos would leak. They prepared the counter-narrative in advance.

Yes. Which means we need more than photos. We need living witnesses. Operators who can testify they were there.

De'Osha Davenport, Michael typed. James saw her. If we can get her off the island—

She's already dead, Martinez interrupted. I checked manifests. Personnel transport to island three weeks ago. Medical disposal logged four days ago.

Michael felt grief hit like a physical blow. "No."

Craig spoke through the vent: "Bad news?"

"The worst," Michael replied.

De'Osha Davenport. Mother of two. Thirty-four years old. Gone.

Worked to death in volcanic tunnels while her daughters waited for her to come home.

Michael added her name to his cloud drive as deceased:

Confirmed Dead: De'Osha Davenport

The list kept growing. The bodies kept accumulating. And the conspiracy kept winning.

On TV, Dickens answered more questions with practiced ease:

"What about Detective Simmons's testimony?"

"Detective Simmons is facing espionage charges. His credibility is non-existent."

"What about Detective Miguel's original investigation?"

"Detective Miguel is awaiting trial for multiple felonies. His allegations have been thoroughly discredited."

"What about Ida Glitter's committee testimony?"

"Ms. Glitter tragically took her own life after suffering from mental health issues. Her testimony was the product of delusion and stress."

Every truth twisted. Every witness discredited. Every piece of evidence explained away.

Michael watched the press conference end with Dickens walking away, questions unanswered, narrative controlled.

The comments section under the livestream filled immediately:

Finally, someone calling out the conspiracy theorists Those photos look fake to me Why should we believe criminals over the governor?

This is just another attempt to attack successful programs

But there were other comments too:

Something doesn't add up–why won't he allow independent inspection?

Those photos look real to me

Where are the operators if everything is legitimate?

Demanding transparency doesn't make you a conspiracy theorist

The public was split. Belief fracturing along existing political lines. People seeing what they wanted to see.

Michael's tablet had a new message. Robert Hayes, his lawyer:

The governor's press conference changes nothing legally. Your trial proceeds as scheduled. Two weeks from today. Jury selection Monday.

Can we use the leaked photos? Michael typed.

Not without provenance. The judge ruled them inadmissible yesterday. Too much question about authenticity and how they were obtained.

So we're going to trial with no physical evidence.

Correct. Which means we're going to lose. I need you to consider the plea deal again.

Michael stared at the message. The plea deal. Sonia had taken the Attorney General's offer. Testified against James. Saved herself by sacrificing everyone else.

And now Robert wanted Miguel to do the same.

Plead guilty. Serve two years. Stay silent forever.

Let operators keep dying.

Let the conspiracy win.

No, Miguel typed. We go to trial. We fight.

Mike, we'll lose. The jury will convict you. You'll get ten years minimum.

Then I'll do ten years, Michael replied. But I won't plead guilty to crimes that were necessary to expose murder.

Robert didn't respond for a long moment, then:

You're the most stubborn client I've ever had.

Good. Stubbornness is all I have left.

Michael lay on his bunk, staring at the ceiling.

Two weeks until trial. Fourteen days to find one piece of evidence they'd missed. One witness they couldn't silence. One thread that would unravel everything.

But every witness was dead or arrested. Every piece of evidence was destroyed or inadmissible. Every thread had been cut.

The conspiracy had won.

Completely.

Perfectly.

And Michael was going to prison for a decade while operators kept dying and the world moved on pretending nothing was wrong.

He closed his eyes and tried to find some reason to keep fighting.

The reason came from an unexpected source.

A letter arrived that afternoon, delivered by a guard who looked uncomfortable handling it.

The letter was already opened.

Inside: a single photograph.

De'Osha Davenport with her two daughters. The same photograph her family had sent him weeks ago. But this one had writing on the back:

Detective Miguel, my mother told us about you. She said you were trying to help. She said you were brave. She said that even if she didn't come home, someone would remember her name. Thank you for remembering. Thank you for trying. Please don't stop.– De'Osha's daughters

Michael pressed the photograph against his chest and felt tears burn.

He couldn't save De'Osha.

He couldn't stop the conspiracy.

He couldn't win this fight.

But he could remember names. He could refuse to let operators become statistics. He could insist that their lives mattered even when the system treated them as disposable.

That wasn't justice.

But it was something.

And sometimes, something was enough to keep fighting.

## CHAPTER THIRTY-TWO

# Evidence Destroyed

James Simmons sat in federal detention, identical to county jail except the crimes were bigger and the sentences longer.

His lawyer—a federal defender named Marice Williams—sat across from him in the attorney conference room, surrounded by papers that all said the same thing: James was going to prison for twenty years.

"The espionage charges are solid," Williams said. "You traveled to a restricted facility in international waters. You photographed classified operations. You attempted to release material designated as national security sensitive."

"I documented genocide," James corrected.

"The government disagrees with that characterization," Williams replied. "And they have better lawyers."

James leaned back in his chair. "What about the fifty photos? The ones that leaked?"

"The ones you claim you didn't leak?" Williams asked.

"Correct."

"The FBI believes you had an accomplice," Williams said. "Officer Linda Martinez. They're searching for her now. If they find her, she'll be charged as co-conspirator."

"She didn't do anything," James said automatically.

"Then how did the photos get online?" Williams challenged. "You were arrested. Your equipment was seized. The memory cards were destroyed. Yet fifty photographs appeared on anonymous file-sharing sites. Someone had access to those images."

James said nothing. Protecting Martinez meant silence.

"James," Williams continued, "if you cooperate—if you identify who helped you, who provided the boat, who leaked the photos—the prosecutor will reduce charges. Five years instead of twenty."

"I'm not cooperating," James said.

"Then you're going to spend the next two decades in federal prison," Williams replied. "Is that worth it? For photos the government is successfully discrediting? For a case that's already lost?"

"The case isn't lost," James said. "It's just harder."

"No," Williams corrected. "It's impossible. Detective Miguel goes to trial in two weeks. He'll be convicted. You'll be convicted. Sonia Miguel testified against you both. Ida Glitter is dead. Every piece of evidence has been ruled inadmissible or destroyed. There's nothing left to fight with."

"There's truth," James said.

"Truth doesn't win trials," Williams replied. "Evidence wins trials. And you don't have any."

James thought about the operators he'd seen on Blind Island. De'Osha Davenport in a gas mask. Justin Jones dying in a medical building. The tunnels. The guards. The systematic extermination.

"What if I could get a living witness?" James asked. "An operator who escaped the island. Who could testify about conditions."

"That would change everything," Williams admitted. "But there are no escaped operators. The facility is surrounded by ocean. Security is absolute. No one leaves except through official transport. And official transport only goes one direction."

"What about someone who worked there?" James pressed. "A guard. A doctor. Someone with a conscience."

"Guards sign NDAs," Williams said. "Violating them means civil liability and criminal prosecution. No one's going to risk that."

"Someone might," James said. "If they saw what I saw. If they understood what's really happening."

Williams gathered his papers. "I admire your optimism. But my job is to prepare you for reality. And reality is: you're going to prison. The only question is how long."

He left.

James sat alone in the conference room, feeling walls close from every direction.

No evidence. No witnesses. No hope.

Just twenty years stretching ahead like a sentence worse than death.

His mind went to Martinez. She was still free. Still out there. Still fighting.

The fifty photos had sparked debate but not action. The governor had successfully framed them as fake. Public opinion was split. No investigations launched. No operators rescued.

Fifty photographs had changed nothing.

Except they'd kept the story alive. Barely. Enough that people were still talking. Still questioning. Still uncomfortable with the official narrative.

That was something.

Not much. But something.

James closed his eyes and thought about Miguel's words during one of their last conversations: The fight isn't about winning. It's about refusing to surrender.

Refusing to surrender meant going to trial. Facing twenty years. Living with the knowledge that he'd failed to save anyone.

But it also meant the conspiracy couldn't claim total victory. Couldn't pretend dissent didn't exist. Couldn't erase his testimony from the record.

That was worth something.

Maybe not twenty years. But something.

His federal cell was smaller than county. Eight by six. Concrete. Steel. Designed to break people.

James lay on the bunk and stared at the ceiling, counting tiles.

Forty-seven tiles. Each one a small perfect square. Each one identical to the others.

Like operators. Like victims. Like everyone the system chewed up and spit out.

His phone call for the day came at three PM. He called Martinez's emergency number—a nontrackable phone she'd set up in her friend's name before going dark.

She answered on the fifth ring. "James."

"Linda. Are you okay?"

"I'm alive," Martinez replied. "FBI is looking for me. I'm staying mobile. Changing locations daily. Living off cash."

"I'm sorry," James said.

"Don't be," Martinez interrupted. "I chose this. I saw the photos we took. I saw what they're doing to those people. I couldn't walk away."

"The photos didn't change anything," James said. "The governor discredited them. People think they're fake."

"Some people do," Martinez corrected. "But not everyone. I've been monitoring social media. There are activists organizing. Disability rights groups demanding transparency. Media outlets digging deeper."

"It's not enough," James said.

"Not yet," Martinez agreed. "But it's more than nothing. And nothing was what they wanted. Total silence. Complete suppression. We denied them that."

"At what cost?" James asked. "You're a fugitive. I'm facing twenty years. Miguel's going to prison. Sonia betrayed everyone. Ida's dead. The operators are still dying."

"Yes," Martinez said simply. "But they're dying with witnesses. That's the difference. Before, they died invisible. Now, they die documented. And documentation matters. Maybe not today. Maybe not in court. But eventually, history will record what happened. And that's justice of a different kind."

"Historical justice doesn't save living people," James replied.

"No," Martinez agreed. "But it prevents future people from being forgotten. It creates a record that can't be erased. And sometimes, that's the best we can do."

James heard sirens in the background on her end. "Where are you?"

"Moving," Martinez said. "Don't worry about me. Worry about yourself. Your trial is in three weeks. Have you considered cooperating?"

"Every day," James admitted. "And every day I decide not to."

"Good," Martinez said. "Because cooperation means silence. And silence is what killed the operators in the first place."

The sirens grew louder on her end.

"Linda, you need to go," James said.

"I know," she replied. "James—if I get caught, finish this. Promise me."

"I can't finish anything from prison," James said.

"Then finish it anyway," Martinez replied. "From inside. By refusing to be silent. By making them work to keep you quiet. By being a problem they can't solve."

"That's not much of a plan," James said.

"It's the only plan left," Martinez replied.

The line went dead.

James returned to his cell and lay down, feeling the weight of promises he couldn't keep and fights he couldn't win.

But refusing to try felt like a different kind of defeat.

So he didn't refuse.

He just kept moving forward.

One day at a time.

One hour at a time.

One breath at a time.

Until either freedom came or death did.

Either way, he'd go down fighting.

Because some things were worth twenty years.

Like truth.

Like justice.

Like the stubborn insistence that human lives mattered more than corporate profits.

Even when the world disagreed.

Even when the system crushed you for believing it.

Even when surrender was the smart choice.

James closed his eyes and tried to sleep.

Tomorrow would bring more bad news.

More losses.

More proof that fighting was futile.

But he'd fight anyway.

Because futile wasn't the same as wrong.

And wrong was what happened when good people chose silence over sacrifice.

## CHAPTER THIRTY-THREE

# Blind Island Name Spreads

The name appeared first on activist message boards.

Then on disability rights websites.

Then in alternative media articles.

Then, finally, in mainstream coverage that could no longer ignore the growing momentum.

Blind Island.

Two words that had been conspiracy theory three months ago and were now entering public consciousness as something that might actually exist.

Michael watched from jail as the narrative slowly, painfully shifted.

The governor's dismissal of the fifty photos had worked initially. The forensic analysis. The claims of manipulation. The discrediting of sources.

But then independent analysts started examining the images. Tech bloggers. Digital forensics experts who weren't paid by the government. Photography professors.

Their conclusion: the images were authentic. Unmanipulated. Real.

The metadata was corrupted—which made sense if federal agents had attempted to remotely wipe files. But the image content itself showed no signs of digital manipulation.

The photos were real.

Which meant Blind Island was real.

Which meant the conspiracy was real.

Public opinion began to shift. Slowly. Not dramatically. But measurably.

Polls showed 38% of people now believed operators were being trafficked. Up from 12% before the photos leaked.

Not a majority. But enough to create pressure.

Enough to make politicians nervous.

Enough to force conversations that three months ago would have been dismissed as conspiracy theories.

Michael's tablet showed a message. Sarah Chen, the reporter:

The Kansas City Star is running a follow-up series. "Where is Blind Island?" Six-part investigative report. Satellite analysis. Shipping route verification. Financial deep dive. We're going all in.

When does it publish? Michael typed.

Starting Monday. Right before your trial. Figure it might help public perception.

Or make the jury think I'm part of a media conspiracy, Michael replied.

Risk we'll have to take, Sarah wrote. Because silence hasn't worked. Caution hasn't worked. Playing by their rules hasn't worked. So we go loud. We go aggressive. We force them to respond.

Thank you, Michael typed.

Don't thank me. I'm just doing my job. You're the one going to prison for it.

The series published Monday morning.

PART 1: THE COORDINATES

The Kansas City Star has obtained shipping manifests showing regular supply runs to coordinates 22.4°N, 157.8°W—a location in the Pacific Ocean roughly 2,000 miles from any major landmass. Satellite imagery of this location reveals an island with industrial structures, mining operations, and what appears to be dormitory housing.

The article included satellite photos. Not as clear as James's ground-level shots, but clear enough to show buildings. Ships at dock. Activity.

PART 2: THE MINERAL

Tenorite is a rare copper oxide mineral that forms in specific volcanic conditions. When processed, it produces semiconductors with exceptional properties for artificial intelligence applications. Unprocessed, it produces toxic dust that causes irreversible blindness. Advanced Semiconductor Technologies—a Fortune 500 company—has purchased processed Tenorite through Pacific Mineral Holdings, a shell corporation with ties to Kansas state government.

The article named names. Provided documentation. Connected dots that couldn't be dismissed as speculation.

PART 3: THE DISAPPEARANCES

Twenty-three blind vending operators have disappeared from Kansas over the past two years. All were subjected to "reassignment reviews" by the BBVP committee. All were transported shortly after disappearance approval. None have been seen or heard from since. The Kansas City Star requested interviews with these operators. State officials claim they're at "training facilities" but refuse to provide locations or allow contact.

The article included photographs. Names. Families. Human faces attached to statistics.

Antony Grumpton.

Justin Jones.

De'Osha Davenport.

Micah Mitchell.

All twenty-three.

PART 4: THE MONEY

Pacific Mineral Holdings has received $47 million in transfers from Kansas state budgets over two years. These transfers are labeled "program enhancement" and "operator support services." Independent analysis suggests the money funds island operations: food, medical supplies, industrial equipment, security personnel, and transportation. Governor Bruce Dickens's chief of staff, Ron Spillwind, serves on Pacific Mineral Holdings' board of directors.

Follow the money. Always follow the money.

PART 5: THE SYSTEM

The Randolph-Sheppard Act grants significant authority to state licensing agencies and blind committees to oversee vending operations. This authority, intended to protect blind operators, has been weaponized in Kansas to identify, isolate, and remove operators deemed "difficult." Committee votes show unanimous approval for every disappearance—statistical impossibility suggesting coordination rather than independent judgment.

The article laid out the entire conspiracy with devastating precision.

PART 6: THE QUESTION

If these allegations are false, the solution is simple: allow independent inspection of the island facility. Allow media access. Allow interviews with transported operators. Allow verification that conditions are humane and participation is voluntary. The governor's refusal to permit any transparency raises an obvious question: what are they hiding?

The series ended with a challenge. Not an accusation. A question.

The comment sections exploded.

Millions of views. Thousands of shares. Debate that couldn't be dismissed or suppressed.

The narrative was shifting. Slowly. Painfully. But shifting.

Michael's trial started Wednesday.

Jury selection took two days. The prosecutor—a sharp woman named Patricia Vance—used every challenge to remove jurors who expressed skepticism about government. Who questioned authority. Who showed any sympathy for Miguel's methods.

The final jury: nine people predisposed to trust institutions and three who seemed genuinely open to evidence.

Not ideal. But not hopeless.

Opening statements came Friday.

Vance stood before the jury, projecting confidence: "Detective Michael Miguel is not a hero. He's a criminal who broke multiple laws under the pretense of investigation. He trespassed on private property. He stole classified documents. He conducted illegal surveillance. He released information that threatened national security. The defendant will claim he was exposing corruption. But breaking the law to fight alleged lawbreaking doesn't make you righteous. It makes you a criminal."

Robert Hayes responded: "Detective Miguel is a decorated veteran who lost half his vision serving his country. He became a cop to protect vulnerable people. When he saw blind operators disappearing through a state program, he investigated. What he found was systematic trafficking. When official channels ignored him, he gathered evidence. When the system protected itself instead of victims, he went public. You may not agree with his methods. But his methods were necessary because the alternative was silence. And silence means death for people no one else will fight for."

The trial proceeded through testimony.

Expert witnesses explaining why Miguel's evidence was inadmissible.

Federal agents describing how he'd stolen classified documents.

SLA administrators claiming the BBVP operated with complete integrity.

Day after day, the prosecution built an overwhelming case that Miguel had broken laws. Which he had. Unquestionably.

The defense's only argument: necessity. Justification. The greater good.

But the judge had ruled that "necessity" wasn't a valid defense for the crimes charged.

Which meant Hayes couldn't argue that Miguel's actions were justified.

He could only argue that Miguel believed they were justified.

Which wasn't enough.

The jury deliberated for six hours.

Returned with a verdict.

Guilty on all counts.

Michael stood as the verdict was read, feeling the words wash over him like cold water.

Guilty of trespassing.

Guilty of theft of government documents.

Guilty of obstruction of justice.

Guilty of unauthorized surveillance.

Guilty of conspiracy to commit fraud.

Five felonies. Consecutive sentences possible.

The judge set sentencing for two weeks.

Michael returned to his cell that night knowing he'd spend the next decade in prison.

Everything he'd fought for had failed.

Every sacrifice had been meaningless.

Every operator he'd tried to save was still trapped or dead.

But at least people knew their names now.

At least Blind Island was no longer a secret.

At least the conspiracy had to work harder to maintain silence.

That wasn't victory.

But it was something.

And for Michael Miguel—convicted felon, suspended detective, abandoned husband—something was all he had left.

## CHAPTER THIRTY-FOUR

# Coordinates Located

Martinez sent the message at 3 AM, knowing Miguel would be awake.

Found it. Exact coordinates. Independent verification. Blind Island is real and I can prove it.

Miguel's prison-issued tablet flashed with the incoming text. He read it three times before responding.

How?

Shipping manifests cross-referenced with satellite imagery and ocean current patterns. The island is at 22°27'N, 157°49'W. Not the coordinates in public records—those were decoys. Real location is 30 miles southeast.

Miguel felt his pulse quicken. Can you verify operators are there?

Not directly. But supply deliveries match our timeline. Food quantities suggest 40-60 people on site. Medical supplies consistent with respiratory treatment and chemical exposure. It's the right place.

What are you going to do with this information? Miguel typed.

Give it to international human rights organizations. UN investigators. Media that can't be blocked by US government. Make it impossible to deny.

They'll come after you harder, Miguel warned.

I know. But I'm already a fugitive. Might as well make it worth it.

When?

Tomorrow. Press conference from undisclosed location. Remote appearance. I'll present coordinates, satellite imagery, evidence analysis. Then disappear again before they can locate me.

Martinez, this is dangerous.

Everything is dangerous now. Staying silent is dangerous. Speaking up is dangerous. At least this way I'm dangerous to them instead of just vulnerable.

Miguel wanted to argue. To tell her to stop. To protect herself.

But he understood. Because he'd made the same choice months ago.

Choose danger over complicity. Choose risk over silence. Choose fighting even when fighting meant losing.

Be careful, Miguel typed.

I will. And Mike—your sentencing is in two weeks. If this works, if international pressure forces investigations, maybe it changes things.

Or maybe I still go to prison and operators still die, Michael replied.

Probably. But at least we tried.

Yeah. At least we tried.

Michael sat on his bunk, staring at the wall, thinking about coordinates and satellites and the thin line between hope and delusion.

Martinez held a press conference the next morning via encrypted video link.

Michael watched from the jail common area, surrounded by inmates who'd grown interested in his case.

Martinez appeared on screen wearing a mask and voice modulation. Anonymous. Protected. Smart.

"My name is not important, I work for law enforcement. I'm the one that sent the photos to the news media of Blind Island. I'm here today to provide additional evidence that the island exists and blind operators are being held there against their will."

She displayed satellite imagery. High-resolution. Time-stamped. Independently verifiable.

"These coordinates—22°27'N, 157°49'W—show an island with industrial operations. Multiple buildings. A mine entrance. Processing facilities. Security perimeter. Supply ships arrive weekly from Long Beach, California."

She overlaid shipping manifests. Supply quantities. Personnel transport records.

"The math is simple: supply deliveries indicate 40-60 people on this island. Medical supplies suggest respiratory illness and chemical exposure. Food quantities exceed what staff would need, indicating a larger captive population."

She displayed comparison analysis. Before and after photos showing island development over two years. Timed to coincide with operator disappearances from Kansas.

"I'm providing these coordinates to international human rights organizations. To UN investigators. To media organizations in countries where US government can't block coverage. I'm making it impossible to continue claiming this island doesn't exist."

She paused, looking directly at the camera.

"To the operators on Blind Island: people know you're there. People are fighting for you. Your names are not forgotten. Your lives matter. And we will not stop until you're free."

The video ended.

Comments flooded in immediately:

Finally, real coordinates we can verify independently Why won't the governor allow inspection if there's nothing to hide?

This is getting harder to dismiss as conspiracy theory Satellite imagery doesn't lie

But also:

How do we know this officer isn't lying?

The island could be a legitimate facility

Supply deliveries don't prove trafficking

This is anti-government propaganda

The narrative remained split. Belief still fractured along existing lines.

But something had shifted.

International media picked up the story. BBC. Al Jazeera. Deutsche Welle. The Guardian.

American outlets could dismiss domestic reporting as biased. But international coverage was harder to suppress.

The UN Human Rights Council announced an inquiry.

Not an investigation. Just an inquiry. A review of allegations. A request for information.

Small. Insufficient. But something.

Michael's sentencing hearing was scheduled for Monday.

He spent the weekend reviewing everything. Every document. Every photograph. Every piece of evidence they'd gathered.

Building a statement. Not for the judge. Not for the jury. For the record.

So that years from now, when someone looked back, they'd see that people had fought. Had tried. Had refused to be silent even when silence was safer.

Monday came.

Michael stood before Judge Hammond again. Same courtroom. Same furniture. Different outcome.

The judge reviewed the presentencing report. Miguel's clean record before this case. His military service. His eight years as a detective. His lack of remorse.

"Mr. Miguel," Hammond said, "the court recognizes that you believed you were doing the right thing. But belief doesn't excuse lawbreaking. You had multiple opportunities to work within the system. You chose instead to break laws systematically and deliberately."

"Because the system protects itself," Miguel said. "Not victims."

"That's not for you to decide," Hammond replied. "The system has mechanisms for addressing corruption. Internal affairs. Legislative oversight. Federal investigations. You chose to bypass all of them."

"Because they weren't working," Miguel said. "Operators were disappearing. The committee is corrupt. The SLA was partially involved. Federal agents were compromised. There was no system to work within."

"So you became your own system," Hammond said. "Your own judge, jury, and enforcement. That's not justice. That's vigilantism."

"It's necessity," Miguel replied. "When no one else will act, someone must."

Hammond set down her papers. "The prosecution recommends ten years on each count, served consecutively. Fifty years total."

Michael felt the courtroom go silent.

"However," Hammond continued, "the court has discretion in sentencing. And while your crimes were serious, your motivation was not personal gain. Your beliefs—were genuine, in this court's view—that you were protecting vulnerable blind people."

She paused.

"Therefore, the court sentences you to three years on each count, served concurrently. Three years total. Eligible for parole after eighteen months."

Michael felt shock ripple through him.

Three years instead of fifty.

Robert Hayes leaned over and whispered: "The international coverage worked. She couldn't give you fifty years while the UN is investigating. It would look like retaliation."

Hammond wasn't finished: "However, Mr. Miguel, you are also ordered to pay restitution for damages caused by your illegal actions. And you are prohibited from any contact with BBVP operators, committee members, or state officials for the duration of your sentence and parole."

"Which means you can't investigate anymore," Hayes whispered.

"The court also notes," Hammond continued, "that if the allegations you've made are ever proven true—if operators are found to have been trafficked as you claim—this sentence will be vacated and your conviction expunged. But unless and until that proof emerges, you are a convicted felon."

She banged her gavel.

"Three years," Hammond said. "Take him away."

Michael was escorted from the courtroom, feeling the weight of three years settle into his bones.

Not fifty. But still forever.

Still time away from Sonia. Away from freedom. Away from the fight.

But at least he'd be alive.

At least he could keep fighting from inside.

At least the sentence confirmed what he already knew: the judge wasn't certain he was wrong. She just couldn't admit he was right without proof.

And proof was what Martinez was working to provide.

Back in his cell, Miguel updated his digital notes on the prison tablet one final time:

Convicted: 5 felonies

Sentenced: 3 years

Eligible parole: 18 months

Operators still missing: 23

Witnesses dead: 4

Evidence: Suppressed but not destroyed

Fight status: Ongoing

Then he lay on his bunk and stared at the ceiling.

Three years.

One thousand and ninety-five days.

Seventy-eight thousand, eight hundred and forty hours.

Time to think. Time to plan. Time to prepare for the moment when he got out and could fight again.

Because the fight wasn't over.

It had just changed venues.

From streets to cells.

From investigations to endurance.

From action to patience.

Three years.

Michael could do three years.

He'd done worse.

And at the end, he'd emerge either vindicated or destroyed.

But either way, he'd emerge still believing blind lives mattered.

Still refusing to be silent.

Still fighting.

Because some things were worth three years.

Like truth.

Like justice.

Like the stubborn insistence that human beings deserved dignity even when systems treated them as disposable.

Michael closed his eyes and started counting days.

One thousand and ninety-five to go.

Starting now.

## CHAPTER THIRTY-FIVE

# Final Confrontation

Sonia Miguel stood outside the federal prison where James Simmons was being held, waiting for visiting hours to begin.

She hadn't slept in three days.

Guilt had become a physical weight—pressing down on her chest, making breathing difficult, turning every moment into a reminder of betrayal.

She'd testified against James. Helped the AG suppress evidence. Saved Miguel's sentence from fifty years to three.

And destroyed every friendship she'd ever had in the process.

James's trial had ended yesterday. Guilty on all counts. Twenty years. No possibility of parole for ten.

Because Sonia's testimony had been devastating. Had confirmed James went to Blind Island. Had admitted helping suppress the photographs. Had corroborated the government's narrative that James was a rogue agent acting against national interests.

She'd done it to save Michael.

And it had worked.

Three years instead of fifty.

But the cost had been James's freedom.

And Sonia's soul.

Visiting hours opened at nine AM. Sonia signed in, submitted to search, and was escorted to the visitation room.

James sat on the other side of the plexiglass, wearing an orange jumpsuit, looking older than he had three weeks ago.

He picked up the phone. Sonia did the same.

"James—" she began.

"Don't," he interrupted. "Don't apologize. Don't explain. Don't try to make this okay."

Sonia felt tears threaten. "I had to save him. They were going to give him fifty years."

"So you gave me twenty instead," James said flatly.

"That's not what I intended—"

"Yes it is," James interrupted. "That's exactly what you intended. You chose Miguel over me. Over the operators. Over everyone. And now I'm spending two decades in prison because you couldn't accept that some things are more important than personal happiness."

"Love isn't personal happiness," Sonia said. "It's survival."

"No," James corrected. "Survival is what you get when you choose the easy path. Love is what you feel when you choose the right path even when it costs you everything."

Sonia wiped her eyes. "I came here to tell you I'm sorry. To explain—"

"There's nothing to explain," James said. "You made a choice. I understand the choice. I even understand why you made it. But understanding doesn't mean I forgive you. It just means I see you clearly now."

"As what?" Sonia asked.

"As someone who broke under pressure," James replied. "As someone who chose love over justice and now has to live with knowing that choice killed people."

"It didn't kill anyone," Sonia protested.

"De'Osha Davenport is dead," James said. "Micah Mitchell is dead. Justin Jones is dead. Twenty-three operators are dead or dying on that island. And your testimony helped bury the evidence that could have saved them."

Sonia felt the words like physical blows. "I didn't know—"

"You did know," James interrupted. "You just decided it didn't matter as much as Michael. And maybe you're right. Maybe one person you love is worth twenty-three people you don't. But don't pretend that's noble. Don't pretend that's love. That's just selfishness disguised as devotion."

Sonia stood, anger breaking through guilt. "I'm not going to let you make me feel worse than I already do."

"Good," James said. "You should feel terrible. You should carry this for the rest of your life. Because those operators don't get to forget. They're dying right now. While we sit here. While you get your husband back. While I spend the next twenty years in a cell. They're dying and no one's saving them. Because you chose silence over sacrifice."

Sonia slammed the phone down and walked away, feeling James's eyes on her back.

She made it to her car before breaking down completely.

Everything James said was true. She'd chosen Michael. She'd betrayed everyone. She'd helped bury evidence that could have saved lives.

And she'd do it again.

Because losing Michael would have broken her in ways she couldn't survive.

So she'd broken everyone else instead.

Sonia drove to the prison where Michael was being held—different facility, different security level, different future.

Three years instead of fifty. She'd saved him that much.

Michael sat across from her in the visitation room, looking tired but steady.

"I saw James," Sonia said.

"How is he?" Miguel asked.

"Angry. At me. He said I chose you over the operators."

Michael was quiet for a moment. "He's right."

"I know," Sonia whispered. "But I couldn't let you spend fifty years in prison. I couldn't lose you like that."

"So you lost everyone else instead," Michael said gently.

Sonia looked up, tears streaming. "Are you angry too?"

"No," Michael said. "I'm heartbroken. Because I understand why you did it. And I understand that you did it for me. And I understand that I made you an accomplice in everything that happened."

"You didn't ask me to—"

"I didn't have to," Michael interrupted. "You love me. Love makes people do terrible things to protect the people they can't live without. I know that because I did terrible things to protect operators I'd never even met. The difference is my terrible things were breaking laws. Yours were breaking friendships. Both hurt people. Both had costs."

"Do you forgive me?" Sonia asked.

Michael reached toward the plexiglass. Sonia matched his gesture, palm to palm separated by barrier.

"I forgive you," Michael said. "But I can't absolve you. That's not mine to give. The operators you helped silence—they're the ones who need to forgive you. And they can't. Because they're dead or trapped. So you're going to carry this. Forever. Just like I'm going to carry every name in my notebook."

Sonia felt something break inside her. "I don't know how to live with this."

"You do what I do," Michael replied. "You keep fighting. You keep trying. You keep refusing to let guilt paralyze you. Because guilt that leads to action is redemption. Guilt that leads to paralysis is just self-pity."

“What can I do?” Sonia asked. “I’m suspended. I’m investigated. Everyone hates me.”

“You wait,” Michael said. “And when I get out—when James gets out—when Martinez resurfaces—you help us finish this. You use your guilt to fuel determination. You prove that betrayal wasn’t the end of your story. Just a chapter.”

Sonia pressed harder against the plexiglass. “I’m so sorry.”

“I know,” Michael said. “Now stop apologizing and start planning. Because I’ve got three years to serve. And when I get out, I’m going to need people who know how to fight dirty. People who’ve made mistakes and learned from them. People who understand that losing battles doesn’t mean surrendering wars.”

“You think we can still win?” Sonia asked.

“The odds are against us,” Michael admitted. “But we will keep fighting. And sometimes, resistance is its own kind of victory.”

Visiting hours ended. Sonia walked out of the prison into afternoon sunlight that felt too bright, too normal, too ordinary for a day when she’d faced both the people she’d betrayed and the person she’d saved.

She drove home to an empty house that felt cavernous without Michael.

Sat at the kitchen table where they’d built their case months ago.

And made a choice.

She could collapse into guilt and spend three years punishing herself.

Or she could use three years to prepare. To gather evidence they'd missed. To build networks they'd need. To become the ally Michael would need when he got out.

Sonia opened her laptop and started working.

Documenting everything she knew. Every conversation. Every betrayal. Every choice.

Building a record of complicity that would either redeem her or condemn her.

But at least it would be honest.

At least it would be active.

At least it would be fighting.

Because James was right: she'd chosen wrong.

But Michael was also right: choosing wrong once didn't mean choosing wrong forever.

It just meant the next choice mattered more.

Sonia worked through the night, building a stronger case and a plan for redemption.

And somewhere in a federal prison, James Simmons sat in a cell counting days until a parole he'd never get.

And somewhere in a state prison, Michael Miguel started serving time he'd earned fighting for people who'd never thank him.

And somewhere in the Pacific Ocean, operators kept mining poison while the world debated whether their suffering was real or imagined.

And somewhere between evidence and hope, truth and belief, justice and survival—the fight continued.

Quieter now.

Smaller.

But ongoing.

Because some fights don't end when you lose.

They just change shape.

And keep going.

Forever.

## CHAPTER THIRTY-SIX

# Eighteen Months Later

Michael Miguel walked out of state prison on a Tuesday morning in August, eighteen months after sentencing, having earned parole through good behavior and overcrowding relief.

The open sky felt too unreal. The air too open. Freedom too big.

Sonia waited at the gate, standing beside a car Michael didn't recognize, wearing clothes that looked new and an expression that looked cautious.

They hadn't seen each other in six months. The last few visits had been too painful—too much silence, too many things unsaid, too much distance that couldn't be bridged through plexiglass.

"Mike," Sonia said when he reached her.

"Sonia."

They stood awkwardly, the space between them filled with eighteen months of separation and decisions that had broken them both in different ways.

"I brought clothes," Sonia said, gesturing to a bag in the back seat. "Your size. And food. Real food, not prison food."

"Thank you," Michael said.

They drove in silence for the first ten minutes, Michael staring out the window at a world that had continued without him. New construction. New billboards. New normal.

"How's James?" Michael asked finally.

"Still in federal prison," Sonia replied. "No parole possibility for another eight years. I've tried to visit. He won't see me."

"Can't blame him," Michael said.

Sonia's hands tightened on the steering wheel. "I know."

"Martinez?"

"Still disappeared," Sonia said. "FBI stopped actively searching six months ago. Officially she's a fugitive. Unofficially I think they're content to let her stay vanished."

"And the operators?"

Sonia was quiet for a moment. "Still on the island. The UN inquiry went nowhere. They requested access. Governor Dickens refused citing national security. The inquiry closed with 'insufficient cooperation' noted in the report."

Michael felt old rage resurface. "So nothing changed."

"Some things changed," Sonia corrected. "Public awareness. Media coverage. Political pressure. Governor Dickens didn't run for reelection. His chief of staff resigned. Pacific Mineral Holdings dissolved under investigation. The BBVP committee was restructured."

"But the operators are still there," Michael said flatly.

"Yes," Sonia admitted. "The operators are still there."

They drove to the house Michael hadn't seen in eighteen months. It looked smaller than he remembered. More ordinary. Like a place where normal people lived normal lives—which they weren't and never would be again.

Inside, Sonia had prepared lunch. Sandwiches. Real coffee. Small gestures toward normalcy that felt surreal after eighteen months of institutional meals.

Michael ate slowly, tasting freedom in every bite.

"I kept your notebook," Sonia said, pulling a familiar leather-bound book from a drawer. "The one you documented everything in. I added to it. Every article. Every development. Every time someone mentioned Blind Island. It's all there."

Michael opened the notebook and saw his handwriting from eighteen months ago, followed by Sonia's neat additions. Dates. Headlines. Updates.

Month 3: Governor Dickens announces retirement, cites health reasons Month 7: Pacific Mineral Holdings files bankruptcy amid federal investigation Month 10: BBVP committee chairman Demetrius Giller resigns Month 12: Advanced Semiconductor Technologies settles civil lawsuit, admits no wrongdoing Month 15: UN Human Rights Council closes inquiry, cites lack of cooperation

Small victories. Insufficient justice. Operators still trapped.

"Thank you for keeping this," Michael said.

"I promised I would," Sonia replied. "I promised I'd keep fighting even if you couldn't."

"And have you?" Michael asked. "Fought?"

Sonia met his gaze. "Every day. In small ways. Legal ways. I've been working with disability rights organizations. Families of missing operators. Building a case for civil litigation. It's slow. It's frustrating. But it's something."

Michael saw the exhaustion in her face—eighteen months of carrying guilt and determination in equal measure.

"You look tired," he said.

"I am tired," Sonia admitted. "Tired of fighting. Tired of losing. Tired of watching the conspiracy adapt faster than we can expose it."

"But you haven't quit," Michael observed.

"No," Sonia said. "Because you wouldn't quit. And if I quit, then everything I did—all the betrayal, all the choices—it all becomes meaningless. At least if I keep fighting, there's a chance at redemption."

Michael reached across the table and took her hand. "You don't need redemption. You need forgiveness. And I already gave you that."

"James hasn't," Sonia said.

"James is angrier than I am," Michael replied. "Give him time."

"Eight years?" Sonia asked bitterly. "That's how long before he's even eligible for parole."

"Then eight years," Michael said. "Or longer. However long it takes."

They kissed and then sat in silence, hands clasped, trying to rebuild something broken.

Michael's phone rang—Michael could not believe Sonia did not allow his phone to be disconnected during his time away. Unknown number.

He answered. "Hello?"

"Detective Miguel." The voice was familiar. Martinez. "Welcome back to the world."

Michael's pulse quickened. "Linda. Where are you?"

"Somewhere safe," Martinez replied. "But I'm calling because we need to meet. I found something. Something big. Something that changes everything."

"What?" Michael asked.

"Not over the phone," Martinez said. "Meet me tomorrow. Two PM. The old railyard on Fifth Street. Come alone."

"Martinez—"

"Tomorrow, Mike. This is the break we've been waiting for."

The line went dead.

Michael stared at his phone, feeling eighteen months of forced patience suddenly irrelevant.

"Who was that?" Sonia asked.

"Martinez," Michael said. "She wants to meet. Says she found something."

Sonia's expression tightened. "It could be a trap. The FBI could be monitoring her communications. Using her to draw you out."

"Or it could be real," Michael replied. "Could be the evidence we need."

"You're on parole," Sonia reminded him. "Any violation sends you back for the full sentence. Meeting with a fugitive would definitely qualify as violation."

"I know," Michael said.

"But you're going anyway," Sonia said.

"Yes."

Sonia closed her eyes. "Of course you are. Because eighteen months in prison didn't change you. Didn't make you cautious. Didn't teach you when to stop."

"It taught me patience," Michael corrected. "Not surrender. There's a difference."

"To you maybe," Sonia said. "To your parole officer, there's no difference. Just violation and consequences."

Michael stood. "I've spent eighteen months waiting. Reading. Planning. Thinking about how to finish this. If Martinez has evidence—real evidence—then meeting with her is worth the risk.

"And if it's a trap?" Sonia challenged. "If the FBI arrests you? If you go back to prison for the full sentence?"

"Then I go back," Michael said simply. "But at least I'll go back knowing I tried."

Sonia stood too, anger and fear mixing. "And what about me? What about us? Do I just watch you throw away freedom for a case you can't win?"

"You don't have to watch," Michael said gently. "You can come with me. Or you can stay here. Or you can report me to my parole officer and end this before it starts. Your choice."

Sonia stared at him, tears threatening. "Why are you making me choose?"

"I'm not," Michael said. "I already made my choice. Now you make yours."

He walked upstairs to change clothes, leaving Sonia standing in the kitchen, faced with the same impossible decision she'd made eighteen months ago.

Love or justice.

Safety or truth.

Michael or the fight.

But this time, Michael wasn't asking her to choose him.

He was choosing the fight.

And Sonia had to decide if she'd follow.

## CHAPTER THIRTY-SEVEN

# Martinez Returns

The old railyard was abandoned—rusted tracks, collapsed buildings, graffiti on everything that didn't move. Perfect place for a clandestine meeting. Perfect place for a trap.

Michael arrived at 1:45 PM, early enough to scope the area. He'd told Sonia he was going alone. She'd said nothing, just watched him leave with an expression that might have been resignation or might have been something darker.

He circled the perimeter, looking for surveillance, for federal agents, for any sign this was exactly what Sonia feared: a setup designed to send him back to prison.

Nothing obvious. Which meant either it was clean or they were very good at hiding.

At 1:58 PM, a figure emerged from one of the collapsed buildings. Female. Average height. Moving with the confidence of someone who'd spent eighteen months staying invisible.

Martinez.

She looked different. Shorter hair. Darker. Contacts instead of glasses. Weight loss that suggested stress and irregular meals. But the eyes were the same—sharp, determined, exhausted.

"Mike," she said, approaching carefully.

"Linda," Michael replied. "You look like crap."

""Eighteen months on the run will do that."

"Why surface now?" Michael asked.

"Because I finally found what we've been looking for," Martinez said. She pulled out a tablet—old model, probably purchased with cash, impossible to trace. "Remember how the committee killed every witness? Darrius Johnson. Kail McDow. John Lizzardo. Ida Glitter."

"I remember," Michael said.

"They made it look like suicide or disappearance," Martinez continued. "But they had to do something with the bodies. Darrius was found. Ida was found. But Kail and John were never recovered."

"So?" Michael prompted.

"So I've been tracking burial records. Death certificates. Cremation logs. Looking for any indication of where bodies went." Martinez opened files on the tablet. "And I found discrepancies. Four unclaimed bodies in the last eighteen months. All listed as John Doe. All cremated without family notification. All with dates that align with our missing witnesses."

Michael felt his pulse quicken. "You think they're our people?"

"I know they are," Martinez said. "I bribed a morgue attendant to pull tissue samples before cremation. DNA analysis confirms: one body was not Kail McDow. Another was John Lizzardo, but one could be Kail's driver."

"How did you get DNA samples for comparison?" Michael asked.

"Kail's brother in Detroit. John's mother in Topeka. I told them I was investigating their disappearances. They cooperated." Martinez pulled up more files. "But that's not the important part. The important part is who signed the death certificates."

She displayed an image: a death certificate signed by Dr. Richard Banks, Medical Examiner.

"Same medical examiner who ruled Darrius Johnson's death a suicide," Michael said.

"Yes," Martinez confirmed. "And same medical examiner who signed death certificates for three other unidentified bodies in the last two years. All cremated immediately. All with cause of death listed as 'complications from pre-existing conditions.'"

"He's covering up murders," Michael said.

"He's part of the conspiracy," Martinez corrected. "And I found his connection. Dr. Banks received payments from Pacific Mineral Holdings. Consulting fees. Over two hundred thousand dollars in eighteen months."

Michael felt the case click together. "He's paid to make bodies disappear."

"More than that," Martinez said. "I tracked his travel records. He's been to the island. Four trips in two years. Always labeled as 'medical consultation.' Always lasting three days."

"He's treating operators on the island," Michael realized. "Or certifying their deaths when they can't work anymore."

"Exactly," Martinez said. "And if we can get him to testify—if we can prove he's been facilitating murder—"

"We can break the conspiracy," Michael finished.

Martinez nodded. "But there's a problem. Dr. Banks is careful. Paranoid. He knows people are watching. He won't talk willingly."

"So we make him talk unwillingly," Michael said.

"That's where you come in," Martinez replied. "You're out on parole. You're clean. You can approach him officially. Request his assistance with a private investigation. Get him comfortable. Then I show up with evidence and we corner him."

"That's entrapment," Michael said.

"That's justice," Martinez corrected. "And it's the only shot we have."

Michael thought about parole conditions. About staying away from investigations. About keeping his head down and rebuilding his life.

Then he thought about all the operators still trapped on the island.

About James serving twenty years.

About witnesses murdered and families destroyed.

"When?" Michael asked.

"Tonight," Martinez said. "He's working late at the morgue. Alone. No witnesses. No surveillance. Perfect opportunity."

"And if it goes wrong?" Michael asked. "If he calls police? If we get arrested?"

"Then we get arrested," Martinez said. "But at least we'll have tried. At least we won't be sitting on evidence waiting for the perfect moment that never comes."

Michael looked at the tablet, at the death certificates, at the proof that witnesses had been murdered and covered up.

“Okay,” he said. “I’m in.”

“Good,” Martinez replied. “Because I wasn’t going to do this without you.”

They spent the next three hours planning. Approach. Questions. Evidence presentation. Exit strategy. Everything they’d learned from eighteen months of watching the conspiracy win.

At seven PM, Michael texted Sonia:

Need to check something. Won’t be home until late. Don’t wait up.

Her response came immediately:

Be careful. I love you.

I love you too.

Michael and Martinez drove to the county morgue in separate vehicles—plausible deniability if things went wrong.

The building was quiet. After hours. One light visible in a back window of

Dr. Banks office.

Michael approached the entrance. Locked. He knocked.

A moment later, Dr. Banks appeared—fifty-eight, gray hair, tired eyes. He recognized Michael immediately.

“Detective Miguel,” Banks said cautiously. “You’re supposed to be in prison.”

"Paroled early," Michael replied. "I need to speak with you. About death certificates you signed."

The doctor's expression hardened. "I don't discuss cases with former detectives."

"Even cases involving murder covered as suicide?" Michael asked.

Banks started to close the door. Michael wedged his foot in the gap.

"Dr. Banks, I'm not here to threaten you. I'm here to give you a chance. To cooperate. To tell the truth before someone else does."

"I have nothing to say," Banks said.

"Then let me show you something," Michael replied.

He pulled out his phone and displayed the death certificates Martinez had found. "Four unclaimed bodies. All signed by you. All cremated immediately. All with payments from Pacific Mineral Holdings arriving in your account within days."

The doctor went pale. "How did you—"

"Doesn't matter," Michael interrupted. "What matters is that I know. And if I know, other people will know. Federal investigators. Media. Families of the deceased. Everyone."

"You can't prove anything," Dr. Banks said, but his voice wavered.

"I can prove enough," Michael replied. "Enough to destroy your career. Enough to open criminal investigations. Enough to make your life very difficult."

Banks hands shook. "What do you want?"

"Testimony," Michael said. "About the island. About operators. About who paid you to cover up deaths."

"I can't," Banks said. "They'll kill me."

"They'll kill you anyway," Michael replied. "Once you become a liability. Once they don't need you anymore. Right now, you have value. You know things. You can trade that knowledge for protection."

Banks stared at Michael for a long moment, weighing impossible choices.

Then he opened the door. "Come in. We need to talk."

Michael stepped inside, feeling the trap close—not on him, but on the conspiracy that had protected itself through silence and murder.

Dr. Banks was about to break that silence.

And when he did, everything would change.

## CHAPTER THIRTY-EIGHT

# The Medical Examiner Talks

Dr. Richard Banks sat in his office, surrounded by death certificates and the weight of complicity, and told Michael everything.

"It started two years ago," Banks said, hands shaking as he poured himself whiskey from a desk drawer. "Governor Dickens's office contacted me. Said they needed a medical examiner who could be discreet. Handle sensitive cases. I thought they meant political scandals. Affairs. Nothing illegal."

"When did you realize it was murder?" Michael asked.

Dr. Banks drank the whiskey in one swallow. "When they brought me Darrius Johnson. Gunshot wound to the head. Powder burns on the hands. Classic suicide setup. Except the angle was wrong. The barrel placement was wrong. Everything was wrong."

"But you signed it as suicide anyway," Michael said.

"They paid me one hundred thousand dollars," Dr. Banks said quietly. "Cash. Untraceable. And they told me if I didn't sign, I'd be next. So I signed."

Martinez recorded everything on her phone, hidden in her jacket pocket.

"Tell me about the island," Michael prompted.

Banks poured more whiskey. "They flew me there three times. Medical consultations. They said operators needed regular health screenings. That I was helping protect vulnerable people."

"What did you actually see?" Michael asked.

"evil," Dr. Banks said simply. "Operators working in gas masks. Respiratory failure. Chemical burns. Malnutrition. Exhaustion. I documented everything. Wrote reports recommending immediate evacuation. They ignored every recommendation."

"Why didn't you report this?" Michael demanded.

"To who?" Banks challenged. "The governor who was funding the operation? The FBI agents who were protecting it? The SLA administrator who was in on it as well? Everyone who should have cared either didn't or couldn't do anything."

"So you kept signing death certificates," Michael said.

"Yes," Banks admitted. "Because refusing meant becoming one of the bodies I certified. And I'm a coward. I chose survival over morality."

"You're choosing morality now," Michael said. "By talking to us."

"I'm choosing self-preservation," Banks corrected. "You found the evidence. Which means others will find it. I'd rather cooperate than wait to be exposed."

Martinez stepped into the room, revealing herself. Banks startled.

"Officer Martinez," Banks said, recognition dawning. "You're a Fugitive," Martinez finished. "I know. But right now, I'm your best chance at redemption."

She pulled out a tablet showing tissue sample analysis. "I have DNA evidence proving John Lizzardo's body was processed through your morgue. I have financial records showing Pacific Mineral Holdings payments. I have travel logs showing your trips to the island."

"You have enough to destroy me," Banks said.

"Or save you," Martinez replied. "Depending on what you do next."

Dr. Banks looked between them. "What do you want?"

"Formal testimony," Michael said. "On the record. Documented. Admissible in court. Everything you've seen. Everyone you've covered for. Every body you've certified falsely."

"That's suicide," Banks said.

"Silence is slower suicide," Martinez replied. "again as Michael said, let me say it slower. The conspiracy will kill you eventually. Right now, you're useful. But the moment you become a liability—the moment they think you might talk—you'll end up on one of your own examination tables."

Banks hands shook harder. "Even if I testify, who would prosecute? The local DA is compromised. The AG is their ally. Federal prosecutors ignored evidence for two years."

"We're not relying on prosecutors," Michael said. "We're going public. Media exposure. International pressure. We make it impossible to ignore."

"They'll kill me before the story runs," Banks said.

"We'll protect you," Martinez assured him. "Witness protection. Secure location. Armed guards."

"You're a fugitive and he's on parole," Dr. Banks said, gesturing between them. "What protection can you possibly provide?"

"Better protection than they'll give you," Michael replied. "Because we care if you live. They only care if you stay silent."

Banks stood and walked to his window, staring out at the parking lot. "I have a wife. Two daughters. Grandchildren. If I testify, they become targets."

"If you don't testify, they become collateral damage when this collapses anyway," Martinez said. "Better to be on the right side when it does."

Banks was quiet for a long moment, weighing survival against conscience.

"I need guarantees," he said finally.

"We can't guarantee anything," Michael admitted. "Except that doing nothing guarantees you end up dead and forgotten. At least if you testify, your death—if it comes—means something."

"That's not comforting," Banks said.

"It's honest," Michael replied.

Banks turned back from the window. "What's the plan?"

"We record your testimony tonight," Martinez said. "Full statement. Names, dates, details. Everything. Then we release it tomorrow through multiple media outlets simultaneously. By the time the conspiracy realizes what happened, the story is already everywhere."

"And me?" Banks asked. "Where do I go?"

"Wherever you feel safest," Michael said. "We'll arrange transport. New identity if necessary. Whatever you need."

"I need to call my wife," Dr. Banks said.

"After we record," Martinez said firmly. "Once you make that call, we won't have long before someone intercepts communication and figures out what's happening. We record first. Hide you second. Contact family third."

Banks nodded slowly. "Okay. Let's do this before I lose my nerve."

They spent the next three hours recording. DR. Banks testimony was devastating—meticulous detail about bodies, causes of death, payments, threats. He named names: Governor Dickens. Ron Spillwind. Demetrius Giller. FBI Agent Rutledge. SLA Administrator Cynthia Delancey.

Everyone who'd pressured him. Everyone who'd paid him. Everyone who'd threatened him.

By midnight, they had enough testimony to destroy careers and open criminal investigations across multiple agencies.

"What happens now?" Banks asked, exhaustion evident.

"Now we get you somewhere safe," Michael said. "And tomorrow, we strike the match and burn it all down."

They escorted Dr. Banks to Martinez's vehicle—a nondescript sedan purchased with cash under false registration.

"Where are we going?" Banks asked.

"Undisclosed location," Martinez replied. "For your protection and ours."

They drove through empty streets, checking mirrors constantly for surveillance.

Michael's phone buzzed. Sonia:

Where are you?

Working on something. I'm okay. I'll explain later.

Mike, your parole officer called. You missed your check-in.

Michael felt ice run through him. He'd forgotten about the mandatory check-in—required within 24 hours of release.

I'll handle it, Michael typed.

You can't handle it. You're already in violation. If they issue a warrant—

Then they issue a warrant. I'm almost done.

Mike—

I love you. Trust me.

He turned off the phone.

Martinez glanced at him. "Problem?"

"Parole violation," Michael said. "Missed my check-in."

"So you're already going back to prison," Martinez said.

"Probably," Michael agreed.

"Was it worth it?" Martinez asked.

Michael thought about Banks testimony. About the evidence they'd secured. About the story that would break tomorrow.

"Ask me after the story runs," Michael said.

They drove until dawn, reaching a safe house Martinez had prepared months ago—rural property, isolated, off-grid. Perfect for hiding a witness the conspiracy wanted dead.

"You'll stay here until the story breaks," Martinez told Banks. "After that, decide if you want to testify formally or disappear permanently."

"What if they find me before then?" Banks asked.

"Then we all go down together," Martinez replied. "But at least we'll go down fighting."

She turned to Michael. "You need to leave. Get back to Wichita. Deal with your parole violation before it escalates."

"What about you?" Michael asked.

"I stay here," Martinez said. "Protect the witness. Release the story. Finish what we started."

"Linda—"

"Go, Mike," Martinez interrupted. "You got out of prison yesterday. Don't throw it away for something I can handle alone."

Michael wanted to argue. Wanted to stay. Wanted to see this through to the end.

But Martinez was right. He'd already violated parole. Staying longer only made it worse.

"Release the story at noon," Michael said. "Simultaneous publication across multiple outlets. Make it impossible to suppress."

"That was always the plan," Martinez replied.

Michael drove back to Wichita as sunrise painted the sky orange and gold. Beautiful morning. Perfect day for a reckoning.

He arrived home at 7:30 AM to find Sonia waiting with two people he didn't recognize.

"Mike," Sonia said, her voice tight. "This is Agent Hayly and Agent Tyler. FBI. They have a warrant for your arrest."

Michael raised his hands. "I understand."

Hayly approached with handcuffs. "Michael Miguel, you're under arrest for violating the terms of your parole. You have the right to remain silent—"

"I know my rights," Michael said. "Just do it."

They cuffed him. Led him to their vehicle. Drove him back to the same jail he'd left yesterday.

Full circle. Twenty-four hours of freedom. Used to secure testimony that would either save everything or prove that fighting was futile.

Michael sat in the holding cell, waiting for noon.

Waiting for Martinez to release Banks testimony.

Waiting to see if eighteen months in prison and twenty-four hours of freedom had been worth it.

He closed his eyes and tried to find patience.

Just four more hours.

Then the world would know everything.

And either justice would follow.

Or it wouldn't.

But at least the truth would be undeniable.

And for Michael Miguel—convicted felon, parole violator, suspended detective—that was enough.

# CHAPTER THIRTY-NINE

## Sonia Calls Governor

Sonia Miguel sat in her car outside the governor's mansion at 11:45 AM, phone in hand, preparing to make the call that would either save everyone or destroy what little remained of her integrity.

Martinez's story was scheduled to publish in fifteen minutes. Dr. Banks testimony would expose the entire conspiracy. Operators would finally be vindicated. The conspiracy would collapse.

Unless Sonia stopped it.

Her phone rang. Unknown number.

She answered. "Hello?"

"Officer Miguel." The voice was male, familiar. Governor Bruce Dickens. "We need to talk."

"I have nothing to say to you," Sonia replied.

"Even if it means saving your husband?" Dickens asked.

Sonia felt her stomach drop. "What are you talking about?"

"Michael was arrested this morning," Dickens said. "Parole violation. He'll be returned to prison to serve his full sentence. Three years. Unless I intervene."

"You can't intervene in state sentencing," Sonia said.

"I can make recommendations," Dickens corrected. "I can suggest clemency. I can suggest that enforcement be... lenient. Or I can suggest they throw away the key. Your choice."

Sonia's hands tightened on the phone. "What do you want?"

"I want you to stop Officer Martinez from releasing her story," Dickens said. "You know where she is. You know how to contact her. Call her. Convince her to delay publication."

"Why would I do that?" Sonia asked.

"Because in fifteen minutes, she's going to publish Dr. Banks testimony," Dickens said. "And when that happens, federal agents will raid every location connected to Pacific Mineral Holdings. They'll find operators on Blind Island. They'll document conditions. And they'll discover evidence that... complicates things."

"Complicates what?" Sonia demanded.

"Your husband's imprisonment," Dickens said carefully. "You see, we've been preparing for this possibility. We have documentation showing Michael Miguel coordinated with international terrorists to sabotage American semiconductor supply chains. We have communications between him and foreign agents. We have proof of espionage."

"That's fabricated," Sonia said.

"Of course it's fabricated," Dickens agreed. "But it's convincing fabrication. And once it's released, Michael stops being a wrongfully convicted detective and becomes a national security threat. Which means he gets transferred to federal maximum security. Solitary confinement. No visitors. No parole. For the rest of his life."

Sonia felt ice run through her veins. "You'd do that? Frame him for espionage?"

"I'd do that to protect national interests," Dickens corrected. "Tenorite isn't just valuable, Officer Miguel. It's essential. Our military. Our technology. Our global competitiveness. All depend on stable supply. If Blind Island operations are disrupted—if operators are removed—if extraction stops—we lose strategic advantage to China. To Russia. To nations that don't care about humanitarian concerns."

"So you're choosing strategic advantage over human lives," Sonia said.

"I'm choosing many lives over few lives," Dickens replied. "The operators on that island number maybe sixty. The Americans who depend on Tenorite-based technology number millions. It's unfortunate math. But it's necessary math."

"You're insane," Sonia said.

"I'm pragmatic," Dickens corrected. "And right now, I'm offering you a deal. Stop Martinez. Delay the story. Give us time to evacuate the island and relocate operations. And your husband goes free. He serves no additional time. His record gets expunged. He lives a normal life."

"And the operators?" Sonia asked.

"Will be relocated to other facilities," Dickens said. "Better facilities. Under better conditions. We'll reform the program. We'll implement oversight. We'll fix what went wrong."

"You're lying," Sonia said.

"Probably," Dickens agreed. "But you'll never know if you don't take the deal. And by the time you find out I lied, your husband will be free and this will be someone else's problem."

Sonia stared at her phone, feeling history repeat itself.

Eighteen months ago, she'd chosen Michael over justice.

Now she was being asked to choose him again.

And the cost was higher. The stakes clearer. The betrayal more complete.

"What happens if I refuse?" Sonia asked.

"Then the story publishes," Dickens said. "Operators are rescued. The conspiracy is exposed. And your husband spends the rest of his life in federal supermax prison as a convicted spy. Your choice."

The line went dead.

Sonia sat in her car, watching the clock tick toward noon.

Twelve minutes until publication.

Twelve minutes to decide.

She pulled out her phone and called Martinez.

Martinez answered immediately. "Sonia? Everything okay?"

"Linda, I need you to delay publication," Sonia said.

Silence.

"What?" Martinez asked finally.

"Delay the story," Sonia repeated. "Just for a few days. Give me time to—"

“No,” Martinez interrupted. “Absolutely not. We’ve worked eighteen months for this. Banks risked everything for this. Mike violated parole for this. I’m not delaying.”

“They’re going to frame Michael for espionage,” Sonia said desperately. “They’re going to send him to supermax. Forever. Unless we delay.”

“Then he goes to supermax,” Martinez said flatly. “Because delaying means operators die. Means the conspiracy adapts. Means we lose our only chance.”

“I can’t lose him again,” Sonia said, tears breaking through.

“You already lost him,” Martinez replied. “Eighteen months ago when you chose him over the operators. Now you’re trying to make the same choice again. But Sonia—this time, he won’t forgive you.”

“He’s my husband,” Sonia said.

“And those are human beings dying on an island,” Martinez countered. “Human beings with families. With children. With lives that matter just as much as Miguel’s.”

“Please,” Sonia begged. “Just a few days. Let me figure something out.”

“There’s nothing to figure out,” Martinez said. “Either we publish and operators get rescued, or we delay and they keep dying. Those are the only options. And I’m not choosing death over Michael’s freedom.”

“Then I will,” Sonia said.

She hung up and immediately called Governor Dickens.

He answered on the first ring. "Officer Miguel. Have you reconsidered?"

"Tell me exactly what I need to do," Sonia said.

"Call the Kansas City Star," Dickens said. "Tell them the story is based on fabricated testimony. That Dr. Banks is mentally unstable. That the evidence is fraudulent. Create enough doubt that they pull the story while they verify."

"That's defamation," Sonia said. "I could be sued."

"You could also save your husband," Dickens replied. "Your choice."

Sonia wiped tears from her eyes and made the call.

She called Sarah Chen at the Kansas City Star.

Sarah answered. "

"The story you're about to publish," Sonia said, voice shaking. "It's based on false testimony. Dr. Banks is unstable. He's fabricating evidence to cover his own crimes. You need to pull it."

Sarah was silent for a moment. "Sonia, are you serious?"

"Yes," Sonia said. "I'm serious. Pull the story."

"I can't pull a story fifteen minutes before publication without cause," Sarah said. "Do you have proof Banks is lying?"

"I have..." Sonia trailed off. "I have concerns about his mental state. About his reliability as a source."

"That's not proof," Sarah said. "That's suspicion. And I'm not killing a major investigation because a cop has suspicions."

"Then double-check everything," Sonia urged. "Delay publication until you can verify independently."

"Why?" Sarah asked. "What's really going on, Sonia?"

Sonia felt tears stream down her face. "Please. Just trust me. This story will cause more harm than good."

"You're wrong," Sarah said quietly. "This story will expose murder. And I'm publishing it. With or without your support."

She hung up.

Sonia called Dickens back. "She won't pull it. She's publishing anyway."

"Then you've failed," Dickens said. "And your husband pays the price."

"Please," Sonia said. "There must be another way—"

"There was another way," Dickens interrupted. "You just chose not to take it. Good luck, Officer Miguel. You're going to need it."

He hung up.

Sonia sat in her car, watching the clock tick to noon.

The story published.

Headlines appeared across every major outlet:

MEDICAL EXAMINER TESTIFIES TO BLIND ISLAND MURDERS GOVERNOR'S CONSPIRACY EXPOSED THROUGH WITNESS TESTIMONY SYSTEMATIC COVER-UP OF OPERATOR DEATHS DOCUMENTED

Within minutes, federal agents were mobilizing. Search warrants being issued. Raids being planned.

The conspiracy was collapsing.

Operators would be rescued.

Justice would finally come.

And Michael Miguel would spend the rest of his life in federal prison.

Because Sonia had tried to stop it and failed.

Had tried to choose him and lost him anyway.

Had betrayed everyone one final time for nothing.

She put her head on the steering wheel and cried.

Not because she'd tried to stop the story.

But because she'd failed.

And failure meant Michael's freedom was already gone.

Already forfeit.

Already beyond saving.

She'd chosen wrong.

Again.

And this time, there would be no forgiveness.

## CHAPTER FORTY

# The Island Raid Preparation

Federal agents raided Pacific Mineral Holdings offices at 12:47 PM.

They raided the SLA administrator's home at 1:15 PM.

They raided the governor's mansion at 2:03 PM.

And at 3:30 PM, they began preparing to raid Blind Island.

Michael watched it unfold from his jail cell, guards bringing him updates because his case had become national news and everyone wanted to see if the convicted detective had been right all along.

"FBI's assembling a task force," one guard said. "Military transport. Coast Guard support. They're treating it like a hostage rescue operation."

Michael felt vindication and terror war in his chest.

Vindication because everything he'd said was being proven true.

Terror because federal raids meant federal crimes meant Michael's parole violation was about to become the least of his problems.

His lawyer arrived at four PM. Robert Hayes looked exhausted.

"Mike, we need to talk about what happens next," Hayes said.

"What happens next is I go back to prison," Michael replied.

"It's worse than that," Hayes said. "The prosecution is filing additional charges. They're claiming you coordinated with Martinez to intimidate a witness. That you coerced Dr. Banks testimony through threats."

"That's not what happened," Michael said.

"Doesn't matter," Hayes replied. "What matters is they can make it look like that happened. And if they do, you're not facing three years. You're facing twenty."

Michael felt the walls close tighter. "Can you fight it?"

"I can try," Hayes said. "But Mike—your best defense just became your worst problem. Dr. Banks testimony is exposing the conspiracy. Which means the conspiracy needs that testimony discredited. Which means they need Banks to be unreliable. Which means they need you to be the bad guy who forced him to lie."

"So either Banks testimony destroys the conspiracy," Michael said, "or the conspiracy destroys Banks testimony by destroying me."

"Exactly," Hayes confirmed.

Michael laughed bitterly. "I can't win. If the conspiracy falls, I go to prison for witness intimidation. If the conspiracy survives, I go to prison for parole violation. Either way, I'm gone."

"Not necessarily," Hayes said. He pulled out documents. "There's one possibility. If the raid on Blind Island confirms everything Dr. Banks testified to—if they find bodies, evidence, systematic abuse—then Banks testimony becomes verified. Which means you didn't coerce lies. You helped expose truth. Which could get charges dropped."

"That's a lot of ifs," Michael said.

"It's the only hope you have," Hayes replied. "The raid happens tomorrow. Military transport to the coordinates. Full documentation. If they find what we think is there..."

"Then operators are saved and I might go free," Michael finished.

"Yes," Hayes said.

"And if they don't find anything?" Michael asked. "If the conspiracy evacuated everyone before the raid?"

"Then you're convicted of witness intimidation and spend the next two decades in federal prison," Hayes said bluntly.

Michael absorbed this. Everything riding on one raid. One chance to verify truth or confirm lies.

"What do I do until then?" Michael asked.

"You wait," Hayes said. "And you hope the operators are still there."

The raid launched at dawn.

Michael watched news coverage from the jail common area, surrounded by inmates who'd grown invested in his case.

Military helicopters. Coast Guard vessels. FBI tactical teams. The full weight of federal law enforcement descending on coordinates in the middle of the Pacific Ocean.

Live coverage from ships just outside territorial waters. Reporters breathless with anticipation.

And Michael, locked in a cell, watching his entire future depend on what they found.

The first helicopter reached the island at 6:47 AM.

Cameras captured the approach: volcanic rock rising from ocean. Industrial structures. Clear signs of habitation.

The island was real.

Agents deployed. Secured the perimeter. Began systematic search.

Michael barely breathed.

Reporters narrated: "Federal agents are now inside the primary structure. We're waiting for confirmation of what they're finding..."

Minutes stretched. Tension built.

Then: "We're getting reports—yes, confirmed—agents have found multiple individuals inside the facility. Details are still emerging, but initial reports suggest—"

The coverage cut to a federal spokesperson: "We can confirm that federal agents have located and secured approximately forty individuals at the coordinates known as Blind Island. These individuals appear to be blind vending operators who were reported missing from various states. Medical teams are assessing their condition. Full statement will be provided once assessment is complete."

The jail common area erupted.

Inmates cheering. Guards stunned. Everyone watching had just witnessed validation of a conspiracy they'd been told didn't exist.

Michael felt tears burn. "They found them. They actually found them."

Craig, his cellblock neighbor, slapped him on the back. "You were right, cop. You were right the whole time."

“I was right too late,” Michael replied. “How many died before this raid? How many didn’t survive to be rescued?”

The celebration dimmed. Because forty rescued operators meant others weren’t. Meant bodies buried or cremated. Meant families who’d never get closure.

The federal spokesperson returned: “Preliminary assessment indicates the rescued individuals have been subjected to harsh conditions. Respiratory issues. Malnutrition. Evidence of forced labor. We’re treating this as a human trafficking investigation. Additional charges will be forthcoming.”

Michael’s lawyer called minutes later. “Mike, you saw?”

“I saw,” Michael replied.

“This changes everything,” Hayes said. “Dr. Banks testimony is verified. The conspiracy is confirmed. You’re not a witness intimidator—you’re a whistleblower who helped expose systematic abuse.”

“Does that mean charges get dropped?” Michael asked.

“I’ll file motions immediately,” Hayes replied. “Request emergency hearing. With this evidence, I can argue you were justified in every action. That parole violation was necessary to save lives.”

“When will we know?” Michael asked.

“Days,” Hayes said. “Maybe weeks. But Mike—you might actually walk away from this.”

Michael hung up and returned to watching coverage.

Operators being loaded onto helicopters. Medical teams providing emergency treatment. Survivors wrapped in blankets, faces hidden, identities protected.

Forty rescued.

Twenty-three disappeared from Kansas alone.

How many from other states? How many total victims?

The math was horrifying.

And Michael had been right all along.

But being right didn't undo the damage. Didn't bring back the dead. Didn't erase eighteen months in prison or the trauma of everyone who'd fought alongside him.

It just meant the truth was finally undeniable.

Finally public.

Finally real.

Michael watched until the coverage shifted to political fallout: Governor Dickens's resignation announced. Federal investigations launched. Civil lawsuits filed. The machinery of accountability grinding into motion.

Too late for most.

Just barely in time for some.

And Michael Miguel—convicted felon, parole violator, vindicated detective—sat in a cell waiting to see if justice would save him like he'd tried to save others.

Or if the system would claim one more victim before admitting it had been wrong.

## CHAPTER FORTY-ONE

# Miguel's Hearing

The emergency hearing convened three days after the Blind Island raid.

Michael sat in the courtroom wearing an orange jumpsuit, hands cuffed, watching Judge Hammond review documents that would decide if he spent the next twenty years in prison or walked free.

His lawyer Robert Hayes stood beside him, radiating cautious optimism.

The prosecution—led by Patricia Vance—sat across the aisle, looking less confident than she had at Miguel's original trial.

"Your Honor," Hayes began, "my client stands accused of witness intimidation. Specifically, the prosecution claims Detective Miguel coerced Dr. Richard Banks into providing false testimony about Blind Island. However, the federal raid three days ago confirmed every detail of Dr. Banks testimony. Forty operators were rescued. Evidence of systematic abuse was documented. Bodies were found. Everything Dr. Banks said was true."

Vance stood. "The accuracy of Dr. Banks testimony doesn't negate the methods used to obtain it. Detective Miguel violated parole to contact a witness. He pressured that witness through threats. He coordinated with a fugitive—Officer Martinez—to intimidate Dr. Banks into cooperation."

"We didn't intimidate," Michael said, unable to stay silent. "We gave him a chance to tell the truth."

Hammond looked at him sharply. "Mr. Miguel, your attorney speaks for you."

"With respect, Your Honor," Michael continued, "I violated parole to save lives. Forty people who are alive today because I didn't follow rules designed to protect a conspiracy."

"Rules designed to ensure justice," Vance corrected. "You're not a vigilante, Detective Miguel. You're a convicted felon who repeatedly breaks laws under the pretense of righteousness."

"I'm a detective who solved a case everyone else ignored," Michael shot back.

Hammond banged her gavel. "Enough. Mr. Hayes, continue your argument."

Hayes pulled out documents. "Your Honor, I have affidavits from the rescued operators. They confirm they were held against their will. They confirm conditions matching Dr. Banks testimony. They confirm systematic abuse. My client didn't coerce false testimony—he facilitated the exposure of genocide."

"Genocide is a strong word," Vance said.

"It's an accurate word," Hayes replied. "Twenty-three operators from Kansas are confirmed dead. Bodies found on the island or traced through medical examiner records. Multiply that across multiple states and we're looking at hundreds of deaths. All covered up by the conspiracy Detective Miguel exposed."

Hammond studied the documents. "Ms. Vance, how does the prosecution respond to the fact that the raid confirmed Dr. Banks testimony?"

Vance shifted uncomfortably. "The state maintains that Detective Miguel's methods were illegal regardless of outcome. We can't allow citizens to break laws simply because they believe they're serving justice."

"Even when breaking laws prevents mass murder?" Hayes challenged.

"Even then," Vance said. "Because once we accept that ends justify means, we have no system. Just chaos."

Hammond closed the file. "The court will take a brief recess to review the evidence. Thirty minutes."

She left the bench.

Michael sat in the courtroom, feeling his entire future compress into thirty minutes of judicial deliberation.

Sonia sat in the gallery behind him. They hadn't spoken since his arrest. She'd tried to visit. He'd refused. The gap between them had grown too wide—filled with her attempt to stop the story, her failure, her pattern of choosing wrong.

But she was here. Watching. Waiting.

The thirty minutes stretched. Lawyers whispered. Guards stood impassive. The courtroom held its breath.

Hammond returned.

"After reviewing the evidence," she said, "the court finds that Detective Miguel's actions, while technically illegal, were performed in good faith to expose systematic criminal activity. The operators rescued from Blind Island validate his investigation. Dr. Banks testimony has been verified. Under these circumstances, the court declines to prosecute witness intimidation charges."

Michael felt relief flood through him.

"However," Hammond continued, "the parole violation stands. Detective Miguel left the state without permission. He contacted individuals he was prohibited from contacting. He engaged in investigative activities expressly forbidden by his parole conditions."

The relief evaporated.

"Therefore," Hammond said, "the court remands Detective Miguel to state custody to serve the remainder of his original sentence. Eighteen months, minus time served on this violation. Effective immediately."

The gavel banged.

Michael stood as guards approached with handcuffs.

"Wait," Hayes said. "Your Honor, my client has already served eighteen months. He was released on parole—"

"And violated that parole," Hammond interrupted. "Which means the time served on parole doesn't count toward his sentence. He serves the full eighteen months from today."

Michael felt the floor drop. "That's three years total. For crimes committed while exposing murder."

"That's the consequence of breaking laws," Hammond replied. "Even when breaking laws achieves good results. Court is adjourned."

She left the bench.

Guards cuffed Michael and led him toward the holding cell.

He passed Sonia in the gallery. Their eyes met.

"I'm sorry," she mouthed.

Michael looked away.

Sorry wasn't enough. Sorry didn't change anything. Sorry was just another word for failure.

Back in his cell, Michael stared at the ceiling and calculated time.

Eighteen more months. Twenty-one if he lost good behavior credit. Almost two years watching the world move on while he sat in a cage.

The operators were safe. That mattered.

The conspiracy was exposed. That mattered.

Justice had partially prevailed. That mattered.

But Michael was still paying the price while the architects of the conspiracy—Governor Dickens, committee members, corporate executives—negotiated plea deals and immunity agreements.

The system protected itself. Always.

Even when admitting it was wrong, it punished the people who'd forced that admission.

His lawyer visited that evening.

"I'm filing appeals," Hayes said. "The sentence is harsh. Given the circumstances, given the rescue, given everything—we have grounds for reduction."

"How long will appeals take?" Michael asked.

"Months," Hayes admitted. "Maybe a year before we get a hearing. But Mike, we have a good case. Public opinion is on your side. The rescued operators are grateful. Families are speaking out. You're being called a hero."

"Heroes don't sit in jail," Michael said.

"Sometimes they do," Hayes replied. "Because the system takes time to catch up to truth."

Michael wanted to believe that. Wanted to think justice was just slow, not broken.

But he'd seen too much. Learned too much. Lost too much to believe in systems anymore.

He believed in people. Individual people who chose courage over comfort. People like Martinez and James and Ida and even Sonia—flawed, broken people who tried anyway.

Systems failed. People persisted.

And Michael would persist through eighteen more months because the alternative was surrender.

And he didn't know how to surrender.

## CHAPTER FORTY-TWO

# Operators Rescued

The rescued operators were taken to a federal medical facility in San Diego for evaluation and treatment.

Michael watched coverage from jail, seeing faces he'd memorized from photographs now attached to living, breathing people who'd survived the island.

One operator agreed to an interview. Her name was Catherine Wells. Forty-six. Blind since age twelve. BBVP operator for fourteen years. Missing for nine months.

The reporter asked gentle questions. Catherine answered with devastating precision.

"They told us we were going for advanced training," Catherine said. "Better opportunities. Better pay. We believed them because we trusted the program. We trusted the committee."

"What happened when you arrived at the island?" the reporter asked.

"They took our phones. Our identification. Everything that connected us to our old lives. They said it was for security. For our protection." Catherine's hands shook. "Then they showed us the tunnels."

"Can you describe the tunnels?"

"Volcanic rock. Narrow passages. Heat from the earth below. Dust everywhere—Tenorite dust. They gave us gas masks but the masks didn't always work. We'd breathe the dust and our lungs would burn."

"How many hours did you work?"

"Twelve hours. Sometimes fourteen. Mining the Tenorite. Filling containers. Carrying them to the surface. The guards watched constantly. If you slowed down, they'd withhold food. If you complained, they'd put you in isolation—small rooms carved into rock, no light, no sound, just darkness and heat."

"Did anyone try to escape?"

Catherine's voice broke. "Marcus tried. Marcus Torres. He was twenty-eight. Blind since birth. He tried to steal a boat. They caught him. Beat him. We heard the screams from the dormitory. The next morning, they told us Marcus died from injuries sustained during an escape attempt. They cremated his body. Scattered the ashes in the ocean."

Michael wrote the name in his notebook: Marcus Torres. Age 28. Murdered for attempting escape.

The interview continued. Catherine described conditions. Food rationing. Medical neglect. Operators dying from respiratory failure, heat exhaustion, accidents in the tunnels.

"How many died while you were there?" the reporter asked.

"I counted fifteen," Catherine said. "But there were others before I arrived. The guards would talk about past workers. About how the island went through operators quickly. About how there were always more coming."

Fifteen deaths in nine months. From one operator's count alone.

Multiply that across two years. Across multiple states feeding operators to the island.

The math was horrifying.

"Why didn't you speak up during medical evaluations?" the reporter asked.

Catherine laughed bitterly. "The medical examiner who visited—Dr. Banks—he documented everything. Respiratory problems. Malnutrition. Injuries. He wrote detailed reports. But nothing changed. We realized he wasn't there to help us. He was there to assess how much longer we could work before we broke."

"What sustained you?" the reporter asked. "What kept you going?"

Catherine was quiet for a long moment. "Detective Miguel."

"What?"

"We heard about him. From new operators who arrived. They told us a detective was investigating disappearances. That someone was fighting for us. That we weren't forgotten." Catherine's voice strengthened. "Even when everything was hopeless, we knew someone outside was trying. That mattered. It gave us strength to survive one more day. One more shift. One more horror. Because someone cared."

Michael felt tears burn.

He'd failed to save most of them. Failed to stop the operation before it consumed more lives. Failed to prevent Catherine and forty others from experiencing nine months of pure evil and slow torture.

But he'd given them hope. And hope had kept them alive until rescue came.

That wasn't nothing.

It wasn't enough. But it wasn't nothing.

The interview ended. Catherine was escorted to continued medical treatment. The reporter turned to camera:

"Forty operators were rescued from Blind Island. Federal authorities estimate another thirty died during the two-year operation. Investigations are ongoing. Criminal charges are pending against numerous officials. But for the survivors, the trauma is just beginning to be addressed. These forty people will carry scars—physical and psychological—for the rest of their lives. The question now: how do we ensure this never happens again?"

Michael turned off the TV.

How do we ensure this never happens again?

The same way you ensure anything doesn't happen: constant vigilance. Refusal to look away. Persistent questioning of systems that demand trust without earning it.

And people like Michael—stubborn, willing to sacrifice everything—who fought even when fighting was futile.

Michael received mail. A letter that read:

Detective Miguel. This is Catherine Wells. I wanted to thank you. For not giving up. For fighting when everyone else looked away. You saved my life. I know you're in jail. I know you paid a price. But please know: it mattered. Thank you.

Michael read the message three times.

Then he saved it.

Because on days when eighteen months felt unbearable, when the cost seemed too high, when doubt crept in—he'd need reminders that fighting mattered.

That justice delayed wasn't always justice denied.

That forty people were alive because someone refused to quit.

Even if that someone was sitting in a cell paying for the crime of caring too much.

## CHAPTER FORTY-THREE

# Conspiracy Strikes Back

The conspiracy struck back two weeks after the raid.

Not with violence. Not with obvious retaliation. With something more insidious: manufactured evidence.

Federal prosecutors announced new charges against Michael Miguel: espionage, conspiracy to commit terrorism, and foreign agent activity.

The accusations were absurd. Detailed. Convincing.

"Detective Miguel," the indictment read, "coordinated with foreign intelligence services to sabotage American semiconductor supply chains. He used the pretense of investigating operator disappearances to access classified facility locations. He shared intelligence with hostile nations regarding Tenorite extraction operations."

The evidence was fabricated. Michael knew it. His lawyer knew it. Anyone paying attention knew it.

But fabricated evidence, presented confidently by federal prosecutors with unlimited resources, could be persuasive to juries who wanted simple answers.

Hayes visited Michael in jail, looking pale.

"They're serious," Hayes said. "Federal terrorism charges. If convicted, you're looking at life in prison. No parole. Maximum security."

"On what evidence?" Michael asked.

"Communications allegedly between you and foreign agents," Chen replied. "Financial transfers to offshore accounts. Encrypted messages discussing facility locations."

"All fabricated," Michael said.

"Of course," Hayes agreed. "But proving fabrication requires forensic analysis. Expert testimony. Resources we don't have. And by the time we could mount a defense, you'd have already spent years in pretrial detention."

Michael understood. The charges weren't meant to convict him. They were meant to bury him. To keep him locked up indefinitely. To make him disappear the way operators had disappeared—not through violence, but through legal process weaponized against truth.

"Who's behind this?" Michael asked.

"Officially? Federal prosecutors acting on national security concerns," Hayes said. "Unofficially? What's left of the conspiracy. People who want Blind Island forgotten. Who need the narrative shifted from 'government trafficked citizens' to 'detective aided foreign enemies.'"

"So they're making me the villain," Michael said.

"Yes," Hayes confirmed. "And it's working. Media is covering the charges extensively. Public opinion is shifting. People who called you a hero two weeks ago are now questioning whether you were a foreign agent all along."

Michael felt rage burn cold. "What do we do?"

"We fight," Hayes said. "We demand discovery. We expose the fabricated evidence. We call expert witnesses. We make this so public they can't sustain the lie."

"How long will that take?" Michael asked.

"Years," Hayes admitted. "Federal terrorism cases move slowly. Especially when the government wants them to move slowly."

"So I sit in jail for years waiting for a trial that might never come," Michael said.

"Unless we find another way," Hayes replied.

"What other way?"

Hayes hesitated. "There might be someone who can help. Someone with resources. Someone who owes you."

"Who?" Michael asked.

"Dr. Elena Vasquez," Chen said. "The Advanced Semiconductor consultant who leaked Tenorite information. Her company settled civil suits but she's still wealthy. Still connected. She's been following your case. She reached out. Offered to fund your defense. Expert witnesses. Forensic analysts. Everything needed to prove the charges are fabricated."

"Why would she do that?" Michael asked.

"Because she feels guilty," Chen said. "Her company profited from Tenorite while operators died. She wants to make it right. And funding your defense is one way to do that."

Michael wanted to refuse. Wanted to say he didn't need corporate charity. That he'd fight without help from people who'd been affiliated with the conspiracy.

But pride was a luxury. And Miguel couldn't afford luxuries.

"Tell her yes," Michael said. "And thank you."

Hayes nodded. "I'll coordinate with her team. But Mike—this fight is going to be brutal. The government will use every resource to destroy you. They'll attack your credibility. Your methods. Your motives. They'll make you look like a terrorist instead of a detective."

"Let them try," Michael said. "I've been called worse."

"But have you been convicted of worse?" Hayes challenged. "Because that's what they're aiming for. Conviction. Life sentence. You disappearing into federal prison where no one can hear you. Where your testimony becomes meaningless. Where the rescued operators' vindication gets overshadowed by your alleged crimes."

Michael understood. The conspiracy couldn't undo the raid. Couldn't bring back the island operations. Couldn't erase the exposure.

But they could discredit the exposer. They could make Miguel so toxic that anyone who cited his investigation looked foolish. They could turn vindication into doubt.

"Then we make sure the rescued operators stay visible," Michael said. "Make sure they testify. Make sure their stories are the ones people remember, not mine."

"That's already happening," Hayes said. "Catherine Wells has been doing interviews. Other operators are speaking out. Disability rights organizations are amplifying their voices."

"Good," Michael said. "Because I'm expendable. They're not. If destroying me protects them, I'll accept that trade."

Hayes looked at him for a long moment. "You really mean that."

"Yes," Michael said simply.

"Then we'll fight," Hayes replied. "Not just for you. For everyone who trusted you. For everyone who survived because you refused to quit."

Hayes left.

Michael returned to his cell and tried to prepare mentally for a fight that might never end.

Years in detention. Fabricated charges. Federal prosecutors with unlimited resources. The full weight of government machinery turned against one detective who'd refused to look away.

It was designed to be unwinnable.

But Miguel had fought unwinnable battles before.

In Iraq. Against soldiers with better weapons and home advantage. He'd survived.

In Wichita. Against a conspiracy with government backing and corporate funding. He'd survived.

He'd survive this too.

Or he wouldn't.

But either way, forty operators were free.

And that was worth whatever came next.

## CHAPTER FORTY-FOUR

# James Freed

James Simmons walked out of federal prison on a Wednesday morning in October, ten years early, his sentence commuted in light of the Blind Island exposure.

The paperwork cited "cooperation with ongoing investigations" and "service to national interests"—sanitized language that erased ten years of wrongful imprisonment and pretended justice had always been the goal.

James didn't care about language. He cared about freedom.

Martinez waited at the gate, still technically a fugitive but no longer being actively pursued. The FBI had quietly dropped its search after the raid, acknowledging implicitly that she'd been right all along.

"James," Martinez said when he reached her.

"Linda."

They hugged—two people who'd sacrificed everything and somehow survived.

"How does it feel?" Martinez asked.

"Surreal," James admitted. "Ten years compressed into ten seconds. I keep expecting to wake up back in a cell."

"You won't," Martinez assured him. "It's over. You're free."

They drove to a diner—James's request. Real food. Real coffee. Real conversations with real people in real places that didn't smell like disinfectant and defeat.

"How's Miguel?" James asked.

Martinez's expression darkened. "Facing terrorism charges. Federal prosecutors claim he was a foreign agent. It's fabricated but convincing. He's been in detention for two months. Trial isn't even scheduled yet."

"Can we help?" James asked.

"We are helping," Martinez replied. "Vasquez is funding his defense. I'm gathering evidence proving the charges are fabricated. But James—it's bad. They're throwing everything at him. Trying to bury him so deep he never surfaces."

"And Sonia?" James asked carefully.

"Suspended. Investigated. Mostly keeping her head down." Martinez paused. "She's been trying to help Michael but he won't see her. Won't talk to her. He's still angry about her trying to stop DR. Banks testimony."

James understood. Betrayal cut deeper than imprisonment. Choosing wrong when choosing right mattered most—that was unforgivable.

"Will you see her?" Martinez asked. "She's been wanting to apologize. To explain."

"There's nothing to explain," James said. "She chose her husband over the operators. Twice. That's clear enough."

"She failed both times," Martinez pointed out. "Tried to stop the story, failed, Michael ended up in jail anyway. Maybe that deserves consideration."

"Failure doesn't erase intent," James replied. "She wanted to silence truth. The fact that truth survived anyway doesn't make her intentions noble."

Martinez sighed. "I'm not defending her. Just saying—we're all broken from this fight. We all made choices we regret. Maybe she deserves the same grace Michael gave you when you doubted him."

"I never tried to suppress evidence," James said.

"No," Martinez agreed. "But you almost didn't go to the island. You almost chose safety over risk. Michael talked you into it. Without him, we'd have no photographs. No proof. No rescue."

James absorbed this. Martinez was right. Everyone had moments of doubt. Moments where quitting seemed rational. The difference was what you did next.

Sonia had tried to stop the story. But she'd failed. And when the story published anyway, she'd lived with the consequences.

Maybe that deserved something. Not forgiveness. But acknowledgment.

"I'll think about it," James said.

They finished breakfast and drove to a small apartment Martinez had rented—modest, secure, off the grid. James's temporary home until he figured out what came next.

Inside, Martinez showed him the evidence wall she'd been building. Photographs. Documents. Timeline. Everything connecting the conspiracy from its roots to its collapse.

"This is my project now," Martinez said. "Documenting everything. Building a complete record. So that years from now, when people doubt this happened, we have proof it did."

"That's important work," James said.

"It's obsessive work," Martinez corrected. "But it's all I have. I can't be a cop anymore. Can't have a normal life. The fugitive label sticks even after they stop hunting you. So I do this. I document. I remember. I refuse to let this be forgotten."

James studied the wall. Names. Faces. Dates. The architecture of atrocity.

"I want to help," he said.

"You should rest," Martinez replied. "You just got out. You've earned time to recover."

"I've had ten years to rest," James said. "I want to fight."

Martinez smiled. "Then welcome to the resistance. Population: three. Four if we count Michael. Three-and-a-half if we count Sonia."

They spent the afternoon organizing evidence. Building cases. Identifying conspiracy members who'd escaped prosecution. Following money trails that hadn't been pursued.

The work was tedious. Painstaking. Necessary.

At six PM, James's phone rang. Unknown number.

He answered. "Simmons."

"Detective Simmons." The voice was familiar. Sonia Miguel. "It's Sonia. I know you don't want to talk to me. I know I betrayed you. But I need five minutes. Please."

James wanted to hang up. Wanted to maintain righteous anger. Wanted to hold the boundary he'd drawn.

But Martinez was watching. And Martinez had advocated for grace.

"Five minutes," James said.

Sonia's relief was audible. "Thank you. Can we meet? In person?"

"Why?" James asked.

"Because I have something to show you," Sonia said. "Something that might save Michael. But I need your help to use it."

James's suspicion flared. "What is it?"

"Not over the phone," Sonia said. "Please. Just meet me. If you don't think it's worth it after five minutes, you never have to see me again."

James looked at Martinez. She shrugged—your choice.

"Okay," James said. "Where?"

"Old railyard on Fifth Street," Sonia replied. "One hour."

"I'll be there," James said.

He hung up and looked at Martinez. "Thoughts?"

"Thoughts are: it's probably possibly genuine, definitely complicated," Martinez said. "But you won't know until you go."

"Come with me?" James asked.

"As backup," Martinez agreed.

Sonia was waiting patiently. She looked older. Thinner. Worn down by months of guilt and isolation.

"James," she said when he approached. "Thank you for coming."

"Five minutes," James replied. "Starting now."

Sonia pulled out a folder. "I have evidence that the terrorism charges against Miguel are fabricated. Communications logs showing the alleged encrypted messages were created after his arrest. Financial forensics proving the offshore accounts were established by government agents, not Miguel. Expert analysis showing the entire case is manufactured."

James felt his pulse quicken. "Where did you get this?"

"I've been investigating," Sonia said. "Using contacts. Burning favors. Trading information. I know I can't undo what I did—trying to stop DR. Banks testimony. But I can try to make it right by saving Michael now."

"Why bring this to me?" James asked. "Why not Michael's lawyer?"

"Because Michael's lawyer is being monitored," Sonia said. "Every communication. Every filing. The conspiracy knows what he's planning before he plans it. But you—you're off their radar. You just got released. You're not officially involved. You can move without being watched."

James studied the documents. The evidence looked legitimate. Damning. Exactly what Michael needed to prove the charges were fabricated.

"If this is real," James said, "it could free him."

"It is real," Sonia insisted. "I've verified everything. But James—I need you to deliver it. I need you to testify about its authenticity. Because if I do it, they'll dismiss it as a desperate wife trying to save her husband. But if you do it—a decorated detective, wrongly imprisoned, recently vindicated—it carries weight."

James looked at Martinez. She nodded slightly—the evidence checks out.

"Why should I trust you?" James asked. "You tried to bury the truth twice. Why should I believe you're trying to expose it now?"

Sonia's eyes filled with tears. "Because I was wrong. Because I chose wrong. Because I failed Michael and I failed the operators and I failed everyone who trusted me. And I can't live with that. So I'm trying—desperately, pathetically—to make one thing right. To save one person. Even if that person won't forgive me. Even if no one ever forgives me. At least I'll know I tried to fix what I broke."

James felt anger and sympathy war in his chest. Sonia had betrayed them. But she'd also spent many, many isolated months trying to redeem herself. Trying to fight when fighting came at personal cost.

Maybe that deserved acknowledgment.

"I'll deliver the evidence," James said. "Not for you. For Michael. Because he deserves better than life in prison for being right."

"Thank you," Sonia whispered.

James took the folder. "But Sonia—this doesn't fix us. This doesn't make us okay. You broke something fundamental when you chose silence over truth. And I don't know if that's repairable."

"I know," Sonia said. "I'm not asking for forgiveness. Just for the chance to help."

"You've helped," James replied. "Now stay out of the way and let people who don't betray their principles finish the fight."

He walked away before she could respond.

Martinez followed, and they drove in silence until they'd left the railyard far behind.

"That was harsh," Martinez said finally.

"She deserved harsh," James replied.

"Maybe," Martinez agreed. "But she also just handed you the evidence that could save Michael. That takes courage. Or desperation. Or both."

James stared at the folder in his lap. "I don't know what to feel anymore. About her. About any of this."

"Then feel nothing," Martinez suggested. "Just act. Deliver the evidence. Free Michael. Feelings can wait until after the fight."

James nodded. "Okay. Let's do that."

But as they drove toward Michael's lawyer's office, James couldn't shake the image of Sonia standing alone in the railyard, broken and desperate and trying anyway.

Maybe betrayal wasn't permanent. Maybe people could change. Maybe grace was possible even when forgiveness wasn't.

Or maybe he was just tired of carrying anger.

Either way, he'd deliver the evidence.

And Michael would finally get the defense he deserved.

## CHAPTER FORTY-FIVE

# Sonia's Final Choice

Sonia sat in her car outside the federal courthouse, watching people stream in and out, and tried to convince herself she was making the right choice.

The evidence she'd given James would save Michael. The forensic analysis proved the terrorism charges were fabricated. Expert witnesses would testify to government misconduct. Michael's conviction would be overturned. He'd walk free.

Unless Sonia did what she was about to do.

Her phone buzzed. A call from the same number that had contacted her eighteen months ago. Governor Dickens—no longer in office, but still connected, still powerful, still pulling strings from behind scenes.

She answered. "What do you want?"

"Officer Miguel," Dickens said. "I hear you've been gathering evidence. Building a defense for your husband. Very touching. Very futile."

"The evidence is real," Sonia said. "It proves the charges are fabricated. Michael will be freed."

"No," Dickens replied. "He won't. Because I'm offering you one final deal. The last one. After this, no more negotiations."

Sonia's stomach dropped. "I'm done making deals with you."

"Even if this one saves everyone?" Dickens asked.

"What are you talking about?"

"The operators rescued from Blind Island," Dickens said. "Forty people. Currently in federal medical facilities receiving treatment. Very vulnerable people. Very easy to... misplace."

Sonia felt ice run through her. "You're threatening them?"

"I'm explaining consequences," Dickens corrected. "If your husband is freed—if he testifies about the conspiracy—if he names names and provides evidence—certain people will be prosecuted. Powerful people. People with resources. People who don't accept accountability gracefully."

"So they'd kill the operators?" Sonia demanded.

"They'd remove witnesses," Dickens said. "Quietly. Professionally. Medical complications. Transport accidents. Nothing traceable. Just forty vulnerable people who tragically didn't survive their rescue."

"You're out of your mind," Sonia said.

"I'm realistic," Dickens replied. "Power protects itself. Always. The question is whether you'll help or hinder that protection."

"What do you want?" Sonia asked, though she already knew.

"I want you to stop helping your husband," Dickens said. "Specifically, I want you to discredit the evidence you gave Detective Simmons. Tell the court it's fabricated. That you manufactured it yourself in a desperate attempt to free Michael. Testify that the forensic analysis is fraudulent."

"That would destroy any chance Michael has at freedom," Sonia said.

"Yes," Dickens agreed. "But it would guarantee the operators' safety. Because with your husband convicted and imprisoned, the threat ends. The rescued operators become irrelevant. They live out their lives in peace, unaware how close they came to being silenced."

Sonia felt tears burn. "You're making me choose between Michael and the operators."

"I'm making you choose between one person you love and forty people who survived the island because of his actions," Dickens corrected. "It's unfortunate math. But it's necessary math."

"What guarantee do I have?" Sonia asked. "What stops you from killing the operators anyway?"

"Nothing," Dickens admitted. "Except pragmatism. If your husband is convicted and imprisoned, there's no tactical advantage to killing witnesses. The story is over. The conspiracy is dead. Moving against operators only creates new investigations. Better to let them fade into obscurity."

Sonia wanted to believe that. Wanted to trust that betraying Michael one final time would actually save the forty people who'd already suffered so much.

But she'd made deals with Dickens before. She'd been promised things before. And every promise had been a lie wrapped in convenience.

"I need time to think," Sonia said.

"You have twenty-four hours," Dickens replied. "After that, the first operator has a fatal medical complication. Then another.

Then another. One per week until either they're all gone or you cooperate. Your choice."

He hung up.

Sonia sat in her car, feeling the walls close from every direction.

Choose Michael and forty operators die.

Choose the operators and Michael dies in prison.

Choose nothing and everyone suffers.

She'd faced impossible choices before. Eighteen months ago, she'd chosen Michael. She'd tried to stop DR. Banks testimony. She'd failed but she'd tried.

And Michael had never forgiven her.

If she chose him again—if she sacrificed the operators for his freedom—he'd hate her. Completely. Permanently. Their marriage would be over not because they'd grown apart but because she'd become exactly what he fought against: someone who chose personal happiness over collective justice.

But if she chose the operators—if she testified against Michael to save forty lives—he'd hate her anyway. For betraying him. For lying. For destroying his one chance at freedom.

Either way, their marriage was over.

Either way, she lost him.

The only question was whether she lost him while saving lives or losing them.

Sonia drove home and sat at the kitchen table where she and Michael had began investigating a case that destroyed their lives. Where they'd chosen truth over safety.

She pulled out her phone and recorded a video:

"My name is Sonia Miguel. If you're watching this, it means I made a choice. A terrible choice. But the only choice that mattered. Tomorrow, I'm going to testify that the evidence I provided was fabricated. That I manufactured forensics to free my husband. That the terrorism charges against him are legitimate. I'm going to lie under oath. I'm going to destroy his defense. I'm going to ensure he's convicted and imprisoned for the rest of his life. And I'm doing it to save forty operators who survived Blind Island. Because Dickens threatened to murder each one of them. I know he is not bluffing. Because power protects itself. Because someone has to choose the many over the one. Michael taught me that truth matters more than personal happiness. That justice requires sacrifice. That some things are worth losing everything. He's right. He's always been right. And I'm finally choosing the way he would choose. Even if it means losing him. Even if it means he hates me. Even if it means I spend the rest of my life knowing I destroyed the person I love most. The operators deserve to live. Michael would agree. He'd hate that I'm the one making the choice. But he'd agree with the choice. So I'm making it. And I'm recording this so that someday—years from now someone — Might understand I wasn't a villain. Just someone who loved two things: my husband and justice. And when I couldn't have both, I chose the one he'd have chosen. I love you, Mike. I'm sorry. Forgive me if you can. Hate me if you must. But know I did this because you taught me what matters. And what matters is protecting the vulnerable. Even when protecting them destroys us. I'm sending this video to Martinez. She'll know when to release it. She'll know how to use it. Trust her. She never betrayed you. Even when I did. I love you so much! You were my first and only love and you always will be. Goodbye Michael."

She ended the recording and sent it to Martinez with instructions: Don't open unless I'm dead or Michael is.

Then she deleted the video from her phone and prepared for tomorrow's testimony.

The testimony that would save forty operators and condemn her husband to life in federal prison.

The testimony that would end her marriage and prove she'd learned nothing from eighteen months of guilt.

Or prove she'd learned everything and finally had the courage to act on it.

She didn't know which.

She just knew she had to choose.

And she was choosing the operators.

Because Michael would have chosen them too.

Even though it would kill him.

Even though it would kill her.

Even though it would kill everything they'd built together.

Some things were worth losing everything.

Michael had taught her that.

Now she'd prove she'd been listening.

## CHAPTER FORTY-SIX

# The Betrayal

The courtroom fell silent when Sonia Miguel took the stand.

Michael sat at the defense table, watching his wife raise her right hand and swear to tell the truth. He'd refused to see her for two months. Hadn't taken her calls. Hadn't read her letters.

But his lawyer Robert Hayes had insisted she testify. Said she had exonerating evidence. Said she could prove the terrorism charges were fabricated.

Michael had reluctantly agreed.

Now, watching her sit in the witness box, avoiding his eyes, he felt unease creep through him.

Something was wrong.

The prosecutor—Patricia Vance—stood to question her.

"Mrs. Miguel," Vance began, "you approached Detective James Simmons two weeks ago with forensic evidence suggesting the terrorism charges against your husband were fabricated. Is that correct?"

"Yes," Sonia said quietly.

"And this evidence included communications logs, financial forensics, and expert analysis?"

"Yes."

"Where did you obtain this evidence?"

Sonia's hands tightened on the railing. "I created it."

The courtroom erupted. The judge banged her gavel. Michael felt the world tilt.

"Order!" Judge Hammond demanded. "Mrs. Miguel, please clarify. Did you create the evidence or obtain it?"

"I created it," Sonia repeated, voice stronger now. "I manufactured the forensic reports. I altered the communications logs. I fabricated the expert analysis. All of it."

Michael's lawyer shot to his feet. "Your Honor, I request a recess—"

"Denied," Hammond said sharply. "Mrs. Miguel, are you saying you committed perjury in providing false evidence?"

"Yes, Your Honor," Sonia said. "I was desperate to free my husband. I used my law enforcement connections to create convincing forgeries. I lied to Detective Simmons. I lied to everyone."

Michael stood. "She's lying now. Your Honor, she's lying to protect—"

"Mr. Miguel, sit down," Hammond ordered.

"She's protecting the operators," Michael continued. "Someone threatened her. Someone made her do this—"

"Bailiff, remove Mr. Miguel from my courtroom," Hammond said.

Guards moved toward Michael. He didn't resist. Just stared at Sonia, trying to understand.

Their eyes met for one second. In that second, Michael saw everything: fear, determination, love, and something that looked like goodbye.

Then guards escorted him out.

From the holding cell, Michael could hear muffled testimony. Sonia explaining her fabrication. Vance asking detailed questions. The defense crumbling in real time.

His lawyer joined him an hour later, looking shell-shocked.

"She destroyed everything," Hayes said. "Every piece of evidence we had. She admitted to fabricating it all. The judge is throwing out the defense. The jury is being instructed to disregard previous exonerating testimony."

"Someone threatened her," Michael said. "Dickens or someone else. They got to her. Made her do this."

"We can't prove that," Hayes replied. "And Mike—even if we could—the damage is done. Your wife just confessed to manufacturing evidence. No judge will believe anything connected to her now."

"So I'm convicted," Michael said flatly.

"Almost certainly," Hayes admitted. "The terrorism charges will stand. You'll be sentenced to life in federal prison. Maximum security. No parole."

Michael felt the trap close completely. "When?"

"Sentencing is tomorrow," Hayes said. "Judge Hammond wants this resolved quickly. Before media attention escalates further."

"And Sonia?" Michael asked. "What happens to her?"

"She'll be charged with obstruction of justice. Evidence fabrication. Possibly perjury. She's looking at five years minimum."

"So we both go to prison," Michael said. "She sacrifices herself and me for nothing."

"Not nothing," Hayes corrected. "The rescued operators stay safe. If Sonia's testimony discredits you, if the terrorism narrative sticks, then the conspiracy has no reason to silence witnesses. They've won. The story is over."

Michael understood. Sonia had chosen the operators over him. Just like eighteen months ago, she'd chosen him over the operators. Now she was correcting that choice. Making the sacrifice Michael himself would have made.

But it didn't feel noble. It felt like abandonment.

"Can you go to see her," Michael said.

"She's in federal custody," Hayes replied. "No visitors until after sentencing."

"Then get me a message to her," Michael said. "Tell her... tell her I understand. And I forgive her. And I love her. Even if I never see her again."

Hayes nodded. "I'll try."

He left.

Michael sat in the holding cell, trying to process betrayal that wasn't actually betrayal. Sacrifice that looked like selfishness. Love that felt like hate.

Sonia had destroyed his defense to save operators.

She'd lied to protect truth.

She'd chosen justice over personal happiness.

Just like Michael had taught her.

And he hated that she'd learned the lesson. Hated that she'd become the person he'd wanted her to be. Hated that their marriage had been sacrificed on the altar of principles he'd insisted mattered more than comfort.

He'd created this. By refusing to take plea deals. By insisting on fighting even when fighting was futile. By teaching her that some things were worth losing everything.

She'd just proved she'd been paying attention.

And now they'd both pay the price.

## CHAPTER FORTY-SEVEN

# Sentenced to Life

The sentencing hearing lasted forty-seven minutes.

Judge Hammond reviewed the case: terrorism charges confirmed by federal prosecutors. Evidence of espionage activities. Witness testimony from Sonia Miguel—discredited but damaging. No credible defense remaining.

"Mr. Miguel," Hammond said, "you've been convicted of conspiracy to commit terrorism, espionage against the United States, and coordination with foreign intelligence services. These are the most serious charges this court handles. They represent betrayal of the nation you once served."

"I served the nation by exposing murder," Michael said. "Everything else is fabrication."

"That's for the jury to decide," Hammond replied. "And they decided you're guilty."

"The jury was misled," Michael said. "By prosecutors who needed me silenced. By a system protecting itself."

"Mr. Miguel," Hammond continued, "I've watched you fight for two years. I've seen your determination. Your refusal to accept limitations. Your conviction that you know better than everyone else. And I've seen the cost. Your career destroyed. Your marriage broken. Your freedom forfeit. All because you couldn't accept that some fights aren't yours to win."

"The fight was mine," Michael said. "Because no one else would fight it."

Hammond sighed. "And that's precisely the problem. You appointed yourself judge and jury. You decided the system was wrong and you were right. You broke laws systematically. And now you want credit for the chaos you created."

"I want credit for saving forty lives," Michael corrected.

"You'll get credit," Hammond said. "In history books. In articles about the Blind Island scandal. In memories of the people you helped. But in this courtroom, in this moment, you're a convicted felon facing sentencing for crimes against your country."

She paused, reviewing documents.

"The prosecution recommends life imprisonment without parole. The defense—what remains of it—requests leniency based on your service record and the operators rescued. I've considered both arguments."

Michael held his breath.

"The court sentences you to life imprisonment in federal maximum security facility," Hammond said. "You'll be transferred immediately to a location determined by the Bureau of Prisons. You'll serve this sentence with no possibility of parole. No visitation rights for the first five years. Limited communication privileges. You'll be classified as a national security risk and treated accordingly."

The gavel banged.

Michael felt the words settle into his bones. Life imprisonment. No parole. National security classification.

He'd be buried in a federal prison so deep no one would ever find him.

The operators were safe. That mattered.

But Michael was gone. Erased. Disappeared into the same machinery that had disappeared the operators.

Poetic justice. Terrible symmetry.

Guards moved to escort him out.

Michael looked back at the gallery. Martinez sat there, tears streaming. James beside her, face grim. Other operators he'd helped—watching the man who'd saved them get sentenced to death by imprisonment.

No Sonia. She was in a different facility. Different charges. Different future.

They'd never see each other again.

Miguel would die in prison. Sonia would serve her time and emerge to a life without him. Their marriage—already broken—would dissolve into legal paperwork and memories too painful to revisit.

But forty operators were alive.

And that was worth it.

It had to be worth it.

Because if it wasn't—if sacrificing everything meant nothing—then Michael had wasted two years fighting for principles that existed only in his imagination.

The guards led him from the courtroom.

Through hallways. Into a transport vehicle. Chains on his wrists and ankles. Maximum security protocols for a man they'd transformed from detective to terrorist.

The vehicle drove for hours. Michael didn't know where. Didn't ask. Just watched landscape blur past tinted windows and tried to prepare mentally for spending the rest of his life in a cage.

He thought about Antony Grumpton. About Justin Jones. About De'Osha Davenport. About all the operators who'd died before rescue came.

At least they'd had hope. Had known someone was fighting.

Michael had nothing. No one fighting for him. No hope of release. Just years stretching ahead until his body gave out and the system erased him completely.

The vehicle stopped.

Guards opened the doors. Michael squinted against sudden brightness—not sunlight, but artificial lights. Industrial facility. Concrete walls. High security.

"Welcome to your new home," one guard said. "Federal Supermax. You'll spend twenty-three hours a day in your cell. One hour for exercise in a concrete box. No contact with other inmates. No visitors. No phone calls. Just you and silence."

Miguel was processed: fingerprints, photographs, medical evaluation, psychological assessment. Everything designed to categorize him, classify him, reduce him to data points in a system designed to forget he existed.

His cell was eight feet by ten. Concrete walls. Steel door. Narrow window that showed nothing. Toilet. Sink. Bunk. Nothing else.

This was his future. This concrete box. For decades. Until death.

Michael sat on the bunk and tried to find meaning in suffering.

He'd saved operators. He'd exposed conspiracy. He'd fought when everyone else looked away.

And now he'd pay for that courage with his life.

Not dramatic death. Just slow erosion. Years in isolation. Madness. Decay. The gradual extinction of the person he'd been.

Maybe that was justice. Maybe people who broke systems deserved to be broken themselves.

Or maybe justice didn't exist. Maybe there was only power and the illusions people told themselves to survive.

Michael lay down and stared at the ceiling.

Day one of life imprisonment.

One down. Twenty thousand to go.

He closed his eyes and tried to sleep.

Tomorrow would be exactly like today. And the day after. And the day after that. Forever.

Until the system finally succeeded in making him disappear.

Just like the operators he'd fought to save.

The symmetry was perfect. Terrible. Complete.

And no one was coming to rescue him.

## CHAPTER FORTY-EIGHT

# The Secret Revealed

Martinez received Sonia's video two weeks after Michael's sentencing.

She watched it three times, each viewing making her chest tighten more.

Sonia's confession. Her reasoning. Her choice to sacrifice Michael to save the operators.

And the implicit question: had she made the right choice?

Martinez didn't know. But she knew the video needed to reach the right people.

She called James. "We need to meet. Now. I have something you need to see."

They met at Martinez's apartment. She played the video.

James watched in silence, his expression shifting from confusion to shock to something that might have been respect.

"She chose the operators," James said when it finished. "Just like Michael would have."

"Yes," Martinez agreed. "Which means we have a problem. If we release this video, it proves Sonia testified falsely. Which means Michael's conviction might be overturned. Which means the operators become targets again."

"But if we don't release it," James said, " Michael spends life in prison believing his wife betrayed him. Never knowing she sacrificed him to save the people he fought for."

Martinez nodded. "So what do we do?"

James stood and paced. "We wait. We hold the video. And when the time is right—when the conspiracy is truly dead, when the operators are truly safe—we release it. We vindicate them both. Sonia for her choice. Miguel for his sacrifice."

"That could take years," Martinez said.

"Michael has years," James replied grimly. "Life imprisonment means decades. We use those decades to build a case so airtight that releasing this video doesn't endanger anyone. Then we free them both."

"And until then?" Martinez asked.

"Until then, we keep fighting," James said. "We finish what they started. We make sure the conspiracy stays dead. We protect the operators that the Miguel's gave everything to save."

Martinez felt determination crystallize. "Okay. We wait. We fight. We finish this."

James nodded. "And we make sure that when Michael finally learns the truth, it's because he's free to hear it. Not because he died in a cell never knowing his wife loved him enough to destroy him."

They spent the next months gathering evidence. Following money trails. Identifying remaining conspiracy members. Building cases that prosecutors couldn't ignore.

The work was slow. Painstaking. Often frustrating.

But gradually, arrests happened. Officials prosecuted. Assets seized. The machinery of accountability grinding forward.

Governor Dickens was indicted on racketeering charges. Ron Spillwind on conspiracy to commit human trafficking. Committee members on accessory to murder.

The conspiracy wasn't dead. But it was dying. Being dismantled piece by piece by investigators who finally had resources and political will.

Six months after Michael's sentencing, Martinez got a call from Robert Hayes.

"I need to tell you something," Hayes said. "About Michael's transfer."

"What about it?" Martinez asked.

"The federal Bureau of Prisons doesn't have a record of him," Hayes said carefully.

"What do you mean?"

"I mean he's not in the federal database," Hayes explained. "He was sentenced to federal supermax. But when I tried to schedule a legal visit, they said no such inmate exists. I pushed. They pushed back. I filed paperwork. It disappeared. Martinez—I think Michael was never actually transferred to federal prison."

Martinez felt ice run through her veins. "Then where is he?"

"I don't know," Hayes admitted. "But I have a theory. A terrible theory."

"Tell me," Martinez demanded.

"What if the terrorism charges were never about conviction?" Hayes said slowly. "What if they were about classification? About labeling Michael a national security risk so he could be moved without oversight? Without record? What if... what if they sent him to the island?"

Martinez's stomach dropped. "No. Blind Island was shut down. Federal agents raided it. The facility was closed."

"The facility we knew about was closed," Hayes corrected. "But what if there are others? What if the conspiracy couldn't sustain the Kansas operation but continued elsewhere? What if they decided the perfect revenge against Michael was sending him to the place he'd fought to expose?"

"That's insane," Martinez said.

"It's poetic," Hayes replied. "And more importantly—it's possible. Think about it. Michael disappears into federal custody. No records. No oversight. Classified location. National security designation. That's how you make someone vanish completely."

Martinez felt panic rise. "We have to find him."

"How?" Hayes challenged. "We don't know where he is. We don't have resources to search international waters. We don't have authority to investigate federal prison systems."

"Then we get authority," Martinez said. "We go public. We demand answers. We force investigations."

"Which endangers the operators," Hayes reminded her. "The same operators Sonia sacrificed Michael to protect. If we create chaos, if the conspiracy feels threatened, they could strike back. And the operators pay the price."

Martinez wanted to scream. Every choice led to impossible tradeoffs. Save Michael, endanger operators. Protect operators, abandon Michael.

"What do we do?" Martinez asked.

"We verify," Hayes said. "Quietly. Carefully. We find out if Michael is actually at a secondary facility. And if he is—we extract him. Not with publicity. Not with investigations. With direct action."

"That's illegal," Martinez said.

"So was everything Michael did," Hayes replied. "And he was right. Sometimes breaking laws is necessary. Sometimes justice requires methods the system doesn't permit."

Martinez absorbed this. "You're proposing a rescue operation."

"I'm proposing we find him first," Hayes said. "Then we decide how to proceed. But Martinez—if Michael is on another island, being forced to mine the same poison he tried to stop—we can't leave him there. We can't let him suffer believing Sonia betrayed him. We can't let the conspiracy have that victory."

"Agreed," Martinez said. "Start searching. I'll start recruiting. James will help. We'll find Michael. And then we'll bring him home."

Hayes hung up.

Martinez sat in her apartment, staring at the evidence wall, feeling everything shift.

Michael wasn't in federal prison.

He was missing. Disappeared. Sent to a place no records acknowledged.

And if Hayes theory was right—if the conspiracy had sent Michael to another extraction facility—then he was experiencing exactly what he'd fought to prevent.

Mining Tenorite. Breathing poison. Dying slowly in volcanic tunnels while the world thought he was imprisoned in a federal facility.

The cruelty was stunning. Perfect. Complete.

And Martinez couldn't allow it to stand.

She called James. "We have a problem. And a mission. How do you feel about international waters?"

"Depends," James said cautiously. "Why?"

"Because we're going island hunting," Martinez replied. "And we're not coming back without Michael."

## CHAPTER FORTY-NINE

# Transported to the Island

Michael Miguel woke in a cell that smelled like salt and sulfur.

Not the concrete box he'd been in. Not federal supermax. Something else. Somewhere else.

His head throbbed. His mouth tasted like chemicals. Memory was fragmented: guards entering his cell. Injection. Darkness. Transport. Voices speaking languages he didn't understand.

Then nothing.

Now this. Wherever this was.

Michael sat up slowly. The cell was carved from volcanic rock. Eight feet by eight. No window. Metal door with a small observation slot. Single bunk. Bucket. Nothing else.

The air felt hot. Humid. Oppressive.

And through the walls, Michael heard sounds: machinery. Distant voices. The rhythmic clang of metal on stone.

Mining.

"No," Michael whispered. "No, no, no—"

The door opened. A guard entered—not American, not military. Private security. Wearing the same coveralls James had photographed two years ago.

“Awake,” the guard said in accented English. “Good. Time to work.”

“Where am I?” Michael demanded.

“Site 9,” the guard replied. “Processing facility. You mine Tenorite. Eight hours per shift. Two shifts per day. Cooperate, you eat. Resist, you don’t.”

“I’m a federal prisoner,” Michael said. “I’m supposed to be in supermax. You can’t—”

“You’re not a prisoner,” the guard interrupted. “You’re an operator. Convicted terrorist. National security classification. Transferred to alternative detention. No records. No oversight. You don’t exist.”

Michael felt horror crystallize. “This is illegal. When people find out—”

“People won’t find out,” the guard said. “Because you’ll die here. Just like all the others. We don’t do rescues twice. We learned. Now we operate in international waters. Multiple small facilities. Harder to find. Harder to raid. Easier to deny.”

“How long?” Michael asked.

“How long what?”

“How long do I have?” Michael clarified. “Before the Tenorite kills me?”

The guard shrugged. “Six months. Maybe a year if you’re lucky. Depends on lung capacity. Depends on mask maintenance. Depends on whether you take breaks you’re not supposed to take.”

Six months. Maybe a year. Then death from respiratory failure while the world thought he was safely imprisoned.

The perfect crime. The perfect revenge. The perfect erasure.

"Get dressed," the guard said, tossing coveralls at Michael. "Orientation starts in ten minutes. Then you mine."

The guard left.

Michael sat holding the coveralls, feeling everything he'd fought for collapse into irony.

He'd exposed Blind Island. Saved forty operators. Destroyed a conspiracy.

And his reward was being sent to the exact place he'd tried to shut down. To experience exactly what he'd fought to prevent. To die the same slow death he'd tried to spare others.

The conspiracy had won. Not through conviction. Not through imprisonment. Through transformation. By making the detective into an operator. The savior into a victim. The witness into someone who'd never testify.

Michael dressed slowly. The coveralls fit. Of course they did. This had been planned. Calculated. Executed with precision.

Orientation consisted of a video—the same video the original operators had watched. Safety protocols. Work expectations. Consequences for resistance.

Then Michael was escorted to the mine entrance.

Volcanic tunnels descending into heat and darkness. The smell of sulfur. The glitter of Tenorite dust in artificial light.

And other operators. Maybe fifteen visible from the entrance. More deeper in the tunnels. All wearing gas masks. All moving with the exhaustion of people who knew death was coming but couldn't stop working toward it.

"Pick a mask," the guard said, gesturing to a rack. "Make sure it seals properly. You breathe unfiltered air, you die faster."

Michael took a mask. Fitted it. Checked the seal.

Then he walked into the tunnel and joined the other operators mining poison while the world above forgot they existed.

His first shift lasted eight hours. His lungs burned despite the mask. His muscles screamed from lifting containers filled with Tenorite. His mind rebelled against the reality: this was his life now. This tunnel. This poison. This slow death.

During a brief rest period, another operator approached. Young. Maybe twenty-five. Hispanic features visible around his gas mask.

"You're new," the man said.

"Yes," Michael replied.

"I'm Carlos. Been here four months. You?"

"First day," Michael said.

"It gets worse," Carlos said matter-of-factly. "The poison accumulates in your lungs. First month is okay. Second month, you start coughing. Third month, breathing hurts. Fourth month..." He gestured to his chest. "Fourth month, you're counting days."

"How many days do you have?" Michael asked.

"Not enough," Carlos replied. "But maybe more than you. You're older. Lungs aren't as strong. You'll deteriorate faster."

"Thanks for the pep talk," Michael said.

Carlos laughed—a bitter sound. "We don't do pep talks here. We do truth. And truth is: you're going to die in this tunnel. Just like me. Just like everyone else who gets sent here. The only question is whether you die fighting or die accepting."

"I'll die fighting," Michael said.

"Good," Carlos replied. "Then when you figure out how to fight, let me know. Because I'm ready."

He walked away before Michael could respond.

Michael returned to mining. Filling containers. Carrying them to the surface. Breathing poison despite the mask. Feeling his body slowly betray him shift by shift, hour by hour, breath by breath.

This was justice. This was consequence. This was what happened when you fought systems and lost.

Not death. Not imprisonment. But transformation into the very thing you fought to protect. Becoming an operator. Experiencing the suffering you'd tried to end. Learning that exposure changed nothing because conspiracies simply adapted and continued.

Michael had exposed Blind Island. So they'd created Site 9. And Site 12. And Site 17. And however many other facilities operated in waters no government claimed and countries ignored.

The conspiracy hadn't died. It had just gone deeper underground. And taken Michael with it.

At the end of his first shift, Michael collapsed on his bunk and tried to remember why he'd thought fighting mattered.

Forty operators saved. That mattered.

But hundreds more were still being trafficked. Still dying. Still forgotten.

And Michael —the detective who'd tried to save them—was now one of them.

Dying in darkness. Mining poison. Forgotten by the world that had once called him hero.

The perfect ending. Terrible. Complete. Undeniable.

And no one was coming to save him.

Because no one knew where he was.

And even if they did, why would they care about one more operator dying in tunnels on an island?

Michael closed his eyes and tried to sleep.

Tomorrow, he'd mine again. And the day after. And the day after that.

Until his lungs gave out. Until his body quit. Until death finally freed him from the fight he'd never been able to win.

## CHAPTER FIFTY

# Sonia's Plan

[Three months later]

Sonia Miguel sat in a federal holding facility, serving time for evidence fabrication, and waited for the signal.

It hadn't come yet. Maybe it wouldn't come. Maybe the whole plan was delusional. Maybe Michael was already dead and everything she'd sacrificed had been for nothing.

But she had to believe. Had to hope. Had to trust that the choice she'd made—destroying Michael to save operators—would somehow lead to salvation instead of damnation.

Her cellmate was named Rosa. Drug trafficking. Seven years. She'd learned to read people during two decades in and out of prison, and she'd been reading Sonia since day one.

"You're waiting for something," Rosa said during evening lockdown.

"No I'm not," Sonia lied.

"Yes you are," Rosa insisted. "You check the mail every day. You watch the news like it's life or death. You're counting something. Days? Weeks?"

“I’m just serving time,” Sonia said.

“Everyone here serves time,” Rosa replied. “But you’re serving time with purpose. Like you’re waiting for a moment. Like you made a deal and you’re waiting for the other side to pay up.”

Sonia wanted to deny it. Wanted to maintain cover. But Rosa was right. And secrets in prison were luxury items Sonia couldn’t afford.

“I did something terrible to save people,” Sonia said quietly. “And I’m waiting to see if it worked.”

“Did it?” Rosa asked.

“I don’t know yet,” Sonia admitted.

That night, the signal came.

A message delivered through a prison guard. From Martinez. One sentence:

The island has been located. Extraction in progress.

The guard did not stop as he walked by Sonia’s cell. He answered no questions as instructed.

Sonia replayed the message in her mind three times before the words made sense.

They’d found him. They’d found Michael. Not in federal prison. On an island. At another extraction facility.

Which meant Hayes theory was right. Which meant the conspiracy had sent Michael to the place he’d fought to close.

But Martinez had found him. Was extracting him. Was bringing him home.

Sonia felt tears stream down her face.

Her plan—if it could even be called a plan—had been simple: sacrifice Michael to save the operators. Let him be convicted. Let him be imprisoned. Let the conspiracy think they'd won.

Then work with Martinez and James to locate him. To verify he wasn't actually in federal prison. To find where he'd really been sent.

And once found—extract him. Rescue him. Bring him home to a world where the operators he'd saved were finally safe and the conspiracy was finally dead.

It was a terrible plan. Required sacrificing Michael first. Required making him suffer months or years believing she'd betrayed him. Required destroying their marriage to save it.

But it was the only plan that protected everyone. The only plan that kept the conspiracy from striking back at operators while buying time to finish the investigation.

And now—if Martinez's message was accurate—it was working.

Michael was being extracted. Would come home. Would learn the truth.

Would understand that Sonia hadn't betrayed him. She'd sacrificed him. Temporarily. Strategically. With the full intention of bringing him back once the path was clear.

Or maybe he'd hate her anyway. Maybe temporary betrayal was indistinguishable from permanent betrayal. Maybe sacrificing someone—even to save them—was unforgivable.

Sonia didn't know. She'd find out when Michael came home. If he came home.

Rosa watched from the bunk across. "Is what that guard said good news?"

"Maybe," Sonia said. "Or maybe just hope disguised as bad information."

"Hope's valuable in here," Rosa said. "Don't discount it."

Sonia closed her eyes and tried to imagine the reunion. Michael walking free. Learning she'd orchestrated his conviction to protect him and the operators. Understanding that every lie she'd told was tactical. That every betrayal was strategy.

Would he forgive her? Would he understand? Would their marriage survive this final, terrible test?

She didn't know.

She just knew she'd made the only choice available. The choice Michael himself would have made if their positions were reversed.

Sacrifice one to save many. Destroy the person you love to protect the people that person loved most. Accept temporary pain for permanent salvation.

It was the right choice. She believed that.

But right choices didn't always feel right. Sometimes they felt like failure. Sometimes they felt like the end of everything beautiful.

And Sonia wouldn't know which until Michael came home and either forgave her or didn't.

Either loved her or didn't.

Either understood or didn't.

The uncertainty was crushing. The wait unbearable. The gap between intention and outcome infinite.

But she'd chosen. And now she'd live with the consequences.

Just like Michael had been living with the consequences of his choices.

Suffering in tunnels. Mining poison. Believing she'd betrayed him.

All because Sonia had decided that some things were worth losing everything.

Including the person she loved most.

Including herself.

Including any chance at happiness.

Because Michael had taught her that justice required sacrifice. That protecting the vulnerable meant accepting personal destruction. That some fights were worth losing yourself completely.

She'd just never thought she'd be fighting alone. Never thought she'd be the one making Michael suffer to save him.

But that was love. Terrible, complicated, impossible love. The kind that broke you before it saved you. The kind that required becoming the villain to be the hero.

And Sonia had become the villain. Had testified falsely. Had destroyed Michael's defense. Had ensured his conviction and imprisonment.

All so that years from now—when the conspiracy was truly dead, when the operators were truly safe, when Michael was finally free—he might understand.

Might forgive.

Might come home to a wife who'd loved him enough to destroy him.

That was the hope. The terrible, desperate, probably delusional hope.

And Sonia clung to it. Because the alternative—accepting that she'd destroyed everything for nothing—was unbearable.

So she'd wait. And hope. And believe that Martinez would succeed. That Michael would survive. That truth would eventually triumph over temporary lies.

And that when they finally reunited—in some future she couldn't yet imagine— Michael would look at her and see not betrayal but sacrifice.

Not abandonment but strategy.

Not the woman who'd destroyed him but the woman who'd loved him enough to let him hate her if that meant keeping him alive.

That was the plan. Terrible. Desperate. Built on hope and prayer and the belief that love could survive being weaponized.

And Sonia wouldn't know if it worked until Michael came home.

If he came home.

If Martinez's extraction succeeded. If Michael survived the island. If the conspiracy didn't strike back one final time.

Too many ifs. Too much uncertainty. Too much risk.

But that was love. That was justice. That was the price of fighting systems designed to protect themselves at all costs.

You paid. You sacrificed. You accepted that winning might look like losing.

And you hoped that someday, someone would understand.

That your terrible choices had been necessary choices.

That your betrayals had been acts of love.

That destroying someone temporarily was better than losing them permanently.

Sonia closed her eyes and whispered into the darkness:

"Come home, Mike. Please. Come home and understand. Come home and forgive me. Come home and let me prove that every lie I told was in service of truth. Come home."

The darkness didn't answer.

It just held her while she waited.

And hoped.

And prayed that extraction in progress meant her husband was already on his way back to a world that had tried to erase him but failed.

Because some people couldn't be erased. Some truths couldn't be buried. Some love couldn't be destroyed even when weaponized.

Sonia believed that. Had to believe that. Would die believing that.

Because the alternative was accepting that she'd destroyed the person she loved most and gotten nothing in return except guilt and loneliness and the slow erosion of her own soul.

And that was unbearable. Unacceptable. Impossible.

So she chose belief instead. Chose hope instead. Chose trust that the plan would work even though the plan had been desperate from the beginning.

And tomorrow, she'd wake up and check mail again. And wait for news. And hope that extraction in progress meant Michael was coming home.

Home to a wife who'd betrayed him to save him.

Home to a truth more complicated than anyone could imagine.

Home to a love that had been tested beyond breaking and somehow—impossibly—survived.

Or didn't.

Sonia wouldn't know until Miguel came home.

And the waiting was killing her.

[END OF BOOK ONE]

[TO BE CONTINUED IN BOOK TWO: THE EXTRACTION]

# ACKNOWLEDGMENTS

I would like to thank my wife, children, family, and friends—everyone who has stood beside me through the challenges of losing my sight and the uncertainty that followed. Your support has meant everything during the ups and downs, the questions that couldn't be answered, and the things I've seen that perhaps I wasn't supposed to see.

To those who have encouraged my business ventures even when they didn't fully understand what I was working on or why it mattered so much—thank you. Your faith in me has been my anchor.

And to the operators and committee members who know what I know, who have lived what I've lived—this story is for you. Some of you will recognize the truth hidden in these pages. Some of you will understand why it had to be told this way.

The rest of you will have to decide for yourselves what's real and what isn't.

# ABOUT THE AUTHOR

Michel Battles was born in Detroit, Michigan, and now lives in Kansas with his wife. He is a serial entrepreneur with diverse business interests, and spent years reading mysteries before deciding to write his own—though "fiction" may not be the right word for what you've just read.

Michel has worked on both sides of the fence: as a blind vending operator within the Kansas Blind Business Vending Program, and later as an employee of the Kansas State Licensing Agency—the first blind person ever hired by the Kansas SLA.

The reader will need to decide what is truth and what is fiction. Michel knows. The people who worked alongside him know. The operators who have lived through "the grievances" know. The committee members who've seen the same patterns know.

And now you know enough to ask your own questions.

Note to law enforcement and concerned parties: I, Michel Battles, love my life. I am not suicidal. I do not go hunting, hiking, or participate in any extreme sports. I do not take unnecessary risks. I stay close to home, close to my wife, close to people who know where I am.

If I should go missing, if my route is suddenly "reassigned," if my family receives a letter with bureaucratic language about compliance reviews or temporary adjustments...

If you're reading this and I'm gone...

THE BLIND CONSPIRACY draws from lived experience, industry knowledge, and a deep understanding of how power operates behind closed doors. This is Michel Battles debut novel.

Learn more at: https://www.IronCaneMedia.com

SERIES NOTICE

THE BLIND CONSPIRACY is Book One
of an ongoing thriller series.

Book Two is forthcoming.

# A NOTE TO READERS

If you enjoyed this novel, please consider leaving a review. Reader reviews directly support independent authors and help ensure stories like this continue to be told.

www.ingramcontent.com/pod-product-compliance
Lightning Source LLC
LaVergne TN
LVHW010628110826
845149LV00014B/2801

* 9 7 9 8 9 9 4 8 7 2 6 1 1 *